MW00488490

ONE KILLER. ONE AGENT.
AND THE WOMAN WHO
TEMPTS THEM BOTH

A
RIGHTEOUS
KILL

By Kerrigan Byrne

0 9 8 7 6 5 4 3 2 1

Editor: Chelle Olson

Published by Gnarly Wool Publishing, an imprint of Oliver Heber
Books

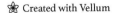 Created with Vellum

To my Anam Cara.
I recognized you instantly and never looked back.

ACKNOWLEDGMENTS

First and always to my little "coven" of witches: Cynthia St. Aubin, Cindy Stark, and USA Today bestselling Author, Tiffinie Helmer. (See what I did there?) You ladies are my sounding board, my inspiration, my sanity, and the source of so many smiles. I'm so excited for the magic we're about to produce together!

A special "Thank you" to Janet Juengling-Snell and Nicole Garcia for all the work you do on my behalf! Also, to my beta-readers who go above and beyond! Namely, Lynne Harter, Emma Elliot, Suzi Behar, Gigi Rivera, Carly Gentleman, Amy Byrd, and Jennie McDuffie Nunn.

Thank you to the WID: Mikki Kells, Ariadne Kane, and H.M. Turner. I'm so excited for what the next years will bring for you all. I'm honored to be a part of it.

PROLOGUE

Forty Years Ago

Russians always sold the best weapons.

He checked his position against the explosive charges he'd hidden beneath where the two gray vans parked. One wrong move and they'd all be squinting up at St. Peter with their ears still ringing from the blast. Heaven's doorman would let old "Danny Boy" through those pearly gates, of course, as he'd be a martyr for the holy cause and all.

That was why he liked to do this kind of thing alone. He didn't ever want to be the reason a brother was blown to bits.

Himself? Well, he couldn't think of a better way to go.

The Russians? Nothing would make him happier

than to blow them to wee pieces. They *were* going to try to kill him first after all.

But a fellow *Sinn Féin*? Wasn't worth the bloody risk to his soul.

Meeting in Switzerland was a brilliant idea on his part. Neutral ground and all that. Plus, a bulk of Irish Republican Army funds were stored here. And on the off chance that this deal went through as planned, he might need quick access to more money.

Checking their quaint, mountainous surroundings, Danny Boy opened the door to his rented Volkswagen and stepped out. His briefcase hung from a hand cuff off his right wrist, bursting with cash. It always surprised people when he pulled his weapon from its holster with his left hand. They didn't stay surprised for long. He only drew if he planned to put a bullet in someone.

Left-handed people were supposed to be artistic weren't they? It fecking applied. He was a virtuoso. A bloody artisan of anything combustible. Explosives, firearms, engines... women.

Lifting his arms out to the side to show the briefcase and the dangerous weapon in the shoulder holster beneath his jacket, he turned in a slow circle.

That's right you double-dealing twats, send out your best to feck with me.

The passenger door to the front vehicle opened. The boot that hit the rocky earth shocked him.

Black leather. With heels that had to be at least three inches.

Tucked into those knee-length boots was the longest pair of legs he'd *ever* seen. And the woman attached to those perfect gams? She could have been strutting on one of Paris' catwalks instead of a damp, nefarious road in the Alps. Long, glossy black hair disappeared behind her slim shoulders. It framed a perfectly symmetrical, delicately angled face with flawless olive skin.

This couldn't be the fabled *Zoya*, could it? The assassin arm of the corrupt KGB general who sold illegal arms to—well—to men like himself.

Her hands remained tucked into the pockets of her short-waisted leather jacket. He'd bet his favorite rosary that she had something sharp in her hand instead of a gun.

That meant she'd have to get close to him. He smiled at the thought.

With the boots he'd put her at almost six foot tall, which meant that she'd have an inch or so on him in her bare feet.

Didn't matter, they'd be horizontal for what they'd spend most of their time doing. Unless she had those fantastic legs wrapped around him while they stood. *That* would bring them face to face. His body responded to that thought.

He couldn't feckin' wait.

She stopped inches from him, her dark almond eyes flicking over him in a quick and dismissive assessment.

He smirked, knowing what she saw. Hell, he shaved his freckled, ginger mug in the mirror every morning. What he lacked in height, he made up for in heft. He had to turn sideways to get his shoulders through doors sometimes. And his heavy arms were the length of a much taller man's with big, ugly hands that were surprisingly deft with things that took precision. He wasn't handsome, but he knew his green eyes sparkled when he smiled.

He put every bit of that sparkling into his grin.

"The very instant that I saw you, did my heart fly to

your service." Danny Boy was shite with words. Only The Bard could express his feelings correctly.

She blinked and cleared her throat but looked unimpressed. "You're Daniel?" she asked in a husky, brusque Russian accent.

"Just *Danny Boy*, I don't use my given name in military operations."

Her full and lovely lip curled at the word *military*. *Huh*. She was one of those who filed the IRA under 'Terrorist' rather than 'Military.'

No matter, now they'd have a subject for pillow talk.

"Is that the money?" She motioned to the briefcase with her chin.

"Aye."

Her eyes snagged with his.

Maybe the old Irish sparkle was working? He amped it up a notch.

She looked away.

Aye, it was working.

"It's my job to take your money and kill you," she informed him. "I'm *very* good at my job." Her stone-faced act was damned adorable. One problem though, her black eyes weren't dead. They crackled with life. With curiosity. With passion. She *would* kill him, given the chance. Of that he had no doubt.

"I know it." He held up the briefcase cuffed to his wrist. "Only I have the key and I'll give it to you when you're done handing me the merchandise."

His eyes were on the long, serrated knife she pulled from her pocket. It was why he didn't see the devastating punch to his solar plexus. He was still fighting for breath when by some act of kung-fu magic, she had both hands pinned behind him and the knife to his throat.

"I could just cut off the arm attached to the money and leave you to bleed out," she purred against his ear in that sexy Eastern accent of hers.

He wished he had his hands free to adjust what was going on in his pants. But, she'd have his jugular spilling on to the dirt, so he let her have them. Besides, her full breasts pressed against his back every time she took a breath. And he liked that.

The knife broke skin.

"Do it, and the explosives beneath both your vehicles will create a new valley for the alp skiers this winter."

She took a breath and let out a stream of Russian words that probably would have made her grandmother blush. "Where's the detonator?" she demanded.

"My boot. If I touch my toe to the top, we'll be incinerated."

"How did you avoid the explosion while we struggled just now?" She sounded impressed. Good. He was getting somewhere.

"We Irishmen are fleet-footed. I'm more agile than I look. I have absolute control of *every* part of my body." He took a chance by stroking the inside of her wrist with the rough pad of his thumb.

She must have understood the innuendo, because she wrenched his arm so hard she would have dislocated the shoulder of a weaker man. But she didn't cut him again. So... progress. "I think you do not," she said wryly. "*I* control some parts of it now, eh?"

And didn't that turn him on more than it should? He'd never let a woman tie him up before, but he'd happily submit to any torture she could devise.

"No one's ever tried *The Tempest* on me before." Her voice had a smile in it.

She knew Shakespeare? Danny Boy decided he was going to spend the rest of his life with her.

They would make beautiful babies.

A door slammed. "Zoya?" a hard, male voice prompted.

"*I'll follow you and make a heaven out of hell, and I'll die by your hand which I love so well.*" Danny Boy decided to stick with what was working. Shakespeare had a saying for just about any situation.

She loosened her grip on the knife. "*If love be rough with you, be rough with love.*" A nip at his ear punctuated the challenge.

"Jaysus woman, if we didn't have company, I'd already have you naked against the first hard spot I could find." Okay, so, Shakespeare never said that, but he'd wanted too.

"Then..." She let him go, altogether. "Get rid of our company."

"Did you actually bring the explosives we asked for?"

"No," she confessed.

"Good." He grinned and took her wrist, sprinting for cover.

The explosion was nothing compared to what would be coming as soon as he got her out of those boots.

1

As flies to wanton boys, are we to the gods;
they kill us for their sport.

— WILLIAM SHAKESPEARE

I f work was calling this time of night, it only meant
one thing. A dead body.

Luca Ramirez ran a tired hand over his face and
blinked hard, trying to clear the fog from his contacts.
Didn't work. Maybe the fog was outside? At midnight,
it could be either. He was so damned out of it, the
streetlights ran together and he'd been doing his level
best not to crash his new government-issued black
Dodge Charger into anything. Thus far, that had been
the extent of his plans to be effective for the rest of the
weekend. The urge to grab his phone and huck it into
the Willamette River seized him with such force, he
white-knuckled the steering wheel and took a bracing
breath before reaching for it.

"Ramirez," he barked.

The feminine voice on the line had become the
extent of his nightlife lately, which was just a damn
shame because she was at least twenty years older,

married twice that long, and a grandmother of twins. "Local PD just received a 10-90 from the river bank. Indigent reported it in from Cathedral Park."

Every now and again, it sucked to be right.

"Figured I'd give you a heads up because that's your part of town." Beatrice Garber, the graveyard dispatcher, knew he was close to Cathedral Park because he'd barely waved goodbye to her fifteen minutes before when he'd finally left his office at FBI Headquarters.

"Uh, Bea, I'm at the ass-end of a fourteen hour day. I *have* to get some sleep." Five years ago, he'd have jumped at the call. Five years ago, he'd still been in his twenties. "Does the dead body for sure fit the M.O.?

Bea paused. "The victim is described as a redhaired female found draped in white vestments and a red robe."

"*Fuck!*" he exploded, pounding on his steering wheel. "Goddammit!" It was what he'd feared. The reason he'd been pushing himself to the limit these past umpteen months. He'd promised himself John the Baptist wouldn't evade him long enough to take another victim. "That cock-sucking son of a—"

"Still here," Bea chirped, her tone half amusement, half censure.

"Responding," Luca flipped the switch to his lights. "Call Di Petro, CSU, the lab and—"

"Already on it."

Throwing his phone to the passenger seat, he jammed the gas pedal to the floor and his car leapt forward like a predatory cat, roaring past thinning Friday night traffic.

With thick clouds threatening to dump their contents any moment, the water of the Willamette River couldn't be seen tonight. Rather, it seemed like a wide ribbon of darkness cutting through the bright lights of Portland. The cityscape downtown would reflect off the water, creating insubstantial renderings of architectural giants of the northwest.

He took the turn onto Pittsburgh Avenue on two tires, cranking the wheel and skidding to a halt next to the only other police unit in the small Cathedral Park lot. Ten more minutes and this place would be lit up with more flashing lights than a downtown rave.

He lunged out of his car. The humid October chill punched into his lungs, making him feel like he inhaled ice cubes. At least it finished the job his adrenaline had started. He was awake and in the moment.

The north side of the riverbank was a swath of inky darkness, despite the traffic lights over St. John's Bridge and some soft, ambient street lamps illuminating the famous stone stanchions bearing the viaduct over the park.

Glancing at the police car as he passed, he saw that the back window of the vehicle had been kicked out, the safety glass one cracked chunk on the ground reflecting the alternating flashes of red and blue from the lights. Luca cased the vehicle leading with his gun, searching for an injured cop. Finding none, he scanned the empty night with his eyes and weapon.

Had they captured the suspect? Had he escaped?

Danger thrummed through his veins as he vaulted over the concrete barrier and plunged through a thin line of trees to the water's edge. He jogged toward the beams of two flashlights several yards down the riverbank, keeping his duty weapon at his side.

Two police beams blinded him and he heard the click of gun safeties being released. "Stop right there," a uniform commanded. "This is a secure scene." A fat rain drop hit the bridge of Luca's nose, amping up his urgency to get a look at the body before any evidence was washed away in a storm.

"FBI. Special Agent Ramirez. I'm going to use my left hand to show you my badge," he warned. He knew better than to make any swift arm movements at a fresh murder scene.

"Let's see it," came the clipped reply.

Luca kept advancing, but reached in his jacket pocket and flashed the badge and ID that clearly identified him as a Fed.

The officers lowered their weapons.

"Is the body one of *his*?" Luca didn't have to say the name.

"Looks like." The uniforms dropped their beams and refocused them on a still, white bundle wrapped in a swath of crimson. Luca had to blink to clear the blind spots and let his eyes readjust to the darkness.

Upon first glance in the darkness, someone could mistake the limp, dirty bundle as a heap of garbage washed up into the narrow bank, but that was blatantly impossible. Luca looked upriver and made a few instantaneous calculations.

Cathedral Park was situated at a bend in the Willamette that gave the cursory illusion of a scenic suburban park. When, in fact, it was positioned between two of Portland's largest water industrial complexes. Around the west bend, Swan Island Basin and Northwest Industrial launched dozens of ships and conducted abundant trade. From the eastern edge of the park, almost all the way to where the Willamette merged with the Colombia, lay several square miles of blue collar paradise, including everything from tire disposal and recycling, to transport management.

Luca noted the shadowed juts of ancient pylons

lining the entire west side of the river and scanned the locations of driftwood along the banks and their distances from the thin tree line. This body would have had to miraculously steer through the maze of pylons to reach the shore, let alone sit three feet clear of the water's edge.

Another cold drop hit the crown of Luca's head. "Did either of you move the body?" he demanded.

The senior partner narrowed his beady blue eyes and hiked his gun belt higher on his considerable paunch. But the young African-American kid with him just shook his head.

"This is now *my* secure scene. Got it?" He was too exhausted and pissed-off to bother with inter-agency diplomacy, taking charge before Officer *McTubby* thought of some bullshit regulation to gum up his night. He was in no mood to wait for more federal back up. "Get on the radio and tell area patrol to be on the lookout for whoever kicked out your window and escaped from the back of your squad car. Then get an ETA on Coroner and CSU."

He and the older officer weighed about the same, but at 6'2" Luca had a good five inches on the guy. Also, Luca's heavy frame was a product of regular weight training and weekend contact sports as opposed to stale doughnuts and a few too many Rueben sandwiches. He'd bet his favorite Sig Sauer the guy was a diabetic. He turned to the kid, dismissing two hundred plus pounds of sputtering temper. "Tell me what we have here."

His eyes widened, showing brilliantly white against his dark face. "He—he escaped?" Looking grim and humiliated, the young officer did his best to recover. "We were patrolling the park when we got the call from dispatch a couple of minutes ago. A local transient who claimed to have pulled her out of the river called 911." Luca started walking toward the body, taking latex gloves from his pocket. He waited for the kid to tell him something he didn't already know. "The homeless guy was in full psychotic meltdown when we got here, I thought O'Reilly had secured him in the squad car."

O'Reilly. The fat bastard was added to his shit list for not securing the indigent. It was a rookie fuck up that could cost lives.

"Well, he didn't," Luca blandly stated the obvious. Despite the distance and the sounds of traffic, the officers should have heard the commotion of the broken window. His face started burning as his blood pressure spiked. "Keep your flashlight on the body," he ordered, furious with their incompetence.

Luca forced himself to notice the small things first. To separate the victim's parts from the whole of a human corpse. He started with her hands.

The nails weren't painted or fake, just shaped and groomed. Not like the others

"Does John the Baptist really drive stakes through their hands while they're still alive?" The officer used the name the public and media had dubbed the most prolific serial killer the nation had seen in decades.

"Like what nailed Jesus to the cross." Luca rolled the gloves on and lamented the light sprinkle of rain he could hear plunking into the river. Though it didn't matter to her anymore, he squelched the need to cover the small and mostly naked woman and protect her from the freezing rain.

Squatting down next to her, he eased the delicate fingers open. Jones gasped and swore. Luca had passed that stage of law-enforcement a long time ago.

A hole about an inch or so long and one-fourth as wide punched through the palm. Blood mingled with water and river filth staining her pale flesh.

There was still some elasticity to her skin and he could move her fingers easily, so rigor mortis hadn't set in.

This was a fresh kill.

Luca squinted as though the night could provide some answers. John the Baptist could be close. Maybe even watching them. He let out an exasperated breath as the sprinkle turned into a drizzle, slicking his thick hair to his skull and making him shiver in his suit coat.

Honestly, the rain wasn't much of a complication. It was wishful thinking on his part that there would be evidence to wash away. The son of a bitch never left any. Just another pretty red-head with holes in her hands and a stab wound to the side before she was baptized in the river. Usually the body was wrapped tight in white and red vestments like a gruesome burrito, but this one was naked to the waist, the vestments tangled with her lower half and mucked up with river sludge and blood.

Sirens wailed in the distance, some coming from the direction of the University, others racing across the bridge.

O'Reilly trudged up to them, slightly out of breath. "This whore must have been one of the high-class, expensive ones," he remarked without taking his eyes from the victim's perfect, pale breasts.

Luca met Jones's look over the dead woman's body. He was glad to see his disgust mirrored in the younger man's eyes. In this job, you met all kinds of cops. They weren't always the good guys. Sometimes the criminals had a more respectable code of conduct.

Luca gathered his fortitude and looked down. Her eyes were closed. Thank God.

O'Reilly had grabbed his camera from his car and began to snap pictures, as per protocol. The idea of the lousy cop having those photos made Luca ill. Objectively, the fucker had been right. This was one of the better-looking victims. She hadn't just been pretty, she'd been beautiful. Young, mid-twenties, with a lithe body that was obviously, he noticed the lack of body hair, well-groomed. The expected stab wound still seeped a little from the left side of her toned waist. The blood mixed with rainwater and ran in chaotic pink rivulets to the vestments beneath her.

Her ivory skin was flawless except for a few bruises and ligature marks around her wrists and ankles. She'd been tied up for an indeterminate amount of time, like all the others.

And she'd gone through hell before she died.

Exhaustion was settling into his bones again. Or was it just weariness? Poor kid. Luca didn't care what life she led before this. She could have been the whore of Babylon for the hell it meant to him. Most of the previous victims had been. Didn't matter. She was alive before now. A person with needs, wants, aspirations, hope—pain. Maybe she had someone who'd loved and missed her. Maybe not. But *she* mattered. She deserved justice. Whoever she was.

Luca could hear footsteps, the calls of his colleagues. He took a painful breath. "We need to ID her as soon as—"

"*Holy shit!*" Jones reared back and pointed in astonishment.

The camera shattered where O'Reilly dropped it onto the rocky bank.

"What the hell's the matter with you?" Luca barked.

Then he saw it. The corpse shuddered. Once. Twice. Then her chest heaved violently.

"Get me a fucking ambulance and do it *now!*" he yelled.

Jones scrambled to yell into his shoulder radio, the broken camera a forgotten casualty of the moment.

Luca dropped to his knees and started chest compressions before rolling her jerking body to the side. Convulsing violently, she heaved up an alarming amount of dirty water before sucking in a screeching breath, only to cough up more. The shock of the freezing downpour must have somehow roused her, and her body struggled to breathe through the water in her lungs.

"That's it. That's good. Keep coughing," he urged, making sure she was posed so as not to aspirate anything she coughed up.

"Th-that's not possible," O'Reilly stuttered. "She was cold. She wasn't breathing. S-she had no pulse!"

"Where'd you check it?" Luca barked over his shoulder, giving her a few encouraging slaps on the back.

"Her right wrist. I didn't wanna disturb the body." O'Reilly's voice lifted to a shrill whine.

"I'm going to have your badge, you dumb-fuck," Luca snarled. Checking the right wrist of a victim who wasn't breathing and bleeding from multiple wounds? Could he have checked a weaker place for a pulse? Anyone who knew anything checked the neck. Could he have even *felt* a weak pulse through his sausage fingers?

Luca wrenched his suit jacket off his shoulders and wrapped her nakedness with it, not just to warm her, but to shield her from the officer's beady eyes. He was pleased to see that more desperate breaths were being drawn into her shuddering body through the coughs.

She wouldn't be alive for long if her wounds weren't seen to. "Where's that goddamned ambulance?" he shouted.

"On its way," someone yelled back. "There's a station not four blocks away, they'll be here in two minutes."

He hoped they had two minutes. The news that they were dealing with a live victim spread through the gathering law-enforcement crowd with the speed of a fire in a library. The more people showed up, the more likely someone competent would get him a mother fucking first aid kit.

"Here." An open black plastic box full of bandages, pills, antiseptic, medical tape, and other first-aid odds and ends was shoved into his hands. He looked up. PPD homicide detective Regan Wroth knelt at the other end of the kit.

Luca liked her. Hell, he'd tried to get into her pants more than once, along with the rest of the Portland law-enforcement community.

"Thanks." He ripped open a few bandages and lifted his jacket to press it to the victim's side. "Put pressure here," he directed. Wroth gave him a *'duh'* look, but didn't mouth off to him. He knew he liked her for a reason other than her looking like a smart version of Emilia Clarke.

As soon as Wroth applied pressure to the victim's wound, the girl's eyes flew open and her arms flailed. A hoarse scream gurgled to the surface and she tried to grab at his shirt. Once she attempted a grip, she cried out again in pain and pulled her injured hands into the cradle of her body. Panic-filled eyes bounced from face to face and sobs of terror were interrupted by another fit of body-wracking coughs.

"Hey. Hey... shhhhh." Luca gently grasped her slim wrists. "I know this hurts. But we have to stop the bleeding." He positioned himself into her line of vision, hoping to block out all the chaos and faces and flashing lights. "Look at me, sweetheart," he crooned as her wide green gaze locked on his face.

She blinked rapidly, but stopped sobbing. She just trembled and stared, her tears mingling with the rain. The surrounding chaos immediately receded into darkness. Luca shivered again, but not because of the rain plastering his thin dress shirt to his body. As their eyes locked, some kind of cosmic puzzle piece snapped into place. The sensation that seized his chest with the force of an iron vice had words like *fate* and *destiny* chiseled into it.

And he didn't even *believe* in that bullshit.

Luca's brain rejected the feeling like an ingested toxin, heaving it with a violent spasm onto the ground. This girl—woman—was not only a victim, she was a witness. His witness. She'd stared into the eyes of the devil. She'd been crucified, stabbed, drowned, and returned from the brink of death. This alien feeling of epic magnitude could only mean that she could be the key to putting an end to the evil terrorizing the women of his city. At least, that's how Luca was determined to interpret it.

"You need a blanket," he noted. "Someone get her a fucking blanket!" he ordered over his shoulder and his ire was somewhat appeased by the frantic movement to comply. It wasn't often that people questioned him on a good day. But on a night like this, he just *hoped* someone challenged him. He needed a direction for his fury.

When he turned back to her, he saw something in the clear green gaze that he'd not expected in the least. Hope. Relief. Trust?

Wordlessly, she offered him the backs of her injured hands, like a child would show an inconsequential wound to a parent. Silent tears still ran down her cheeks. They wrenched at his insides, but he was just so damned relieved to see her reacting at all.

"I know," he murmured to her, gently pressing gauze into her palm. "I know. The ambulance is on its way. Can you hold on for me until then?"

She gave him what might have been a watery nod.

"Good girl." He laid a hand on her hair and looked back over his shoulder. "Goddammit!" he exploded. "It's like, twenty fucking below out here and not one of you fuck-nuts can find a blanket? *Aye Chingau pendejos!* She was just pulled from the goddamned river! I swear to the *Madre de Dio*—"

A blanket appeared in his hands. One of those coarse wool emergency jobbers that people kept in their trunks and hoped to never use.

What, did they have to *weave* it first before getting it over here?

Whipping it open, Regan helped him settle it over the victim. At least the girl still trembled beneath his hands. If she suffered complications from hypothermia, he would beat O'Reilly to death with his own baton. Hell, if this situation went any further south, that fat fuck would face his wrath—

Luca took a deep, cool breath through his nose and let it hiss through his throat on the exhale. What had he learned in Anger Management? While counting to ten, in English then Spanish, he gently tucked the edges of the blanket around where Wroth still held pressure on her stomach wound.

She said nothing, but raised a chocolate eyebrow at him.

"Was I yelling in Spanish?" He busied himself fussing with the blanket way more than was needed. He'd forced himself to drop all traces of a Hispanic accent in college. It was only when he lost control of his temper that he ever reverted to his first language. He'd been better at that lately. Mostly.

"Uh huh."

"Sorry," he muttered, more to the victim than the detective.

She just blinked at him, seeming to focus more on panting and shivering than anything else. A reckless and distressing urge to pull her shivering body into his arms and share his heat with her had Luca clenching his fists at his sides.

Someone yelled that the paramedics had arrived. He couldn't complain about their timing, but the woman's pallor was seriously starting to alarm him.

"You look like you've had a hell of a day, Ramirez." Wroth used that silky voice on him, the one that lulled many an unsuspecting criminal into a false sense of security. "Go home and cop a few hours of sleep. I'll go with her in the ambulance and call you—"

"No!"

They both looked down in surprise.

The victim was frantically trying to roll her body toward him, reaching out to him with her injured hands again, causing the gauze to loosen. The wild look returned to her eyes. "No. No! *You*." Her head shook wildly.

"Hey. It's all right. Calm down." He took hold of

her shoulders gently and tried to subdue her thrashing.

She obviously struggled to speak around her chattering teeth. "Don't. Leave. Me," she pleaded.

"Okay. I'm going with you to the hospital. I need you to lay still, sweetheart. Your side is starting to bleed again."

She complied immediately, relaxing beneath his hands.

He snagged gazes with Wroth. She'd just shocked the hell out of them both. Why not go with the kind and pretty, but capable woman detective instead of his vulgar ornery ass?

Secretly, Luca suspected he would have argued the point regardless of what the victim wanted. Hell, it really wouldn't have been much of an argument. He would have just strong-armed his way into the ambulance. For some ridiculous reason, the thought of leaving her care to anyone else made him crazy. What if something happened on the way to the hospital? Who was going to make sure the paramedics did their job? Or the doctors once they got to the Emergency Room?

It wasn't because of the lead weight in his belly every time he looked at her. Or due to the unreasonable primitive instincts that seemed to ripple through his blood. It had nothing to do with either of those things. She was his first and only lead on this case. He'd be damned if he let her slip through his fingers for a few hours of sleep.

"Excuse me, sir." A tiny, honey-colored female paramedic and her blonde male partner shouldered him aside in their hurry to place the stretcher on the ground. They worked efficiently together, and didn't seem to mind him hovering.

"You can help carry her up the hill while I see to these," the woman commanded Luca while addressing the open gashes.

Luca liked her right away. Why *didn't* they have more women in their profession? In his experience, they tended to keep cooler heads in times of crisis and fall apart later. He would rather deal with that then colossal fuck ups like O'Reilly.

Once they were settled into the ambulance and racing for Legacy Emanuel Medical Center, he leaned in close to the victim, trying to keep her from sinking into shock or some shit.

Warming her up would mean more blood flow. Though the paramedic seemed to be doing a good job and the victim's vitals were stronger than he'd expected, he was still scared shitless she might not make it.

"What's your name?" he asked her, reaching up to smooth a grimy lock of hair away from her forehead.

She searched his face with unfocused eyes before whispering, "Hero."

A sad smile tugged on the corner of his mouth. "I'm no hero, girl. Don't ever mistake me for one."

2

*"What's in a name? That which we call a rose
By any other word would smell as sweet."*

— WILLIAM SHAKESPEARE, ROMEO AND
JULIET

Hero Viola Katrova-Conner. Fucking bizarre name.

Sprawled in the uncomfortable vinyl ICU recliner that farted loudly every time he shifted, Luca zoned while he watched the stable rise and fall of her chest. Along with the steady sounds of the monitoring machines, the rhythmic movement hypnotized him. He'd been staring like this for—he checked his watch —a good half an hour now. Damn. He'd have sworn not 5 minutes had passed since they'd wheeled her into this private room.

She'd freaked out when the ER staff had separated them. He couldn't get the terror in her eyes out of his mind. She'd begged to let him stay with her. And they had allowed it until she'd been properly sedated. He'd become her security blanket, Luca guessed, but he couldn't for the life of him understand why. Most people that met him in a professional capacity couldn't wait to get *away* from him.

His gaze drifted to her hands tucked limply to her sides and wrapped in heavy bandages. It made him want to throw something, so he shut down the impulse and used the moment to really study her. Her nose, now hooked to oxygen, was small and pert and smattered with just a few freckles he hadn't detected before. Her oval face had a sweet curve to it, lending her a youthful innocence. Her body was compact and generously curved, but sinewy, he remembered, like an athlete.

As a prostitute, she would make a killing.

She'd been in emergency surgery for three excruciating hours. After she'd been wheeled into the ICU, one of the clerical assistants, Barbara, of the cat-like fingernails and Texas bouffant, had recognized her as someone who regularly volunteered at the hospital. Something *else* that didn't jive with John the Baptist's *modus operandi*. Salivating over the prospect of a lead, Luca had spent a good hour grilling poor Barbara. By the time he finished, the office assistant didn't like him either. Big surprise.

He'd gleaned through her tears and redneck accent that the victim was a yoga instructor and popular local artisan. Pottery, it seemed. Barbara had even held up a bright pink coffee mug with yellow swirls that had been bought at a Christmas charity auction the year before. Holding the coffee mug had made her cry harder, which caused her eye makeup to goop and run into the wrinkles and grooves that branched out from her eyes.

No, she didn't know if Hero was involved with someone.

No, it was inconceivable that she had any enemies.

No, she couldn't say where Hero lived or what else she did for a living. And Luca was a bastard for even implying she was anything but a right and proper angel.

The woman had been useless after that. Luca dismissed her to go fix her face.

Background checks were being propagated, and Hero's past was now being compiled by an army of federal office clerks and paralegals. He'd know everything from where she lived, to her medical records, to what kind of nail polish she preferred.

By the time the surgeon emerged to deliver a prognosis, Luca had paced a new path in the well-worn carpet of the waiting room. They'd had to reconstruct some of her large intestine and sew a small laceration to her kidney. A few pints of blood had been replaced and they still worried about infections or parasites from the river water. However, the fact that she'd spent time in the freezing water likely saved her life. Her body was strong and healthier than most, so they expected her to pull through. This seemed to be her lucky night.

If you put aside the whole victim of a psycho killer part.

Luca collapsed with relief into the chair and not moved since. He stared at his Bruno Magli *Palatino* Cap Toe Boots. Studying his shoes always helped him think. The rain and mud had done a number on them. Luca sighed. That's what he got for wearing four hundred dollar boots to work.

He couldn't make sense of this one. Thus far, John the Baptist's victims were hookers. Or in one case, an escort, and if everyone was being completely honest, there wasn't much of a difference. Maybe in the way they filed taxes. Perhaps Hero prostituted to supplement her artist lifestyle? Hey, if college chicks were doing it nowadays, it wasn't past the realm of possibility. But still, more and more about this particular victim didn't add up.

Then there was her family. No Katrova-Conners were listed in the phone book. Oddly enough, he knew of one other person with that distinctive last name and the menacing bastard just *happened* to be a fellow FBI agent. And Hero's brother. Maybe that meant something?

Because of the public outcry over John the Baptist, it was pretty common knowledge Luca was lead on the case. He'd done a few bullshit press conferences. Was it a possibility this hit was more of a taunt to the FBI? A copy-cat maybe?

While Hero had been in surgery, Luca had called his partner, Vincent Di Petro, to ask what he could about Hero's brother. He'd seen the guy around, but they'd never really had the opportunity to work together.

His partner was at the scene, coordinating the evidence collection while Luca stayed with the victim, but he was able to give Luca the info he needed on Hero's brother.

Berowne "Rown" Katrova-Connor worked in the White Collar Division and on the International Crimes Task Force. He was ex-military, a crack shot, fantastic grappler, and some sort of computer whiz. The whole *famn damily*, which he understood to be prolific, was military or law-enforcement.

Except for Hero, looked like. And what the hell was up with their weird ass names? Hero? Berowne?

Luca took a sip of shitty hospital vending machine coffee. It was luke-warm now and tasted like grit and ashes. The grounds at the bottom stuck in his throat and he had to chew a little and force them down. Then, he stood and tossed the Styrofoam cup at the trash can across the room by the door. God, he was sick of bad coffee. But he wasn't going to wait in line at some uppity, beat-nick coffee house full of stoners and students—not that the two were mutually exclusive— just for a decent cup of joe. He had shit to do.

"Made it." The smile in her weak voice made him think that maybe he'd gone without sleep for so long, he'd started hallucinating.

Luca spun back around as if he'd heard a gunshot. "What?" The bleary jade-green eyes that met his gaze suffused him with a barrage of disturbing sensations. "Ms. Connor, I—"

"Where's everybody?" she slurred slightly while looking around her dim room in bewilderment.

"Who?" Were there more women floating in the river tonight? Had she been held with someone else? Did she mean the rest of the first responders?

"Knocks," she mumbled. "Brown. Rohm. Dim tree. Dra. Pop. Mmph." Her eyes clouded with worry and confusion.

Okaaaay, now she was just speaking nonsense. He should probably go get a doctor and let them know she was awake. And had a possible brain injury. God, he hoped not. He needed the horrible information she carried in her memory. He needed every little detail. The shark in him wanted to attack her with a million different questions.

A booming voice threatened from the direction of the nurses' station. "I don't give a ripe shit about visiting hours *or* who's already in there. They're not family, and they can get the hell out!"

"But Mr. Connor, he's FBI." Barbara's frazzled response came closer, along with the clacking of her ridiculous shoes as she chased the determined voice down the hall.

"Well, so the hell am I." This was obviously said through clenched teeth.

"And he's a *Mexican*," she stage whispered in her southern drawl.

Luca rolled his eyes. He was half Euro-Brazilian, half Puerto Rican, but whatever.

Hero's head fell back to the pillow, and she relaxed.

Apparently, Di Petro had made good on his promise to call Rown and the concerned brother had flown here and apparently called in the rest of her clan.

It surprised him how badly he didn't want anyone else in Hero's room. Even her family. She'd clung to him so ferociously, and he wasn't ready to give that up. So—this was new and dangerous emotional territory.

Hero was a piece of priceless evidence, nothing more. He had no business going all white-knight and shit.

"In here, man," he forced out, walking to the door to wave the brother in. It was that or slam and lock it against him and the rest of the world.

Yeah, he was one tired bastard if he was considering something so stupid.

"Ramirez." Rown's amber eyebrows lifted in surprise as he narrowed green eyes identical to Hero's. He wore workout sweats, a T-shirt that struggled to contain his muscle, and flip-flops. He'd likely been roused from bed by Di Petro's call. Luca had never seen him out of his cheap ass Men's Wearhouse suits. The same ones that hung in Luca's own closet, or the one he wore now. The man was built like a comic book hero with crazy-wide shoulders and a disproportionately lean waist. He shoved past Luca into the room.

Were it not his sister lying on the bed, Luca would have shoved the guy back. Right out the third story window. He let it slide though. For now. The wild, frenzied worry in the other man's demeanor told him his fellow agent was ripe for violence. And this big mother-fucker may not work homicide, but Luca couldn't predict the outcome of that particular battle.

"Hero? Hero, what the—" As if on instinct, Rown reached to take her hand, then recoiled when he saw the thick bandages covering all but the tips of her fingers. "What did he do to you?"

Hero didn't answer as she had sunk back into unconsciousness.

Her brother leaned over as if looking for a safe place to touch her. With the scratches and contusions now swelling and coloring her face, her injured hands, and the various tubes attached disappearing beneath the covers to God-knew-where, he obviously didn't dare.

"*Damn.*" Turning away from her, he seemed to search for something to throw. Or smash. Luca knew the urge all too well.

"She woke up a second ago." He kept his voice even and non-threatening. The situation between them could go south very quickly. They were on the same side here. No reason for their respective testosterone to clash. "I think she was asking for you. She's pretty out of it."

Rown turned and his eyes focused as they zeroed on him. He seemed to get a hold of himself and nodded, his jaw still clenched. Luca spoke this language all too well. Don't unlock the teeth until you can trust yourself not to do something ridiculous like snarl or roar.

Make gestures instead.

Luca answered the question in Rown's eyes. "She was pierced in the hands and the left side, then nearly drowned in the river. Lost a good deal of blood, but they replaced it and fully expect her to pull through. Here's the surgeon's cell number. He went home, but said to contact him anytime."

Vibrating with obvious rage, Rown looked at the extended card for a sec and then took it. "Thanks."

"Yeah."

"And for..." he gestured to the chair.

"Yeah." Luca stuck his fists in his pockets. "She was pretty scared. I didn't want her to wake up alone."

A spark of defensive anger flared in Rown's eyes.

"We didn't recover a purse or any identification," Luca explained. "You were called as soon as we knew who she was."

After a quick mental evaluation, Rown nodded and ran frustrated fingers through short, auburn hair and linked his fingers behind his head, causing his biceps to threaten the seams of his sleeves. "John the fucking Baptist?"

Luca nodded. "Looks like."

"That makes no damn sense. Doesn't he only kill hookers? How the hell did this happen? My sister is no prostitute."

Luca cleared his throat. "How... sure are you of that?"

"Sure as shit." Rown pushed an extra folding armchair out of the way hard enough that it bounced off the wall and advanced on Luca, who just shrugged and stood his ground.

"I have to ask. You know that."

"Oh dear," Barbara moaned from the doorway. Luca thought it was because she caught the murderous glint in Rown's eyes. But at that moment, either a rioting mob had gathered, or the rest of Hero's family stormed through the halls of the ICU. God, he hoped they didn't traumatize the other occupants of the unit with their noise.

"Where is she? Where's my baby girl?" Was that an Irish accent in a booming baritone?

"What the fuck did Rown say on the phone?" Came the irate, gravelly question. Someone hadn't shaken the sleep from their voice, but the accent was American.

"Watch your mouth in front of your mother. You may be Special Forces, but I'll still wipe your arse on the floor, boy."

"It's *'wipe the floor with your ass'* pop." Came yet another deep, male voice. This one calmer. Darker.

"Calm down, Dad. I'll find the night ICU doctor and he'll tell us what's going on." A woman's voice. The obvious force of reason in the chaos.

"All Rown said was she'd been stabbed and found in the river and that she was alive," said calm-and-dark.

"Lennox is going to be so upset when he hears about what happened to his Hero." How international *was* this family? That trembling female voice had a faint, Eastern European tinge to it. Russian maybe?

Wait. *'His Hero?'* Was this Lennox asshole Hero's man? Why the hell wasn't *he* here yet? Wouldn't he notice his lady was missing all night? Didn't matter, Luca wasn't in a hurry to meet him.

Couldn't say why.

"Look here, Ramirez." Rown used his family's distraction to get up in Luca's face.

Not appreciated.

"You breathe one word about the possibility of Hero being a prostitute in front of my mother and dad, I'll rip off your head and spit down the stump, got it?"

His sharply angled face couldn't be more dead serious.

Luca could respect that. "Step back and we've got a deal." Two could play the stone-face angle. But he could be decent without being intimidated into it, thank you very much.

Rown jutted out his chin, but took a retreating step before turning to meet the crowd in the hallway. As it turned out, only five extra people crammed into the small ICU room instead of the six Rown had predicted.

"Where's Knox?" Rown demanded to no one in particular.

"London." The biggest of the five men present wasn't the tallest at maybe six foot, but his shoulders blocked the entire doorway. His matching green eyes were dead, though, and a disconcerting chill settled around him like an aura.

"We were waiting to call him until we knew more." The obvious patriarch of the family also happened to be the shortest in the room. If one discounted Hero. At about five-seven, he stoutly led the three Katrova-Connor men.

Christ, was Hero related to SEAL Team Six?

"Jesus, Mary and Joseph... my sweet child." The older Irishman crossed himself and kissed his fingers before grabbing the hand of a tall, classically beautiful, sixtyish brunette and rushing to his daughter's side. The others present dutifully followed suit with the crossing, the kissing, then the hovering.

Luca made his own cross, for Hero's sake. The motion was so alien to him now. Most of the time, he contended that if there were a loving God, shit like this wouldn't go down. But a part of him still expected to be hit by lightning even as the thought rolled through his mind.

Dead-eyes lingered at the edge of the group and didn't miss Luca's movement. As his gaze zeroed in on him, Luca felt as though he'd just been marked for death. "Who are you?" the broad man asked with that gravelly voice. Something was wrong with this guy. Dangerously wrong.

Rown deftly commandeered the introductions. "This is Special Agent Luca Ramirez from the Bureau. He's lead on the John the Baptist case." He gestured to his father and the lovely dark-haired, black-eyed woman tucked into his brawny side. "My parents, Eoghan and Izolda Katrova-Connor."

That was the cause of the hyphenated last name, huh? How progressive of them.

"My little brother, Demetri." He pointed at a black-haired, black-eyed carbon copy of his mother. "Little" must have been an ironic statement. The guy was decked in jeans, heavy leather and carried a black motorcycle helmet with the skull and crossbones on the back.

They exchanged nods. This one belonged to the dark, silky voice.

"The oldest, Romeo." He nodded to the muscled equivalent of a storm-cloud.

"Connor," the husky voice corrected, his flat affect never once changing.

Sure. The scary bastard wouldn't want anyone getting the wrong idea, after all. This guy was no poetry spouting lady-killer. Luca looked at Hero who still slept as peacefully as a child. Yeah, wrong choice of words. Even on the inside.

Luca had never been so grateful that he was tall and built like a linebacker. He might need it in this crowd.

"Oh and that's Andra." Rown threw a hand toward the slim red-head now standing in the doorway. Thick-rimmed librarian glasses framed her whiskey-colored eyes. Her hair, a little darker red than Hero's or Rown's, was drawn back into a tight knot that went with her smart slacks and shirt.

"Timandra Katrova-Connor." She walked in briskly, followed by a middle-aged doctor who looked fresh enough to just be coming on shift.

"As in—"

"Assistant District Attorney Andra Connor, yes." She offered him her hand and he took it in a congenial shake. He couldn't believe he didn't put that together before. Damn.

So, Hero hadn't been spouting nonsense after all. *'Brown, Rohm, Dim Tree, Pop, Tmmm, and Mmph'* turned out to be Rown, Romeo, Demetri, her father, Timandra, and Mom.

Wait a sec. He took that class in college. Some of these names were like, from plays and shit. Shakespeare, right?

"Now that's out of the way," Izolda said, her husky Russian accent taking command of the room. "Tell us what is going on here."

Luca cleared his throat, squirming a little beneath her cat-like gaze. She carried a lot of presence by herself, but flanked by her enormous sons and attached to a husband that could have been a ginger gorilla in another life, she was downright venerable. "We believe your daughter, Hero, has been the attempted victim of John the Baptist."

The next silent three seconds must have been the eye of the storm. In all of his experience with college sports and Law-Enforcement, he'd never heard so much cursing packed into one space. Even the doctor's ears turned a little red. The general sentiment seemed to be the expected questions. What happened? Was Hero going to be all right? Did they catch the perpetrator? Et cetera.

"I'm sorry!" The doctor's tag read *Karakis*, which kept in bearing with his Mediterranean looks. "This is not good for the patient. Please follow me out into the consultation area and I can give you more information."

"I'm not leaving my daughter." Eoghan visibly dug into the ground, gently laying his meaty hand on Hero's forearm. "You can *consult* with us right here."

"I really must insist." To his credit, the doctor remained undaunted.

"Look let's not make an incident out of this." Luca looked to Rown for back-up. But the guy had rallied around his parents. Traitor.

"You can keep the hell out of this." Connor shoved a finger in Luca's direction. "If you'd been doing your job instead of thumbing your dick for the last six murders, my little sister wouldn't be lying in that bed."

"Hey." The weak voice from the aforementioned bed startled them all into silence. And likely saved ole Romeo's life. Hero lifted her head to spear her oldest brother with gentle reprobation. "Be nice."

3

"Thy drugs are quick."

— WILLIAM SHAKESPEARE, ROMEO AND JULIET

The ruckus had been pleasant, at first, as Hero swam in the soupy remnants of whatever painkillers or sedatives the hospital had given her. These voices were so beloved to her. She was alive. Safe. She wasn't dead or staked to a cross anymore. No reason to think about that now. Then her heart would start to pound, her limbs would tremble. And she would sweat. She was always a nervous sweater, and if that beautiful Latin cop was still with her, she didn't want him to see her all sweaty. So, she'd just float here, wrapped in the warmth of her family's presence and concern.

And likely Vicodin.

Hero pictured the gentle dimpled smile of her wrathful savior. Probably gentleness didn't come easily to him. Or smiles.

Speaking of... somewhere beyond her soft nebulous, the masculine voices started to churn with aggression. Hero decided to surface so she could mediate. She allowed herself a long-suffering inward sigh before opening her eyes. Good, they were functional, if somewhat blurry.

Telling Conner to mind his manners worked, for once, she noted smugly. So, she'd found a silver lining to this whole business of being in a hospital bed. Of this, she would take great advantage.

As soon as her vision cleared, Hero used the shocked silence to search the familiar faces for *him*. Ah, there he was, looming in the corner. The avenging angel with tempting mocha skin and glittering black eyes.

God, she was going to sculpt him naked someday. And, if he didn't let her see him naked? She'd just have to use her imagination, her very *vivid* imagination. She was probably going to try to get him naked, though.

"Hi." She attempted an engaging smile but her numb face refused to cooperate. What did they have her on, anyway? This was some good shit. Hero refrained from taking anything inorganic into her body, but this counted as a medical emergency. And, in truth, she was kind of enjoying herself. It didn't matter, she'd do a juice cleanse upon her release from this fine establishment and get any harmful chemicals out of her system.

Tall, dark, and dangerous was adorable when flustered. "Hi," he responded in that silky baritone of his. He cast a sheepish glance at Rown and her father. A smile fought at the corners of his lush lips and showed off that one great dimple on the left cheek of his chiseled face.

She wished he didn't have his suit jacket on, then

she'd be able to tell if all that width was pure shoulder and not padding.

"Christ, she's high as a kite." Rown rolled his eyes.

No she wasn't.

"No, I isn't," she insisted. Her nose itched like crazy, but her hands felt like they were weighed down with bricks. With all her attention focused on lifting one of them, she effectively ignored everyone. She smiled triumphantly—probably—as her right arm lifted and she directed it toward her nose. It frustrated her when she poked herself in the eye. You'd think finding your own nose on your face would be easy. "Well, maybe a little," she admitted. If not being able to feel your extremities meant you were high. Holy balls! Those bandages were huge! Only the very tips of her fingers were visible and the bandages were tight enough that she couldn't wiggle any of them.

But her nose didn't itch anymore, so she shrugged. Mission accomplished.

"That might not be a bad thing right now, Berowne," her mother said softly and petted her hair.

Hero loved her mama and told her so.

"I love you too, my darling." Her mom kissed her hair. Hero also loved that whenever her mother said "darling" it still sounded like "*dar link*." She wished her mother didn't look so sad, though. That everyone didn't. She was fine. She was safe now, and would just focus on recovery. No need to dwell on anything unpleasant. They should be celebrating. She survived, beat the odds. That was kind of a big deal.

"Ms. Connor, are you in any pain?" Dr. Karakis squeezed his way past Rown and Andra to the left side of her bed. Seeing as how everyone else was on her right, he'd taken the path of least resistance. Smart guy, her doctor. Handsome too, kinda.

"On a scale of one to ten, rate the pain you're in," he ordered gently, while checking her monitors and IV, looking satisfied.

"I can't even tell I'm attached to my body, doc." She tried the smiling thing again. Probably she was doing okay at the smiling. She had enough practice. Didn't your muscles just retain the memory of stuff you did all the time? "You're doing a *great* job," she encouraged Doctor Karakis. He really was a nice man. She wondered why she'd never met him from her volunteer work. She remembered to thank him for his time.

A choked noise drew her attention. Her father had started to cry. Why was he doing that? She was fine. Couldn't he see?

"It's okay, Pop," she tried to reassure him. "Don't cry." It made this whole thing really awkward.

Andra had tears running down her face too and Andra *never* cried. Even at sad movies. She usually served as Hero's human Kleenex as she was a big ole' baby. Her brothers just stood around and looked grim. So business as usual, then.

She missed Knox. He would have smiled at her. He was the only other one that was also as good at smiling.

"I need a number," Doctor Karakis gently prodded, "for your chart."

"Oh, of course." Why hadn't she thought of that? "*Liiiiiiike,* a two, and mostly because I just poked myself in the eye. Also, my throat is sore."

"That's because of the breathing tube," the doctor explained patiently. "It was difficult to keep you breathing on your own, at first, and you needed it during surgery." Hero found it hard to ignore her families' horrified reaction. She didn't want to hear this stuff yet. She just wanted to ride out her sweet drug-induced mellow.

Motioning him closer with her head, mostly because her hands were still refusing to work, she was pleased when he bent down to her.

"Why don't you take everyone out there and tell them how okay I'm going to be," she suggested in a conspiratorial whisper. He hadn't yet told *her* she was going to be okay. But, likely someone would have mentioned it if she were dying. "Also, you can tell them exactly how to pamper me while I get better."

She attempted a wink, but her eyelid just trembled and she had to blink rapidly.

Dr. Karakis patted her on the shoulder and offered her a warm smile that deepened the attractive brackets around his mouth. "I'll be in the consultation room to the right. How about *you* tell them to meet me there? Maybe they'll listen to you." His wink was successful.

Show off.

"It's very important that you don't strain your abdomen, understand? I'll leave the rest to tell you later." He nodded to the room at large and strode out the door and to the right.

"Mama..." Hero blinked up at her mother.

"I know, *Malyshka*." Her mother kissed her forehead and nuzzled her cheek. She felt warm and soft and familiar. She stood and threw her statuesque shoulders back and regarded her brood. "We're going to get information from the doctor," she commanded. Coming from Mom with her husky voice reinforced by steel, it sounded like there might be waterboarding involved during the procurement of said information. But there wouldn't be. Mom was smooth.

"We'll be right back in, wee one." Pop kissed her. His graying ginger bristles didn't tickle her cheek like they usually did. Stupid numb face. But he smelled like Irish Spring soap, engine grease and Guinness. All was right with the world. He followed Mom out the door.

Demetri held his glossy, black, shoulder-length hair back from his face and bent to kiss her. His jacket clinked and creaked. *He* smelled like leather and asphalt and nighttime. "You're such a bad ass," he murmured, pressing his broad forehead against hers.

Hero ignored the darkness and vengeance lurking in his eyes. "I had you for an example," she whispered.

The corner of his mouth lifted in his signature devastating half-smile. "I'm glad you're going to be okay." He slapped Connor's shoulder as he passed him on his way to the door. "C'mon, big guy."

Her eldest brother loomed at her feet, all rumpled and bleary, like he'd also been roused from a pill-induced sleep. Which was more than likely. His hands curled into fists and he might as well have been chewing on nails. Hero tried to understand him. But they rarely agreed on anything. In his mind he exacted death and formed a battle plan. He was gathering intel and securing the high-ground. He'd never come home from the war. It still raged within him. "I swear to God, I'm going to—"

"Not now." Andra grabbed his arm.

His jaw ticked. "Later then," he promised.

Andra patted Hero's forearm. Her fingers were moist from wiping the tears off her cheeks. Red patches of skin crept up her elegant neck as she fought her emotion. Andra was a blotchy crier like her. Huh. You learned something new every day. "I'm just going to make sure the poor doctor is okay," she sniffed.

"Maybe he's single," Hero suggested through tingling lips. Uh oh, maybe the drugs were beginning to wear off. No good could come of this.

"Why don't *you* go for him, then?" Andra visibly brightened and hid her worry behind a prolonged blink. Andra could play anyone like Darol Anger's fiddle and could read a person with Shakespearean accuracy. She'd honed her acting skills in the courtroom and, at this moment, Hero was glad. "You've got to be the hottest patient he's had in a long time. Plus, you look pathetic enough to pull the sympathy card."

"I have too many tears in me." Hero held up her bandages for inspection. Hey, it worked! "I'll give you the advantage point, this time."

Andra blinked again, but her smile remained. The corner of her lip caught the tear that escaped. But bless her for trying.

"Now, go arbitrate," Hero demanded, before she ended up crying too. If she started now, she'd not stop until her bones wrung dry.

Andra collected Connor on her way out.

Now she was almost alone with *him*. If she could only get rid of Rown. She looked up at her brother who stood with his arms crossed over his chest and glared down at her.

Didn't seem likely. Dammit. Hero frowned right back. If he said something to harsh her buzz, she'd never forgive him.

"Who's your friend?" she spoke first, looking past Rown to the mysterious man who regarded her with what she imagined to be a fascinated expression. Some people would say he looked at her like she was crazy. But she was an optimist. Life was all about per-spective, right?

He gave her a startled blink, but quickly recovered and cleared his throat. "I'm Special Agent Luca Ramirez." He stepped out of the dark corner toward the foot of the bed. He moved like a panther might. Sleek. Predatory. Deceptively loose-limbed and re-laxed, until you were lying with your throat torn out wondering what just happened. "I have a few ques-tions for you."

"Absolutely not," Rown snarled.

She didn't like where this was going at all.

"She doesn't want to go there right now," Rown said.

"You know the longer I wait, the less likely it is we catch this guy." Agent Ramirez stepped toward her.

"Tough shit." Rown stepped closer, as well, her wall against reality and the horror that faced her in remembering it.

"What's with you, man?" Luca threw his hands out. "What if someone else is already in danger and she holds the key to apprehending this sick bastard? You of all people should appreciate that."

"That someone else isn't my sister," Rown said. "She almost *died* tonight, for chrissakes and she's trip-ping balls. Nothing she says can be admissible in court. You can wait until tomorrow."

Hero shrugged. She didn't want to face this. Not now, not *ever*. But Agent Ramirez had a point. The dill weed. What if she decided to be an ostrich and an-other woman died? She'd have that on her conscience.

"It already is tomorrow," she sighed and motioned to the dim silver light at the window that threatened dawn. "And I'm only going to feel worse." She'd at-tended this dance before, she knew the steps. A brief relationship with horseback riding had left her with screws in her hip and some herniated disks. You felt the best the moment after you woke up. It was all downhill from there. She took a deep breath, knowing that she was most definitely not high enough for this. There was no such thing. "Tell me what you want to know."

LUCA LOOKED from a glaring Rown to Hero's expectant, affable expression. How did this pretty, cherubic woman belong to such a hardcore family? Maybe it was just the drugs talking. Hell, for all he knew, she was a criminal or a prostitute and her good nature was chemically induced. Either way, she was feeling talkative and the investigator in him smelled blood in the water. With each passing moment, John the Baptist slipped farther and deeper into his impenetrable lair. The bastard probably spent the night somewhere celebrating a job well done before lining up the next kill.

According to the criminal profiler, their killer was a single white male, mid-thirties to late-fifties. Charming, unassuming and socially adept, but lived alone. He would be a religious fanatic, obviously, with a job or obsessive hobby related to the study of history, theology, or the humanities. Unlike most serial killers, he would be the opposite of a sociopath. He'd feel very strongly regarding his victims. His neurosis and emotions would run very deep. He'd probably have delusions of grandeur or megalomania.

This was JTB's first official fuck-up, and Luca planned to be all *over* his shit. Rown could just get over it.

"If you could start from what you were doing before you were taken," he prompted. "Just do the best you can and tell me everything you remember, even if it doesn't seem important."

"Don't worry." Her voice's airy levity was replaced by something deeper, more haunted. "I remember everything."

4

"Pluck from the memory a rooted sorrow."

— WILLIAM SHAKESPEARE, MACBETH

"I remember thinking how incredibly strong he was." The medications caused the pupils of Hero's eyes to constrict to the size of pinpoints. The vivid color stood out even more striking against her pallor.

Luca got lost in them for a moment before remembering himself. He didn't dare look at Rown as he cleared his throat. "Can you describe your attacker at all?"

She sighed and rested her head back against the pillow, closing her eyes as if to conjure an image. "I never saw his face, but he wasn't a big guy, you know? Not like you or my brothers. I remember looking at him from where I was... tied to a-a beam and thinking: *How could someone so* average *be so incredibly strong?*"

Luca noted the suspect's "average" specs on his legal pad, more than a little disappointed that she didn't have any features to describe. Wasn't her fault. But still. He didn't forget the hitch in her voice when she'd mentioned her captivity. They'd get there. Just not yet.

He set his phone on the small rolling table by her head. He'd told her that he was recording this, but she hadn't seemed to notice.

"You asked me to start at the beginning, didn't you?" She squinted as if it helped her go further back. "After about seven I was at St. Andrew's helping Father McMurtry and Father Michael get started with preparations for the Christmas pageant this year. Knox and I usually go a week or so before Thanksgiving to get set up. Sometimes it takes us that long."

"Knox?" Luca tried not to put as much interest into the question as he felt.

"We've been going since we were young. I design and paint the sets and Father Michael builds them. He says that doing carpenter work makes him feel like a true apprentice to Christ." She smiled fondly.

Luca wrote: *Father Michael – St. Andrew's Catholic Church*

"Then what does this Knox do?" he asked.

"He bakes," she said matter-of-factly.

"Excuse me?" She visibly fought the effects of the sedatives, but it was unsure at this point who was winning. At least she wasn't slurring her speech anymore.

"He makes all the pies and muffins and coordinates the menu with Father McMurtry and the church ladies."

Luca rolled his eyes. "And Knox is *what* to you, exactly?" Jesus, why couldn't he let this go?

"He's the brother closest to me in age," she explained. "We've kinda always done everything together."

He shouldn't feel as relieved as he did, either.

Pull it together, man. God, he felt like a rookie. Time to get back to the important stuff before she needed another dose of pain meds and they lost her for the night.

"Okay so, Knox is out of town. Who was there with you last night?"

"Just Father Michael and I, at first. We drank a glass of wine while we brainstormed some ideas about the set. Then I drew a couple rough drafts. Father Mc-Murtry came in later." She paused. "He seemed upset or distracted about something, but was reluctant to talk about what."

Luca added Father McMurtry's name to his page and slashed two lines beneath it.

"Do you think that either priest could have been your attacker?" he asked.

"Hell no," Rown spoke up for the first time. "Father McMurtry christened most of us. And Father Michael, he's just a good man. There's no way that—"

Luca didn't have to say anything. Just cut Rown a look that spoke volumes.

The fellow agent had the courtesy to look ashamed. He knew better than to compromise any part of an investigation. It became more and more obvious he was a big brother tonight rather than an FBI agent.

"He's right," Hero admitted. "We've known Father McMurtry forever. And, Father Michael is newer, but he's done so much for St. Andrew's, for the community in general. There's just no way. Besides, I probably would have recognized their voices."

Luca and Rown shared a look. They both knew that meant nothing. But he read a stubborn reluctance in the other agent's eyes.

"Did anything happen at the church that might have seemed strange or out of place?"

She shook her head and then winced as though it caused her pain. "No, Father McMurtry got over whatever it was and helped us finish the bottle of wine. I left at about eleven."

Making note of the time, Luca didn't look at her as he asked, "Where did you go after that?"

"I'd planned on working all night, so I stopped at the gas station on the corner of Lomond and Broadview because they sell those organic green-tea energy drinks that don't have the dangerous stuff in them."

Luca smirked. He'd read those articles too. It's why he just stuck with coffee. Coffee probably never killed anyone. He wished like hell he had another cup now. He looked toward the garbage where he'd thrown his last cup and shuddered.

Maybe not.

He took a deep breath, not looking forward to his next question. "I want you to answer me honestly, without any fear of legal reprisal. You said you planned on working all night..."

Hero nodded, and Rown un-folded his arms and put his fists at his sides.

"Would you, by any chance work in the sex-trade industry?"

"Dammit, Ramirez," Rown growled.

Hero blinked a few times, as though she were thinking about the question very carefully. Which made him wonder... it was a pretty simple 'yes or no' question. "It's okay," she said finally. "You have to ask right? Because all those other poor women did."

"Right." Luca sat back and tried to look non-judgmental. There was a part of him wound tight as a fucking bow-string. The thought of this woman in any of the salacious situations that seemed to take life of their own in his mind's eye made the coffee turn sour in his stomach. But that dark, evil part of him, the one he never could truly rid himself of. The one beaten into him by his father that stained his immortal soul —just wanted to know what her rates were.

She took longer to answer than Rown obviously expected. "I've never in my life been paid for *sexual* favors. But..."

Rown turned several different colors of the red/purple spectrum. His fists, though, were pure white. "*But?*" he hissed through clenched teeth.

She swung her eyes to her brother in a ponderous, unfocused way. "I'm no Catholic-school virgin," she said with sisterly derision. "*None* of us are."

Rown looked away and mumbled something foul.

She rolled her head back toward Luca. His fists were turning white too. But he kept them wrapped tightly around his pen and legal pad. "I worked as a nude model for a sculpting class more than a few times, and was commissioned to pose nude for a professional painting after that." Her shoulder lifted. "It was no big deal, and I'm not ashamed of it."

"Do you have the name of the artist?" His voice was tighter than it should be.

"Julia Danforth. She's local." Hero shrugged. "We had a short-lived, casual thing in college, and we keep in touch sometimes."

Rown and Luca both stared at her with slack jaws for a moment. Luca was pretty certain the thoughts going through their heads were vastly different.

At least, he hoped so.

Luca recovered first, shifting uncomfortably.

"What about pictures, could anything be up on the internet?"

"I can't fucking hear this." Rown turned away, but stopped short of leaving her bedside.

Her brows furrowed. "No. I've never had nude photographs taken of me. At least to my knowledge. I walk around my apartment naked sometimes, especially when it's sunny out. I have a lot of windows so I guess it's a possibility... but I don't have a lot of people close by—"

"Ew, Hero. God!" Rown turned back, looking more like a disgusted teenager than a thirty-something special agent.

"What? *You're* not there. I'm alone. Usually. Tell me you never walk around your apartment naked."

The smug face she directed at her brother made Luca smile in spite of himself. He couldn't help but like her. He choked back a laugh when he saw the blush beneath Rown's already ginger complexion.

A sudden and absurd gladness seized his breath and surprised the hell out of him. Thank God she'd survived. Even in the aftermath of her ordeal, she was so full of light and vivacious personality.

Of life.

It would have been the most terrible crime to snuff that light out. He was going to bring down the man who'd attempted to. He made a quick and silent vow as he stared into her sparkling eyes. Her smug expression and half-smile faded as she stared right back. He didn't know what she was thinking, but he got the distinct impression that she'd read him like an open book.

They'd strayed from their purpose. He broke eye contact and poised his pen against the paper, willing the intensity of the moment to pass. "What happened after you left the gas station, Ms. Connor?"

"It's Katrova-Connor, and I never left the gas station," she said. "At least, not on my own. He took me from the parking lot."

Luca shifted, trying to hide his excitement. Circling the name of the gas station, he wrote: *Subpoena parking-lot camera.*

"This is where I need as many details as you can remember." He leaned forward. "Start from when you walked out the door of the service station. Which way did you turn?"

Hero's nose scrunched, and she looked to the right. She studied the machine monitoring her vitals with a stony silence. Though her affect never varied from serene, her blood pressure rose a quick ten points.

"I turned left—er—west. I was parked on the west side of the building, not by the pumps. I didn't get any fuel, just an energy drink and one of those gluten-free raw coconut cookies that they had."

Rown rolled his eyes but stayed silent.

"I got to my car and opened the door when—when he called my name."

This was important news. Luca wrote: *Attack not random. Perp had previous knowledge of victim. How much more did he know than her name?*

"I turned around. I saw a man coming toward me, but he was wearing a black hood and it was so dark. There were no lights on that side of the station, and he was back-lit by the gas pump area."

She looked at the bandages on her hands which rested in her lap. "To be honest, I didn't really pay attention as he approached. I put my cookie in my purse. I figured it was one of my students, a customer, or an acquaintance that recognized me and wanted to chat. That happens sometimes. I was preoccupied with thoughts of work and being hungry. I was a little impatient." She shrugged. "I didn't even try to make eye contact or anything. I thought if I was aloof, whoever it was would just say a quick 'hi' and I could be on my way."

Her eyes sought Luca's. Apparently, she hadn't missed his eyebrow raise when she'd said *customer*. "When I said I had to work, I meant I had some pottery to throw. I have a wheel at my apartment and I do my best work at night. The Christmas season is my busiest time of year. Plus, I have a downtown gallery show in December, and I wanted to finish some pieces for that."

"I understand," Luca nodded. He hoped his skepticism didn't show on his face. As much as a part of him wanted to believe her, the possibility that she actively hid the truth from her brother and family still existed. "Can you describe what the man was wearing? Was it a hooded sweatshirt or coat? Possibly with a brand?"

She chewed her lip. "At first, I thought it was a duster or a long coat, you know, but it ended up being a black cassock."

"A what?"

Rown cleared his throat. "A cassock is the robe of a Catholic cleric. Some of them don't have hoods. Some of them do." He looked at the two names so far on Luca's legal pad and frowned. "It's pretty easy to get your hands on one. You don't have to be a priest."

Luca wrote the word next to what little description he had. "So, the hooded man called your name and walked toward you. Then what?"

"He punched me." Instead of pain or fear, Hero's voice conveyed sheer amazement. "Like, in the *face*." She lifted her chin where an angry bruise was gaining some vibrant color. It stood out even more against her white skin. "I'm shocked it didn't break my jaw, but it knocked me out."

Luca flinched for her. "You lost consciousness?"

She nodded. "When I woke up, I was in the back of a long van, you know, like those child-molester vans? But without any seats."

Luca smiled at her descriptive metaphor. He wrote: *Knowledge of fighting techniques? Boxing? Accurate punch to the jaw causing a jolt to the brain and spine resulting in instant but unstable unconsciousness.*

Also known as "the button." This guy took risks.

"Can you remember any details about the van, or its interior? The route you took to the river?"

"There were no windows—" She halted. Her breath rattled out of her lungs as tremulously as a long-time smoker's would.

Luca waited patiently. This was always the hardest part of a victim interrogation. His humanity would war with his duty as an investigator. Forcing a victim to revisit their crime sometimes felt like perpetrating it. Alternately, wading through the often unreliable memory of a mind that was actively trying to suppress a trauma had to be the most maddening part of his job. Either way, he struggled.

Then, he'd feel like a complete douche for even considering his own frustrations.

"Take your time," he said.

"I was already tied up when I opened my eyes," she blurted. "My arms were stretched wide and—my wrists and ankles were tied. It was too dark to see anything." She started moving her feet, as if to prove to herself that she could. "I didn't believe it, at first. I thought for a second that it was some strange sort of prank or whatever. Like, someone set me up for that cable show where they scare the shit out of you and laugh about it. I didn't mean to be naive, but you just don't want to accept it... not when it's happening to you."

Luca nodded. "Did he say anything?"

"He wouldn't shut the hell up," she said roughly.

Rown moved to her shoulder, laying his hand on her arm. She leaned into him, and then winced as though the movement was too much for her stomach wound.

"Do you remember what was said?"

"No, it sounded like it was all in Latin. Kind of sing-song like the prayers Father Michael does at church."

Conversational knowledge of Latin? Luca scratched onto his pad. When he looked up, Hero was staring at him with such hope and intensity, it stunned him into stillness.

"Did anyone find my purse?" she asked with absolute solemnity.

"Not that I know of, not at the scene anyway." Luca had been e-mailed the evidence list from the Crime Scene Unit a few hours back. "We'll track down your car and check in that vicinity."

A tear finally escaped the corner of Hero's right eye. Luca tracked its path as it cut over the curve of her high cheekbone and angled down her wobbly chin.

"I really could have used that cookie right now."

Rown bent at the waist and kissed the top of her head. Resting his cheek against her hair that had dried into auburn mats and likely still smelled of river water, he glared at Luca. "We can be done if you want Hero. You can rest and do this later."

"No, I can finish." She frowned. "But my nose itches again."

Rown sighed and reached down to her face, using the pads of his fingers to pinch and do a little comprehensive rub. She gave a delicate sniff when he finished.

"Thanks." She rested her head against his broad shoulder and they stayed like that for a long moment.

Luca's throat closed off and he averted his eyes, feeling like a shameless voyeur. He'd had a sister once. He'd never showed her that kind of tenderness. Maybe things would have ended differently if he'd known how.

He shifted in the embarrassingly loud chair.

Rown's eyes had softened, but when he straightened and crossed his arms, he fixed Luca with a chilly glare. *Don't push her,* it warned.

"Um," Hero looked up at Rown with huge, shiny eyes. "Do you think they have those cookies here? Maybe in a vending machine? I'm so starving, I'm shaky."

Rown hesitated. "I don't know if you can eat anything, Hero. You had stomach surgery."

Her crestfallen look would have melted the polar ice caps.

"I'll go and ask the doctor, 'kay?" he rushed.

She brightened and gave him a wobbly smile. "I love you."

Rown cleared his throat and glanced at Luca, who schooled the threatening smile out of his face. "*Lovey-outoo,*" he lifted a shoulder and retreated.

Hero turned her attention back to him with a big sigh.

"You're good." Luca let his smile escape. He didn't miss how her eyes zeroed in on his mouth.

"I don't want him to hear the rest. Not any of them." She stared out the door.

"I understand," he nodded.

She rested her head deeper into the pillow and shut her eyes. "It happened quickly, you know? I expected to be taken to some kind of cultish lair or underground stone room or something. I kept waiting to be raped or tortured, but he barely touched me through the whole thing. I guess I've seen too many movies." She opened her eyes to stare at the ceiling. "He took me straight to the river bank, parked, and came into the back of the van to gag me. He was chanting the whole time."

"Still in Latin?"

"I think so," she nodded. "His voice was so... beautiful. It almost lulled me, made me feel, I don't know, passive?" She lifted her head. "Isn't that horrible?"

"Of course not," Luca murmured.

"Anyway, when he pulled me out of the back of the van, that's when I knew we were by the river. He dragged the wooden cross, with me tied to it, to the edge of the water. I kept thinking that he was *so* strong. You have to be freakishly strong to drag me *and* that cross made of heavy wood. But he did it." She shook her head, as though this was the most unbelievable part of the entire story.

"Do you know what part of the river?"

Hero nodded. "It was beneath the Burlington Railroad Bridge."

Luca made a note. That bridge was less than half a mile from St. John's and Cathedral Park and the banks were perfect to release a body from if you wanted it carried on the currents. "Go on," Luca prompted.

"I knew the moment the van's back door opened that I was going to die." She swallowed. "I was so mad, because I kept thinking that I am too young to die." Half of her mouth twisted upward into a wry smile. "How cliché is that?"

She didn't wait for an answer but sped up her speech pattern as though in a hurry to get through this next part. "He dropped me onto the river bank, which was incredibly painful, and then took out a big, flat-head hammer, and two nails. I'd never been so afraid in my entire life. I remember hoping he'd kill me first and *then* pierce my palms."

She looked down at the thick and immobilizing bandages around her hands. They lay on her lap, palms up, as though in supplication. "He didn't, though. I couldn't beg through the gag. But I tried really hard. I screamed. I struggled. I cried. I feel like I embarrassed myself, you know? I like to think I would have showed more dignity than I did. That I wouldn't have given him what he wanted. Like, some people get off on the struggle, right? But I tried everything. I wanted to live *so badly.*"

The tears flowed freely now, but she showed no signs of slowing down, so Luca listened quietly, not wanting to interrupt her memory. She wasn't in the room anymore. She was back on that river bank, fighting for her life. Every word pinned Luca to his chair. He forgot to take notes. He forgot to make any affirmative noises or comfort her in any way. He just listened to her horrible story, a black, aching pit opening up in his chest.

"He never let me see his face. I wanted to. I wanted to look him in the eyes. But he kept his hood down really low and stayed with his back to the light. There were a lot of clouds. He just knelt by my left hand first." Her eyes clouded with confusion, then with disgust. "He was crying. At first I thought it had started raining but it was his tears landing on my wrist, which just made me beg harder.

Stunned, Luca leaned forward intently. Serial killers didn't usually cry. They enjoyed what they did. "Did it seem your pleas had any effect? Did he pause or apologize?"

Hero shook her head. "He drew a cross on the palm with his—his finger and then... Then he poised the nail at my open palm and I was screaming and crying, but he just—drove it in."

Luca winced.

"The first hit hurt the most. After that, it was just dull and achy. I was so angry because I thought, *'what if I can't sculpt anymore?'* Which was stupid, because I was about to die, or whatever."

She sighed and continued. "He stood and moved to my right hand and I was so focused on trying to free my left one that I didn't even see him drive the nail in until I felt the pain."

"I couldn't breathe through my mouth because of the gag, and my nose was running everywhere because I was crying so hard. I kept thinking that I was so embarrassed and all I wanted to do was wipe my nose. Maybe I would seem more like a human being to him if I didn't have snot everywhere and then he wouldn't kill me."

She let out a self-deprecating laugh, then sniffed and cleared her throat. "When he took this antique-looking spear out, I closed my eyes. It was kind of like when I get blood drawn at the doctor's office. I'm fine with it as long as I don't watch. I didn't want to watch him stab me to death. I remember being stabbed in the side. I remember how much it hurt, and how afraid it made me. But after a moment I just thought, *'Well, there it is. There's no going back. I'm done.'* I think I passed out at that point because I don't recall how he got me off that cross and into the river." She sighed, as if the telling had exhausted her. "I guess I lied to you when I said I remember everything. Not very *heroic* of me was it?"

Luca didn't know what to say. The fact that she was retelling this made her a damn hero in his eyes. Also, her status as a John the Baptist victim had just been undoubtedly confirmed.

The fact that he stabbed his victims with an ancient Roman spear had never been released to the press.

"I appreciate you going over that with me, Ms. Katrova-Connor." Luca stood and grabbed his phone from next to her head. "Last thing; is there anything you can remember about the van? A color, a license plate, an identifying sign, words, or even letters?"

Aggrieved, Hero shook her head. "I only saw the inside. When he dragged me away from the van, it was dark and I was really disoriented. I was so busy trying to get a look at *him* I didn't even... I'm sorry."

"It's okay. That's everything I need for now." She'd given him more information in a few minutes than he'd collected in a few months. She couldn't know how grateful he was for that. "I'll leave you to rest and work on recovering."

She nodded before sniffing in a very unladylike manner and tilting her head to wipe a tear on the shoulder of her gown.

He couldn't bring himself to move, though. He just stood there like a chump, looking at her stunningly beautiful face and her small, still body. He knew she had a brute squad for a family, but once she was out of his sight, he couldn't be sure of her safety and Luca found he didn't like that one little bit.

She needed a tissue. He couldn't leave before getting her one. Grabbing a handful from the box next to her bed he held them out to her, and then performed a mental facepalm when she glanced down at her bandaged hands.

"Here," he murmured, holding the bunch up to her nose. She raised her eyebrows, but gave a dainty blow, which he wiped and chucked the wad into the garbage. This stunned him. Usually, that kind of stuff squicked him out, but with her, he didn't seem to mind. It was kind of cute, even. With a mental shrug, he grabbed another tissue and covered his finger with it.

"Can I ask you one last thing?" He blurted the question before his mind had the chance to talk him out of it. Lowering the back of his finger to her face, he used the tissue to gently wipe her damp cheeks, just so they wouldn't get itchy if the tears dried. No other reason.

"Sure," she whispered, her eyes locked on his. Damn, those things were like heat seeking missiles. Once they had you, there was no escaping them.

"Why me? Why did you want me with you last night? Regan, er, Detective Wroth would have been better. Hell, anyone would have."

She looked thoughtful for a moment. Then shrugged. "When I came to, your voice cut through everything else. I knew I'd been saved. That I *was* safe. And there aren't words for the relief I felt." She smiled, which pushed her cheek against his hand. He didn't move it. "You've seen the men I've lived with for most of my life. After feeling the most helpless I could ever imagine, I felt safe with the one in command, who got things done while shouting obscenities. It felt like being home."

Luca frowned, unsure of how he felt. Flattered? Had she just said he made her feel like home? That was probably a bigger compliment than he was willing to accept. All he knew was he didn't want to stop soothing her, touching her, now that he'd started.

And that was fucking dangerous.

"Hero, the doctor said—" Rown's voice cut off.

Luca snatched his hand away and took a hurried step back. He didn't really want to turn around. He knew what Rown's face would look like. Never one to be intimidated, he nodded a goodbye to Hero and spun to face the agent blocking the door.

Yup. Suspicious and threatening.

"I'll be in touch." He nodded at Rown.

Rown nodded back.

He could feel *her* presence at his back. The tingle of awareness started at his neck and shot down his spine. It took Herculean effort not to look back at her. His exhausted brain fired all kinds of fucked-up synapses. He couldn't trust his feelings or instincts. He needed to leave.

Like *now*.

Tucking his legal pad under his arm, he did just that, putting one foot in front of the other in the general direction of his car. The checkered floor blurred in front of him. Thank God he had to grab a taxi on the way home. He probably wouldn't make it alive, otherwise.

Keys? Check. Shades? Check. Gun, badge, wallet? Check. Check *annnnnnd* check.

A weary sigh escaped him as he stepped into the morning downpour. The press already gathered like starving wolves ready to collectively tear their prey asunder, but hospital security kept them at bay. He'd bet his left nut that Barbara had blabbed.

He called his partner, Vincent, to update him, then his boss.

Hero Viola Katrova-Connor would be his unavoidable obsession for the foreseeable future. She was his weapon against John the Baptist.

If they were lucky, no one else would die.

"True is it that we have seen better days."

— WILLIAM SHAKESPEARE, AS YOU LIKE IT

Seven Weeks Later

Home had never looked so damn good, but the smell assaulted her right away. Closing the door behind her, she clicked the button on her key that disarmed the alarm for thirty seconds and threw them into the catch-all pottery bowl. Hero dropped her rolling suitcase and carry-on and took cautious steps around the entry corner into her cozy loft.

Why the hell hadn't she thought to send someone over here to clear out her fridge? Just when she was certain she'd thought of everything.

The romantic anticipation of seeing her apartment again was certainly a confused one. This place held nothing but happy memories. Dinners and friends gathering to sing, create, play music, and dance. Drum circles and costume parties. Hangover breakfasts and laughter.

She needed to be here. To remember what it was like to feel comfortable and carefree.

If only she'd thought to bring a gas mask.

Hero wrinkled her nose. The undeniable scent of death and decay emanated from the kitchen. Putting her purse on the lamp table and throwing her coat on the couch, she headed toward the windows. The three-inch heels of her boots echoed loud as gunshots on the hardwood floor.

In the middle of the living room, a cold blast of fear made her hesitate.

Her kitchen and living room were separated by a half-wall that had a granite countertop for a bar. It had never occurred to her before that it could hide a human being. What if someone was waiting to jump out at her? John the Baptist had called her by name. Did he know her address too? They'd recovered her purse the night she'd been attacked and her ID had still been inside, but that didn't mean he didn't have her information.

She couldn't call someone, could she? Not because of a rank smell and a panic attack. Knox would come, any one of her family would. But, chances were they'd tell her she wasn't ready to be on her own and harass her into going back to her parent's house.

She loved her parents dearly, but after six weeks of recovering with them, she'd had enough of their hovering.

It was time to take back her life.

Hero felt a sudden surge of unfamiliar anger. How had this bastard turned her cozy sanctuary into a sinister place? Her breath sped and her throat constricted as she turned and took a few hesitant steps toward the swinging kitchen door. Her heart beating in her ears muffled the silence, and her muscles went painfully rigid as adrenaline spiked.

Wait. Wasn't this how the pretty girl died in all the movies? Was her hypothetical audience yelling at the screen?

Don't go in there! If you do, you're too stupid to live!

Run out the door and don't look back!

Where's your fucking weapon?!

Oh—a weapon. Good idea. She looked around her clean, bohemian-style living room for something she could use to defend herself.

Hmm, she sure had a lot of useless pillows.

Hero hurried back to the door and grabbed her umbrella from the coat/hat/umbrella stand, and brandished it in front of her. It had a metal pointy end, and she would face whatever was dead or alive in her kitchen. Her parents forced her to take martial arts with Knox and Demetri as a young teenager. It had been years and years, but probably she could kill someone with an umbrella.

Probably.

She wanted Agent Ramirez here. Luca. He would keep her safe.

Quickly pushing that thought away, she inched closer to the kitchen door on wobbly legs.

Pressing her back against it, Hero took a bracing breath before exploding into the kitchen, the point of the umbrella preceding her, ready to skewer any assailant.

Her war cry cut short when she faced an empty, albeit stinky room. Feeling foolish, she leaned the umbrella against the counter and reached for her stainless steel fridge. Yup, this was the culprit. She hadn't stepped foot in her home for six weeks, of course every vegetable, fruit, organic cheese, marinated olive, and leftover would be rotten by now. She closed her eyes and groaned. Her last meal of wok fried tofu Pad Thai was only covered with plastic wrap and not in a container.

Dear sweet Jesus, all the rotten fish sauce.

Before she could stomach cracking the fridge, Hero opened the small window above the sink and hurried to open the living room windows to create a cross-draft. What had she been afraid of? Whoever may have been hiding behind her kitchen wall would have asphyxiated at the stench.

Throwing back her fringed, beaded blue and purple drapes, she was captivated for a brief moment by the blue of the Willamette River. Hero loved her view. In the unseasonable warm December weather, a few hardy souls still took their boats out on the choppy river, bobbing like rubber toys in a rowdy child's bath. As much as she loved to watch, Hero doubted she'd ever dare go in the river again.

Averting her eyes and the direction of her thoughts, she lifted her gaze to the fluffy clouds drifting overhead. The weather channel called it partly cloudy. She preferred to think of it as partly sunny.

Renting a top floor, one bedroom, mother-in-law apartment off Riverside Drive had been the biggest stroke of luck. Situating it above a posh mansion overlooking the country club dock and the sparkling waters of the Willamette, well, that had been just brilliant.

It took all her body weight to open the stuck latch on the window. She loved to listen to the sounds of afternoon lake traffic. But there would be time to enjoy the view later. First, she had to get rid of whatever was making her apartment smell like a landfill.

Snatching the essential oil air freshener in the bathroom, she sprayed a liberal path into her bedroom and opened the window in there, as well. Clove and mulberry tinged the air but failed to dissipate the awful stench.

Puffing out her cheeks on a beleaguered sigh, she tried to steel herself for what she must do. No getting around the fact it was time to tackle the fridge. Hero groaned as she remembered the Kim Chi experiment waiting for her. It would be a dismal failure now, ruined by the extra five weeks it spent marinating.

Stef will have a good laugh at this, she mused.

Stef and her sister, Andra, had her undying gratitude for taking her on that Mexican Rivera Cruise. It had been just what she needed to clear her head, escape the smothering sympathy of her family, and finish healing.

Hero remembered how angry Agent Ramirez had been at her for going to Mexico without his permission. She could remember the pure, hot fury in his silky voice when she'd called him from the airport to tell him she was boarding the plane.

"*Like hell you are,*" he'd growled.

"*Oops, can't hear you, air traffic radio interference!*" She'd hung up on a string of curses that would have impressed a prison inmate.

She couldn't depend on his incredible strength for everything. She needed to face her own fears. John the Baptist had been quiet since her attack. He'd never threatened her or acknowledged his failure. Even after the media furor. And he hadn't killed anyone else.

That they knew of.

The FBI pulled their official protection from her a month after her attack. No more drive-bys, no more check-ins. The Bureau's Senior Special Agent could no longer excuse the allocation of resources anymore.

Agent Ramirez had been angry about that, too.

Stalling, Hero leaned her hip against the sink and looked around her kitchen. It looked like a coffee commercial had frag-bombed in here.

Luca would look good in this room. It matched the mocha color of his smooth, perfect skin.

Hero shook her head to scrub away unruly thoughts. She had to be careful about this line of thinking. The many times they'd been together since her attack had been so perfunctory. They focused on the statements she needed to sign. They went over her story. And over. And over. Studied pictures to see if anything jogged more memories. Visited the crime scene once she'd been well enough to leave the house and drew diagrams. The whole time, she should have been focused on the despicable reality of what has recently happened to her.

Instead, her mind seemed to wander to the veins in Luca's muscled forearms that rolled and flexed when he took hand-written notes on his yellow legal pad. She'd never seen him without that memo pad, actualizing his thoughts in strong, decisive scrawls. The greatest distraction was the way he smelled invariably of coffee and fresh linen. It was like a damn aphrodisiac.

Okay, *this* smell wasn't going to dissipate without some help, and mentally conjuring any other scent with the cloud of rank organic death floating about was impossible. She hoped her landlord wouldn't be stopping by to welcome her home and offer well-wishes. That would be so embarra—

Hero opened the stainless steel door and gagged.

So much blood. Another death. Strange, yellow, life-less eyes fixed in the stare of the dead.

Her lungs emptied and refused to inflate again. Purges of cold and hot alternated over her skin and her extremities lost all feeling as they began to shake uncontrollably as she stared at the gore. Her throat clogged on a scream and a sob.

Dear God. She'd thought she was safe. That the nightmare was over.

But it was just beginning.

*"In the affliction of these terrible dreams
That shake us nightly. Better be with the dead."*

— WILLIAM SHAKESPEARE, MACBETH

"Hero!" Luca called as he burst into her apartment. His semi-automatic did a quick sweep of the space. He gave an involuntary flinch at the scene. More from the odor than the sight of the dead goat head in the open fridge. He'd known what to expect, more or less, from Hero's borderline incoherent phone call.

"Ms. Conner?" Vincent Di Petro called from behind him. She was no longer in the kitchen and the living room and bedroom were also empty.

Luca's heart rate spiked. Were they too late? He'd raced over here as though demons from the seventh-level of hell gave him chase. He'd never forgive himself if she—

A flush from the adjoining room and a beleaguered feminine groan gave away her position. Luca sprang for the door.

She knelt with her forehead resting on the pristine

porcelain of the bowl. The faint bitter smell in the room suggested she'd just tossed her breakfast. Her hair was secured in a loose bun skewered by a thin paintbrush. A few long tendrils tangled with her extravagant earrings.

"Are you all right?" he asked lamely.

She took a few deep breaths through her nose and hissed them out her throat before answering. "I'm okay." Her voice echoed in the toilet bowl.

"We're clear," Vince's Boston accent, tinged with some east coast Italian descent sounded more like *'Weah cleah.'* "I'm calling forensics and securing the scene."

"Copy that," Luca called over his shoulder, unable to take his eyes off of Hero. He moved deeper into the bathroom to stand beside Hero on the shaggy, lime-green bath mat.

Bent over like she was, her short, flowing green sundress shared a hemline with her jacket, barely covering her round ass. That sure meant a lot of leg showing, and anything below the knee was covered with sexy brown leather boots. Hmm, the Mexican sun had dusted her skin with gold.

Goddammit. He averted his eyes.

"Let me help you up."

She lifted her head and regarded him for a second before accepting his outstretched hand. Luca had braced himself for the inevitable electric contact of her skin. He'd experienced chemistry with women before, but nothing like this. It was like he could feel every swirl in the pad of her fingers, every line in her palm, because they were all alive with kinetic energy. That same energy flowing from her fingertips jolted through him like a taser burst, not leaving any muscle, sinew, or piece of connective tissue unfazed. He'd been fighting this feeling for almost two months now, and he was damn tired of it.

Luca helped her stand, catching a flash of teal lace panty in the process. He squeezed his eyes shut and tried to think of the dead animal head in her fridge.

Boner killer.

"Agent Ramirez?"

He opened his eyes and cleared his throat. She looked pale beneath her tan. Her eyes had sunken back into her skull a little too much for his taste and her cheek bones stood out more prominently than they should. She was still the most temptingly beautiful woman he'd ever seen up close, but damn, she needed a cheeseburger and some sleep.

"Tell me what happened," he demanded more tersely than he'd meant to.

Her eyes didn't tear up. In fact, they narrowed on his face. "He *found* me."

"There's a note in here," Vince called from the kitchen.

"Did you read it?" Luca asked Hero.

She nodded and stepped around him, heading for her living room. "It was some kind of bible verse," she said as Luca followed her. "He still wants me dead."

"Maybe you should sit in your bedroom," Luca suggested, trying to prevent her from seeing the gruesome scene again.

"I want to look out the window," Hero insisted, plopping onto the ridiculous, overstuffed sage green couch and refusing to look in the direction of the kitchen.

Jesus, how many funky pillows did one couch need?

"He was in my *house*." She began to itch at the

raised scars on the back of her hands. They were still pink, but had healed very well, considering.

"We can't say that for sure." Luca tried to sound reasonable. "It could be a copy-cat, or any sick fu—, er, weirdo who'd seen you on T.V. We need to verify it was him. That's why we're getting the Crime Scene Unit down here."

She nodded, looking hopeful and frightened at the same time.

Luca couldn't stand it, so he turned and stalked to the kitchen to examine the typed note Vince was studying.

LET NOT SIN THEREFORE REIGN *in your mortal body,*
     that ye should obey it in the lusts thereof.
     But yield yourselves unto God.
     For he that is dead is freed from sin.

I WILL SET YOU FREE.

"SO FREE EQUALS DEAD. EASY ENOUGH," Vince whispered.

Luca cursed. "This is from the bible?" No wonder he didn't read the thing.

"Been too long since I cracked open one of those," Vince snorted. "We'll have the nerd herd back at headquarters look it over."

The shrill wail of sirens sounded in the distance and quickly drew closer.

"Sure." Luca glanced up at Hero. She was staring out at the beautiful river, stubbornly avoiding her kitchen. Her hand idly rubbed at the side of her slim waist, where he knew a deep scar still healed.

Had that only been less than two months ago?

Luca told himself the tightness in his chest was just pity. He'd been eating, drinking, and sleeping John the Baptist for the better part of a year. More so these last two months. Living every moment trying to beat some invisible countdown to another dead body was taking its toll on his sanity. He'd chosen this, though. He could walk away from it anytime. Dump the file in another poor sucker's lap and wash his hands of this job.

As a victim, Hero didn't have that luxury. On top of it all, her home had been invaded.

Luca never had to grapple with the fear of impotence, but this shit was every bit as emasculating as a limp dick. He couldn't very well hand-cuff her delicate, bangled wrists to his. No matter how badly he wanted to. And short of doing that, he couldn't be sure of her safety. Since the night he'd spent with her in the hospital, she'd been part of his every unfettered thought. If he wasn't pouring over case files, notes, photographs, profiles, and forensic evidence, he was wondering if she slept okay. If nightmares plagued her. If her body recovered properly.

What she wore to bed.

He knew what transference was, hell he'd deflected it a time or two. He couldn't twist his obsession with catching John the Baptist into an obsession with the madman's alluring victim. When she looked at him like she did now, like she trusted him implicitly, it made him want to run like hell. It scared the holy bejeezus out of him and conflicted the two halves of his nature. Part of him wanted to be what she saw when she looked at him like that. The rest of him knew what he actually *was*. A man on this side of a monster, using the rigid rules and protocols of the law to harness the taint of evil within himself.

The direct imperative to keep Hero at arm's length became his daily mantra. They would keep things professional. He would do his best to keep her safe, whatever it took, but there were lines he would absolutely not cross.

Rule number one: Avoid being alone together at all costs.

Rule number two: Refer to rule number one.

The Special Agent in Charge of the Portland FBI Headquarters, Hank Trojanowski, charged into the apartment with all the grace of a stampeding rhino.

"Ramirez. Di Petro. As of right now, you're taking 12 hour shifts as Ms. Connor's personal shadows. Either one or both of you will be glued to her side until this evil bastard makes his move. This is our chance to catch this killer."

A LOOSE SEAM in Director Trojanowski's suit jacket shoulder drove Hero to the brink of madness. The late afternoon sunlight kept glinting off the string which was the same color of grey as his thinning hair. Her fingers itched to pluck it for him, but she folded them tightly in her lap to stifle the urge. Her hands were clammy and her mouth was dry. She desperately wished it could be the other way around. She needed a drink. A stiff one. She looked at Luca who urgently argued with Director Trojanowski regarding all the reasons he shouldn't have to stay with her.

What the hell was with him? It seemed that he even found her *handshake* distasteful and took special precaution to keep any physical interaction very brief. She tried not to be offended. Maybe she wasn't his type? Maybe he only liked Latino girls?

That was an awfully racist assumption to make, she chided herself. She knew from Rown that it was against most law-enforcement policy to "fraternize" with suspects or victims. But Hero had never been much for rules or policies. Especially when they made no sense. Oh, and when they got in the way of something she wanted.

"How am I going to conduct an investigation if I'm not in the office during the day?" Luca challenged his boss, crossing thick arms over his chest.

Director Trojanowski was built like a string bean, kinda thin with lumps in unexpected places. He sounded like Darth Vader, though, and Hero imagined that most people found that unsettling. "Well that's easy. Di Petro will take the day shift, six to six, while you put in your time at the office and have a few hours to yourself. Then you'll be here from around six p.m. to six a.m. You two can adjust hours as needed."

"Sounds good, boss," Di Petro piped in from where he was directing the different field units that now crowded her home.

Luca pinned an accusing stare on her. "What about weekends?" he continued stubbornly.

"One of you takes Saturdays off, one of you takes Sunday." The Director shrugged. "It's undercover field work, Ramirez, it's not like you haven't done this for weeks on end before."

"Yeah man." Di Petro wandered over. "Think of all the wicked sweet overtime." He waggled his dark brows. "You paid off your bike with what you earned on that human trafficking case a year ago." Point made, he popped his gum and plunged his hands into the pockets of his slacks. "Besides, now we might actually be able to catch this prick."

Luca ignored him. "Wouldn't it be more appropriate if a woman spent the evening hours here— wait —*undercover*?"

Trojanowski turned to Hero then, joining her on the couch at a circumspect distance. "Tell me what you think of this, Ms. Conner."

"It's Katrova-Connor," she corrected. "But you can call me Hero." She liked the Director, and did her best to muster up a smile to give him.

"Thank you." He patted her hands in a fatherly gesture. "I know you're an artist by trade, but according to your profile, you do most of your work during the day and much of your socializing and running around in the evenings, am I correct?"

Hero tried not to be disconcerted that the Federal Bureau of Investigation had a profile on her. What else did it say in there?

"Generally," she shrugged. She did some of her best pottery work in the middle of the night and usually slept in until about nine-thirty or ten. She liked to sculpt during the day when the sun helped to direct her with shadows and shades. Two nights a week, she taught a yoga class. Early mornings were pointless and had no use to her at all. She had to do shipping during banking hours and could work on her website whenever. However, those hours didn't include gallery shows, art exhibits, weekend farmer's markets and festivals, which accounted for a ton of her income. She traveled to several of those pretty much everywhere along the coast, especially in the summer/autumn months.

"My schedule is all over the place. Anyone who thinks I'm an idle starving artist has another thing coming." She winked up at the agents. "You two will have to keep up."

Trojanowski smirked. "We're well aware of that. We've seen your income tax history."

Her brows drew together at that and she hoped she hid her wince. Did they know about all the stuff she *didn't* claim?

"We're not the IRS," he chuckled.

She let out a nervous laugh. Guess you didn't get to be where he was in the Bureau if you weren't damn good at reading people.

"Anyway, in light of recent case developments we at the Bureau feel it would be safer if you took an agent with you everywhere."

"Does *recent case developments* mean the dead goat head in my fridge?" That poor goat. It had to have been huge, judging from the size of his horned head, and pure white, with those creepy, grey, square-shaped pupils. Despite that, Hero mourned its pointless death. Had it been afraid? Had it struggled for its life as she had?

"Uh, that would be correct." Their conversation was interrupted as Hero's entire refrigerator rolled by on a dolly pushed by a man and woman with "PORTLAND CSU" reflecting off their police jackets. Roger Daltry's voice screamed through her mind.

Who are you? Who, who? Who, who?

God, she was losing it.

At least they wrapped the fridge closed with crime scene tape.

"It's difficult to explain a Federal tail to those in your social group or professional life, and it tends to make people jumpy," Director Trojanowski was saying.

Hero squinted at him, trying to reach his point before he did.

"Which poses a public safety issue. Also, a *uniformed* body guard might scare off the perpetrator."

"Wait." Hero worried about where this was going. "Isn't that the idea?"

"Well Ms. Katrova-Connor, Hero, ah, our best chance of catching John the Baptist is if he attempts to... contact you again."

"You mean attempts to *kill* her again," Luca interjected. His demeanor had been stormy before. Now it was thunderous. "We're not using her as live bait. There has to be another option that doesn't involve—"

"I'm sorry, but does your name title have 'Director' in front of it? Because it damn well better if you're issuing orders, Ramirez." Trojanowski stood and drew himself up to his full height, which was still considerably shorter than Luca.

Luca's jaw set forward, a muscle working furiously on the left side, "No *sir*, but we can't—"

"Yes," Hero interrupted. "I'll do it. I'll do whatever you think is best."

"Hero, you should think carefully about this." Luca insisted, his black eyes glittering with warning.

"What's there to think about? I'm not living like this. And I don't want another woman to go through what I did. For whatever reason, this ass hat picked me, and I intend for that to be the biggest mistake he ever made. You know, other than killing people." She stood up, because it seemed like the thing to do. "I'm in. I'll be your bait."

"Right on, sister." Di Petro clapped her on the back. "You've got a pair on you."

Hero smiled at Agent Di Petro. She'd had an easy rapport with the East Coast transplant since they'd met at the Bureau offices when she'd given her first statement. She liked his sharp, lanky Italian good looks and his laid back, easy smile. He reminded her of a thirty-something Mark Wahlberg and she got the impression that he hid his keen intelligence behind his thick Southie accent and inappropriate humor. He liked people to underestimate him. And that made him dangerous.

"Excellent." Trojanowski looked pleased. "So, like I said, an obvious agent would be difficult, but if he were to be something closer, like say, an artist's assistant or a boyfriend, it would explain their constant presence. Agent Di Petro has consulted for Interpol on some international art theft cases back in Boston and Philadelphia. I feel that he's more suitable to act as your protégé."

Vince nodded, eyeing his partner with a knowing smirk.

That left Luca as the love interest.

Hero bit her lip. Her temperature spiked. How could it be that her body responded to him even in the middle of such chaos and danger?

The agent in question looked like he could spit nails.

Every cloud really *did* have a silver lining. Sure, a psychopath wanted her dead, but she'd also get to watch the tight-assed Agent Ramirez squirm. He'd spent weeks infiltrating a human trafficking operation without complaint, but he was pissed about pretending to be her boyfriend? What was so wrong with her? Better yet, what was *his* problem? She was an excellent girlfriend. In whatever capacity. He should *be* so lucky.

"Sounds perfect," she agreed. "Agent Ramirez can sleep on my couch."

The men all dubiously eyed the couch in question.

The director shrugged. "He's slept on worse, I'm sure."

"Yeah, he has." Vince clapped Luca on the shoulder, losing the battle with his mocking smile.

Luca just glared at the couch in pure disgust, his crossed arms straining the sleeves of his suit coat.

Hero looked over her shoulder. What? Her couch was comfy. Well, it was more pretty than practical. And now that she looked closely, she doubted Luca could stretch his six foot plus frame end to end. Maybe if he moved some of the pillows.

Oh hell, she'd offer him the air mattress in her closet. But only after he stopped being a pouty dickweed.

"Hero, this is *very* important," Director Trojanowski claimed her attention with the grim severity in his voice. "Intelligence has gone over your case and they strongly feel that John the Baptist is someone you know. Or, at least, have met in a personal or professional capacity."

Hero's heart stalled. "How does that figure?"

"To start with, the extreme differences between you and the previous victims. You're not a sex worker. You have a strong religious background. No addictions. You don't come from a broken or abusive family. You're educated, successful, et cetera."

Didn't coffee count as an addiction anymore? Hero pressed her lips between her teeth. "My religious background isn't *that* strong," she confessed. "I'm more of a Christmas and Easter Catholic. For my parents, mostly. I mean, I'm more spiritual than religious."

"Either way, the psychological profile suggests that John the Baptist has likely been close to you this entire time and that something you did drew his... attention. We believe he kills these women in the way he does to save their souls. He's just never left any indication as to why. If this is the case, then he won't stop until he feels as though he's *saved* you."

"Until he kills me, you mean." Hero rubbed at the scars on her hands again, her eyes flicking to Agent Ramirez.

In that moment, with his intense black eyes boring into hers, Hero knew they both wondered the same thing.

What had she done to make this fanatic want her dead?

7

*"I am a great eater of beef
and I believe that does harm to my wit."*

— WILLIAM SHAKESPEARE, TWELFTH NIGHT

Luca stepped out of his car and checked his watch. Six o'clock, dead on. Grabbing his overnight bag, laptop, and briefcase, he looked up at the mansion. The dark grey brick seemed blue in the waning light. It matched the cherry wood pillars and window accents.

Hero's apartment was around the back through a narrow pathway between the house and the extra garage. The one big enough for boats and shit.

Long way from where he grew up. His parent's trailer back in El Paso could have fit in the extra garage like—he leaned over and looked in the dark window—at least three times.

His Ferragamo Tosco Leather Oxfords made a smart clip he enjoyed on the slate flagstones of the drive. He had about a hundred more steps to get his head in the right place. Something he always had to do before seeing Hero. He sure as shit hadn't been prepared this afternoon. He'd just rushed over, afraid for Hero's safety. Everything had spun out of control from there.

So he had to sleep in the same vicinity as Hero. No big deal. She was nothing more than a breakable object that he needed to keep intact. She was the job. He just needed to do his job without— *doing* his job.

The covering over the oval pool flapped in a sudden gust of winter wind, and Luca turned to scan the shadowed forest guarding the acre back yard and a view of the river. A tactical nightmare, this house. Almost impossible to protect from all sides. Like all these umpteen million dollar homes off Riverside Drive, any assailant could melt into the trees and escape through the Highland Forest with no problem.

Luca climbed the few steps to her arched door and paused in front of it, willing the anticipatory heat in his blood to calm. Taking a breath in through his nose he exhaled slowly through his mouth.

One... Two... Three... Four...

The door jerked open and Vince greeted him with his hand reaching into his suit coat for the Beretta he holstered next to his shoulder.

"Oh it's you," Vince said. "I thought it might be, but then you didn't come in." He reached to help with Luca's bag and stepped back to let him pass into the small, cozy entryway. "It's been bugging the hell outta me that this door doesn't have a peephole."

Luca almost forgot the townie had the hearing of a fucking owl. "Sorry, man." He received a fist bump. "I was preparing myself for the smell."

He inhaled. Her apartment smelled nice. The rank odor of death had been vanquished by lemons and something sharper, earthier.

"How is she?" Luca asked, surprised by how anxious he was for the answer.

"She's acting just fine," Vince shrugged. "She bought everyone processing the scene some lunch. Then, when they all split, she changed and I helped her clean up fingerprint dust and what not. She wiped everything down with essential oils and got rid of the smell. Either she's coping very well, or she's in denial."

Luca tried not to let that trouble him. "Did CSI find fingerprints on this guy? Anything?"

"Do they ever?" Vince frowned.

"What about on the note?" A message was new. They could examine the handwriting. Process the paper and the ink. Maybe it would give them *something*.

Vince just shook his head.

"Is that you, Agent Ramirez?" Hero's voice called from inside.

"Yeah." Luca stepped around the entry wall into the living room and his jaw hit the floor.

Hero bent over the ornate black table, her weight resting on her elbows, studying some papers spread out in front of her. She'd changed out of her dress into a maroon tank and grey, stretchy yoga pants that clung to her ass like a second skin.

All the muscles clenched in his stomach. He tried to block out all the dirty things he could do to that—

"You hungry?" she asked, throwing a glance over her shoulder.

Moisture flooded his mouth. Fuck yeah, he was hungry. But it wasn't dinner he wanted to eat on that table. He dragged his gaze away from her tempting curves. Her eyes. He should be looking at her eyes.

"I was just about to order out for dinner." Her mouth lifted in an inviting smile.

Christ, he was in so much trouble.

"Sure," he called, turning to Vince. "You staying for dinner?" Careful to keep his tone casual, he hoped his desperation didn't show. *Don't leave me alone with her yet.*

"Nah. Semester finals just ended and I have plans to get rowdy with some graduate students at O'-Hearne's tonight. New England Revolution is going to beat Real Salt Lake on the big screen and I'll be in the mood for a victory dance after." Vince clapped Luca's shoulder and wagged his brows before grabbing his suit jacket from the rack. Luca knew what *dance* was a euphemism for. "But you kids have fun."

Almost supernatural hearing but the observational skills of an ostrich. Wasn't it their job to read people?

"Thanks for everything, Agent Di Petro," Hero called without looking up from her menus.

"You're going to have to start calling us by our first names, especially in front of people." Vince threw a flirty smile in her direction. "I'll show up tomorrow in appropriate artists attire."

"Maybe I'll even teach you something," she volleyed back.

"Yeah, good luck with that." Vince lifted his chin at Luca. "It's been quiet, but I'll be close if anything goes down. Later, *homes.*"

Luca had changed his mind. It was time for Vince to take his easy wit and wicked smile somewhere-not-Hero's-house. He shut the door behind his partner more firmly than intended. Then locked it. And put the chain on.

"So what are you in the mood for?" Hero asked from the table.

Was she kidding? Even if she offered what he

knew she wasn't offering, Luca wouldn't have been able to decide. Naked. He was in the mood for naked, hard, and wild. And that was a fucking dangerous mood.

"I've got Chinese, Thai, Indian, pizza…"

She shifted her weight from one bare foot to another and scratched an itch on her calf with a manicured toe. The movement did something amazing to her ass. He got a little lightheaded as all his blood rushed south. What was the last thing she said?

"Pizza's good," he managed. Besides, she should probably eat something carby and greasy. It'd do her some good.

He stooped to grab his overnight bag and move it next to the detestable couch, hoping to avoid looking at her as much as possible. He leaned to set it and his laptop down, trying to find a pillow that didn't have some kind of East Indian pattern, fringe, or sequins on it.

He failed.

"Great. Gino's makes this veggie pesto and pine nut pizza on a gluten-free crust that is just incredible."

The needle scratched on his inner soundtrack and he straightened. "Pesto and pine nut better be some kind of chick code for pepperoni, sausage, and extra cheese," he warned. "And what's wrong with plain old red sauce?"

"Do you know how much processed sugar they use in those sauces? Besides, I'm a vegetarian. Doesn't it say *that* in your little FBI profile?" She turned to face him, her eyebrow cocked in a dare.

"Vegetarian?" He made a face. It was kind of like she'd just told him she believed in fairies but not shaving.

And he *knew* that wasn't true. Well, at least the shaving part.

"Yeah. If you knew what digesting meat did to your insides you'd give it up, too."

He snorted. "I'd rather die."

"And you will. Slowly. Of stomach cancer."

This conversation just went somewhere he really hadn't wanted it to. And he sure as shit wasn't eating pesto and pine nuts on gluten-free cardboard. Why did she have to mess with pizza? It was an absolute good.

"What about Chinese?" he suggested, hoping he conveyed more diplomacy than disgust.

"Okay," she picked up the Chinese menu and handed it to him. "Great idea, I'll grab the phone." Brushing by him, she snatched her cell off the bar counter.

He inhaled. Because of her, the smell of earth, herbs, and cocoa butter would be permanently tattooed in his nasal cavity.

That was okay by him.

"Hi, Mr. Huang? Yes, it's Hero, how are you?"

Obviously she ate Chinese a lot.

"Mexico was beautiful..." Her face fell and she took a long breath. "Yes... I'm glad to be home. It's been..." Her eyes flicked to where her missing fridge had gone. "eventful... Yes, delivery." She brightened again. "I'd like the wok-fried veggies with tofu, no sauce and..." She looked at Luca expectantly.

Blech. Luca grimaced. That didn't count as food. That was just roughage you put down to help you digest real food. But he was hard pressed to argue in front of Mr. Huang.

"Beef lo mein," he supplied, going for the meat

and gluten double-whammy. "With a side of those cream cheese wontons, extra deep fried."

She narrowed her eyes at him, but repeated his order into the phone. "Yes, I am entertaining company... Okay, thank you, Mr. Huang. You tell Mrs. Huang and Johnny Li that I said 'hi' okay?"

She hung up. "I need a shower, do you mind listening for the door?"

"Of course not." Luca eyed the door to the bathroom that also connected to the apartment's one bedroom. Hero's bedroom. "I was just going to do a little work. Do you mind if I spread out on the floor here?" He pointed at the Persian-looking rug in front of the couch.

She paused for a moment, studying him, and then looked at the floor. Luca could only guess what she was thinking.

"Of course not," she echoed.

Luca glanced around her apartment. It looked like Bollywood barfed all over the Tai Pan Trading Company in here. Aside from the ridiculous couch facing the wall of windows on the side of the house overlooking the river, a few papasan chairs and a gigantic Lovesac completed the receiving ensemble. All were strewn with loud-colored throws and—what do you know—more pillows. Some bookshelves lined the wall by the entry door, mostly stocked with books on art, pottery, random new age topics, and romance novels with no apparent organizational system. He looked closer. Maybe they were color coded? Other arbitrary tables and surfaces were littered with countless pieces of pottery, vases, dried flowers, and weird trinkets that ranged from Indian deities, to Buddha, to a crushed velvet picture of Jesus in a garish frame.

The dark wood doors to her bedroom and bathroom huddled next to each other on the long wall that ran from the entry all the way past the kitchen and created the shortest hallway in the world. At the end of that hall, Luca knew a small cellar-like room held her pottery wheel, an electric kiln, and floor to ceiling shelves full of pottery in different stages of becoming.

Luca liked how the kitchen, tiny dining room, and living room all shared one huge loft space with high ceilings. Sure as hell blew his beige apartment with beige walls and beige furniture out of the water. Just one thing was missing.

"Do you have a TV? I'd like to catch the game while I sort through some papers."

"I don't." She walked to a closet with funky handles, pulling out a large, fluffy teal towel and a candle. "Don't really need one."

Wait. What? "You never watch TV?"

She shrugged. "I'm usually too busy, and if I have a show I'm following or something I just watch it on my laptop or someone else's house.

"Oh." Luca supposed he could watch on his tablet, but he missed his fifty-five inch flat screen with a physical ache.

Hero paused in front of the bathroom, her hand on the doorframe. An uncomfortable awareness paralyzed Luca and from the worry in her eyes, he could see she felt it too.

This was probably a bad idea.

Other than the fact that the very sight of her affected how his pants fit, they were incompatible in every way. No one would believe that they were lovers. Let alone in a committed relationship.

He was in the FB-*fucking*-I. Couldn't they come up with a better cover than this?

"All right, well... I'll be out in a bit." She shut the

door behind her and the sound of the shower starting broke his daze.

He dropped onto the couch and sank in way further than anyone should be able to. The only thing to recommend this piece of furniture was that it faced away from the bathroom. Only a thin slab of wood separated him from Hero's naked body. This very moment she'd be stepping into the hot spray, water sluicing down her lithe body, dripping into the hot crevices he'd yet to explore. He shouldn't be contemplating pitting his strength against the door. Besides, she didn't lock it.

He clenched his jaw and started counting to ten.

Luca looked up at the wall of windows and remembered something she said at the hospital. For the millionth time. Hell, sometimes in dark moments he'd close his eyes and picture it. Hero admitted to walking around naked in her home sometimes. Unconcerned that anyone with a telephoto lens or a penchant for roaming the woods alone could watch her every move.

The thought chilled him. He stood to let down the blinds and closed the curtains, but paused to scan the tree line and the swath of river turned black by the gathering shadows. If John the Baptist was out there watching, he'd already know that their relationship was a hoax. They were too careful not to touch. They never kissed. Didn't act like two people in love.

Because if they did, there was no way he wouldn't have followed her into the bathroom.

HERO STEPPED from the steam into her bedroom and made her way to the dresser. She grabbed a lacy matching pair of panties and bra. Just because Agent Ramirez was in the next room.

It wasn't that she *planned* to show them to him. You just never knew.

The shower had washed away fingerprint dust and negative energy. Hero hummed as she lathered with lotion and threw on black silk pajama bottoms and a grey cotton top with a black shiny *om* symbol. Running her hands through her wet hair, she padded into the living room.

Eschewing all the uber comfy furniture, Agent Ramirez sat on the floor in the middle of an organized mess of files, legal pads, and paperwork. His laptop glowed to one side, and an almost finished box of Chinese food was discarded to the other. Though he'd abandoned his suit jacket, he still wore his work clothes and shoes, which were *nice*. His only concession to comfort was rolling up his shirtsleeves and loosening his tie.

Hero liked how the creamy almost-white of his shirt contrasted with the light brown of his skin and shadowed his dark eyes with something a little sinister. She had to admit to herself that if she'd met him in a dark alley, she wouldn't assume he was fighting for the good guys. Not because of his race, but because of the tension coiled in his muscles. Because of the simmering heat rolling beneath the smooth skin. Because every feminine instinct she had warned her of an approaching predator every time he was in the room.

"Your dinner's on the table." He never looked up from the report he read.

"Thanks." She picked up the recyclable brown box —Thank you Mr. Huang—and grabbed some chopsticks before walking over and plopping herself, cross-legged, on the edge of his organized chaos.

"What are you reading?" She popped a baby corn cob and some watercress into her mouth.

Luca looked up from his report, but his eyes snagged on her lips closing over the chopsticks.

She drew them out slowly. Just because. Then licked them.

"Father Michael's interview report." He fixed his stare firmly back on the paper. "He left the country two days after your attack, the morning after we questioned him."

Defensiveness for Father Michael surged inside her. "He always goes to Rwanda for a few weeks before Christmas to take the money and donations from the Thanksgiving fundraiser. He wants to make sure they get to the women and orphans."

"How do you know that's what he *always* does? This is only his second year with your church." Luca challenged. "John the Baptist started killing almost a year to the day after Father Michael showed up in Portland."

"He's taken this trip for two years straight." Even to her, the argument sounded weak. "He brings back pictures and letters from the people he's helped."

"We told him not to go *anywhere*. It makes him look suspicious. Besides, he's the only one without an alibi for *any* of the nights John the Baptist struck." Luca looked up and met her eyes this time. Snared them, was more like it. "Including yours. He was the last person to see you before you were attacked and, remind me again what he was wearing while you shared that glass of wine?"

Hero looked at her food. "A black cassock... but all priests do." She hated that he did this. He turned everyone that she loved and trusted into a potential serial killer. Who were they going to suspect next? The nuns? Her brothers? Her parents?

"I'm just saying, don't trust anybody, Hero. Not while you're still in danger."

A small thrill went through her at sound of her name on his lips. "What about you? Can I trust you?"

Luca shuffled some papers and picked up another folder. The silence screamed his answer.

Hero munched quietly for a bit and watched him work. He set down the yellow legal pad he'd held in his lap and picked up another one. Each of the notepads spread around him had dates on the front pages. One of them had the date of *her* attack at the top.

Father Michael's name was scrawled beneath the date.

Hero didn't want to look at that one, so she picked up the folder right in front of her and flipped it open. A pair of soft green eyes looked out at her from a hard female face. Across a pair of ginormous fake breasts, a Portland PD sign tagged the picture as a mug shot. The name "Jensen, April" spelled out in white letters above the arrest date. Her haphazardly lined lips tilted into the kind of smile produced by illegal chemicals. Flaming red hair curled wildly around her equally wild eyes.

Abandoning her dinner to the floor, Hero looked at the picture behind it. She gasped. Bled dry and snagged on a piece of driftwood, April's sightless eyes stared into the camera. Her hair, still half submerged in the river, flowed away from her with the current, still trying to escape the horror her body had succumbed to.

Those eyes. They could have been her own. The water had turned April's copper hair darker and straightened out the curls. Hero ran her fingers through her own wet, straight, auburn locks.

Behind that unsettling picture, she found others, other women, some mug shots, one high school picture, and a few that looked like they'd been taken by friends or family.

Hero's chest tightened as she rifled through them, not stopping on any particular one, but searching each pair of eyes for any signs of life. For redemption.

The folder ripped from her grasp and she jumped. "Hey!"

"Don't." Luca leaned and snatched April's picture from her other hand. "Don't do that to yourself."

"Those were the other victims." Hero knew they were. She'd seen some of those very pictures on the news before she'd been attacked. She studiously avoided the news now. Even NPR. "Where are their reports? Why isn't anything else with them in this file?"

"I don't need their reports." Luca's hand tightened on the manila folder.

"Why?" Hero demanded. "Because they're dead? Or because they were whores?"

Luca's features hardened.

Where would her report be if she hadn't survived? Would she be tucked into a gruesome folder and shoved aside? She abruptly wondered which living picture of her would have made it into the discarded file that sat as far away from his body as possible. She'd never been arrested. And maybe it wouldn't have even mattered. "Don't you even look in there? Don't those women still matter?"

Luca stared at her for a full minute, then ripped open the file and held up April Jensen's mug shot. "*This* is April Jensen. Her birthday is April seventeenth. She was thirty-six years old when she died, but she was still telling everyone she was thirty. She lived in an apartment off Rosemont Street. Parents' names are Frank and LaVerna Jensen. Their birthdays are October fifth and January second. They live in a farmhouse south of Bend where Frank keeps a bunker full of illegal weapons, food, and Ku Klux Klan robes. He was on the suspect list until he had an alibi for the murders of Jessi Scott and Amber Wilcox. After a secretly rebellious teen life, April ran off with a black man, Antony Hines, who became her pimp. *His* DOB is August Eleventh and he lives in Vancouver. He isn't John the Baptist, but I did enjoy putting him in jail for a while. April worked the streets for almost two decades and had a bad addiction to pain pills and to the men who would supply them to her. When she was a child, she wanted to be a veterinarian. She still collected horse figurines."

He stuffed her picture back into the file and grabbed the high school photo. Gritting his teeth, he thrust it in front of her. "*This* is Janelle Kennedy. She was born June fifteenth. She was proud of being a Gemini and had the sign tattooed on her lower back. Her mother died and her father was a stock trader for a bailout bank. His DOB is July twenty-seventh. He lost everything her senior year in prep school so she auctioned her virginity online for a few thousand dollars. In two years she made almost a hundred thousand dollars prostituting herself online and was a freshman at University of Portland studying economics. She wanted to transfer to OSU. She essentially lived down the street from me. Her father had no idea what she did and he now works for a tech support call center in—"

"Okay!" Hero held up a hand. "All right," she said

more softly. "I'm sorry. It's just been... a really long day."

Luca shocked the hell out of her by gently taking her wrist in his large hand. His skin was cool and dry against her flesh which still threw off warmth from the extra-hot shower. He silently turned her wrist until her palm faced up.

Hero let him, transfixed by the broad planes and sharp angles of his face. All anger had fled his features, replaced by a curious emotion she could only describe as reverence. She closed her eyes. Blood pounded through her veins, concentrating in the wrist he held, pulsing beneath his long fingers.

"To answer your questions: Yes, they all matter. And yes, you can *trust* that I'll protect you with my life." Luca's murmur slid across her senses like silk over flesh. His other hand enfolded hers, the pad of his thumb running next to the raised ridge permanently slashed through her palm.

She opened her eyes as goose bumps flared over her skin, tightening her nipples and speeding her breath. Hero tried not to think of how close the bedroom was. Or the kitchen table. Hell, the floor would do.

She glanced down. Maybe not the floor. Sex on the case files would be creepy. But the couch...

Luca abruptly released her hands. "I'll clean these up and take them back to the office. You don't need them here."

"No." Hero tucked her hair behind her ears and stood, taking her food with her. "You work. I have a kiln to load and some bowls to throw. I'll just work down the hall." *Trying not to melt into a puddle of hormones*, she added silently. "Just let me know how much I owe you for dinner."

Luca smiled. "Don't worry about it, it's on the Bureau."

Hero summoned a smile and turned her back, making her way to the studio down the hall from the kitchen that she planned on avoiding for the rest of the night.

The sincerity of Luca's promise echoed through her.

I'll protect you with my life...

She prayed it didn't come to that.

8

"This above all: to thine own self be true,
And it must follow, as the night the day,
Thou canst not then be false to any man."

— WILLIAM SHAKESPEARE, HAMLET

Luca hunched over his unfolded map of Portland and checked his watch. 9:30 a.m.

A caffeine headache pricked behind his eyelids and started to spread over his skull cap. He'd showered, shaved, manscaped, dressed, and read over the detailed pathology reports from Hero's refrigerator all in the last hour and a half.

A muffled noise from the direction of her door suggested she was awake. Finally. He'd lain up half the night on that godforsaken couch listening to the white noise of her potter's wheel and her off-key sing along to alternating indie rock and dub step remixes. Luca rubbed at his left eye. Somewhere between midnight and 2 am he'd developed a twitch.

Hero's door opened and Luca twisted his head around as she lurched into the loft toward the kitchen.

"Good morn—"

She cut him off by lifting her hand and squinting a grumpy scowl at him as she passed. "Don't talk. Coffee," she croaked.

Luca shot a glance over the half-wall at the shiny piece of machinery with a myriad of knobs and leavers that seemed to be the centerpiece of her entire mocha-colored kitchen. Which was basically a coffee shrine.

With her eyes still swollen half-shut from not enough sleep and motions that were jerky and dangerous, Hero performed a ritual Luca found so fascinating, he forgot to be miffed that she'd just shushed him.

Besides. She just said the magic word.

Three different whole beans from separate local coffee houses mixed in the grinder while she took down two hand-made mugs, some sugar, a bag of stevia, and poured cold water into the machine.

Luca stood very slowly, careful to make no sudden movements as he meandered toward the aromatic kitchen in the most unthreatening way.

Hero unceremoniously dumped the coffee into the filter and pushed a button. That handled, she leaned her forehead against the cupboard above the sink and let out a groan worthy of the walking dead.

So little Miss Sunshine wasn't a morning person. Good to know.

Luca popped his head around the door and when she didn't bite it off, he followed with the rest of his body. She'd yet to look in the direction of her missing fridge, so he was probably safe over there. Leaning his hip against the counter, he studied the back of her. Couldn't complain about the view.

They listened to the trickling promise of future happiness in silence and Luca was just fine with that. Hero's hair fell behind her in a tangled braid. He fought the urge to reach out and unknot the elastic. She looked so tiny hunched over like that, her shoulders rolling forward and her whole small, sinewy frame somehow deflated.

The urge to reach out and pull her against his solid body gripped him so hard his skin itched with it. Muscles twitched. Teeth set. He pulled in tight and shut it down, all the while watching her even breaths as she stared through the hair that fell in a curtain over her face as though the dark liquid in front of her offered some kind of salvation.

"What are you still doing here, anyway?" she grumbled. "Isn't Agent Di Petro supposed to be here at six a.m.?"

A tight, unpleasant reaction twisted in his gut. Just how eager was she to see Di Petro? "Ah, Vince texted me this morning. He won't be able to make it until noon."

"Too much victory dancing?" she asked wryly.

"I'm not sure."

The moment the drizzle slowed to a few bubbles, Hero lunged at the pot and dumped it into both cups. Doctoring hers with a bit of the stevia, she inhaled the steam from the cup before taking a tiny, tentative sip.

Luca watched the rapture on her face. Like a fucking coffee commercial. Consider him sold.

Like some kind of arabican magic, her eyes instantly cleared and she handed him his mug. "Tell me this isn't the best cup of coffee you've ever had."

"Smells good," he shrugged and picked up the cup without touching the sugar. A wave of ecstasy overtook his entire body at the first sip. It was still a little too hot, but Luca didn't care. He wanted the taste branded into his tongue forever. When he opened his eyes, Hero was smiling at him over her mug.

"I know, right?"

"Oh. My. *God.*"

She smirked and turned to push through the doorway, plopping into one of the dining chairs. Luca followed her, still trying to wrap his mind around the awesomeness in his cup.

"How do you make this?" he demanded.

Hero took another sip. "It's my special blend. I usually reserve it for the morning after."

Luca almost dropped his mug. Some coffee sloshed onto his map. "Morning after?"

"Well yeah, I like to leave someone with a good taste in their mouth, you know?"

Heat that had nothing to do with the coffee scalded his insides. If this was the morning after coffee, then the night before really must be— His free hand curled into a fist somewhere over the Columbia River as he fought an intense hatred of every man who'd ever tasted this particular blend. His next sip was bitter.

"So, what are you doing with this?" Hero motioned to the map.

Luca stared down at his city, collecting himself. How the fuck did she break his concentration over a cup of coffee? He needed to focus on business, which was keeping her alive.

"These are the residences of all John the Baptist's previous victims." Luca pointed to six different black X's on the map. "These are where we found each of the bodies." Luca gestured to five red X's scattered along the riverfront. One had even reached the Ocean and been found in the net of a fishing dory.

Hero reached out and placed her finger on the one green X next to Cathedral Park. "That's me," she murmured.

Luca nodded. "You weren't a body." *Thank God*, he added silently.

"I like that it's green." Hero rubbed at it absently, as though trying to erase the mark. "The black X's, they're all concentrated in one area of the city."

"Yeah." Luca cleared his throat. "At first I thought JTB had some connection with the University of Portland because all of the women grew up, lived, or—worked their trade at or around the University. You and Janelle were the only women who'd ever actually attended the college, but neither of you finished with a degree and, as far as I can tell, you don't have much of a connection with it anymore, if at all."

Hero shook her head. "The classroom is more Andra's department. I never really did well in such a structured environment. But you said 'at first' which means you don't think it's the University anymore?"

"I haven't ruled it out, but take a look at this." Luca pointed to the black X's again. "There seems to be a correlation with parks in the area, too. Janelle lived by Portsmouth Park. Another victim, Amber, constantly met clients at Columbia Park. April Jensen, she went missing near Northgate. Now, you grew up near St. John's Park and were—rescued in Cathedral Park. That's looking less and less like a coincidence to me. Of course, there's always a chance neither the University nor the parks have anything to do with the location of the murders but rather that whole area's proximity to the two rivers." Luca pointed to where the Columbia and the Willamette converged, right above the neighborhood where Hero grew up. Less than two miles from Cathedral Park. "You were reportedly pulled out of the river by a vagrant who called in to the authorities. He disappeared before he could be identified, but we have a good sketch from the officers on scene. As of right now, he's a very strong suspect and he'd be familiar with the area parks."

Hero took another sip of her coffee, prompting Luca to do the same. Jesus, did she put crack in there?

"I suppose that's possible." Hero's teeth captured her lower lip as she ran her finger over well-worn creases in the map. "Isn't there like, an app for this? Same with your notebooks and paper files. Can't you use a scanner and lap top to organize most of this instead of carrying around a briefcase? It would save a few trees."

Luca carefully folded the map, painfully familiar with the bends in the paper. "I could and I do scan electronic copies of everything." He lifted a shoulder. "But I don't like the idea of all my work disappearing into some electronic netherworld when I power down. I need it to be tangible. I can only trust what I see with my eyes. Feel with my hands. Write in *my* words. Call it old fashioned, but it's how I work my cases."

Hero's eyes were soft as she regarded him, turning Luca's insides to liquid. "I understand," she murmured. "I think it's—beautiful."

"Yeah, well—" Luca tossed back the rest of his coffee, which had cooled enough to only resemble magma, but he liked how the pain distracted him from how adorable she looked in the morning. "What's on the agenda for today?"

Hero brightened. "I'm taking some of my pottery to a friend's house who has a Tunnel Kiln. I need to get a second fire on a few pieces for my upcoming exhibit." She reached out and gave his bicep a few squeezes. "You can help me carry them to the car."

An hour later, Luca shut the door to Hero's funky blue Juke and turned to see her jogging down the driveway after her third trip back to the loft after something she forgot. Was it her purse this time? She looked like a ray of autumn sunshine in a flowing gold peasant blouse and bronze skirt. Some kind of fringed, Asian-looking bag swung from her right shoulder and, apparently she'd decided to thread some kind of scarf through her hair while he loaded the car.

He'd better get breakfast out of this. Heavy on the meat.

"Just one more thing before we go," Hero called. "I have to talk to Angora about you staying here. She just returned from Morocco, and I don't want to freak her out."

Luca reluctantly followed her up the pathway to the front entrance of the mansion. He flipped through his mental rolodex to Angora Steinman, Hero's landlord. From what he could remember, she'd been a cabaret dancer forty years ago, who claimed to be a stage actress before becoming the third wife of a Hollywood producer after the scandal of their affair broke in the media. She'd been born Ida Kreuk, but a glamorous name change and several Jewish weddings later, she settled in Portland with twice as many million dollars as she'd had husbands. Now content to serve on local art and drama councils, she still boinked rich older men she met at the local country club.

Hero just let herself in with a key. "Angora? Are you awake?" Her voice echoed off the marble entryway and carried above the chandelier to the second floor walkway.

Luca whistled. Nice digs.

"Hero is that you I just saw out the window owning the walk of shame?" A disembodied voice barreled down the stairs. It was two parts long-time smoker, one part sex-kitten. "Who was that beautiful man you were with? I could watch him carry heavy things all day."

Hero threw a smirk to Luca over her shoulder and walked to the bottom of the grand staircase. "That's what I wanted to talk to you about, do you have a minute?"

"Is he still with you?"

"Yes."

"Then let me finish putting on my face and I'll be right down. Take a seat in the solarium!"

Luca snorted. Who had a solarium anymore? "Is she for real?" He followed Hero through gilded French doors into a garish room that could only be categorized as a shrine to the past.

"I don't think there's much left of her that is, actually," Hero laughed.

Chaotic portraiture of a woman who very much wanted to look like Marilyn Monroe littered the French wallpaper. Some of them were black and white, some of them in Technicolor. A few included other people, but only celebrities.

"I love that she kept these costumes," Hero commented. "And look at all the wigs! Angora's done everything from blonde bombshell to Arabian nights."

"The mannequins are creepy." Luca fingered a red wig belonging to a naughty mermaid costume. The "fins" had nothing in the way of substantial fabric. Had the mannequin been a real woman, he'd have known her *true* hair color.

Luca wandered toward the wall of photos, not trusting the delicate, no doubt expensive, furniture to hold his weight. Angora smiled expansively back at him through twenty years of big blue eyes. Though, as the years wore on in the pictures, certain aspects of her figure and face became much more accentuated while others chipped away.

"You're missing out, young man, I just rotated out some of my nude portraits." Angora floated into the room on feathered high heels sporting more pearls than had possibly ever been found in the Pacific Ocean. "I'm sleeping with this Republican Senator who is inviting too many friends to my Christmas Party. You know how *they* are about indecent exposure."

Luca smothered his laugh with a cough.

Hero hurried over to her and the women air kissed on opposite cheeks. "Angora, this is my—boyfriend, Luca Ramirez. Luca, this is Angora Steinman."

"Mrs. Steinman." Luca held his hand out.

"*You* can call me Angora, darling man." She extended her hand to him in an over-dramatic movement and he shook it gently, avoiding the mile-long crimson nails.

"Hero, my dove, he has the look of a Mediterranean God with the proud forehead and bladed nose of a native savage."

Luca swallowed, frozen in place as she circled him as though studying the lines of a stallion. "Tell me you're capturing this man in a sculpture. I'll buy the original, but only if it's *en dishabille.*"

Hero crossed her arms as Angora reached her and studied him intently.

Luca started sizing up which windows to break in his escape.

"Actually, I've been considering a sculpture since we met." Hero winked at him.

"Well, you couldn't have picked a better muse. The clay would positively quiver to immortalize this specimen. In fact, I'd pay double to play voyeur to the sitting."

Jesus Christ. This wasn't part of his job description. Did the FBI have a sexual harassment policy? Couldn't someone just shoot him? In the head.

"But lo!" Angora flung her arm with a flourish. "A man who blushes! A rare find, indeed."

Luca frowned. He didn't fucking blush. His face was hot because old people kept their houses a balmy seventy-five degrees.

"What do you do, Luca?"

"Actually, Luca was one of the agents assigned to my case." Hero rescued him. We just couldn't deny our chemistry." She sent him a look that could have set his shoes on fire.

"Scandalous!" Angora grinned, and then took both of Hero's scarred hands in hers. "How are you doing with all that, my pet? I heard what happened yesterday and I've already ordered you a new refrigerator."

"You didn't have to do that."

Angora held her hand up. "I'll hear none of it. Besides it'll soothe my conscience. I didn't arm the alarm system last night because I had a late visitor." This was said with a meaningful, salacious smile.

Luca narrowed his eyes. He'd been wondering why the alarm hadn't been triggered during the invasion.

"I know," Angora pouted an overfilled, overglossed lip at him. "I was naughty. But I promise that I'll not be remiss again. Not until this villain is brought to justice."

"I would caution you to be careful, too, Mrs. Steinman. You should be worried about your own safety as well as Hero's." Luca put his hands in his pockets, caught the appraising look she sent his zipper, and promptly took them out again, thankful for his suit coat.

"You're so kind to worry about an old woman." Angora stepped to him and planted a kiss on his cheek. It would have been his mouth if he hadn't turned his head at the last moment.

"About that." Hero cut in. "I was going to ask if you minded Luca staying with me for a while, you know, for safety's sake."

Luca glared at the smile on Hero's face. She was enjoying this.

"Mind?" Angora laughed and put a flirty hand on Luca's shoulder. "Just give me time to install cameras in the bedroom."

Luca coughed again and tugged on his collar. Why *did* old people keep their houses so warm?

"That's what I thought you'd say." Hero gave her a hug.

"Well, you two young, beautiful people enjoy your day. I'm off to the Tea Garden for lunch with Josiah Winthrop." She clip-clopped toward a side entrance that Luca guessed went to the garage.

"Another late-night visitor?" Hero asked.

"Not yet." Angora winked from the door. "But there's always hope."

9

*"To my sick soul, as sin's true nature is,
Each toy seems prologue to some great amiss:
So full of artless jealousy is guilt,
It spills itself in fearing to be spilt."*

— WILLIAM SHAKESPEARE, HAMLET

Hero kept sliding her gaze from the road to the sexy FBI agent in her passenger seat. If she thought he looked good in a suit, she should have known that jeans and a button-up over a tight t-shirt would be *so* much better. The V collar of the t-shirt exposed muscled curves and sinew that she'd never before noticed in a man. Who'd have thought clavicles could be so arousing?

One could tell a lot about a man from his eating habits, and like everything else about Luca, mealtime was all about control and efficiency. His sharp jaw flexed as he devoured his breakfast-of-death sandwich, balled the wrapper in his hands, and put it back into the oil-stained paper bag.

He took a swig of the coffee he'd pilfered in one of

her to-go mugs and let out a huge sigh of satisfaction. "Now *that's* breakfast."

Hero rolled her eyes. He was, of course, referring to her prior meal of fresh, sugar-free organic fruit crepes and homemade Kefir yogurt from the raw deli on the waterfront. He'd turned up his nose at the menu and demanded drive-through. "What I ate was food. What you ate was fat, meat, and preservatives."

"In a flaky biscuit." He flashed his teeth.

God, that dimple did something to her that was completely unfair. "The eggs weren't even real. When I get my new fridge and can actually store stuff, I'm going to make you meals full of things your body needs."

"How do you know what my body needs?" The silky darkness in his voice caused her thighs to clench together.

"Trust me." She added a husky thread in her reply. "I *know*." Her daring glance clashed with the wry masculine challenge in his black eyes. If he didn't wipe away the pure sex on his face, she was going to pull over and climb into his lap.

He must have ascertained her thoughts because he powered down like someone had released the pressure valve.

Yeah, batten down the hatches, sailor, she thought. *There's a storm a-brewing.*

Trying to ignore the inconvenient warmth in her panties, Hero turned down a private drive where willow trees danced with alders.

"So, where is this?" Luca asked.

"Sea Crest Manor."

"As in..."

"No, this house was built and named before that particular Seacrest was born." Hero chewed on her lip.

How much did she need to tell Luca about this place and the man who owned it? He seemed more relaxed now that he'd eaten and was enjoying the picturesque tunnel of trees. So maybe nothing? Maybe Alec wouldn't even be home. She could just use her key to the side door and they'd be in and out with little fuss. For some reason, she didn't want the two men to meet.

When the tree line opened onto a spacious yard, Hero pointed at a large, circular wing of the stately Tudor style mansion. "Whoever built this house was a glass and pottery worker. A walk-in tunnel kiln is installed right there. Because it is gas-powered instead of electric, it gets a gazillion degrees hotter than mine at home. The heat brings out bolder colors than my kiln at home."

"Oh yeah?" Luca tilted his head like he was trying to take all eight thousand square feet at one time. "Who owns it now?"

Hero forced a smile. "Professor Graham. He taught an ancient European Myths and Legends course and also Renaissance Art History that I took back in college. We've kept in touch. He lets me use the kiln from time to time."

"How does a local college professor afford a *manor*?" Luca's tone made it abundantly clear he found the word pretentious.

"Family money, I think." Hero shrugged. "I never really asked. I believe Alec just teaches for love of the subject matter. He is to history what Trekkies are to ComicCon. I heard he was a fellow at Duke University and sometimes consulted at the Smithsonian. Who knows why he ended up here?"

The temperature in the car dropped maybe fifty degrees and Hero fiddled with the windshield wipers, unwilling to meet dark eyes that always saw too much.

"Alec?" Luca repeated. How could one man pack so much skepticism, accusation, and disgust into such a short word?

Hero parked her car behind the brand new yellow Fiat and reached for the door handle.

"Is there something I need to know—"

"It's starting to rain for real now. Let's try to keep the pottery dry as we transfer it inside." Hero dove out of the car and into a pair of painfully familiar arms.

"Hero!" The smell of tweed, cigars, and Brandywine engulfed her. Once, she'd found the scent alluring and mysterious. She couldn't really decide what emotion it evoked now. "My God, it's so good to see you alive and well. Did you get the flowers I sent?"

She pulled back and met a familiar pair of liquid brown eyes set in the unassumingly handsome face she'd seen so many times.

In so many positions.

"I did. Thank you."

Alec cupped her face in his gentle, scholarly hands. "I've been worried. You haven't been returning my texts."

Therein lay the problem, didn't it? She's brutally attacked by a serial killer and he sends her flowers and texts? No phone calls. No dropping in. No offers of help of any kind. Just enough effort to be socially apropos but deftly avoiding any real physical or emotional responsibility.

Things never changed, did they?

Alec kissed her on the cheek, right below her lashes. Her car door slammed so hard she seriously feared for the pottery in her back seat and trunk.

Hero jumped out of his arms. "Alec, this is Luca, my..."

"Boyfriend." Luca helpfully supplied for her.

Alec winced as he and Luca gripped hands.

"Alexander Graham." Those liquid-brown eyes masked a flash of surprise and displeasure behind a very practiced and professional geniality. "Any man who can buy a pair of Cole Haan's in that size is a man I can respect."

Hero looked down. Luca *did* have big feet...

"I thought you rejected the relationship labels that denoted ownership and fortified the oppressive patriarchal values of our society." Alec turned to her, his perfectly shaped eyebrow arched in a way that told her she'd be hearing about this later.

Hero tossed her hair and slipped her arm around Luca's back. His spine was ramrod straight, and she knew he held a pressure cooker beneath that amiable demeanor. "Yeah well, sometimes you just find that person who changes everything."

For a split second, Alec looked like she'd kicked him in the nuts.

"Your tastes always did trend toward the exotic." His smile could have fortified the Bering Glacier.

Whoa. Did he just go there?

Chancing a look at Luca, she was surprised by his lack of umbrage. Instead, keen interest sharpened his dark gaze. He wasn't so much glaring daggers, but razors, ones he used to cut away the meat and expose the nerve.

"*Anyway.*" Hero stepped around Luca's wide shoulders and opened her car door. "I appreciate you letting me use the kiln for these." She carefully lifted the fragile glazed pottery out of the secure nest of blankets and such that she'd crafted around it, hoping to signal the men to do the same.

Luca grabbed the largest vase and turned to Alec. "Lead the way." Against bronze skin, his sharp teeth flashed white in what was supposed to be a smile. He'd made it a point to identify himself to her as an unapologetic carnivore. Hero never believed that more fully than this moment.

They followed Alec to the garage entrance, which would lead them to the basement. Hero didn't miss the fact that the professor didn't offer to help carry anything in. She wondered about the reasons. Was he being bitchy? Oblivious? Or insecure?

Despite his brilliance, she remembered his unerring capability for all three traits.

As the garage door trundled open, Hero fought a sudden and intense chill as she remembered his reasons for parking the Fiat in the driveway. The sleek, silver Maserati he owned napped like a great cat on its padded floor on the right. To the left of that, the vehicle the college supplied him for trips, digs, and field work nearly glowed white against the well-painted grey-blue concrete of the garage.

Even as Hero told herself she was being ridiculous, a tight band began to squeeze her chest and weaken her arms.

A utility van. Probably full of tools like hammers and nails and... cross beams?

God. She was *not* this person. This paranoid, suspicious, fearful child always waiting for the boogey man to jump out of the shadows.

Alec opened a door leading downstairs, and Hero fought the feeling gripping her insides. The one where her imaginary audience was yelling at her not to go in the basement.

"So Luca, what do you do?" Alec made a stab at being conversational as he disappeared down the wide concrete staircase.

Hero inched around the van, as far away from it as

possible, and followed Luca's broad back into a familiar basement.

"I work for the FBI."

Alec paused on the bottom step for one beat longer than needed. "Oh yeah?" He didn't turn around. "Probably means you're packing heat all the time then?"

"Usually."

Why would Alec want to know that? He wasn't particularly a gun enthusiast. The way he'd said *packing heat* made her eyes disappear into her skull. He really shouldn't try to pull off that kind of vernacular.

The men turned the corner at the bottom of the stairs, and Luca set his load carefully on the long fold-out table next to the kiln. He turned to Hero and took her burden, as well.

"I'm going back up for the rest." He flicked his gaze toward Alec, though he addressed her. "Do you want to come with me?"

Hero seriously considered it, but shook her head. "You go ahead, I'll start loading these. You can hear me if I need you," she felt compelled to add.

"Do what you gotta do." Leaning down, he pressed a light, familiar kiss to the corner of her mouth. His warm, full lips promised the kind of sin that no amount of confession could rectify. Hero formed a desperate wish that their audience would go away so she could explore that mouth's capabilities. She wanted a full kiss, Dammit.

With tongue.

Except—their audience was the entire reason for his affection. She needed to remember that.

"Thank you." Her breathless whisper echoed off

the bare walls and through skeleton beams of the vast unfinished basement.

Then she made a mental note to clarify later that she meant thanks for carrying heavy things. Not for the kiss. His smirk caused her to doubt he understood the distinction.

She studied the fit of his pants as he walked away. Could that man *be* any more genetically gifted?

"I remember a time you used to look at me like that," Alec said.

Hero jumped. Her *ex*, for lack of a better word, had moved uncomfortably close without her noticing.

"That was two years ago before you decided twenty-three was inching toward geriatric and slept with that eighteen-year-old freshman." She picked up what was going to look like a Grecian jug, and walked over to the kiln, if only to put some space between them.

"Biggest mistake of my life."

Wrenching the heavy, fire-proof door open, she stepped onto the grated floor of the circular kiln. Even for someone her size, there was barely enough space to turn around. Carefully setting her work on the shelves, she returned to the table for the other piece without looking at the only man who'd ever come close to breaking her heart.

"Why, because you were five months from committing a felony?" she snarked.

God, she was such a cliché, sleeping with the handsome professor. Who *did* that and actually expected it to work out?

"That isn't fair, Hero." The hurt in his voice could have been real. "You never said you wanted us to be exclusive. In fact, I remember you being very adamant that I not 'own you.'"

He actually used rabbit ears. Was there anything more annoying? Hero sighed, unwilling to get into this right now. "We agreed to still be friends, Alec. Friends don't bring up the past, not after it's been forgotten."

"What can I say? History is sort of my thing."

Ugh. Had she found him charming at one point? Lame.

She carried the heavy vase to the kiln while he stood there with his hands in his khaki pockets.

"Why did you bring *him* here?" Alec turned on the intellectual condescension she'd mistakenly found sexy two years ago. "Is this an intimidation ploy? Are you trying to make me jealous? Tell me what you want from me."

Hero turned on him and froze. His body blocked her exit. Alec wasn't sculpted like Luca, but tailored to fit expensive clothing like a department store mannequin. A narrow waist helped to accentuate moderate shoulders rounded by hours spent in the pool. He was strong for his forty years and a medium build. Hero hated that she looked at every man like a suspect. Could he have carried her on that cross? Was he plotting her death even now?

"I don't want anything from you. Luca's a gentleman who offered to help." She hoped he read the underlying meaning in her nonchalant words. "He doesn't like me to go very many places alone, not with John the Baptist still out there."

Alec nodded, but didn't budge. "Did you get a good look at him, John the Baptist?" His shoulder was only inches from the burn switch, and this kiln was old enough not to have any installed safety measures.

Her heart sputtered.

"No." It would take nothing at all for him to slam the door and lock her inside. She stood and studied

Alec's casual posture, telling herself she was being paranoid and ridiculous. This was a man who was a card carrying member of the ACLU. He strongly opposed the death penalty. The only time he handled dead bodies was if they'd been worm food hundreds of years ago. Plus he got squeamish at the sight of blood. How could he handle driving huge nails through someone's hands?

"He's been quiet for a long time after your attack. Some people say that he's moved on."

"What do you think?" she asked.

His hand inched up the metal door frame. "I think it's impossible to move on."

LUCA DUCKED his head beneath the basement doorframe and shifted the massive, weird-shaped plate in his hands. Voices echoed off the concrete walls and, though he couldn't make out their words, Hero's tone conveyed equal amounts annoyance and alarm.

He strode into the dimly-lit basement where the kiln grooved out of the far corner of the room surrounded by a wall of stone and mortar.

The professor crowded Hero into the kiln, way too close in Luca's opinion.

Instead of drawing his .45 on the guy and yelling '*Back off her, dickbag!*' as was his first instinct, he said, "Do you want me to put these here?"

The surprised jerk of the douchebag's shoulders as he turned around caused Luca inappropriate amounts of pleasure.

Maybe it was because these two had obviously slept together. And the good professor's eyes didn't hide the fact that he wanted to do it again.

Well, I'm drinking 'morning after' coffee now, moth-erfucker.

When Alec moved, Hero lunged out the door and didn't stop until she was at the table. "Yes! Go ahead and set that down. I have one more coat of glaze to add before it goes in." She smoothed her hair, patted the table, and grinned at him, but Luca didn't miss the bloodless pallor of her skin.

He didn't take his eyes off Alec as he gingerly set the piece down. The guy looked like one of those sullen Tommy Hilfiger models who'd just lost their favorite yacht.

Luca had a feeling he should have overheard their conversation, but he'd taken a few extra moments to check out the van in the garage. With only two windows on the driver's and passenger's side, it matched Hero's description of her transport vehicle perfectly. The doors had all been locked when he'd tested it, and he couldn't take an *official* look inside without a warrant.

Who locked their vehicles while parked in a garage?

Guilty people. Okay, and most cops.

"You okay?" he asked, rubbing an affectionate hand down her shoulder. "Need any help?"

Hero stepped into his touch and Luca couldn't help a triumphant glance at Alec.

"Actually, this is mostly a one-person job but will take me a minute to finish." She patted his chest. "How would you like Alec to show you his collection of ancient weapons?"

A chance to shove imaginary sex with Hero into his smarmy, worthless, trust-fund-baby face? "I'd *love* it."

"Certainly." Alec tried to meet Hero's eyes, but she avoided looking at him. "This way."

Luca followed him down the long stretch of basement. His fingers still itched for his gun, but he kept them balled at his side as he looked back at Hero. She paused in her bustling to meet his eyes, and what he read there told him everything he needed to know. She was suspicious of this man, whether she admitted it to herself or not.

Luca sneered at the patches on the elbows of Alec's cardigan as they climbed to the first floor of the house. This guy sure bought into his own image.

Did Hero?

"So what are you a professor of, specifically?" *Come on, buddy, give me something to hang you with.*

"I hold double doctorates in cultural anthropology and Western European history with a specialty in religious iconography and theology from Harvard." He epically failed the false modesty angle. "That qualifies me to teach a myriad of subjects."

"Impressive." Luca probably failed to sound all that genuine either.

"Thank you. It was a lot of hard work." Alec wound Luca through a largely unused palatial kitchen and formal dining room to a hallway mounted with what Luca assumed were antique knockoffs of famous paintings and sculptures he recognized from his own required art and culture classes in college.

Now he wished he'd paid more attention.

"So with those credentials, why settle here in Portland? Wouldn't the East Coast afford you more options for advancement in your career?"

Alec opened an oak-paneled door and gestured for Luca to enter with that frigid smile. "Am I being interrogated *Agent* Ramirez?"

Luca shrugged and stepped into an enormous study, angling himself so he never gave the man his back. "Just a question."

"Well, let's just say the answer is complicated and leave it at that, shall we?"

"Sure."

The green walls and mariner wood décor of the professor's study didn't make much of an impression. But the shadow boxes, glass cases, and antique columns displaying every conceivable instrument of death sent his spidey senses into overload. Along with the multi-cultural arsenal, Roman coins, different coats of armor, antique parchments, and various other ancient-looking bibelots littered the room.

Despite his suspicion and enmity, Luca's inner twelve-year-old just wanted to be friends with this yuppie so he could come over and play with all his cool shit. Emitting a low whistle, he wandered to the window where a half-rusted sword hung mounted on the wall in a bronze velvet case.

"A Roman Gladius." Alec joined him. "Judging by the steel construction rather than iron and taking into consideration the location of the find, it's believed to be used by Julius Caesar's Legionnaires in the Gallic wars around 58 BC."

Luca nodded. "Still considered one of the best close-combat weapons ever devised."

Alec's eyebrows shot up. "You know your ancient weaponry."

"Only as taught by the History Channel."

"Then you might appreciate this." Motioning to the middle of the room, Alec hurried to a case supported by a faux Grecian column.

Luca ambled after him, noting the change of energy between them. In his lair, surrounded by his treasures, the professor was master of his domain. Relaxed in the knowledge that here he reigned, intimately connected with his surroundings.

Good. He was just where Luca wanted him. Guard down and ripe for a sneak attack.

"This is one of my rarest finds. I had to fight to keep it from the museum." Alec removed the glass case top and lifted the delicately arched sword with both hands, much in the way Hero had handled her fragile pottery earlier. "Used in feudal Japan, this Katana was dated back to fourteen fifty." He released the sword from its case. "This steel is some of the purest in the world. In fact, our modern technology hasn't been able to duplicate the high, black sand carbon content of the blade in the way they processed and hand-folded the metal back then."

Distracted by the ancient piece of bad-assary, Luca drifted forward. "Holy. Shit."

"I know," Alec agreed with a self-satisfied smile. "Want to hold it?"

Hold it? He wanted some time alone with it.

"If I could." Luca reverently wrapped his hand around the hilt, feeling like he may have reached through time. Turning, he held it out in front of him, all Akira Kurosawa style. Looking around for a mirror, Luca's notice snagged on a wide display behind the executive desk.

What had Rown called that? A cassock?

Stretched out and pinned to some sort of display board, the thick black robe hung next to a white collar and what appeared to be some colorful scarves. Luca searched his memory. In church as a boy he remembered some of these jewel-colored sashes hanging around the necks of catholic clerics.

Boo yah.

Not wanting to alert the man who was fast becoming a major suspect, he made a show of scanning the rest of the office.

"I've numerous objects of the like." Alec seemed to buy it. "A cavalry mace from the Byzantine empire, a saber used by sixteenth century Atlantic pirates, a French Fauchard and over there." Alec pointed past a pole arm with a bladed point. "A hauberk belonging to a Templar Knight."

"Nice." Luca handed the katana back to its owner.

"Most of my relics are Medieval European, as is my passion."

"I see." Glancing around, Luca motioned to the cassock with his chin. "That's catholic isn't it? Do you have a lot of religious artifacts?"

"You could argue that all my artifacts are religious." Alec smirked. "As most of these weapons were used in religious conquests, holy wars and the like. Pagans versus early Christians. Christians against Jews and Muslims. Catholics against Protestants."

"Which holy war would you have taken up arms for?" Luca asked.

Alec crossed his arms, adopting a thoughtful posture. "Ironically, I'm against war. Though, it has shaped the world we live in. I would say there's an ongoing war that we fight every day. One of enlightenment against ignorance. Of good versus evil."

"Isn't evil subjective?" Luca argued. "Take John the Baptist, for example. In his eyes, he's fighting a war against evil. But to the rest of society, he is the one perpetrating it."

"Interesting perspective." The professor's gaze eyes sharpened with interest. "If I may ask, how close are you to apprehending John the Baptist?"

Luca's chest burned. He wasn't as close as he

wanted, as he *needed* to be. "I'm not allowed to discuss an ongoing case," he evaded.

"But you're allowed an intimate relationship with the victim?"

Luca shrugged. "It's a free country."

"Well, I suppose life can't always be a Dan Brown novel, can it?" Alec studied him in kind with a look of cool superiority that made Luca want to grab the Katana back and see if it was still as lethal as it looked. "We don't always capture our quarry."

Unwilling to let his gall show, Luca stepped past Alec and nearly ran into a glass case containing exactly the kind of confirmation he'd been looking for.

He looked up and locked eyes with the professor, unable to keep the triumph from glittering in them.

"*I* do," he promised.

10

"Do you not know I am a woman?
When I think, I must speak!"

— WILLIAM SHAKESPEARE, AS YOU LIKE IT

"Tell me about *this*." On point, Luca watched the professor's reaction very carefully.

Alec meandered to the case Luca stood in front of and stared down into it with his lip curled. "This isn't much of anything," he answered. "It's a replica I bought at an antiques auction in Antioch years ago. Barely worth the cost of the display case."

Luca studied the specks. Flat, screwdriver-shaped iron point flared to sharp precision for the distinct purpose of wreaking more damage on the way out then at penetration. Long, octagonal wooden pole likely made of ash.

Just like the one used on John the Baptist victims.

"Then why did you buy it?" Luca pressed.

"I couldn't resist due to a personal obsession of mine," the Professor admitted. "Have you ever heard of the Spear of Longinus?"

Luca grimaced and shook his head. Sounded like it belonged in a dirty limerick.

"It's known by many names. The Holy Lance of Antioch, the Hofburg Spear, the Vatican Lance, the Spear of Destiny."

That last one sparked his memory. "The Roman lance that pierced the side of Christ."

Alec glanced over. "Color me impressed. You've really paid attention to your history."

Luca tried to keep smugness out of his answering smile. History. Wolfenstein SoD first person shooter video game in Junior High. Potato. Po—tah—to. "If this is a replica, where is the original?"

Alec leaned against the case. "That's widely debated. Speculations range from a Vatican conspiracy to a treasure cache containing it along with the Holy Grail and Crown of Thorns. You can trace it's mythology from fifth century Jerusalem to eighth century Constantinople, thirteenth century Paris all the way to Vienna. Most recently, rumors are that Hitler invaded Europe seeking the Spear's fabled powers."

"You're shitting me," Luca said, throwing a bit of awe into his voice so professor blowhard would continue.

"I shit you not. A sunken German U-boat was retrieved in the early nineties because of first-hand reports that it carried the spear."

"Where do *you* think it is?" An image of Hero flashed across Luca's vision. Blood leaking from her naked waist, mingling with dirt and rain. Her trembling sobs as she reached for him with skewered palms.

One... Two... Three...

"I could only guess at this point. I think the Spear's power lies in its own mythology. As with all religious relics, the mysterious miracles are likely wrought by the true faith of the believer more than the inanimate object, itself." Alec ran an elegant hand over the glass of the spear case. The smudges he left contrasted with his obviously fastidious nature. But his intense stare penetrated the glass to the object contained within. "Although, the sacrament dictates that you symbolically eat the flesh and drink the blood of Christ. In doing this, you atone for your sins and receive His grace. That in itself is powerful if only because of the absolute belief and practice of billions of people on earth."

Luca wrinkled his nose. Cannibalism, even of the symbolic Demigod variety, kind of made him want to yark.

"Imagine a relic that touched both the holy flesh and the sacred blood at the very *moment* Christ was supposed to be fulfilling his greatest sacrifice for the souls of mankind," Alec continued on as if Luca had disappeared. "Charlemagne believed the power of the spear would help him conquer the world. Others believe the spear would absolve them of any sin and return them to heaven. Or even cast out Demons. Regardless of whether I believe in the spear's more mystical power or not, it would be a potent object to possess."

"What sins of yours would you hope to absolve?" Luca's voice sounded too leashed in the open room, even to him.

As if returning from a hypnotic journey, Alec blinked a few times and swung his gaze toward Luca with a chilling smile. "Too many to confess to the FBI, I'm afraid."

HERO CLIMBED up on the side rail of the van and angled her distorted wire hanger closer to the van's door handle. Biting on the skin of her cheek, she reached the inside the handle, held her breath, and— *Click*.

Taking one final look around, she opened the driver's side door and leaned inside.

The front seats and the floor of the van remained undistinguishable though the clutter of maps, water bottles, a discarded back pack, some books, and a few rolled up duffel bags of field tools. Possibly the only chaotic space in Alec's life.

If Hero remembered one thing with abject clarity, it was the abrasive, grey-lined upholstery on the floor of the van which she'd spent the most terrifying moments of her life.

She peered through the crisscrossed lattice of black metal separating the front seat from the back of the van, her heart performing a little tap dance on her lungs.

Teal. An ugly, albeit clean teal carpet spread over the floor. It reminded Hero of a carefully preserved rug from the seventies, complete with swirling cuts to add some funkiness. Not shag, by any means, but definitely too long to be practical. Especially in a van often assaulted by dirty archeology and/or anthropology students.

A silent shadow fell behind her. A strong hand silenced her shocked cry as she was wrenched out of the van and against a warm stone wall.

"What the *hell* were you doing?" Luca hissed against her ear.

"Nmmphing," she said against his hand.

A callous on his palm abraded her lip. It sent shivers straight to her lady bits.

"Breaking into his *locked* vehicle without a warrant

isn't *nothing*." He held her secure against his body as he reached out and locked the door with his elbow before closing it as quietly as he could. She noticed he took care not to touch it with any part of his skin.

Hero was surprised he could pull this off what with all the struggling she did. The wall of hard muscle pressed against her back reminded her just how thin the fabric of her skirt was.

And she thought the inside of a kiln was hot.

Before she did something crazy, like bend over and offered her ass like a bitch in heat, Hero jabbed his torso with the sharp wire hanger still clutched in her hands.

"Goddammit," he barked.

Her inner victory celebration was cut embarrassingly short when, instead of released, Hero found herself face first against the van window, disarmed, and pinned with the full weight of Luca's body against hers.

His hand was still over her mouth. His other arm banded her elbows to her sides effectively rendering her immobile.

She'd never been so turned on in her entire life.

Thoughts along the lines of, *Yes, Agent Ramirez, I've been a naughty girl,* crowded out all the reasonable ones.

"Do you know how much trouble you're in?" Luca growled against her ear.

Do you? She smiled against his palm, enjoying the balmy moisture of her breath against the flesh of his fingers. She snuck her tongue out and gave him a wet lick much like she had to her brothers when they were kids.

It produced a similar effect. He jerked his hand away and wiped it on his pants.

"The kind where you put me in handcuffs?" She did little to keep the hopeful note out of her voice.

Luca took a moment too long to reply. Speaking of long... something the size of her curling iron—the big one— pressed against her back. "The kind where a possible suspect sues the department because you illegally broke into his van with the FBI present." He lifted off of her, retrieved the wire hanger, and none-to-gently guided her toward the car.

"I didn't *break* into anything. Nothing *broke*. I was just—looking around." Hero held her hands up in supplication.

Luca growled. Like, for *real* growled at her, then put his cell phone to his ear with a free hand. "I need a sneak and peak search warrant, ASAP."

A search warrant? What had he found? What was he looking for?

"Specimen collection off of a weapon and a full sweep of a utility van." Hero listened to him list the van's license plate information and the layout of the home. "I'll send you a picture of the weapon." He checked his watch. "Suspect won't be on the premises between thirteen hundred and eighteen hundred hours. I'll need to request a delay in notification. Ninety days if the judge will allow it. I'll e-mail the Probable Cause Statement."

Hero lifted her brows as she unlocked the Juke and slid into the driver's seat. Her heart turned that little tap dance into a full length *Stomp* performance. Trash can lids and everything. Making sure not to peel out in reverse, she tried to keep her speed somewhere between mach and warp as she fled.

Could FBI agents write traffic tickets?

"What's going on?" she asked when Luca hung up.

He brandished the folded wire hanger. "Where did you learn to break into a locked vehicle?"

Hero shrugged. "My brother, Demetri."

"The one with all the black leather?"

She nodded.

"Figures." He cursed. "Why the hell didn't you ever mention Professor Pansy Ass back there? Did it ever enter your mind that he might be at the top of the fucking suspect list?"

"No," Hero answered honestly. "He may be a self-important pervert, but he's no serial killer." She sounded more sure than she felt.

Luca's eyes glittered with black fire and something a little more wild. "Then why break into his van?"

Hero gripped the steering wheel. The trees whizzed past, blending into one green corridor. "Just because," she evaded. "And for your information, the inside of the van didn't match at all. The carpet was totally different and there were seats in the back. The van I was in didn't have seats."

Luca snorted. "Any criminal worthy of the name would have had that van reupholstered, and seats can usually be removed."

"Yeah, but, Alec's van just didn't—*feel* like the one," Hero insisted. "It didn't have the same evil energy."

Hero didn't have to glance over at him. She *felt* his eye roll.

Which proved her point.

"Well sure, that'll hold up in court," Luca snarked, adopting a mocking fake girl voice. "I'm sorry, Your Honor, I have no evidence against this suspect, but his vibe is like, totally creepy and my spirit guides confirmed that he's guilty."

Hero ran a stop sign on a hard right turn, just to irritate him.

"Jesus Christ, woman, who taught you how to drive?" Luca lost his grip on his cell and Hero took a smug amount of pleasure in how ridiculous he looked trying to keep his eyes on the road and search for the lost phone at the same time.

"Connor, actually, and he used to drive tanks and shit."

"Well, this is no tank. It barely qualifies as a car." Luca threw his disapproving glare around the eclectic interior, his eyes finally landing on her ceramic moon dangly she'd hung from the rear view mirror.

"You don't have to be such an asshole."

"And you don't have to be so oblivious."

"Ob-liv-i-ous?" Hero annunciated every syllable. "*Oblivious?*" Damn him for bringing out her high-pitched voice.

"*You* don't want John the Baptist to be someone you know, especially Professor Cradle Robber back there," he accused.

"Wow, those detecting skills they taught you at Quantico really paid off." Okay, now she was just being a bitch, but at least she could fortify the moral high ground by avoiding being childish.

Because *he* started it.

"They're a damn sight better than your 'energy' verdicts." He used finger rabbit ears, which, again, totally pissed her off. "You'll be grateful for my instincts when they're keeping you alive."

Hero skidded around a chipmunk in the road and narrowly missed an oncoming semi. "*Instincts? Really?* How do those differ from energy? It's the same fucking thing, you're just arguing semantics."

"Wrong," Luca maintained a death grip on the *oh shit* handle above her window and braced his long legs against the glove box. "Instincts are based on sound reasoning skills and common sense in the face of missing evidence. Both of which you're sadly lacking."

"Oh yeah?" Hero sped up to a good fifteen miles over the posted speed limit, hugging the twists of the tree-lined, one-lane highway with reckless miscalculations.

"Tell me you've never seen the Roman spear in the Professor Twat Waffle's study, or did you just *divine* that it wasn't the one that nearly spilled your insides into the Willamette?"

Hero's hand flew to her side, pressing against the healed wound as though to keep her internal organs where they were supposed to be. "His name is *Alec*." She sailed through an orange light. Okay it was red by the time she reached it, but close enough.

"Pull over!" Luca ordered.

"Screw you!"

"Pull the fuck *over*." Luca seized the steering wheel, forcing Hero to stomp on her breaks if she wanted to avoid kissing a tree with her face as she sailed through the windshield.

They stopped on a soft shoulder she hadn't seen coming but he must have noticed.

Fucking instincts.

"What the hell's the matter with you?" Hero screeched.

"With *me*?" Before she could stop him, Luca grabbed her keys from the ignition and wrenched his door open, a terse string of Spanish words spewing from his mouth like the lyrics of a familiar song.

Loca. She recognized that one.

Getting out and stomping around the car, she found him with both hands braced on the trunk. "I am *not* crazy. And, it's not polite to swear at someone in another language. I at *least* have to know what you're calling me, or it's not fair."

Luca blinked at her for a moment. "I'm not—po-lite?" he said through gritted teeth. "Well neither is ve-hicular manslaughter."

"Oh, don't get you're handcuffs in a wad, you're fine."

"You're damn right I am, because *I'm* driving." Luca headed for the driver's side. "Now, get in the car."

"The hell you are." Hero reached for her keys, but he quickly held them above him where she'd have to throw her body against his in order to get them.

Oh why did she have to get her height from her father?

"I said, get. In. The. Car," he repeated, a dangerous warning flashing in his eyes.

"You're being unreasonable," she accused. "And don't tell me what to do. It's *my* car."

"I'm the fucking FBI, I'm appropriating it for offi-cial reasons. That's perfectly *reasonable* considering I just watched you commit a felony and four serious traffic violations." He jerked open the driver's side door then turned to jab a finger at her. "You sped past unreasonable to delusional about five miles ago and that terrifies me because it's going to get you *killed!*"

"It *wasn't* Alec," she shrilled, advancing on him and jumping for the keys, which he deftly kept out of her reach. "I would have *known* if he stabbed me!"

"Why?" Luca sneered. "Because you'd willingly let him do it so many times before?"

That was *it*. Before she could think the better of it, Hero balled her fist and wound up for maximum dam-age, aiming right for his solar plexus.

Luca caught it easily, his long fingers wrapping around her entire fist.

"You are *such* a douche," she snarled, trying unsuccessfully to wrench her hand back into her possession. "You think you have it all figured out. You don't trust anyone, not even *yourself*, and all you do is wait for the next monster to jump out of the shadows. Well you're not *that* smart, Agent Ramirez. If you suspect everyone of being a criminal, then you're bound to be right, on occasion. But this is my *life*, and if you think I'll allow you to turn everybody I know and love into a villain, then you don't know anything about me."

Luca stared at her with demon-black eyes for ten full seconds. She counted. And had a feeling that he did the same.

"I know enough," he growled. In a lightning-quick move, she found herself pinned against him and a car for the second time that hour. His dark head dipped low as he crushed his mouth to hers.

Her hands were both imprisoned by his. Her body seemed so small and insignificant against his unyielding bulk. Hero didn't dare move, didn't want to, because Agent Luca Ramirez kissed like he did everything else.

With his entire being.

His tongue tangled with hers, exploring, claiming, leaving no place untouched. But the kiss didn't stop there. His chest rubbed against hers and the heat of their skin melded between the thin cotton of their clothing. Her nipples beaded from the intense friction. The hard length of his erection dug against her belly, and Hero had to stop herself from climbing him like a pole to press against where it belonged.

Every sense not dominated by him melted away. A car flew past on the road, birds and insects made noises in the trees, but her ears were full of her own heartbeat and the sounds of their desperate breaths.

They didn't need to come up for air, they shared it. She filled her nostrils and lungs with him, with chocolate and coffee and the subtle masculine spice of his aftershave. The cold, damp of the light sprinkle didn't register, but the pleasurable rasp of his invisible stubble drove her to the edge. She wanted to feel it everywhere. On her neck, on her breasts, on the inside of her thighs.

A sound, wild and throaty, broke through their fused lips but she couldn't be certain who initiated it.

Fuck it.

She surged against him, trying to force them closer. Her arms struggled against his hold as she lifted one leg around him, forcing her skirt up her thigh. To her shock, he read her mind and released her wrists to mold his large hands to her ass. Lifting her, he ground his pelvis against hers, pressing the hot flesh behind his zipper *right* where she wanted it. He kept her in place with one hand, the other reaching to the exposed skin of her smooth thigh and pushing her skirt higher. One more inch and his pants and whatever he wore beneath would be pretty much the only thing separating them. What she had on didn't really qualify as panties.

Hero clutched fistfuls of his shirt, then his hair, and everywhere she could possibly touch while nipping at his mouth and reveling in the building sexual frenzy she could feel beneath his skin.

Now Hero understood why Luca kept such strict control over his every move. Beneath the suit-coat and rigid restrictions was a demon, a beast of such insatiable appetites that it would devour anything it wanted.

Much like he devoured her now.

It awed and terrified her, how much she wanted to

be the one to unleash that and see what happened. That streak of self-destructive thrill had been with her since she was a child, and for the first time, Hero could see it consuming her and leaving her a quivering casualty of this dangerous heat.

11

"A thousand kisses buys my heart from me;
And pay them at thy leisure one by one."

— WILLIAM SHAKESPEARE, VENUS AND
ADONIS

It was a car that broke the moment. Or, more accurately, the teenagers inside who honked and yelled "Woooooooooooooo!" as they passed, probably saving them from going at it right there on the highway.

Luca acted like a man who'd just put his hand on a hot stove, jumping away from her as though she'd singed him.

Licking his taste from her lips, Hero remained against the car, watching the intermittent raindrops all but evaporate once they hit her skin. Lord, but that was the most erotic experience of her life. How could one kiss get her so aroused? She couldn't *wait* for that to happen again.

"That can't *ever* happen again." Luca gripped the open driver's door until his knuckles cracked. "Just chalk it up to an inappropriate reaction to a tense situation, and we'll move on."

We'll see. "Whatever you say," she lied. "But bet your tight ass that you can't just use distraction techniques like that every time you're losing an argument." Not that she minded him trying, it just wouldn't work. She was still mad as hell, maybe angrier now that he lit a fire he obviously wasn't planning on putting out.

In her panties.

"You just don't know when to give up, do you?" He turned and pinned her with an accusing stare. The fire hadn't left his eyes, but had banked into something less volcanic and more slow burn. How did anyone keep their legs closed around him?

Two could play at that game. She thrust her hip into her hand and held up the car keys dangling from her finger. He wasn't the only one with skills. "Giving up isn't really in the Katrova-Connor vocabulary. A fight is over when blood is spilt or someone's on their knees." She gestured to the ground in front of her with her chin.

To her utter shock, Luca's moist lips threatened a smile that melted her ire like butter on a hot skillet. That fucking dimple. No fair.

"Noted." With an exhausted sigh he opened the driver's door wider, putting it in between his body and hers. "Just promise not to kill us."

"Seriously?" She stood there like a disbelieving idiot for a second before jumping into the driver's seat. He could have easily taken the keys away from her again. But the slight tremor in his hand caused her to suspect he was avoiding skin to skin contact.

"I don't think I'm capable of driving at the moment," he muttered before slamming the door.

Hero watched him all but limp around the car. It

surprised her he could walk at all with what he was packing between his legs.

He folded himself into the passenger seat and made a show of putting on his seatbelt. "Just do me a favor and obey traffic laws, will ya? You're already at three strikes."

"Three strikes?" Hero fastened her own seatbelt and checked behind her on the highway before pulling onto it. "There's *unlocking* a car door and lewd behavior." She held up two fingers. "Traffic violations don't count as they're only misdemeanors at best."

She'd been through enough traffic court to know.

Luca added his thumb to his first two fingers. "Strike three, attempted assault on an officer of the law."

Oh yeah. Hero grimaced. "That doesn't count if it's justified, which it was."

"I'm only not arguing because my brain isn't getting all the blood it needs right now." Luca ran a hand over his skull and face. "That would have been a decent hit had I let it land. Who taught you to throw a punch like that?"

He was trying to be nice, the asshole. Hero's blood still thrummed with roused heat and here he was trying to shift the atmosphere out of turbo overdrive.

"Knox," she answered.

He shifted in his seat. "I'm beginning to think those brothers of yours are bad influences."

A smile found her and she began to relax. "Probably." She took in a deep, cleansing breath through her nose and let it out of her mouth. Using her yoga techniques, she applied biofeedback to slow her breathing and the beating of her heart. It worked better when the cause of the stimuli wasn't sitting within arm's reach.

She tried a diversion tactic. "Look, I didn't mention Alec before because at the time, I thought I knew him enough to recognize him, even in the dark. His body, his voice, and the way he walked, they were familiar to me. But I'll admit that seeing him today made me realize how little I really knew about him, and how different people can be even from recent memory. On top of all that, it had been so long since I'd interacted with him, he never really came to mind before."

Hero thought she heard Luca mutter something like, "Good," as he quickly thumb-typed an email on his phone.

She ignored the pleasure that evoked.

"What did you find in his house?" she asked again. "What weapon were you talking about when you called in for a search warrant?"

Luca looked up. "You're telling me you never saw the Roman spear he has in his study?"

Hero shrugged. "Not really my thing. I've peeked in there, but instruments of violence and death never interested me."

"It very possibly could be the weapon that stabbed you in the side and killed the other victims." Luca was all business now, never looking up from his phone.

A chill of fear spread through her, but Hero still couldn't bring herself to believe Alec was capable of such violence. She didn't care what Luca thought about her intuition, it had served her well up until this point. For the most part. And even though she'd made a few mistakes in life, if she couldn't continue to trust herself, then she truly could trust no one.

And that terrified her more than anything.

FOR THE YEARS Luca had spent at the Portland Bureau, his commute served as an exercise in introspection and self-awareness. A sort of ritual in place of prayer or ecclesiastical guidance. Though he rarely worked the composite eight to five gig, the custom seemed to follow a pattern of its own. Often, the drive to work consisted of pep talks, recall drills, and memory organization. The trip home sort of worked in reverse. His focus turned to repairing the fractures in the damn containing the deep pool of darkness in his psyche. The way he pictured it was kind of like examining the structural deficiencies causing the leak and figuring out what epoxy to use to plug the darkness back inside.

Some days it worked better than others.

Law enforcement illuminated certain unpleasant truths about the nature of a man. Among the most difficult aspects of the job was facing the sometimes insignificant threads separating champion from criminal. Or man from monster.

More than the dose of blood, corruption, cruelty, and deceit that wound through daily life, the small moments of appalling self-illumination became the foremost disconcerting aspect. It remained a shameful, abstruse facet of the job. Never discussed. Never revealed. Like the unexpected arousal at a crime scene or during an explicit interview. Or morbid curiosity choking out feelings of humane sympathy at the most inappropriate times. Occasionally, it went beyond that to empathizing with a sadist or envying a crime boss.

For whatever reason, be it fear, faith, or simple rectitude, a man could fight the more degenerate instincts of his nature. The difference between a good cop and a bad guy all came down to the choices they made in the face of that innate human depravity.

Luca understood this concept better than most. Which was why he spent the entire drive to Hero's apartment thus far berating himself for his dangerous slip of control the day before.

Just what the fuck had he been thinking?

He hadn't, of course. He'd been too busy feeling. In the two long months he'd known Hero, that kiss brewed between them like a fine ale. The ingredients of trauma, survival, gratitude, physical proximity, and a bit of a victim/savior complex capped and fermented for the appropriate amount of time to create some incredible pressure.

Their heated confrontation shook the contents of the bottle and the cap popped off. That was all. These things happened, and they didn't mean anything. Now that the pressure was released, their feelings would turn flat and lose that explosive, unstable element.

They could do this.

He needed to screw the top back on, in a manner of speaking. Using his very helpful self-control techniques, he'd carefully construct a place in his mind where all inappropriate thoughts of Hero would be stored and filed away, like forgotten cold case files.

The feel of her lips, the warmth of her thighs, the incomparable taste of her. These memories would be locked up and *never* investigated or examined again.

When he'd dropped her off that afternoon to Vince, who'd been waiting at her apartment when they'd returned from the professor's, his partner had offered to take his entire shift that night, as well, to make up for his absence that morning.

Luca jumped at the chance. He wanted to be on site for the search warrant at the professor's house.

Also, he needed the space from Hero to clear his head and get some sleep. To shore up his mental and emotional resources for the indefinite amount time he'd have to stay by her side. He'd just have to ignore the fact that he'd been attacked by an extreme bout of insomnia last night. The things they'd said to each other before their kiss echoed off his bare walls. Had she been right about him? Had he traded thorough, impartial investigative skills for paranoid indiscriminate suspicion? Whatever his perspective, he closed cases. His stats were among the top in the department. He had the commendations to prove his efficiency. But maybe his decade at the FBI had altered him in more ways than one. Or maybe he'd always been this way.

Twisting and thrashing in his bed, his flesh maintained the uncomfortable warmth of perpetually heightened arousal. Yet inside he'd been cold, empty. The exposed walls of his apartment expanded into a stark, vacant space. Devoid of life or color. It was funny how he'd never noticed that before.

Maybe he'd have to get some movie posters or some shit. Spend some shoe money at an art gallery? Luca scowled as he pulled into the mansion's long driveway. What the fuck was happening to him? Next he'd be ordering umbrella drinks and paying more than twenty bucks for a haircut.

He started his slow count the moment he got out of the car. This way, he'd reach ten *before* he reached her apartment.

Vince greeted him again at the door and stepped aside to let him through. Instead of his suit he wore faded jeans, work boots, and an unzipped hoodie over an overpriced vintage tee. He could almost pull off college art student.

"You seem relaxed," Luca noted.

"Yeah." Vince rolled his shoulders. "It's been quiet."

Luca scanned the empty loft. "Where's Hero?"

"She's in her room changing for the yoga class she's teaching tonight." Vince examined Luca's uniform of baggy green Notre Dame basketball shorts over tighter shorts beneath, black ribbed tank, and dark Adidas Porsche cross trainers. "*That's* what you're wearing?"

"What?" Luca looked down. "It's *just* a yoga class. Isn't it like glorified stretching?"

Vince snorted. "Better not let your girlfriend hear you say that."

"Don't call her my girlfriend. She's the job."

"Hey man, I'm part of this whole clambake. Just playing along." Vince held his hands up. "Where you going to put your gun?"

Luca grinned. "Guess."

"I'd say up your ass if that was an option," Vince laughed. "What went down at the professor's house?"

Luca's smile evaporated. What had Hero told Vince? Had she spilled about the kiss? Vince wasn't a stickler for protocol, but he also wasn't known for discretion. "It was nothing," Luca defended. "Just a little fuck up, you know? In the heat of the moment. It won't happen again."

"I was asking about the Search Warrant, but now I kinda want to hear what's doing with this other thing." Vince's gaze sharpened, though his smile remained unperturbed.

Luca mentally beat the shit out of himself.

"Search Warrant was a complete waste." He tried misdirection, hoping Vince would forget about his quasi-confession.

"I *knew* it." Hero was a flash of energy across her loft, gathering a bag from the couch, her mat from a corner, keys off the table. "Alec isn't John the Baptist."

It took an inordinate amount of time for Luca to process her words as his entire focus zoomed in on her incredible body.

The white leggings clinging to her skin tinted with green when they caught the light from her Moroccan chandelier. The spandex-type fabric hypnotized both the men into silence. The same color graced her spaghetti-string top along with some dark green Indian-style accents that clung so close to her perfect shape they could have been tattoos.

The memory of her strong, lithe leg hitched around his hips wiped any other thought from Luca's mind.

"Where was I?" Luca asked quietly.

"Who knows?" Vince's eyes started at Hero's face and drifted south in an appreciative inspection.

Luca hit him in the ribs with a sharp elbow.

"You were telling Vince that I was right about Alec." Hero threw on a long, thick sweater, breaking the spell. Her smile was smug and radiant as she pulled her loose hair from beneath the collar and fiddled with the ginormous buttons.

"Not necessarily." Luca dropped his gym bag and tried to collect his thoughts. "You're professor *is* a double-dealing blowhard."

Vince snorted. "Did you use your ivy league doctorate to figure that out?"

"Wait." Hero put up a hand. "You're a *doctor*? Of what?"

Luca looked heavenward. "Criminal Psychology with a lesser degree in Forensic Pathology. We both have post-graduate degrees. You have to in order to get where we are in the Bureau." He gestured to Vince.

"*Seriously*?" Hero gawked. "Why don't you introduce yourself as Doctor Ramirez?"

"That's easy," Vince said. "Because 'Special Agent' gets *way* more play." He stuck out his tongue and made a lewd gesture.

Hero nodded as though that was sound and acceptable reasoning.

Luca made an impatient sound in the back of his throat. "So the forensic team processed the weapon and the van on scene." He steered the conversation away from himself. "Turns out the antique spear *Doctor* Graham claimed to have acquired in Antioch is actually some cheap knock-off he probably bought at a Scottish Festival or Renaissance Faire."

"No shit?" Vince whistled.

"Not only did it have no blood on it, but if someone attempted to stab a person with it, the superglue holding the spearhead together would malfunction."

Hero narrowed her eyes. "Ugh. It was a knock-off of a knock-off? What a pretentious dick. I'm so embarrassed I ever fell for his—"

"Hey." Vince slung his arm around her shoulders, and she smiled up at him. "We all have a few bangs in our past we're not proud of. He was no Special Agent or anything, but he *was* a doctor." He reached out and nudged at Luca with a playful wink.

All Luca knew was his partner needed to get his hands off Hero before he knocked him into next week. "Let's get going," he urged.

"What about the van?" Hero asked.

Luca shook his head. "They found nothing. No blood, no tools, no traces of you or ties to the other women." He held his hand up to cut off Hero's incoming I-told-you-so. "That doesn't necessarily clear him as a suspect. He's a smart and careful man. He could have plenty to hide."

"I'll look deeper into his background for ya," Vince offered.

Yeah, he should *so* get started on that. Like right now.

"Thanks, man." Luca reached into his bag, pulled out his gun, checked the magazine, and began to secure it to his thigh holster.

"You can't do yoga with your gun strapped there," Hero cautioned.

"Watch me." He flashed her a confident smile. "How hard could it be?"

12

"Let me embrace the sour adversity,
For wise men say it is the wisest course."

— WILLIAM SHAKESPEARE, KING HENRY VI

Luca found the seventh level of hell somewhere between plow pose and eagle pose. While he attempted to balance on one foot while trying to wrap one leg around his other leg and turning his arms into a pretzel, he cursed the entire country of India. All of their gods, their incredibly addicting food, and any past and future incarnations of whoever thought up this bull shit exercise. His holster was chafing his thigh raw and fighting his every movement. The oppressive smells of patchouli, essential oils, and goddamn hippies were exacerbated by the fact that the room had to be at least a million degrees. To add insult to injury, his undershorts kept crawling up his ass.

Whatever happened to going to an air-conditioned gym and throwing heavy weights around, or doing plyometrics? If you wanted to get sweaty, go outside and use a pig skin as an excuse to beat the shit out of your friends.

Luca snuck surreptitious glances at the two other men in the class. He had to admit they were both in decent shape. One looked kind of like a young Lenny Kravitz with dreadlocks and a nose ring. He was way too proud of his underwhelming six-pack and made a point to be shirtless in a room full of ladies.

The second was lean and rocked a pink belly-shirt printed with the words "Namaste Bitches" coordinated with some kind of yellow Thai-looking lounge pants. He seemed *much* more like someone who'd go to a class called "Kick your Asana" than Luca or Kravitz over there. The electric blue tips of his carefully mussed hair matched his manicured nails and pretty much cleared him as serial killer material. Besides, Stefano St. James was a close friend of Hero's whom she regularly referred to as Stef. They'd gone on that ill-advised Mexican Rivera cruise together. Luca still hadn't forgiven him.

"Releasing that pose with mindful breath, let's move into half moon pose and hold for seven breaths," Hero's gentle voice urged before bending herself in half *sideways* and lifting one leg off the floor. "I want to see your legs trembling with effort, but your faces calm and relaxed."

"Oh, for fuck's sake," Luca murmured under his breath, earning him a sharp look from Hero. He returned it with a scowl of his own. *Who* bent like that? He looked around. Other than everyone in this room besides him? Keeping his four-letter words to himself, he let out a loud, irate breath from his throat, which in this crowd got him exactly zero attention. He tried not to kick the blonde standing next to him in the head while he attempted the pose. Come to think of it, he was way too tall to be in the front row. Also, if he wasn't mistaken, blondie kept scooting her mat closer to him and checking out his ass.

Luca hated to admit it, but Vince had been right. Advanced yoga was harder than it looked. Sporting a firearm and a continual hard-on, it was damn near unbearable.

He'd spent the last forty-five minutes watching Hero do things with her body that shouldn't be humanly possible, or at the very least should be illegal. Hell, the first time he saw her in downward dog he all but fell over, and it only got worse from there. The curve of her ass, the flex of her thighs, the lean sinew of her strong yet soft body revved him up like nothing else. He certainly had a few positions *he* wanted to teach her, and now he had irrefutable proof she could pull off every single one. And then some.

A groan escaped him and from the mirth sparkling in Hero's eyes, Luca knew she'd misinterpreted it. This particular sound of suffering had nothing to do with his straining muscles and everything to do with the fact that he could see the outline of her sex through those poor excuse for yoga pants, when she parted her legs like that. They cupped her perfectly, creating a delineation he wanted to explore with his mouth more than he wanted his next breath.

It was official. This case was going to be the end of him. How would he keep her safe if his focus was so trained *on* her that he missed the danger surrounding her? Something to think about. He was a damn good agent with one of the best investigative records the Bureau had seen. It was the reason he got away with being such an asshole. He got results, confessions, and closed cases despite his personality "liability." The complaints against him had never turned into lawsuits and therefore he'd skated around the word *brutality* with a good boss and a little luck.

His size, racial ambiguity and, let's face it, *mad skills* had seen him embroiled in covert operations as everything from a Middle East Terrorist sympathizer to the Mexican Mafia. He'd lived through shootouts, explosions, gang wars, and political nightmares. So why did going quasi-undercover as one tiny yoga instructor's boyfriend feel like the most dangerous thing he'd done thus far? A better man would—would what? Recuse himself? The word had been dancing with Luca ever since the night Hero had been fished out of the river.

A few things stopped him, though. While he was a fan-fucking-tastic Agent, he wasn't necessarily a better man, and he'd be goddamned before he let the interests of his pecker conflict with the interests of justice.

Who *else* could he trust with this case? With Hero's life? Not one person came to mind. Even Trojanowski had seen that he was the best man for this job. So he was going to just have to nut up, so to speak, and keep his eyes where they ought to be. Trying to recognize and anticipate a serial killer's next move. For example, identifying cars that drove by the window of *The Crane and Lotus Yoga Studio* more than once. Checking student rosters against the criminal database. Scanning her students for any strange and obsessive behavior.

Though how he could do that with the lights so low and his head down by his knees was beyond him. Not that his head got *that* close to his knees.

The next pose was some kind of warrior lunge series that allowed him more freedom to look around. The yoga studio wasn't exactly rife with suspects. The women were rejected out of hand along with Stefano, the fabulous, and that only left dreadlocks two mats down from him as the slightest person of interest.

The man *was* medium build, and Luca had to admit that his impressive pound for pound strength and balance was evident in his yoga skills. Though his features were decidedly African-American, his skin was more caramel than chocolate. Apparently he shared one disturbing feature with Luca, a hard-on for Hero. His gaze ventured to the same inappropriate places Luca's had been glued to only moments ago. When she looked in his direction, the smile they shared was warm. Familiar. They knew and liked each other.

Luca's already foul mood darkened. Just *how* familiar were these two? Hadn't the professor said something about her tastes leaning toward the exotic? Was this yahoo some other part of her past that she'd neglected to mention? This time, when Hero abandoned the front of the class to drift through the rows of students to make adjustments and give encouragement, Luca watched their interaction with different eyes. When she neared dreadlocks, the guy broke his excellent form, tilting his hips at an odd angle.

Hero zoned in on the movement, and she walked over to him, placing her hands on his hip flexers and squaring them with the floor. Another shared smile. A few whispered words. Hero touched his shoulder with affection and moved on to another student.

This guy was smooth.

The loaded weapon strapped to Luca's thigh bothered him less now, in fact, it just became downright comforting. As soon as this class ended, he was going to find out just who this guy was to Hero.

As she padded toward Luca in the semi-darkness, she said something to the class that he didn't catch because he was bracing himself for the intense sensation that came with her touch.

She gripped his shoulders pressing down gently and, what do you know, a jolt of pure, electric energy shot down his spine straight to his dick. "Relax these," she urged. "And you'll have more strength and stamina in your legs."

He wasn't relaxing *shit* while her hands were on him. The look he threw her must have told her as much, because an answering heat sparked in her eyes and her fingers tightened on his shoulders.

That was the problem, wasn't it? This thing. This primitive, explosive attraction. It wasn't one-sided. She met his every hot glare *quid pro quo*. She embraced and encouraged his attention, and if there was even the whisper of heat between them, she flipped the knob to broil.

Luca hoped the warning he put into his stare would douse the heat. Keeping a lid on this was his responsibility. He was bound by the law, procedure, duty, honor, and whatever other words meant "hell no" when it came to her. Years of therapy, training, practice, and field work had imbued him with some epic self-control and a high tolerance for torture. As he forced his shoulders to relax, Luca vowed that she could throw whatever she wanted at him and he'd never break.

"Excellent." Her smile told him she'd accepted the challenge, and dread battled with anticipation deep in his gut.

Needing another place for his eyes than her retreating backside, Luca checked in with dreadlocks. What he saw in the other man's striking face was as pure, familiar, and flame-inducing as lust.

It was violence. And it was directed at him.

13

"False face must hide what false heart doth know."

— WILLIAM SHAKESPEARE, MACBETH

As he grabbed a towel from the front desk and wiped the sweat from his face and neck, Luca looked outside the wall of windows and identified one more thing to dislike about hippies. They were overly fond of what he considered to be inappropriately long hugs.

He hung back to observe Hero in her environment. She seemed to know and nurture everyone in her class. She remembered their names, incidentals about their lives, and even so much as physical maladies. Luca had to hand it to her, she was great at what she did. As people filtered out and wandered into the studio, the majority stopped to receive her heart-felt smile and a warm hug.

Taking advantage of a lull, dreadlocks stepped into her arms and enfolded her in a shirtless embrace.

Luca took that as his cue to introduce himself.

Stepping outside, he came up behind Hero and slipped a possessive arm around her waist. She stiffened for a second, and then relaxed into his side as though it was the most natural thing in the world. And didn't it just feel that way? Disturbingly natural.

"Rivers, let me introduce my—boyfriend, Luca Ramirez." Hero put a hand on his chest.

They were really going to have to get rid of that hitch in her voice every time she called him her boyfriend. That didn't sound natural at all.

"Luca, this is a long-time student and friend, Two Rivers." Student first. Friend second. Luca relaxed a little.

The man looked up at Luca for a silent moment with a decidedly un-hippie vibe. This cat was street, or had been. He was trying to seem as though he was still in his twenties, but Luca had him pegged early thirties. He'd learned the same posturing, death-glare, and shoulder position that was the uniform of thug life. His relaxed stance effectively hid an entitled defiance. Schooling his features into the beat-nick squint of pot enthusiast, he switched his clove cigarette to his left hand and offered Luca his right. "Friends call me Rivers."

Luca shook and fist-bumped. "Nice to meet you, man." He didn't call him 'Rivers.' They'd never be friends.

"Pleasure," Two Rivers lied, and then turned to Hero. "I thought you didn't allow men to claim you under the oppressive titles of our Patriarchal society, girl. What changed you?"

Luca slanted a look at Hero. He was starting to see a pattern emerge with men in her orbit. Hero's answer shocked him just as thoroughly as it did the man who'd asked the question.

"Love." She wrapped her arms around Luca's torso and pasted on the dreamy smile of the infatuated.

"Love changes everyone, doesn't it?" She lifted her eyes to meet Luca's, but some kind of heart-pounding weakness kept him from looking down. Instead he offered a tight smile at the brother in front of them, whose own easy smile had faltered.

"That's right, babe." Luca threw sex into his reply, just to be an asshole. Also, because he wasn't sure what love sounded like.

Rivers's smile disappeared altogether, and his brows began a long journey up his forehead. "Babe?"

Hero winced.

"Something wrong?" Luca asked.

Two Rivers shrugged. "Never thought I'd see the day, is all."

"That Hero would be someone's babe?"

The guy flicked some ash and took a long drag. "That Hero would allow someone to *call* her 'babe.'"

"What's wrong with babe?" Luca feigned some bewilderment of his own.

Adopting the posture of a sage, Rivers rested his back on the brick of the building. "I mean no offense man, but it's such an unenlightened term to encompass all that is your lady, you know? It denotes a lack of respect for the feminine divinity."

It took every ounce of Luca's training to maintain his easy-going posture. He'd spent entire weeks drinking with human sex traffickers without a crack in his façade. He'd sidled up to con artists and serial killers. But Luca had little patience for sanctimonious ass clowns. This guy was going to learn about *respecting* his fist in another two-point-five seconds.

Hero laughed to break some building tension, looking between the two men with a mixture of intrigue and bewilderment. "It's charming when Luca does it."

River's striking hazel eyes latched on to the raised scar on the hand that Hero had rested on Luca's abs. He took another drag of the clove, the smoke hiding a deeply camouflaged psychotic rage the likes of which Luca hadn't seen for a long time. Not since he'd last glimpsed it in the mirror years ago.

This man was *not* who he appeared to be. Of the three of them, Rivers was the least genuine, and Luca's instincts were arcing higher than a Geiger counter at Chernobyl. Rivers had a past, and Luca needed to know what it was.

"So, Two Rivers, those were some creative parents you had." Luca put more ease in his smile and less teeth.

"I'm sorry?"

"Your name. It's pretty unconventional."

A mask of complete calm crept across the hippie's face, the persona he'd constructed lying on his features as though it belonged there. "I was not born with this name, with this soul, or this body." His voice had become smooth as glass. "My previous menial existence was one without purpose above my own base pleasure and monetary gain."

Luca suppressed a snort, urging Rivers to continue with a feigned vaguely interested nod.

"One day, overcome by the chaos and negativity that was my life, I found myself at the sacred place where the two Great Rivers converged into one."

"You mean at Kelly Point Park?" Luca asked.

Hero nudged him with her elbow.

Two Rivers narrowed his eyes with condescension. "In that moment, I was truly born. I *became*. And I am named for that sacred place."

That *sacred* place was right in the middle of where

nearly five dead John the Baptist victims were recovered. Including Hero.

"What happened there?" he kept his voice soft, like maybe he bought it.

"The most spiritual experience of my life."

One that involved dead prostitutes and a Jesus complex maybe?

"Which was?" Luca pressed.

"It was there that I saw the face of God, bro. I melded with the universe and understood my place within it."

"Oh yeah, what did God look like?" Luca held his breath. Was this deity nailed to a cross? Did he offer him women to 'save'?

"It's something I can't talk about. Something you don't share, you know? It's too personal, too *real*. Pearls before swine and all that." Rivers put his clove out against his boot and palmed it.

Luca nodded. "I understand." What a fucking poser. "So, what was your name before?" he asked casually.

"I do not speak of the dead, bro." Rivers shook his head as though still mourning the tragic death of a friend. "That incarnation is gone, never again to be named."

Oh, for the love of—

"Look at that, Hatha Yoga meditation starts in five minutes." Hero seized Luca's hand and pulled him toward the studio entry.

"Righteous, I'll go grab my Jung-jungs." Rivers headed for his hippie crossover.

"I'll just bet you will," Luca said under his breath after he memorized the old Subaru's license plates.

"Does he use his handcuffs?" Stef whispered against Hero's ear. "Do you guys play—I don't know, what's the FBI equivalent of dirty cop and *dirtier* criminal? Drug lord and captured agent? Terrorist and infidel?" He bent over the yoga studio's bathroom counter and shook his booty at her. "Please, Agent Ramirez, please don't take me to Guantanamo, I'll do *anything*."

Hero dried her hands beneath the air dryer then spanked Stef on his offered ass. "Stop it, you."

"Mmmm, I'd let him *interrogate* me—"

Hero clapped her hand over his glossed lips. "Hush your mouth. He's right outside the door!"

Stef slapped her hand away. "So what? He knows he's *fine*." Checking and reapplying his lip gloss in the mirror, he twinkled his eyes at Hero. "So tell me everything. How did you two actually get together? When did it happen? Where did it happen? And where did he put it? And *why* didn't you tell me right away?"

Hero stalled a little. In theory she'd thought she was ready for this, the pretense of being *with* Luca. But she hadn't counted on the fact that she wasn't a very adept liar, and these incidentals really shot holes through her story. How would it have happened? When she'd visited the offices? The crime scenes? In the hospital? She'd been back from Mexico with Stef for less than a week. So to him this seemed rather sudden.

Luckily, Stef didn't wait for her reply. "He looks like one of those that fucks *real* gritty." He humped the edge of the sink for effect. "Like all, angry, violent, hold-on-to-your-knickers, I'm-gonna-take-my-issues-out-on-your-business kinda sex. Then again, you never can tell. Sometimes you're expecting that and all the sudden some bad ass goes all tender and starts crying." He rolled his eyes. "Gah. That's the worst."

"If you don't shut up, I'm going to get you banned from the girl's bathroom." Hero was only half joking. She knew Luca stationed himself a circumspect distance from the bathroom door and hawkeyed Two Rivers and the rest of her students as they left for the night. However, this building wasn't known for its sound insulation. Part of her chagrin stemmed from the fact that she actually wasn't sure where Luca stood on the whole gay issue. She'd hate to cause trouble between her dear friend and her fake boyfriend. It wasn't like she could dump him.

"Few have tried, many have failed." Stef flashed her a brilliant smile.

"That doesn't even make any sense."

"So, are you bringing him to every class?" He linked his arm with hers. "Because I have more incentive to work hard if his fine ass is right in front of me. Talk about your af-*firm*-ative visualizations." He pushed open the restroom door.

Luca stood across the hallway looking like a bouncer in basketball gear, his face completely expressionless.

Oh shit, he'd heard every word. Hero's features fell. *Please don't be an asshole. Please don't be an asshole.*

"Is that a gun in your shorts, or are you happy to see me?" Stef put extra wattage into the shameless smile he pointed at Luca and winked.

Hero tensed.

To her complete shock, Luca gave a sexy smirk while he reached deep into the waistband of his basketball shorts and produced the intimidating semi-automatic he'd earlier strapped to his thigh. "Sorry to disappoint." He returned the wink.

Stef's laughter was husky and delighted.

This unpredictable agent constantly surprised and intrigued her. Probably more than he should.

"Oh well." Stef tossed his head in a gesture that imitated a woman with long hair. "A girl can dream."

Luca lifted the leg of his shorts to re-holster the weapon.

"Oh dear lord, he has thighs like a vice." Stef feigned a swoon.

"And, apparently, a top shelf, praise-worthy ass." Though Luca didn't exactly smile, his dimple appeared. "By the way, Guantanamo is more a military facility than anything to do with the FBI."

"If you say so." Stef looked dubious, but his eyes still twinkled up at Luca. "I've learned not to argue with a man packing *heat*." He shot a look at Luca's shorts, and not where he'd holstered the gun.

Hero laughed and enjoyed her entourage while she flipped off lights and the heater and locked up the studio. Stef lingered to give her a warm hug and a sloppy kiss. "We're on for the gallery show next weekend?"

"Of course, and all the shopping that goes with it."

"I'm not saying that I support you putting more clothes *on*, I'm just saying that I'm excited to see you all dolled up." Stef threw his arms out to Luca in the universal sign for "give me a hug" and puckered his lips.

Apparently, that was where Luca drew the line. He opted for a strong handshake.

"Thanks for keeping my girl safe," Stef beamed.

"Always," Luca returned seriously.

He had his cell glued to his ear before Hero had her seatbelt on. "Bea, I need you to run a license plate for me." He listed off a plate number and the description of Rivers's car. "Start a file on the owner, a man who operates under the alias *Two Rivers*. He's probably mid-thirties, five-ten, one-seventy, African-American male, possibly mixed race. Look for a history of violence, assault, or burglary. I'd like you to run nationwide warrants search and full background including credit history and weapons transactions."

Silence.

"Yes, possible person of interest."

Hero rolled her eyes, but it was with a smile. This wouldn't have to do with their little pissing contest, would it? Hero had known Two Rivers for going on a year. He was another of Luca's suspects she found preposterous.

Once the call was disconnected, both hands returned to the steering wheel and he stared wordlessly out the windshield.

Uncomfortable with the silence, Hero turned to him. "I don't want to seem like I'm questioning your instincts," she began diplomatically.

"Then don't."

"It's only that, do you really think that *Rivers* is a prime candidate for John the Baptist? I mean, he hardly fits the profile."

"He's a killer," Luca said without inflection. He remained motionless except for the deft movements that maneuvered his dark car through the darker night. Rain clouds threatened above and blocked out the sky, a common occurrence in the Northwest, but Luca kept his eyes trained on them as though he'd never seen such a thing before.

"How can you be sure?"

"Did you fuck him?" His lips barely moved, but the question ricocheted like a gunshot inside the car's interior.

"What?"

"You heard me." Still no movement. But the creases in the big hands around the steering wheel whitened.

She sighed, missing the easy-going Luca who'd bantered with Stef. "Rivers? No. He's so deep in the friend zone he couldn't afford the equipment to climb out."

"Why?"

"Why does it matter?"

"It's obvious he's at least tried. So answer the question."

Hero thought about it. "Two Rivers is a little *too* laid back for me, you know?"

Luca glanced at her then, but only to lift an eyebrow.

"Look, this shouldn't matter, but I work really hard. I know not in a conventional eight-to-five kind of way, but my work as an artist and instructor is very important to me. Rivers is somewhat aimless, irresponsible, and most important, chronically *unemployed*. I hate to be judgmental, but that's a gigantic turn off. Money isn't everything me, but what I find very sexy in a man, is a passion for what he does, who he is. I'm not looking to find a man who hasn't found himself."

Her words seemed to please and trouble Luca simultaneously. "He certainly has a passion for you."

Hero wrinkled her nose. "Doesn't make him JTB. I mean, he's a vegan. He probably *would* murder a hooker before he'd hurt a goat and stick his head in my fridge." Luca's dark frown caused her to wince, and she held up her hands in surrender. "Okay, yeah, bad joke. But what makes you so certain he's a killer?"

The silence hung as low and heavy as the clouds for a moment. Luca could do that. Whatever storms raged inside him affected the climate surrounding him. As stoic as he could be, one didn't need a meteorology degree to predict the forecast. And yet, when she expected thunder, his silken voice was nothing more than a low, ominous breeze.

"I never applied to work violent crimes, or homicide."

Puzzled, Hero just shook her head.

"In my personnel file, it is noted that I have an 'aptitude for profiling violent offenders.' I was recruited against the recommendation of my field training agent and the psychologist who performed my competency evaluation. In my file it says a lot of things. Things like: Type-A personality, impulse control issues, violent tendencies, anti-social behavior, and liability. I think *liability* was underlined a few times."

Hero hadn't known that, but she couldn't say she was surprised. "Then why—?"

Luca's jaw hardened. "When Special Agent Trojanowski recruited me, I asked him the same question, and do you know what he said to me?"

He seemed to be waiting on her, so Hero shook her head again.

"He said, '*Simile videt Simile*. Like recognizes like.' And ever since he's assigned me the most dangerous, violent cases in the western United States." They stopped at a red light and he turned to her, his expression intense. "So trust me when I say that I know that man is a killer, because we're two monsters who instantly recognized each other."

Hero stared at him. In that moment, she believed his every word. He looked like a monster. The vibrant red of the stoplight fragmented through the windshield and cast the left side of his face in crimson. He reminded her of one of Bouchardon's satyrs. His dramatic brow illuminated from beneath by the color of blood sculpted his features with demonic shadows. Was it just her imagination or the strength of his words that conjured the image? Or was this a rare glimpse into his soul? If he were the Satyr, wouldn't that make her the Nymph? Hero shrugged, if the cloven hoof fits—

"Are you a—that is, have you ever killed anyone?"

The demon became more grim, if possible, the shadows across his face were more prominent, but still the color of blood. "Ironically, I have the same body count as John the Baptist."

"Six?"

He shook his head. "Five." Reaching out, he ran a finger down her cheek and Hero remembered that she wasn't technically a body. "All in the line of duty. *Righteous kills*, our secular government still calls them."

"Is there such a thing?" Hero wondered aloud.

His short laugh was devoid of any mirth. "I sometimes wonder."

"But you were protecting others, weren't you?"

The Satyr had a dimple, this one appearing through a wry smile. "That's what I tell myself." He didn't give that time to sink in. "Can I ask you something?"

Hero nodded. Her thoughts as laborious as chewing on salt water taffy.

"Do you want John the Baptist dead?"

Hero shrugged one shoulder. "I want him stopped. I don't suppose that necessarily has to be the same thing," she answered carefully.

Luca studied her face as intently as she had studied his.

"That's where you and I are very different, Hero. I might be on the right side of this case, but it doesn't make me one of the good guys. I want John the Baptist killed for what he did to you. To those other women. Beyond that, I want to be the one who drills the bullet through his eye."

It seemed an inopportune moment for the light to turn green, but it did, breaking the demon spell. Luca shot through the light, returning to his previous posture of keeping both eyes on the road and both hands on the wheel.

Hero chewed on her lip and ran fingers over the raised scars on her palms. Tonight they felt extra tight, itchy, and hard. Like great, yawning fissures instead of small seams. "Do you think you will?" she asked quietly, watching street after tree-lined street whiz past in a vibrant blur of golden metropolitan lights. "Have the opportunity to kill John the Baptist, that is? Do you think you'll be the one to do it?"

He made a dismissive movement with his chin. "Like I said, I'm good at finding monsters."

Hero frowned. Not exactly an answer, which seemed to be the *status quo* with him. "Aren't you afraid that if you spend your life looking for monsters, you'll start finding them in everyone?"

Luca was silent a long time. "Not everyone," he finally murmured before spearing her with a glance so naked and honest that tears pricked the backs of her eyes. "Not you."

Unable to think of a single thing to say to that, Hero watched the white lines of the road blip past the hood of the car in rhythmic passages of distance. She let them hypnotize her into a sort of introspective trance where she could retreat from the intensity of the moment.

One of the many reasons Hero needed Agent Ramirez in her life right now had been illustrated in their conversation on many levels. Luca was looking for a monster amongst her friends and associates, something she couldn't seem to bring herself to do no matter how much she understood the imperative. And yet his role overreached that in her estimation. This self-imposed savior, this John the Baptist, thought *she* was the monster. If Agent Ramirez was some kind of evil bloodhound, she was glad he didn't bark up her tree, so to speak. She hadn't known it until this moment, but she'd needed to hear his reassurance that her intentions to be a kind and positive person exempted her from his dark brand of cynicism. His words pleased her more than any compliment she'd ever received.

Not you.

Sometimes in her most quiet, solitary moments, she wondered if she'd truly deserved to be spared. If her life was worth the trouble and cost of all this. Father Michael had told her she'd been saved for a purpose, that God had blessed her with a second chance at life. At redemption. Often, she found herself wondering from what sin she needed to be redeemed. Or if she believed in the concept of sin at all.

So she didn't allow herself many quiet, solitary moments. Hell, she barely allowed herself sleep anymore. Because that line of thinking was a rabbit hole to madness and she didn't have the strength. Not while trying to stay one step ahead of a serial killer.

When Luca turned onto her street, it wasn't just the interruption in the lines of the road that jerked Hero out of her reverie. Splashes of red and blue painted alternating warnings across the tree tops.

Luca's curse was long and foul as he sped down the lane almost choked with greenery.

Hero's throat closed and she had to breathe through an open mouth. She shouldn't make assumptions. A lot of wealthy older folks lived on this road, including Angora. The emergency response could mean anything. A house fire. A heart attack. A security system malfunction. Mrs. Gardner, her neighbor two doors down, could have gone into premature labor with her twins. Wasn't her husband away until Sunday?

But even as she tried to reason herself through panic, a chilly intuition seized her spine in its unrelenting grip and was validated as they took the corner with a squeal of tires. The lights of several Portland PD patrol cars reflected off the rain-slicked street in front of Angora's grand estate.

"No," Hero croaked through her tight throat.

Her home had become a crime scene. Again.

14

"The attempt and not the deed confounds us."

— WILLIAM SHAKESPEARE, MACBETH

Every light in the mansion blazed as shadows moved from window to window, though the major contingent of police seemed to be focused on the front porch. Someone had smashed Angora's prize azaleas. She was going to be so pissed, that is if she wasn't— Oh God.

Hero threw off her seatbelt, and leapt out of the car before it even came to a full stop, ignoring Luca's barking protests. Plunging through a group of her gathered neighbors, she thought she'd have to duck under crime scene tape, like they did on TV, but there was none. She ran uninhibited toward Vincent Di Petro, who was standing on the porch at the periphery of six or so officers with a phone to his ear. He hung up the moment he saw her and stowed his phone in time to catch her shoulders.

"Angora?" Hero cried by way of panicked question.

"She's inside," Vince said. "No one's hurt." His grey

eyes found a point above her head. "I was just calling you. Bea said your cell was off."

Hero remembered asking Luca to silence it for the meditation class.

"What happened?" Luca demanded from behind her.

One of the uniformed police officers turned from the cluster to face the Feds. At well under six feet, he had to look up at everyone but Hero. "My partner, Crandall and I were performing our hourly drive by and Crandall saw a figure run into the woods from the yard." The officer's nameplate said *R. Daniels*. Daniels and Crandall, that would never be a primetime crime fighter show. "We called for backup and followed on foot, but he had already disappeared into the trees."

Hero didn't understand. "All this for a shadow that ran into the woods?" She motioned to the umpteen police cars.

Daniels scratched his scalp through prematurely thinning hair that clashed with his round yet handsome young face. "Well, Miss Connor, there was a message."

Hero had to swallow her heart as it tried to leap into her esophagus. Good thing her throat was still mostly blocked by her initial surge of anxiety. "A message?" she whispered. Not another animal head. Not more blood. She couldn't take any more blood.

Daniels didn't take his eyes off her as he motioned for the officer behind him to give him something. A bouquet of wilting purple Rhododendrons was pressed into his latex-gloved hand. The plastic around the blooms crinkled noisily. "Not those, the note!" he gestured impatiently. A note card appeared, already protected in a clear plastic evidence bag.

"The note came with the flowers?" Luca clarified.

"Excuse me, but who are you?" Daniels didn't meet Luca's eyes as he asked the question. Hero still thought he was very brave.

"I'm Special Agent Luca Ramirez, the lead investigator on the John the Baptist case." Luca's voice was closer behind her than she realized. She assumed he produced identification, but couldn't imagine from where. He sounded pissed, but in control. Hero became very aware that if she leaned back, his solid, warm body would be there to prop her up.

Swallowing the overwhelming impulse, she reached for the note, instead.

Daniels glanced at Vince, who nodded, before handing it over.

The nondescript card had no florist imprint, just a little embossed curly border. In hurried, blocky, handwritten capital print it said:

I'M WATCHING YOU ALWAYS.
I PROMISE TO SAVE YOU AGAIN.

BELOW THE SCRIPT was a three-lined smiley face, which Hero found the creepiest about the whole thing. She stared at the flowers. Such a lovely vibrant purple color, but for the brown patches of decay beginning to eat away at the blossoms.

"Which way did he run?" Luca demanded.

Daniels pointed northeast into the back yard. "We combed the woods all the way down to the riverbank. There are just too many places to hide."

Luca said something evocative in Spanish. A Latino officer who was helping to fingerprint the porch covered a laugh with a fake cough.

Hero scanned the precisely groomed tree line and shivered again. He could be out there in the darkness. Watching.

"This handwriting doesn't match that of the note left with the goat head," Vince pointed out to Luca. "What do you make of that?"

"Could there be two JTB's?" Daniels speculated.

"That's not the assumption the FBI is working under," Vince said carefully. "Serial killers are known to work alone."

"What about Dean Corll?" Crandall joined the conversation, looking rather hard and military next to his baby-faced partner. "Didn't he have a few accomplices? Same with the Freeway Killer in California, didn't he recruit young boys to help him?" He looked over Hero's head and gave an involuntary jerk. "I—uh —I read a lot about this kind of stuff," he seemed compelled to add.

Hero turned to look behind her. What was it about Luca that caused these negative reactions? His expressionless face wasn't exuding any particular kind of menace. At least, not more than usual. Sure his black eyes were glittering with a cold and deadly glare but they kind of always did. Maybe she and Vince were just used to it? She mentally shrugged and handed him the note.

"I'd better not hear anything about accomplices in the press," he warned the officers before studying the note.

"Course not," Daniels rushed to comply.

Crandall nodded vigorously, though Luca wasn't looking at him.

Vince put on latex gloves and reached for the bouquet still clutched in Daniels' hands. "I'll take these to the lab. I want to process them for more than prints."

Daniels eagerly handed them over. "Rhododendrons. The flowers mean *beware*." He nodded ominously. At everyone's incredulous stare he added sheepishly, "My fiancée owns a Florist shop in Laurelhurst."

Luca grunted in response, but stepped away, staring at the note as though it held the answers he'd been looking for.

Vince picked up the investigational ball. "You get a good look at the trespasser?"

Abashed, both officers shook their heads.

"It's a real dark night and I only caught a glimpse," Crandall said by way of apology. "He seemed big, but not *that* big." He gestured toward Agent Ramirez. "And tall, but not *that* tall." Again, the head inclined toward Luca.

Vince gave him his quintessential East Coast smirk, disarming and dangerous all at once. "Would you say he was medium height and build? Average, maybe?"

"No," Crandall didn't sound too sure. "He was definitely taller than average, but bulky too, like he might have on a huge coat or something? So his size was somewhat hard to make out."

"Jesus Christ," Luca muttered in disgust, which surprised Hero, because he hadn't looked like he'd been listening. Neat trick, that. Something she'd have to remember.

"Well excuse the fuck out of us, Agent Observant, but its dark out here with barely a streetlight. I was driving and Crandall said he had nothing with which to gauge approximate height."

Hero was trying to decide if Officer Daniels was courageous or just plain stupid. If she'd have pegged either of them with bravado, it would have been Crandall, but the hard-looking man just stared at Luca with an equal mixture of trepidation and anticipation.

She knew exactly how he felt.

Luca's head lifted very slowly from the note, and Daniels' indignant scowl faltered a little, but he stood his ground.

"You had the trees," Luca said after ten full seconds, his genial smile showed just a few too many teeth and was a shocking contrast to the cold fury in his eyes. "Why don't you show me about where he disappeared and maybe it'll help you to remember where the top of his head was in relation to the forest."

The partners glanced at each other before Daniels took in a deep breath and stepped off the porch. Hero kind of wanted to give him a hug. He looked like he needed it.

Crandall followed reluctantly. If he hadn't been the one to spot the intruder, Hero doubted he would have gone. Which went to show how wrong first impressions could be.

Hero found herself thinking that, despite his height and lack of obvious physical prowess, Officer Daniels's fiancée was a protected and lucky woman. She hoped the florist realized that.

"And its Agent *Ramirez*, for future reference," Luca added with a chilling half smile when Daniels reached him.

The officer nodded once, and in the puzzling way of men, the moment was over and they went to work.

Hero shook her head, feeling a little whiplashed.

The flower paper crinkled as Vince stepped closer to her. "How you doin'?" he asked. "Need to sit down?"

She smiled up at him, but it felt brittle. "I need to check on Angora."

"I'm here, darling." The woman in question tottered toward her, gaining four inches from platforms that belonged in the seventies beneath flowing fawn cashmere slacks. "I had to reapply my face. Those first two officers caught me in such a state of *déshabillé*." She tossed the hair of her shoulder-length platinum wig behind her shoulder, uncovering an indecent amount of diamonds hanging from her ears.

Hero threw her arms around the woman, careful not to disturb her artful appearance. "Are you all right, Angora? I'm so sorry about all of this."

Angora cooed and patted her back a few times. "Don't be. Anything that brings Portland's own Italian Stallion to my door..." Hero took her cue to pull back so Angora could receive her due from Agent Di Petro. The Bostonian didn't disappoint, he laid it on thick, twinkling grey eyes and everything.

"Mrs. Steinman, don't you look a picture." He pressed her offered hand between both of his, flashing a flirty smile.

"Oh, I just love your accent, it's so—crude." Enough sex dripped from the last word, there was no way it could be insulting.

"Really though, Angora, I think we should talk about me moving out until this is all over. These flowers were left on *your* porch, not mine," Hero insisted gently.

Angora pursed her rouge lips and *tut-tuted*. "Are you kidding? This is the most excitement I've had in *ages*. I can rub it in Angelique de la Croix's botoxed face. She's always bragging about her *liaison* with that dangerous mobster in Chicago. Like we care who she slept with thirty years ago."

This time when Hero smiled, it felt genuine. "Consider it, seriously," she urged. "I worry about your safety."

"You're such a love." Angora squeezed her hand. "But as they say, *Mi casa es su casa*, no matter what. Which reminds me, where is that tall Latin lover of yours?"

Vince chuckled and motioned over to the trees where Luca and the two officers were measuring approximations. "Careful, Mrs. Steinman, I might be the jealous type."

Offering him a beatific smile, Angora took his arm and led him down the front porch toward the gawking neighbors, leaving Hero to look after them. "All men are the jealous types, Vincent, regardless of what they may claim. Now tell me, when is the press going to get here?"

Hero's eyes watched them the entire way down the front walk, her eyes glued to the rhododendrons clutched in Vince's gloved hands. He stopped at his SUV and took longer than a minute to secure them into whatever storage the lab would require.

The activity of the surrounding officers processing the crime scene turned into a distant buzz. Hero wanted to be rid of them all. She didn't want to talk to the press. Didn't want to see anyone right now, but couldn't bring herself to go into her apartment without Luca. So she stood on the porch and watched him, his vibrant green shorts glowing when they caught the light from the house.

One word echoed through her mind again and again as she clutched at a pillar in order to remain upright, made all the more terrible because of Officer Daniels's young and airy voice.

Beware.

EXHAUSTED AND STARVING, Luca left Hero with Vince in the entry while he did a quick sweep of her loft before letting them in. He knew it was redundant, but that didn't stop him.

"We're good." He said, and collapsed deeper into the Lovesac than he'd meant to. That might have been a mistake, but he couldn't bring himself to move. He'd let Vince and Angora handle the press as neither he nor Hero was really dressed *or* up for it. They'd stayed through the entire processing of the porch and the final sweep of the house to make sure Angora was safe. Luca didn't know the time, but midnight was a distant memory.

Vince took up a standing vigil by the kitchen table, a sure sign he was also hungry.

Hero, on the other hand, reminded him of a butterfly on crack. She flitted around her apartment in a flurry of activity, not really accomplishing anything or staying in one place long enough to be caught.

"You know what pisses me off the most about tonight?" she finally exploded, but didn't wait for a response. "Just what the hell does he think he means by those flowers? *Beware.* I have become the personification of *ware*. The embodiment of *ware*. Tell me, Agent Ramirez, just how frigging much more *ware* could he expect me to *be*? I let two FBI agents move in to my *house*. I wake up *ware*. I go to bed *ware*—"

"It's wary," Luca corrected without thinking.

Hero paused in her tirade and Vince made frantic neck slashing moves from behind her.

"What did you say?" she asked slowly.

"Nothing. You want to take a shower before bed, you know, wash off the day?" He threw an arm over his exhausted eyes. Maybe if he avoided eye contact he wouldn't be turned to stone.

Hero was quiet for a moment, and Luca didn't dare look. "Actually, yes. That sounds incredible." Luca didn't so much as twitch until the bathroom door closed and the water went on.

Vince let out a loud breath. "Close one. I was about to duck and cover."

Luca thought about shrugging, but it seemed like it would take too much effort. "I didn't want to give it much precedence in public, but what do you think about this accomplice idea?"

The couch offered its own sigh as Vince sat down. "Fucking A, you had to *sleep* on this thing?"

Luca just moaned in response.

"I think this is a one man job but I'm not willing to rule out any possibilities." Vince got down to business. "An accomplice would help explain how the girls are moved in and out of the van and on and off the cross and what not. But Hero never mentioned anything about a second assailant. Not even extra footsteps in the dark or what have you."

"I'm trying to figure out how the hand writing on the notes could be so different." Luca sat up with a lot of effort. "I'd never let Hero hear me say this, but it just—*feels* different. I mean, it could be as simple as the flowers aren't from John the Baptist."

"If not from him, then who? A copycat maybe? Some sick piece of shit just trying to freak her out?"

"Could be." Luca shook his head. "But it just feels too personal for that. You know, I remember studying the Freeway Killer in Quantico and what's sticking in my mind is that he recruited fucked up, weak-willed, like-minded kids to help him."

"Sounds right." Vince was waiting for him to get to the point.

"Remember when we interviewed Father Mc-

Murtry and Father Michael? They were the last two to see Hero the night she was attacked."

"Sure."

"I recall Father Michael stating something about being hand-picked by Father McMurtry and groomed to take over his job when he retires."

"After everything that's happened with Professor Alec, and the fact that the hobo that supposedly called in the crime is still at large, you still want to pin this on the priests?" Vince sounded unconvinced.

At the sound of the professor's name, Luca's body involuntarily tensed. "I'm so tired, I don't know what I'm saying, but it might be worth looking into."

Vince looked at his watch. "Can't hurt."

"Before you leave, did Bea tell you about the new suspect?" Luca asked.

The sound of the shower died in the middle of his update regarding Two Rivers. As Luca talked, he was dimly aware of the sounds Hero made in her room as she dressed in her sleepwear.

"I'm not one to second guess your instincts," Vince said. "They've been my constant companion for two years and I've developed a healthy respect. Besides, with a name like *Two Rivers* this *Eat, Pray, Love* mother fucker most definitely has something to hide."

Luca had known Vince would agree.

"But he has an alibi for the flowers. He was at the yoga studio with us." Hero said as she emerged from her room in her night uniform of flowing cotton pants and a tight tank. She walked to the fridge and took out some carrot juice, kale, and a banana. "Want a smoothie?"

"We didn't leave the yoga studio right away," Luca pointed out. "And the incident was fresh when we pulled up. *Rivers* had plenty of time to get over here and be chased off by the police by the time we pulled up. And I'd rather eat my own gym shorts, but thanks for offering."

Hero put too many green things into a blender, and then threw in the banana, some honey, and the carrot juice. "That would be awfully risky."

"The gym shorts or the flowers?" Vince joked.

Luca was too tired to examine the urge to drown his partner in shallow water every time he made Hero laugh.

"Both, I guess, but I was talking about the flowers."

"More risky than crucifying prostitutes and dumping them in a river?" Luca asked.

Hero paused. Her smile suffered a painful death and she looked at him as though to ask him *why*. Instead she murmured, "Good point," and flipped on the noisy blender, a troubled frown creasing between her eyebrows.

"Smooth," Vince smirked.

"It's not my job to be smooth. It's my job to keep her alive."

Vince shook his head.

"You mind sticking around while I shower?" Luca stood.

"Sure. It's the least I can do since I'm grabbing a burger and fries on the way home, and I know what's waiting for *you* in the fridge."

Luca's dirty tank slapped him in the face as he made his way toward the bathroom Hero just vacated.

The better part of a half an hour and an empty hot water tank later, Luca stepped from the sauna he'd created. Vince was nowhere to be found and the rhythmic spin of Hero's wheel competed with her Indie rock from the workshop.

He padded past the kitchen clad in only his

TapOut sleep pants. She didn't look up when he leaned against the entry. Damp hair held back by Mr. Huang's chopsticks, her freshly scrubbed face already sported a streak of red clay. The lithe muscles in her arms flexed with the push and pull movements of her hands. Her thighs were parted around the machine and she gripped it with her knees. As Luca studied her, he realized that she was using her entire body to shape the spinning clay. Her breath synchronized with her actions. Her skilled hands pulled at the cylinder, coaxing it to lift higher, then smoothed back down with even, constant pressure. The movements were so sexual; wet and strong and rhythmic, a little messy and slippery, needing practice and skill to truly master.

Hero was an artisan. And he was toast.

Adjusting his posture to allow for less room in his pants, he broke the moment as only he know how. By opening his mouth.

"Where's Vince?" he asked.

Hero didn't look up. "I told him I was going to sleep and sent him home."

"But you're not sleeping," he pointed out the obvious.

Her unbound breasts bobbed beneath her tank with her careless shrug. "I'll sleep when I'm dead." She let out a dry, humorless laugh. "Which could be sooner than later. Want some coffee?"

"I'm not going to let anything happen to you." She could take that to the fucking bank. "And don't think you can distract me with amazing coffee. I'm starting to become familiar with your diversion tactics." He schooled his voice into a gentle reprimand. "It's two a.m., Hero."

"Only in this time zone," she said brightly.

"Hero."

"There's no time like the present, right?"

"*Hero.*"

"Someone wants me dead," she said as though she was informing him that he'd missed a phone call. "And I want to finish my flower vase right now, okay?"

He winced. "Flower vase? Isn't that kind of—"

"Ironic?" she supplied.

"I was going to say *masochistic*, but let's go with your thing."

She finally spared him a glance, which turned into a second lingering one when she realized he wasn't wearing a shirt. "Either way, I'm working. So go away or pull up a chair. But don't just lurk all dark and shirtless in the doorway, speaking of unfair diversion tactics."

Okay then. Luca debated for less time than he should have while staring at the packed dirt floor of her little cellar-turned-workshop. It was late. He wasn't in a strong frame of mind and she looked like a disheveled pinup girl. He should plant his ass on that godforsaken couch and go to sleep like a good agent. "Let me get my shoes." He turned around.

"Don't," she softly called after him.

"What?"

"Don't get your shoes. Let your feet enjoy the fine-grain clay earth, it'll help ground your energy."

He cast a dubious frown at the dirt. "I'll have you know, my energy is *plenty* grounded."

Her dainty hand disappeared inside the vase and the entire shape of the thing magically changed. "You wouldn't want those expensive shoes of yours to get stained or ruined, would you?"

That would be a *negative*. He stepped down into the damp and chilly workshop. She was right though, the cool packed dirt felt great against his bare feet, still warm from a punishing shower.

The cellar was square, no bigger than twenty by twenty. Surrounded by so many breakable objects, Luca felt like the proverbial bull in a china shop. Tall silver metal shelves lined every wall and held their *objects d'art* in a manner suggestive of the red light districts of Amsterdam and Copenhagen. Curves. They were everywhere. Shamelessly displayed in an endless array of shapes and sizes, each piece of pottery advertised the colorful fulfillment of a different utility. Their coils and curvatures all reminiscent of their creator; vibrant, feminine, sensual, and beautiful in a way that was indefinably complex and unique.

He needed to sit the fuck down before he initiated a *Ghost* moment or some shit. No offense to Swayze, may he rest in peace, but he hated that damned movie. He was more of a Roadhouse kind of guy.

Luca slowly reached for a folding chair, conveniently tucked between a shelf and the wall. Unfolding it, he placed it facing her on the opposite side of the wheel and sat, elbows on his splayed knees, hands hanging loose between them.

He should be thinking about the case. Going over files. Checking on flower shops. Refreshing his email until the reports from the scene processors started to flow in. If he wasn't sleeping, he should be useful.

Moments like this disturbed him. The rhythm of her wheel, the sight of her working was starting to lull him into a warm sort of oblivion. That place where it felt safe to desire. To examine the epoxy that held the cracks together and contemplate the thoughts that got lost in the every day. The way he lived, case to case, arrest to arrest—kill to kill if need be— didn't leave a lot of opportunity for introspection. Which was the point. He avoided words that needed avoiding. Words like *home, future,* and *family.* To a man like him, those words were radical ideals, something he fought for, but never truly intended to have.

The items surrounding him in this room, they belonged in a house, matching a color scheme picked out at the Home Depot. Mugs would be used for coffee accidentally spilled on laptop keyboards. Dishes of all shapes would fill a kitchen and be called upon to entertain guests. Vases would hold flowers or different arrangements, maybe to be broken by a rowdy child. These were the pieces of a life he didn't have. Luca tried to remember the last time he'd eaten anything that didn't come out of a flimsy cardboard box or wrapped in paper. He drank out of the same stainless steel coffee mug and reused gas station plastic water bottles. He never spent money on things like this. He never wanted anyone he brought back to his apartment to feel at home, because then he could be sure they'd leave.

"What's up with that, anyway?" Hero asked him, still absorbed in her work.

He had to take a few moments to assure himself that he'd said nothing of his inner thoughts out loud. "Uh—what?"

"Your shoes, you're more of a girl about them than I am." She flicked a perceptive look from beneath her lashes before returning to her project. "Why is that?"

"I have to dress professionally for my job," he said dismissively.

"There's professional, and then there are seven hundred dollar shoes."

"What else do I have to spend my money on?"

She raised her eye-brow.

"I like to be stylish *and* comfortable." He didn't like the defensive note edging into his voice.

She snorted.

"I have a foot condition?"

"Oh yeah? What's it called?"

He thought about it, trying to come up with a convincing lie. Corns? Bunions? No. Too gross. Bone spurs? Would he be limping?

"You're so full of shit," she accused with a warm laugh. "Come on, Agent Ramirez, you have me at a disadvantage here. You have files full of information about me. You probably know more about me than my own parents." Her smile faltered, and still her hands never wavered from the clay's relentless formation. "You've seen me naked, half-dead, ripped open and bleeding. You witnessed the most— incomparably horrible experience of my lifetime, but I know next to nothing about you that I haven't put together by observation."

Luca's palms began to tingle and he realized he'd been holding his breath for a while. What had she observed? He squeezed his hands together and reminded himself to exhale slowly as she continued.

"Now I've had kind of a bad night and I want to talk. It's not like I asked you to bare your darkest secret or anything, I just asked you a simple question and *now* I know it has a complicated answer. So let's hear it. I'm in the mood for a confession."

Luca blinked at her. He'd never thought of it quite like that before. His knowledge of her was about as intimate as it could get without being downright biblical. It wouldn't hurt to give her something small. Something real.

He cleared his throat and looked down at his bare

feet, smooth and brown and cared for, his big toe digging a little at the packed cellar floor.

"I grew up in El Paso, Texas, in a crime-ridden East Paisano neighborhood along the border of Mexico. My parents spent most of their money on alcohol and my mother had a pill addiction, so that meant my sister and I often went without shoes, especially when we were really little. I remember if I had a pair, the soles would be worn so thin that the pavement would still blister my feet in the summer." He looked up from his feet for just a second. Hero's eyes remained intently on her hands, but her fingers curled inward a little, centering the measurement of the vase. Her silence pressed him to continue.

"When I was ten, I saw a hundred dollar bill left in the cup holder of a car parked next to my school. I stared at that money for a full half an hour before I found some rebar and broke the passenger window. I used that hundred dollars to buy my first real pair of shoes."

"What were they?" Hero asked, surprising him a little.

"Black and orange Reeboks with the air pump in the tongue," he recalled with a nostalgic smile. He'd walked on them for miles. He'd gone to the cracked and weed-choked basketball court in his neighborhood to see if they really helped him to jump higher, and he'd sworn they'd blessed him with a half a foot. "Two days after I bought them, I was jumped by three Junior High kids who beat the shit out of me and took them. But they were mine for two days and those were the best two days of my fucking life."

"Did you steal more money to buy other shoes?"

Luca listened for judgment in her voice, but found only concern. "Later on," he admitted. "But first I realized, if I was going to take money or nice things, I needed to learn how to fight to keep them."

Hero glanced up at him, her eyes round. "Did you?"

"My nickname growing up was *Peleón*. It roughly translates to scrapper or brawler." He flashed his teeth. "Let's just say, about a week later I used that rebar to get my shoes back."

She blinked, but didn't seem surprised.

"Problem was, my old man caught me with them and—" Luca cleared his throat against an unexpected intrusion. "Anyway those shoes caused me more trouble than they were worth. My mother ended up selling them to help pay for my broken arm."

Hero made a soft sound in her throat and her eyes were liquid before she returned them to her wheel. She didn't give him pity or bullshit platitudes. And he didn't want them. Couldn't even figure why he'd gone there.

"Was your family...?" She trailed off, seeming to change her mind from what she was about to say. "From Mexico?"

Luca shook his head. "My mother was an underage Puerto Rican stripper in a border club and my father was from Brazil, but worked in a custom auto body shop that laundered money for the drug trade. He married her to avoid a statutory rape charge when she became pregnant with me."

She blinked a few times. "Do you have family in Brazil? Do you speak Portuguese?"

"Don't know about my family. My father said if he ever went back to Brazil, he would be instantly killed. And no, I only speak Spanish. My mother never talked about her family."

"Where are your parents now?" she asked gently.

Luca cleared his throat and made a dismissive gesture. "My mom took a deadly cocktail of pills and tequila ten years ago and, last I heard, my father was serving two consecutive ten to twenties in the maximum security New Mexico State Penitentiary after a shootout with the police." It had been long enough that Luca could talk about it without flinching. "Son of a bitch was shot three times but, in the end, I think he's just too mean to die."

"How old were you when that happened?" she asked, sounding truly horrified.

Luca didn't look up from his feet. "That was right before my mom—anyway it was a bad year."

"I'd say," she murmured, dipping her hands into a bowl of water and rewetting the clay in front of her, to keep it pliable, he suspected.

"So, your father was violent with you?"

"You could say that." And so could the ER doctors and x-ray techs that'd stitched him up and set his bones over the years. In fact, he was pretty sure he invited the radiologist to his high school graduation. "My father taught me to be violent. It was about the only thing he taught me, and I was for the longest time. Violent and angry. Still can be. My father relied on us all being afraid of him. He hadn't counted on creating someone as vicious as he was. I reached over six feet tall the summer I turned seventeen. I caught him hurting my pregnant fourteen-year-old sister and I threw him through our sliding glass door onto the pavement in the back yard."

"Good." Hero shocked him with the approval in her voice. "I would expect the same from my brothers."

Luca remembered her alpha-male siblings and smirked. "Your brothers probably wouldn't have left you there. I disappeared before my old man woke up, but couldn't convince my mom or sister to come with me though, God knows, I tried. But I knew that if I was still there when he came around, I was a dead man... or he was."

"Where did you go?"

"When I was a sophomore, I almost got expelled for fighting. At the underfunded school that I attended, our counselor was also our football coach. Coach Peck said if I trained with the varsity team, he'd help me stay in school. Maybe make something of myself. He was the only adult I trusted, so I showed up on his doorstep that night. He let me stay with him my whole senior year. He got me a job, trained me day and night, rode my ass about homework and damn near filled out my college applications."

"He sounds wonderful," Hero said warmly.

"He was," Luca cleared his throat.

"Was?"

"We stayed in constant contact until he died of a heart attack four years ago." Funny, out of everything he'd said tonight, that had been the hardest. Luca stunned even himself as he delved into a childhood he rarely visited in front of someone. In front of a victim of more extreme violence, no less. Hell, he'd just told Hero more than he'd told the psychologist. Maybe because she wasn't looking at him, or trying to use his past to explain his present. She didn't scrutinize his motives or ask him how he felt, which was good, because most of the time he still didn't know. She just listened as it all spilled out of him, reminding him of the hot, melted black tar of the desert roads he used to wander as a kid. Dirty and sticky, melding into whatever it came in contact with, filling any surface with a rank, grimy substance that was impossible to be rid of.

But it made him tough. It made him hard. It made him dangerous, and not just to criminals, but to himself and those who were close to him.

"What about your sister?" she asked. "Are the two of you close?"

Luca shook his head, a familiar pang of guilt clenching his gut. "She showed up at Coach Peck's once to tell me she'd lost the baby that day. I didn't see her again until she showed up at my dorm room in college demanding money. I gave it to her and she just... disappeared." Years later, Luca had traced her trail to the border of Tijuana, where it had gone cold. She'd likely slipped the country and the many drug-related warrants she'd had against her.

"You must get very lonely." Hero took her hands off the spinning vase and flipped a switch to cut the engine.

"I get very busy," he hedged. "I don't have time to be lonely."

Hero stood and went to the worktable in the corner, stacked neatly with stamps, tools, brushes, and other instruments. She selected a wire tool that looked like a very efficient garrote, then returned to the wheel and used it to separate the vase from the wheel by sliding it beneath the base of the object.

"You may not have time to be lonely, but you spend much of your time angry."

Didn't take a genius to figure that out. "I'm not angry right now."

"Yes, you are." She gingerly picked up her vase and turned to set it on a stone slab with other pieces in various stages of drying. "Anger is your constant companion, you're just better at burying it some days than others, but I always feel it like a vibration or a wave of heat rolling off of you. I think it builds inside of you. It threatens to overtake you sometimes."

She wasn't wrong. And didn't that just piss him off? Luca stood abruptly, no longer relaxed, hackles raised.

"Can I ask you what you do to relieve that stress? What is your emotional outlet? Other than shoe shopping, which is totally effective." She turned to him with another disarming smile.

She was so goddamned beautiful. Luca stood there, digging his toes in the ground, almost like he was gripping it to keep them planted where they were. Where they should be. He searched his memory for an answer. "Working out. A lot of meaningless sex." Taking a stab at self-analysis he tried one better. "I don't know, maybe—meting out justice to violent criminals that I never got as a kid?"

Hero shook her head. "Your brand of justice has a body count comparable to that of a serial killer." She held her hand up at his dark look. "I'm not judging you, I'm just saying that kind of thing adds to the rage, and though the kills maybe have been, for all intents and purposes, 'righteous', they felt to you like vengeance rather than justice, am I wrong?"

Luca's nostrils flared. His fists clenched. His heart pounded. He *wanted* her to be wrong. Needed her to be wrong. How did they get here? Weren't they just talking about shoes? He glanced over his shoulder at the door, wondering how he could extricate himself from the situation without being a total douchebag. One thing stopped him from giving in to his initial impulse and telling her where to go.

She *was* absolutely right. And she was telling him, in her own way, that she saw through his bullshit good guy façade. She knew him for what he really was. And the way she looked at him now, with her fine brow wrinkled and her eyes pinched with worry rather than pity told him that, in some way, she feared him.

He should have kept his damned mouth shut.

"I'm good at what I do. The best, actually." He moved toward her, and she stood her ground. "I don't want you thinking that I'm somehow damaged goods or dangerous to you. I *handle* my *shit*. Which means, I'll keep you alive. What happened in my youth was a long time ago. I *refuse* to be the monster my father tried to create, so I don't have a wife, I don't have kids. I have a purpose, and that's why I'm the best."

Her eyes widened as he came to a stop in front of her, his body filling her space, his breath teasing the few wisps of baby-fine hair that curled at her temples. He reached out and wiped at the smear on her cheek, which only made it worse. "I don't want you to be afraid of me," he admitted. He spent enough time being afraid of himself.

Hero stared up at him for a long moment, her lips parted.

Luca wanted her to say something. *Needed* her to break the silence before he did something stupid.

"I want to show you something." She stepped away from him and it took all his self-discipline to let her. She turned to the shelf behind her, reaching for a bowl with an odd orange coating and some intricate engravings. Handling it gingerly, she held it out to Luca and he took it, looking to her for an explanation.

"This bowl has some serious imperfections," she explained. "And they're *my* fault. The shape is too thick in some places, and I used the wrong type of glaze for the clay, which in the eyes of most potters is a waste and an abuse of my clay and my equipment." Her lip quirked sadly, then she reached back behind her, bending down to drag a very large box from the bottom shelf. "Chances are, when I put it in the kiln and stress it with a fire hot enough to melt your DNA, it'll crack or explode under the pressure, like all of these did." She pointed to discarded pieces of sharp and colorful shards of broken pottery.

"*But...*" Her eyes twinkled mischievously and she returned to her shelves with a lighter step, reaching to the back and pulling out what looked like a small urn. "Maybe one time in fifty, if I'm *lucky*, the piece survives the fire and the cooling aftermath. What I'm left with is a masterpiece like this."

She held up the urn. The distressed cracks in the cobalt glaze gave it an ancient look, as though it had been pulled out of a dig site and displayed in a museum. Inside the fissures, a bold earthy bronze peeked through the vibrant blue and the effect was absolutely stunning.

"This piece will sell for more than any on that shelf, maybe all of them combined, even though it will require more upkeep, and more careful handling."

She set it down and Luca handed the bowl back to her, uncomfortable now with the pressure of holding it, maybe a little anxious for its future.

"In my opinion, people, especially children, are a lot like my pottery. They're shaped and molded. Sometimes by a gentle hand, sometimes not. Their chinks and imperfections can create volatile and unpredictable outcomes. Once they're fired, those imperfections become permanent one way or the other. But who's to say, that sometimes it doesn't make them all the more... valuable?"

Luca appreciated the metaphor. He looked down at the box of garbage, then to the priceless urn displayed on the shelf. "Which one are you saying I am, the broken shards or the masterpiece?"

"I think you're still in the kiln. I think you walk through the fire every day." Hero reached up to touch her cheek where his fingers had lingered a moment ago. Her eyes roamed him, suddenly flaring when they touched on the bare skin of his torso. Smoldering with dangerous intent, she sashayed toward him. Reaching a finger out to hook into the loose waistband of his sleep pants, she lifted her face and offered her ripe lips to him. "*I* say, we turn up the heat and see what happens."

15

"'Tis one thing to be tempted,
Another thing to fall."

— William Shakespeare, Measure for
Measure

"Hero." Luca's warning sounded more like a plea.

"What do you say, Agent Ramirez, to some good old meaningless, stress-relief sex?" She pulled on his waistband a little, nudging him in the direction of the door. "I think it would do us both some good."

At her proposition, Luca's ever-ready body sprung to life. His pecker didn't seem to care that he hadn't slept in twenty-plus hours. It sent him pulsating images of all the things she could probably do with that infuriating mouth.

"Can't," he gasped, grabbing her wrist and pushing on a pressure point, forcing her fingers to release his waistband.

"Can't? Or won't?" she challenged.

His teeth ground together. "Would. Can't. Go to bed."

"You sure?" Her tongue ran a wet, glistening sheen across her full lower lip.

"Goddammit, Hero," he growled.

She stepped back, putting her hands up in teasing surrender. "Okay, Agent Ramirez. I'll behave." Turning from him, she stepped up into the house and waited for him to follow before turning off the light.

Luca silently shadowed her down the hallway, his stomach bunched into knots, his dick throbbing at him in punishing, masculine protest.

She paused in her doorway and threw a sultry look over her shoulder. "I'll probably just... relieve my own stress then. By *myself*..." She raised her eyebrows and let that thought trail to him in the darkness. The images almost drove him to his knees.

"I'm going to sleep on your fucking uncomfortable couch," he informed her. "And you'd better stay in that bedroom." His self-control was fraying at both ends. He didn't know what would break first, his libido or his temper.

THE NEXT MORNING, Hero emerged from the bedroom trying to do the clasp on her peacock feather earrings. "You sure you don't want to come to church with us, Vince?" she joked.

Di Petro looked up from where he commiserated with Luca over case paperwork spread all over her table. Luca kept his eyes on the yellow pad with some kind of diagram on it, so Hero allowed herself to enjoy the friendlier agent's warm and appreciative glance her way before his wry mouth twisted into a grimace.

She loved this sweater dress, just the right mix of buttoned-up-catholic-school-girl collar, with a hemline that would shock a go-go dancer. She toned it down with nude leggings tucked into winter boots that buckled a little above her knee.

"It's the Sunday around the Immaculate Conception celebration." She threw mock encouragement into her tone. "Which means an extra funny sermon from Father Michael. If that isn't enough to tempt you, we're doing the big Feast of the Immaculate Conception slash pre-Christmas Katrova-Connor holiday practice dinner at my parent's house afterward. It'll be good times. Knox is cooking this year and we'll be drawing names for Christmas presents."

Vince shook his head. "Much as I would like to have my dinner cooked by a two time Light-Heavyweight Champion, all of *this*—" he motioned to his body, draped in his "artist" garb of loose jeans and a vintage t-shirt—"is just too much genuine *wicked* locked in one tempting package to step foot in a church. Besides, I kinda have an issue with the whole Immaculate Conception thing. I mean, without—maculating, what's the point, *amiright*?"

Hero laughed and shrugged making a beeline for the coffee maker. "You have me there, I just go to see everyone and for Knox's incredible holiday Guinness chocolate potato cake. Want some coffee before you go?"

"Is the Pope Catholic?"

Catching Luca's dark scowl, she said, "I'll make you both a cup."

It had been a relief to wake up to Vince's presence Saturday morning to ease her into the weekend. For once, she'd been glad he had the entire twenty-four hours with her. Everything that had happened Friday night: yoga class, the creepy *beware* bouquet, and Luca's confessional in her pottery studio had left her feeling keyed up and emotionally vulnerable. She and Luca needed a break, and his easy-going partner was one hell of a palate cleanser.

Using some new and ardent inspiration, Hero had broken out her sculpting clay and began a new project in the enormous garage that Angora allowed her to use as a studio. Vince had entertained them both by reading particularly naughty parts of her collection of historical romance novels in an exaggerated Southie accent. She'd never be able to curl up with another Regency without giggling at the romantic hero's '*thrabbing cack*'. Bless him, she'd needed the laughs.

Vince slept like a baby on her air mattress and all her good feelings for him evaporated like Guinness at her family parties. He hadn't stirred once as she'd restlessly lurked through her loft until almost four in the morning, and some sadistic part of her really wanted to startle him awake. She rarely slept anymore, but the insomnia seemed to reach a maddening zenith last night.

She'd tried to read, but none of her books held her attention. One frustrating and pointless hour at her potter's wheel had left her irate and troubled. She made tea. She took calming herbs. She did yoga, applied essential oils, meditated and even masturbated. But the name that escaped her lips in a scorching whisper at her climax hung in the air like a delicious vapor afterward, and it had been like she'd invited him into her bedroom. He invaded her thoughts, and at the same time his absence became a conspicuous negative space. A tall, dark, brooding question mark with cold black eyes and rich warm skin.

She'd finally dropped into an agitated doze and didn't wander from her room until well past 9 a.m.

She knew Luca would be there. Sunday was his day to stay with her full-time. But a curious dread clenched in her stomach at the thought of losing Vince's easy presence. She was afraid to be alone with Luca. Not because she didn't trust him, but because she didn't trust herself. She knew a violent demon lurked beneath the suit and tie and impenetrable firewall he'd coded and reinforced. It was that reckless, prying, utterly female part of her nature that wanted to unleash that demon. And she *would*, if she kept poking at it. It was just a matter of time. The knowledge made her feel sensual. Powerful. Dangerous. Nothing at all like a victim, but instead like the circus ringmaster, inciting the powerful lion.

Except Luca was more panther than lion, and his claws would probably leave her heart in shreds when he was through with her.

"I talked to the profiler yesterday." Luca threw his yellow legal pad on top of the pile of paperwork and pinched the bridge of his nose.

Hero's attention returned to the moment, but she remained silent, making a production of the coffee. The agents rarely discussed the case in front of her. Sometimes she appreciated it, other times she wanted to know everything and their tight lipped policy was frustrating. Today she was hungry for some information, some progress, anything that would bring them closer to ending this nightmare.

Vince made a gesture that showed what he thought of profilers.

Luca ignored him and shuffled papers around, picking up another yellow pad. "It made me realize what part of the motive we've been missing. We have the *who*, red-heads in the sex trade." He flicked a glance at her. "Mostly. The *how* is blatantly obvious."

"That sick stigmata bullshit," Vince agreed, unobservant of Luca's attempt at tact.

Hero traced the scars on her hands, a clammy moisture blooming on her palms. "We have the *where*." He motioned to the map with the macabre body markers along the rivers. "So I found a pattern in the *when* yesterday, but only *after* I realized the pattern had been broken."

"Oh yeah? What's that?" Vince's mild tone sharpened with interest.

"Saints."

"Come again?"

"More specifically, canonized female Catholic saints." Luca licked his fingertip and flipped a few pages on his legal pad. "The dates of the murders until now have seemed insanely random, a few happening in clusters with months stretching in between others. I believe I've found the reason. Check it, Amber Wilcox, the transplanted street walker from Jersey, she was killed on February first."

"The feast of St. Brigit," Hero murmured, forgetting her intention to stay silent.

Both agents looked at her with more than a little surprise. "Every good Irish Catholic girl knows Brigit... and most of us not-so-good ones."

Luca made an affirmative noise in his throat. "Janelle Kennedy was found on February eleventh, which is apparently St. Abigail's feast day. March twenty-ninth, the day we found Cheyenne West, is the feast of St. Eithne. April Jensen died May fifteenth, the feast of St. Dymphna. Jessi Scott, August eleventh, feast of St. Athracht. Jesus, I don't even think I'm saying that right." He scowled at his hand-scrawled notes.

Hero pressed the button on the coffee maker and

the familiar sound of it coming to life offered a slight comfort. "Admittedly, I'm not so much a Catholic as my parents are, but other than Brigit, I've never even heard of these saints, or their feast days."

"You know how it is," Vince made a dismissive gesture. "There's like twenty saints to feast every fucking day of the year. Catholics tend to only celebrate the real important ones."

"I considered that." Luca didn't seem to mind Vince playing the devil's advocate, as he was born to the role. "But bearing in mind the very strong religious tones of these murders, I Googled each of these saints and they all have disturbingly similar stories of canonization."

"Martyrs?" Hero guessed.

Luca shook his head. "Very few of them, actually, but aside from all being medieval female saints, they're specifically Irish women who lived, and sometimes died, as bastions of sexual purity."

Vince put up his hand in a staying motion. "Isn't sexual purity what *every* female catholic nun and saint stood for from the beginning of time to kingdom come?"

"Probably," Luca conceded. "Though each of these women have a specific story attached to them in which they make a very large sacrifice for purity. Take Brigit. According to the church documents, she was so beautiful she'd been promised to a chieftain. She prayed for her beauty to be taken away so she could better serve God. Legend says, it worked. She refused to marry, and she ended up one of the Patron Saints of Ireland. And here it says that St. Eithne was a rich and beautiful Irish Princess who was converted by St. Patrick and demanded to immediately become a nun. Once she'd pledged her virginity to Christ, she became so enraptured that she died on the spot and was instantly sainted."

"The fuck?" Vince muttered.

"Then there's Dymphna, who chose death by her father's hand rather than submitting to an incestuous marriage. All these women were renowned and sainted in the middle ages for their so-called sexual virtue."

"So do you think he's offering these prostitutes as sacrifices to these sainted women?" Skepticism colored Vince's words, but his brows rose as though the idea impressed him.

"Sainted *Irish* women," Luca corrected.

Something Luca said before tripped through Hero's racing thoughts. "You mentioned the pattern had been broken. Since I don't fit any of the other victim—*women's* personas, was the pattern of the Saints interrupted by me?" She refused to think of those who hadn't survived her ordeal as prostitutes or victims. They were women and deserved to be remembered as such.

"No, actually." For the first time that day, Luca's eyes met hers. They were opaque. Cold. Though a flare of hunger tightened his features before he smothered it with annoyance and continued with his work. "October Fourteenth is the Feast of Saint Cyra, one of the most famous Irish Abbesses and alternately known as 'The Virgin Saint.'"

Vince snorted. "Like I said, aren't they all?"

"I guess she was extra especially virginal?" Luca made a dismissive gesture. "Anyway, when it comes to breaking the pattern, I have a theory on why he did that, but testing it is impossible."

"What do you mean?" Vince looked uncomfortably at Hero.

"At least two female Irish Saint Feasts have passed in October and November with no incident. I'm guessing it's because John the Baptist is focused on his one sacrifice that failed."

Hero could feel the blood draining from her face as both agents turned to look at her. She made a great to do about arranging coffee mugs and gathering sweeteners. Why should that bother her? She already knew the bastard was still after her.

"How do you plan to test the theory?"

Luca studied her intently. "Who is the woman *most* adored by all Catholics as the paragon of purity? The blessed virgin. And what miracle did she bring about?"

"The immaculate conception," Hero answered, stunned at how neatly Luca's theory fit together.

"Exactly, and if JTB were to make another kill, it would most likely be tonight. I think he's been waiting for the perfect chance to get to you, but if he can't, I'm wondering if his obsessive nature would allow him to pass up a sacrifice to the Virgin Mary on her special day."

"Have you run this past Trojanowski?" Vince asked. "There might be something to this."

"I called him this morning. He's stepping up patrol of the river and putting a few extra agents on watch duty along likely body disposal banks. I don't know how much a deterrent it'll be, but at least it's something."

A sudden fierce pricking of tears burned in Hero's eyes and she blinked at them rapidly. "You think... that maybe... that he's to kill again tonight? That another woman is going to be crucified?"

Vince suddenly looked uncomfortable and shot Luca a voluminous look, which, as usual, he ignored.

"It's possible," Luca answered bluntly, but his dark eyes softened a little as he noted the dread in her demeanor and the slight tremors that had begun in her hands. "It depends on how deep his obsession with you really is. Also my theory could be just that, a coincidence of correlation. There's no way of knowing unless..." He let his insinuation trail off to a troubled silence.

"But, *I'm* supposed to be the bait," Hero insisted. "I want him to be after *me* not anyone else. This *has* to stop. *He* has to be stopped before he hurts another woman." She had the impression she'd shocked them both as the two tall FBI agents in her dining room just stared at her, unblinking for a couple of breaths.

"Hero, we're doing everything we can," The gentleness in Vince's voice softened his accent. "We don't want this to happen to anyone else."

"But our first priority is keeping *you* safe and alive." Luca insisted, crossing his arms over his chest. "So don't go around taking unnecessary risks."

Hero warmed just a little at the concern lurking beneath the warning in his voice.

Vince offered her a careful smile. "Don't go trying to be a hero."

"Good one," she snarked, though sarcasm and gratitude mingled in her short laugh. Hero rolled her eyes as she reached for the coffee pot and filled three mugs, managing not to spill too much of the precious brew regardless of how badly her hand shook.

"That priest, Father McMurtry, is from Ireland, isn't he?" Vince motioned to the name on one of Luca's many legal pads.

"Yes, and Father Michael went to Seminary School there," Luca answered, anticipation coloring his tone for the first time that morning.

"And my actual *father* was born there, too," Hero reminded them. "What's your point?"

The agents traded an entire conversation with a protracted glance. Hero didn't like the suspicious assumptions and speculations floating like errant bullets between the two.

"Don't look at each other in that tone of voice." She pointed a bossy finger at them both. "Tell me what you think we should do about tonight."

Luca stood and put his suit coat on, then walked toward her with a stride so predatory, she was abruptly glad the kitchen half-wall stood between them. He took the coffee she offered and blew on it. A strange smile of anticipation tugged at the corner of his full, exotic mouth and his black eyes flashed dangerously. "We should try not to be late for church."

16

"The Devil can cite scripture for his purpose."

— WILLIAM SHAKESPEARE, THE MERCHANT OF
VENICE

The silent drive from her neighborhood took its place as the second most brutal torture Hero had ever experienced. It was no stake through the palm, but the scraping of the windshield wipers against the chilly rain grated at her nerves. The blinker clicks were cannon shots in the terse quiet. Luca didn't engage her attempts at conciliatory conversation and she'd quickly given up, too tired and anxious to deal with his distance and broodiness.

Oh whom was she kidding? When had she been able to keep her mouth shut for longer than a few minutes?

"I know what you're thinking," she announced as they pulled up in front of St. Andrew's Cathedral.

Luca's nostrils flared, but he made a show of looking for a parking spot rather than at her. "Im-fucking-possible," he said blandly.

"You think Father Michael is John the Baptist."

Luca didn't respond as he slid into a tight space, leaving the comfortable room on her side of the car, whereas his exit would be a squeeze. He was being a gentleman.

Asshole.

"You can't possibly suspect Father McMurtry. He's like—ninety gazillion years old and has walked with a cane since I've known him." His cryptic half-shrug had her wondering if she could remember that karate chop thingy she'd learned in self-defense that dislocated people's shoulders. "Use your words," she snapped, instantly hating her bitchy tone.

His lip quirked in a surprising gesture of amusement. "They're both toward the top of my list."

Hero blinked at him, waiting for him to go on. He didn't.

"Well, I'm sure that list is written on some freaking yellow legal pad somewhere." She undid her seatbelt and twisted her body around, reaching into the backseat for his briefcase. Her breasts rubbed against his arm, the coarse fabric of his suit-coat abrading her through her dress until her nipples were as hard as diamonds.

"Hero!" He seized her arm and firmly planted her ass back in her seat. "What the hell is your problem?"

"You!" she exploded. "*You*, goddammit." She crossed her arms over her sensitive breasts, swearing that she'd damn his soul to the seventh level of hell if he made her go into church with her high beams on.

He was facing her, though his thick black lashes fanned over his smooth caramel skin as his gaze never lifted above the parking break. "Are you mad at me because I didn't fuck you the other night?"

Hero's eyes peeled wide and her mouth dropped open. He'd said fuck. Not *make love to,* not *sleep with* or *go to bed with*, but *fuck*. Because that's what it would have been, what it would *be* with him. Fucking. Dirty. Primitive. Dominant fucking. The vulgarity of his question was intensified by his even, toneless voice. He'd done that on purpose. In the church parking lot, no less.

"No!" she denied, and then reconsidered. "Actually, yes, but we'll address that later. My *problem* is that someone might *die* tonight, and we're wasting time suspecting two priests who are unutterably dear to me. We should be out *there*." She pointed toward the city. "Warning every street pimp and escort service to hold on to their redheads. We should put out a fucking news bulletin. We should be *doing* something to stop the murder, regardless of whether we catch the killer!"

Luca kept careful control over his stony features which just lit her ass on fire. "Are you done?"

A strange and awful vibration seemed to rattle Hero from inside her chest, like someone had plugged a battery into her bones. She tightened her arms around herself. "No, no I'm *not done*. What I am is pissed. You want to know why? Because there is a *serial killer* after me, and no one can seem to figure out the reason. Not only do I *not* fit the profile, but I'm a *nice* person. I love my family. I help out at church. I donate to charity. I volunteer. I watch my karma. I cook for sick people. I *fucking* recycle. And all I can do when you're around is try to figure out a valid reason why every man in my life under six feet tall might want me dead. Can you even comprehend what that's doing to me? Do you know what you're turning me into?" Hero thought tears would accompany her sudden tirade, but her eyes remained curiously dry and narrowed on the taciturn man in front of her. "This!" she pointed at herself when he didn't answer. "This crazy bitch right here!"

Her breaths were quick and spastic and the vibration in her chest turned into a pulse, thrumming outward until it spread through her veins and curiously diminished.

"Feel better?" Luca asked, quirking his eyebrow.

She checked before answering honestly. "A little." Then shame escaped on a deep exhale and served to temper her angst even further. "I usually handle negative situations more productively."

"You have every right to be angry," he said softly. "I've learned that anger is a secondary emotion, usually a response to primary emotions like hurt or fear. After all you've been through, you've got to be feeling a great deal of both."

"What, you're saying I'm mad because John the Baptist hurt my feelings?"

"That's exactly what I'm saying." His tone remained utterly reasonable, intriguing Hero to no end. "You feel that you don't deserve to be targeted."

"I'm not saying those other women *did*," she amended desperately.

"Of course not."

"I'm just saying... oh hell... *I* don't even know what I mean." She clenched her eyes shut and ran her hands through her hair, pulling the silky strands in frustration. "Just, don't shut me out anymore. I have to know what you're thinking, what you're planning. You're supposed to be my boyfriend for Christ's sake."

That tense, heavy quiet settled over the car again, and Hero clamped her mouth shut, instantly cursing herself.

"I'm not your boyfriend, Hero." Luca's voice

dropped lower, as though talking carefully to a trau-matized child. "We're pretending."

"I know that," she snapped, ineffectually glaring at him.

"Do you?" Luca's gaze lifted to collide with hers and she absolutely understood why he'd avoided eye contact until then. The incredible dichotomy of icy fury and banked heat filtering through his black irises would have terrified her into silence. His face made the coolness of his voice all the more chilling and un-natural. He'd been letting her finish. Because if she'd seen the raw intensity controlling his sharp features, she might have fled.

"Yes," she miraculously gasped the answer to his question, though her lungs refused to inflate.

"Then you listen up." The behavior installed by what had to be years of therapy and training began to disintegrate in front of her eyes as his lips pulled tighter and a vein pulsed in his jaw. His voice, though, remained lethally soft and he punctuated every an-nunciation with sniper precision.

Hero sat pinned to the seat, dumbfounded.

"The FBI and local PD are doing everything in their power to prevent another murder tonight. But if you want to know where I stand, I'll tell you." He leaned in closer, until she could smell the delicious coffee on his breath. "I don't give half a *shit* what hap-pens to anyone else. This cock-sucker is after *you*, Hero. Do I want anyone else to die? Hell no. But my first, my *only* priority is making sure you survive this. If that means suspecting your priest, your friends, your father, or the *goddammed* Pope, himself, I'll do it because it's my job."

Stunned by the force of his cold expression and blazing eyes, Hero could only nod. Her heart pounded, her lungs constricted, and she could feel sweat blooming across her skin despite the icy rain's symphonic staccato on the car.

Luca yanked on the door handle and unfolded himself from the driver's seat with stiff, jerky movements, shutting it with more force than necessary and walking around to her side of the car.

After jerking open her door, he leaned down close as the rain began to turn his short hair glossy. A few drops caught on the lashes above his smoldering eyes and had to be just about the sexiest thing Hero had ever seen.

"Now about the other reason you're pissed." His lips flattened even more, whitening at the edges a little. "I vow on this holy ground that when this is all over, I'm going to bend you over the first available surface and fuck you sideways. Got it?"

Hero blinked. The carnal words and the hard tone didn't match his callous voice at all, causing her to question what she'd just heard. Had he just said...?

"Wait. W-what?" she stammered.

"You heard me. Now get out of the car, we're going to church."

Hero got out of the car, then paused, berating herself for instinctively obeying his order. She obeyed no one. Her legs were weak and between them flooded in with insistent, slick heat.

Just who the hell did Agent Ramirez think he was? He couldn't just *decide* when and how they were going to do it. He thought they were going to wait until this was over, huh? Well what if *she* didn't last that long? What if John the Baptist got to her somehow? What she had was here and now. And God only knew she was good and ready.

Her eyes skipped over the full parking lot, including her parent's sensible Subaru, Demetri's bike, Connor's truck, and the stone spires of what seemed like a monolithic cathedral for a neighborhood church. Well—maybe not *here* and *now*. But if Luca thought he could hold out on her indefinitely, he had another thing coming.

LUCA DIDN'T PARTICIPATE in the service, but sat respectfully at the edge of a corner pew, damn near dominated by most of the Katrova-Connor clan. Hero sat on his right with Rown stationed on her other side. Even in the relative safety of the crowd, Luca liked her placement and was comforted by the slight bulge in Rown's jacket. If someone wasn't trained to recognize the shoulder holster, they wouldn't have, but Luca's own weapon happened to be tucked in the exact same spot.

Next to Rown, Eoghan and Izolda Katrova-Connor sat holding hands. Connor and Demetri's wide shoulders rounded out the row. Timandra and Knox had apparently stayed home to prepare and monitor the meal.

Luca stared forward, glowering a hole through the back of some old lady's head. He was miserable. Hero's body pressed against his side. The words they'd tossed at each other in the car squished between them right there on the church bench, waiting to be turned into action. He was in over his head, and not just with this case. He was too damn close. Too close to figuring this shit out and nabbing the killer to give up now. Too close to Hero to maintain composure. He was the best man for the job, in danger of making the worst kind of mistakes. So where did that leave him? He sighed and tried to keep his eyes on the elderly woman's Q-tip do, rather than Hero's tight ass as she slipped off the bench and knelt on the velvet bars for yet another prayer.

Luca wasn't the only one on the row that declined to kneel. When the family dutifully followed the congregation, he glanced across the bench at Connor, who sat unnaturally still, staring into palms that lay open in his lap. He didn't look over at Luca. Didn't acknowledge his mother's soft pat on the knee after she'd returned to the bench. His brown hair resembled that of an unkempt sheepdog and contrasted with the more russet shades in his unruly beard. His breathing seemed to be elevated for a man at rest, but other than that, Hero's oldest brother didn't so much as twitch a muscle for going on an hour now.

Hero, however, squirmed and fidgeted next to him. She surreptitiously checked her phone and returned a text. Crossed and uncrossed her legs. Checked social media. Ran restless fingers through her damp, glossy hair, braiding and unbraiding a strand. Chewed off seven fingernails and was well through her eighth when Rown grabbed her hand and held it tightly encased in his much larger one.

Her brother's dark amber head had to bend far as he murmured something into Hero's ear that made her smirk. In answer, she reached across his body and poked the ribs beneath his arm causing him to flinch and release her with a jerk. But immediately after, she rested her head against his shoulder to smooth away the offense. They both smiled.

Luca watched the exchange with a queer fascination. He *should* be scanning the crowd for someone who seemed out of place. Studying the two priests at the dais for signs of maniacal obsession with Hero.

Playing the concerned but relaxed boyfriend for her family. But he'd spent the past hour doing that, to no discernible outcome, and he was getting tired of sitting in the stuffy room and trying to keep his eyes off of Hero's intriguing hemline.

Rown leveled an inscrutable green gaze at him over Hero's head, and Luca found it hard to meet. But he did, thrusting his chin out in acknowledgment. The fellow agent was the only one who knew of their deception, and he'd made it clear that he didn't like it. In the end, he'd accepted that constant, twenty-four-hour monitoring was the only way to ensure Hero's safety. Of course, he'd demanded Vince's position for himself, and was denied for obvious reasons. He'd definitely given the keep-your-filthy-hands-off-my-little-sister schpeel to both Luca and Vince before they'd taken their places in her home.

Apparently, he'd neglected to give the same lecture to his not-so-saintly sister. Or she'd ignored it, which was the more likely scenario.

A guilty flush crept from beneath his collar. So they'd kissed. So what? They'd have to do that and more in public if anyone was to believe they were in a relationship. Besides that little mistake, what other carnal sins had they committed? None. Words. Just words. Fantasies, innuendos, and salacious promises did not a slimy bastard make.

His notice slid back to where her dress crawled up her thigh.

Yeah, keep telling yourself that, homeboy. See how far it gets you.

The stress was getting to her. Though she tried to hide it behind a cheerful disposition and positive affirmations, the wear was finally beginning to show.

Hero's little display of temper in the car had con-firmed it.

Her willful denial was frustrating, but Luca couldn't blame her. She had a lot to lose. Besides her life and her dignity, she clung desperately to her opti-mism and illusions. To her, the world was a place full of promise and potential, full of colors she could cap-ture and objects she could shape with clay. She'd grown and flourished in the protective bubble of her rare and devoted family. The indulged and adored baby, easily able to charm and smile her parents and older brothers under her complete control, careful to never use her powers of manipulation for evil.

Up until that horrible day in October, she'd had the advantage of a completely clear conscience. A spotless record. Maybe a few white lies or a smudged relationship karmically smoothed over by a volume of unpretentious kind services and selfless good-nature.

Her place in heaven was assured, though she didn't worry about what form that would take, pearly gates or a fortuitous reincarnation. What did it mat-ter? Death was always a distant abstract to someone so young. A thing that happened to the elderly and the careless.

Now she faced violent mortality. The possibility of leaving a life unfinished. Not only that, but the cheery world into which she'd been born, full of life-long re-lationships and loving trust-worthy people was sud-denly shadowed by an unknown and constant threat.

Luca hadn't realized just how much that aspect af-fected her. Of course, the idea that someone you knew and trusted wanted you dead would be horrible for anyone. But for someone like her, it was devastating. An inconceivable mind fuck. And not for the first time he wished like hell it had happened to someone else.

God he was in trouble.

To his exquisite relief, the benediction began and he planted his thoughts firmly back to where they should be. On the case. This afternoon he needed to speak with the intrepid priests of St. Andrews. Tonight he would play devoted and respectful boyfriend to Hero's family, all the while keeping one ear to the ground in case a killer should decide to make his move.

After the benediction finished, Connor shot to his feet, startling everyone in the surrounding pews as he cleared Demetri's knees in one long-legged stride. His hasty exit was covered by the bustling of the congregation at large. Luca regarded his broad, rumpled retreating back as the rest of his family exchanged concerned glances. The guy looked like a giant running from midgets, his shaggy head and shoulders carrying over the sea of people. Something wasn't right there, and Luca started to wonder if he should be worried.

Hero stood and turned, holding her hand out to him with a sunny and inviting smile that stopped the heart in his chest. "Let's go, I'm *starving*."

Luca unfolded from the bench and took Hero's hand, pulling her to the side where they wouldn't hinder the rest of the row's exit.

As they filed down the crowded aisle at the pace of a stoned turtle, it was agreed they'd all congregate back to Hero's parent's house for the sake of expediency. Luca bent to murmur into Hero's ear, enjoying the feel of her small hand in his. "Hang with your brothers for a minute. I need to ask a few questions while I'm here."

She smiled at him over her shoulder. "Sure. I'll stay with Rown."

The Katrova-Connor clan walked to the door where the two Priests stood offering handshakes, blessings, and well-wishes. They each perfectly represented the two ages of the modern Catholic Church. The traditional and the progressive.

Father Michael easily and graciously accepted compliments regarding his charismatic sermon on having faith in miracles and strength in the face of adversity. His disarming brown eyes crinkled with genuine pleasure as he greeted Hero's parents. His cheerful voice seemed to carry regardless of the noise level. White vestments and purple sash seemed at odds with beach-blond good looks that would take a good couple of decades to gain maturity.

In opposition, Father McMurtry was a stooped, soft-spoken old man. Though he rarely smiled, kindness and compassion sparkled from startling blue eyes, whose glimmer of youth contrasted with the deep grooves of his aging skin.

Luca detected the differences in their response as they noticed Hero simultaneously. They each deftly masked their initial reactions to the amount of thigh exposed by her dress, enough to raise eyebrows at a church, but not necessarily on the streets. Father McMurtry smothered a mild look of disapproval as he accepted a warm and familiar hug from her, and Father Michael struggled with a look of not-so-mild masculine interest. All interest evaporated like a Texas turd-floater when he caught sight of Luca's own not-so-mild look.

"I see you brought your new lad," Father McMurtry's voice danced with similar Irish inflection to Hero's father. "Nice to see you again, Agent Ramirez."

"*Padre*," Luca acknowledged.

The old man kept Hero's hands clasped in his

gentle one, the other leaning heavily on his cane as he leaned forward conspiratorially. "Izolda tells me your young agent is also a doctor. I think you'd better keep this one."

Hero laughed merrily, the sound drawing the appreciative notice of those close by.

"It's a PhD," Luca muttered, wondering just how in the hell a fake boyfriend could feel real embarrassment.

"Even so." The ghost of a smile touched his thin, weathered lips. "Agent Ramirez—I have plenty of Latin folks in my fold. We even do a separate Mass in Spanish on every second and fourth Sunday. One of Father Michael's many visionary suggestions." He lifted a voluminous eyebrow at them both. "I hope to see you two around more often. I feel like Hero's a little lost lamb of my flock."

"Aww." Hero offered him a tender smile. "Not lost, Father, just wandering. And you'll see us Christmas Eve for Midnight Mass."

Little lost lamb? His dying ass, she was a succubus in the form of a fucking saint. "I'd like to see you in private actually." Luca told the priest.

Father McMurtry faltered. "How about tomorrow afternoon? I need to say goodbye to everyone and then I have a few—"

"I can wait." Luca knew the savvy priest understood exactly what he was saying. They were going to talk here. Today. One way or the other.

Blue eyes that sparked with intellect narrowed into his with challenging assessment. The kindness and compassion had disappeared, replaced with pious condemnation. "All right," the Priest finally conceded in a soft tone laced with steel. "All right, my boy, follow me to my office. We'll chat there. Father Michael, if you'll excuse us, please."

Luca sent a look to Rown, who nodded and took up watch behind his sister. "I'll be a few minutes," he said to them both, ignoring their nearly identical frowns.

The old priest set a maddeningly slow pace as he limped the way from the vaulted opulence of the hand-some grey stone chapel through a short maze of simple but elegant dark wood hallways. St. Andrew's was more than a stained-glass and stone cathedral. During the week it offered such services as day care for low-income working mothers, Sunday school, confessional, and a rec room provided an open space for everything from youth basketball summer camps to nighttime Alcohol and Narcotics Anonymous meetings.

Father McMurtry's office was exactly how Luca remembered it. He couldn't decide which was older, man or desk. They both looked like they'd once been large, thick and well-built, but were now lined and weathered with much time and use. The somber wood-paneled walls were bare but for an intricate Celtic crucifix over the large executive chair tucked neatly into place.

Father McMurtry pulled it out, and motioned to one of the two studded universal office chairs facing the other side of the desk.

Luca remained standing.

The glint of assessment was back in the old man's eyes, but tinged with a bit of amusement. "I assume you're here to talk about making an honest woman out of our Hero?"

"I'm here to ask you where you were Friday night." Luca kept his tone light, un-menacing, but serious. He retrieved a yellow pad from its case, using the action to press the button on the hidden recorder inside.

"Oh?" His bushy eyebrows crawled up toward his hairline, and he paused in the middle of divesting himself. "In that case, I think we'll need a drink." His limp was more pronounced as he left his cane leaning against the desk and hung his vestments on a special rack on the wall before making his slow way to the old cupboard. "Hero's father, Eoghan, gifts me with a bottle of Middleton every Christmas. It's about time I lay this old soldier to rest, don't you think?" He shook the almost empty bottle at Luca and grabbed two whiskey glasses with his free hand before making his painstaking journey back to the desk.

"Well now!" he exclaimed with the force of settling his brittle bones into his chair. Setting one glass in front of him, and the other at Luca's end of the desk, he uncorked the bottle and poured the last of the fine Irish whiskey in equal amounts. "So this is a visit much like the one you paid me the day after that tragedy at the river."

"I'm afraid so." Luca stepped in front of the visitor's chair to the left and conceded enough to lower his frame into it.

"A pity, I'd like to see that girl settled down. Let's see... Friday." The priest took a sip, and Luca followed suit, enjoying the smooth velvet bite of the fine liquor. "We didn't have anything going on here at the church, so Father Michael and I spent a quiet night at our residence in back of the rectory."

"Scripture studying? Praying? Writing sermons?" Luca prompted.

McMurtry chuckled and took another sip. "Actually, Agent Ramirez, Manchester United beat the socks right off Ireland and I was eating dinner and shouting blasphemy at the television."

"Soccer?"

"'Tis not all sermon writing and do-gooding around here. We do enjoy ourselves from time to time, you know. I even watch every single one of young Lennox's fighting bouts. Religiously, if you'd believe it. I was quite the pugilist back in my day."

Luca smirked in spite of himself. The old Irishman had a charisma all his own. Quieter, introspective, and ultimately likable. Though Luca wrote on his pad that Father McMurtry had once been a boxer. "So, you two were here together, all night?"

The priest leaned forward, his eyes as brilliant as Irish crystal. "Not exactly all night. Father Michael was called away rather late to help in a domestic dispute."

"How late?"

"Ohhhh, about eight thirty or so."

Maybe eight thirty was late to someone like Father Michael, but that gave either priest plenty of time to leave the rhododendrons at Hero's door. Luca watched Father McMurtry's features very intently as he asked his next question. "You or Father Michael visit any flower shops lately?"

"Definitely not. No need."

Nothing. Not even a flicker of guilt or fear. He was either really *really* good, or he told the truth. "What was the name of this family that Father Michael was called to visit?"

A shrug upset the McMurtry's glass, as though he'd forgotten it was still in his hand. He saved any liquid from risk by lifting it to his lips. "I don't know. You'll have to ask Father Michael."

"Don't you think that you two should encourage people to call the police rather than a priest during a domestic dispute?" Okay, so it was off topic, but this kind of thing really chapped his ass.

Father McMurtry remained unruffled by his obvious disapproval. "We believe that sometimes conflict and danger is better solved by God than by guns," he said gently.

"Not in my experience."

"Well..." The old man let the gentle word trail into a voluminous silence, the useless argument passing between them without a word spoken. For neither of them would change their minds.

"What are your plans for tonight?" Luca asked pointedly.

"I've been invited to the O'Rourke's for dinner, and before you ask, Father Michael is planning to feast at the Mendez household, or was it the Murphy's?"

"What about after?" Would there be a little stigmata and a quick 'baptism' for dessert?

"Well, after committing the sin of gluttony, Father Michael and I will absolve each other and likely go to bed and sleep it off. We're not without our own weaknesses, you know. I'll confess to feeling some envy of you and not a little bit of lust when it comes to Lennox's chocolate and Guinness potato cake. So that's three serious sins in one night for me."

Would murder make it four?

"Father McMurtry." Luca leaned forward in his own chair, grasping his glass with both hands. "Do you think Father Michael is capable of being John the Baptist?"

"Absolutely not." The answer was brusque, sincere.

"What about you?"

To his surprise, the old priest's wrinkled features arranged themselves into a droopy kind of wistful smile. "'Twould be difficult for a man of my age and—limitations to crucify six grown women, don't you think?"

Luca left it there. According to his file, Father Alistair Patrick McMurtry immigrated to the states about thirty years prior. He aged early and handsomely like Patrick Stewart or Anthony Hopkins, perhaps adding only a decade to his features in that span of time. His driver's license put him in his mid-seventies, but he could have been a younger or older man.

"If you don't think Father Michael did it, why not provide him an alibi on Friday night? Why not protect him?"

"My boy, the truth has a way of eventually coming out. Why cast suspicion on either of us by lying to you? Investigate our whereabouts on Friday night. I have absolute faith in Father Michael, and therefore don't have a reason to resist bearing false witness to you."

Luca nodded thoughtfully, and they each took a sip.

"May I ask what happened on Friday? What's this about flowers?"

Luca considered him. A genuine anxiety shined in the elderly priest's eyes. "Hero was threatened on Friday, that's all I can tell you."

"What a shame. I pray for her every night and every day. Always such a sweet girl. She doesn't deserve this." Shifting in his chair, McMurtry winced and clutched at his hip, before settling.

"If I may ask, how did you injure your hip?"

The priest considered him for a long moment over his glass, swirling the amber liquid and breathing in the sharp fumes. He seemed to come to a decision and set his glass down on the desk. "I'm going to share with you something that I tell no one. Not since I confessed it and made it right with the Lord. You'll be the only soul on this continent who knows."

Luca leaned intently forward. This was either going to be a murder confession or one of those stories that old people tell that had nothing to do with the original question and was never simplified for context.

"I was born in Belfast, Ireland, in a time when the city was split by war. When I was a boy, my father was hanged for violent crimes he committed during The Troubles. The loss broke my mother, and she turned to the bottle." Father McMurtry stared at the glass in his hand with a wry sort of sadness. "She also turned to any man who would provide the next drink. Needless to say, life was a struggle and I became an angry and violent youth, roaming the streets up to no good. When I came of age, I left whatever squalid hell my mother had moved us into, and made my living as a disreputable boxer with a gambling addiction." A surprising sparkle of humor worked its way into his features.

"I had many Gods before I found this one, Agent Ramirez. Money, violence, women, thrill, and pain. I worshiped them all. My hip was shattered and some of my spine broken when my book maker hit me with his car over a five hundred pound debt. I was told that I would never walk again. And wouldn't you know they sent me to the St. Andrew's Hospital to recover. It was there I found my calling in life, and my salvation. It was in that hospital, through pain and loss, prayer and miracles, that I purged myself of my demons and regained the use of my legs. I joined the clergy the moment I could stand on my own. Once my mother's own demon claimed her life, I made my way to

America to let go of the past. The rest, as they say, is history."

The silence between them was comfortable as they each nursed their drink. Luca searched the priest's eyes for signs of the man he'd just described, and found only knowing, compassionate regard.

"The reasons I have for revealing my past to you are two-fold. You're a sharp and determined lad. I believe God has chosen you to help put a stop to the evil threatening these women. I want you to be looking in the correct direction for this evil, not sidetracked by personal causes, temptations or needless questions. I believe you are strong. That you'll overcome."

Strange and pervasive warmth spread through Luca that had nothing to do with the heat of the whiskey. It made him uncomfortable and quiet. It was the same kind of feeling he'd get from Coach Peck from time to time, an unfamiliar sense of accomplishment at receiving the praise and trust of a respected elder. Not that Luca respected the old priest, he *suspected* him and would do well to remember it. He looked down, inspecting the toes of his *Berluti Brunico* Tobbaco *bis* ankle boots.

McMurtry continued as though unaware of Luca's discomfiture. "I also shared this because I have the suspicion that you and I have more in common than you might think. Similar childhoods, maybe? Perhaps we've even made some similar choices when it comes to the directions our lives have taken us?" He waggled bristled eyebrows at Luca, daring him to put the parallels into place.

Luca shot the rest of his drink and set the glass down on the desk harder than he may have meant to. "Trust me, *Padre*, I am *no* priest."

This pulled a warm laugh from McMurtry, lent a

rich note by the strong drink. "Of that I have no doubt, but maybe we've both devoted our lives to the same goal. Bringing hope to the downtrodden. Trying to facilitate a sense of balance and justice. Battling the darkness threatening the souls of this city, each in our own way."

Luca's eyes narrowed at that last one, suspicion warring with a growing admiration for the man. "Maybe we're both fighting on the wrong side of a losing battle." And maybe Hero had been right. Was he looking for a killer in the eyes of a saint? Or did he recognize a killer with a soul like his own? The jury was still out.

"You say that like a man who's lost his faith," Father McMurtry said softly.

Luca made a caustic sound. "You have to have faith before you lose it."

The old man tutted and sighed, regarding Luca with something akin to long-suffering pity. "Faith is not possession, son, it's an action. 'Tis why they call it *a leap of faith*. You cannot simply stand on the ledge and expect it to find you. You have to jump. You have to fall. It is in the plummet that you will find your soul."

Luca stood, deciding he'd had enough. "This is where you lose me, *Padre*. Thanks for the drink. And... thanks for the confidence."

Father McMurtry also stood, using the desk for support.

"I'll see myself out." Luca didn't want to cause him any pain.

"Agent Ramirez." The old man put out a hand as though to stop him. "I recognize the demons in your eyes as the same ones that used to live in mine. Anger, violence, wrath, hatred, of yourself and of others. They'll consume you if you're not careful."

Luca fought a spike of temper, but shoved it back down with both hands, not willing to prove the sanctimonious, frighteningly observant priest right. "I don't know if I believe in demons. No offense, but I tend to believe that a man is the master of his own actions and emotions. His choices belong to him, alone, along with the consequences."

"I don't disagree. Demons can be figurative as much as literal, lad. We all likely have a few of both kinds."

Compelled by an overwhelming urge to escape the conversation, Luca strode to the door and opened it, inviting in the cool, circulating air of the hallway. It swirled into the room like a ghost, cooling skin warmed by good liquor and elevating blood pressure. Something caused a catch in his step before he could make a full retreat, and he turned back to the priest.

"How do you propose I do it, *Padre*?" he asked quietly. "How do I rid myself of these demons?"

The old man's smile was filled with an almost divine tenderness. "There are many ways to exorcise a demon, Agent Ramirez. Though I have a feeling yours could be chased away with a little hope, dare I say some faith? In yourself, in others, and in the forgiveness of Heaven."

Luca let a sarcastic laugh that came out sounding bereft. "Just like that, huh?"

"If you think that's too difficult, we can consider some of our more traditional ways to exorcize demons." McMurtry gave a mischievous wink.

"No thanks, I've seen the movie." Luca paused. "Thank you again—for—for the drink."

"Come and see me any time."

Nodding, Luca left, closing the door firmly behind him. He stood on the flip side for a moment, his composure rattled. He couldn't shake the feeling he hadn't been the only examiner in the room. The priest's story intrigued him. The injury, in addition to his age, did cast off a good deal of the suspicion. Didn't mean he wasn't going to try to get his hands on some medical records, and perhaps even put a call into the Irish Embassy to request some verification. He'd been a boxer. Hero had been punched in the face by a man wearing a cassock. Too many parallels to ignore.

"Demons," he muttered, feeling a little foolish. "What a load of—"

His phone vibrated against his jacket pocket and Luca took a few long strides away from the office before answering it, making his way back to the front of the church to collect Hero from her brother.

"Why didn't you tell me the news about our bendy friend, Two Rivers?" Vince quipped into his ear.

"What news?"

"Didn't you get the email? It was sent yesterday."

"I have twenty million emails in my inbox. I'm only caught up on the urgent ones." Yesterday was mostly spent researching saints, working out, and catching up on some recorded HBO as it was supposed to be his day off.

Luca usually left the correspondence to Vince. He got off on it. Another reason their partnership worked out so well.

"This one's not marked urgent, but it snagged my eye."

"And?"

"His name is Reese Donovan. He's wanted in California and Arizona for some violent crimes dating back eight years, including three separate cases of sexual battery against women. In fact, there's an extradition order already signed by a federal circuit court judge because one of the Arizona cases has a suspicious death attached to it. Get this, it's a drowning."

"I knew it!" Luca victoriously slapped one of the open doors to the rec room. "I knew that tree-hugging, hippie son of a—"

"Are you still at church?" Vince cut in.

"Oh. Shit—*I mean*—shoot." Luca glanced around, relieved to find he was alone in the hallway.

The smile in Vince's voice carried through the receiver. "Anyway, the field agents and Portland's finest are keeping their eyes peeled for Donovan, but heads up in case he's got a hard-on for our girl."

An urgency to have Hero back within his sights intensified at the news, and he sped through the labyrinth of halls back toward the chapel.

"Still...I don't know if I like him for this," Vince continued. "I mean, he has no documented religious background and his other crimes are kind of small-sauce, you know? Violent, spur-of-the-moment, my-mom-didn't-hug-me-enough bullshit. JTB's so methodical, so precise, and there's the opposite of sexual intent apparent in his crimes."

"I've been thinking along the same lines," Luca agreed. He reached the chapel and made his way across the nearly empty room and down the center aisle. A few people lingered in conversation. "But this Donovan is in Hero's orbit and either way, I want him *gone.*"

"Then again... What if he *is* JTB?" There he went, playing devil's advocate again. "What if this *Two Rivers* is a front for a serial killer and we extradite him to become another state's problem? What if he's released and reinvents himself again? He'll have slipped through our fingers."

"Let's worry about getting him into custody first. *Then* we'll have some decisions to make."

"Sure. Good plan," Vince said. "How did church go?"

"Weird." Luca answered.

"How weird?"

"Like show-me-on-the-doll-where-the-priest-exposed-your-demons, weird."

"That's wicked weird," Vince laughed. "What do you think we should do about the two intrepid Fathers tonight?"

Luca thought about it. "We should put a tail on them both, and the professor, if we can. Even though we won't be there, I want someone on Hero's house. Trojanowski is all over this, so we should be able to scare up the man power, you think?"

"Oh yeah, shouldn't be a problem."

Reaching the doors, Luca found Rown chatting with the grey-haired women from the row in front of them. He'd recognize the back of that head anywhere. The rain had cleared up, but the clouds still hung low in the sky. Hero was conspicuously absent. Luca made a *what the fuck* gesture.

"She's with Demetri," Rown said over the matron's heads. "They both needed to hit the head."

The news didn't distress Luca, as Demetri worked private security, among other things, and was an acceptable guard for Hero in his opinion. Though Luca would kill to see what was on her brother's expunged record.

"All right. I got to go do dinner with the parents," he told his partner.

Vince laughed again. "You've had worse gigs, right?"

"Can't think of any at the moment," Luca grumbled. Meeting the parents wasn't exactly his *modus operandi*.

"Just give them your best I'm-not-banging-your-daughter smile, you'll be fine."

"I'm *not* banging their daughter."

Vince snickered, "Yeah, but they don't know that."

Luca turned around to find the bathrooms when the unmistakable roar of a Harley coming to life in the parking lot drew his attention. A leather jacket filled to the brink over loose-fitting black slacks straddled the heavy bike. Demetri slicked his shoulder-length black hair back with one hand, and wedged his helmet on.

Where was Hero?

"I gotta go." Luca hung up on Vince's reply. Heart slamming against his ribcage, he jogged down the short expanse of lawn, holding a hand up for Demetri to wait.

The visor went up, revealing dark, deep-set eyes.

"Where's Hero?" Luca asked.

"I left her behind Rown, up on the stairs..." His words faded. "She was there a minute ago."

Rown had seen them and also noted Hero's absence. He excused himself from the conversation and made his way toward the bike.

"You check the chapel and offices," Luca snarled to Rown across the lawn, a foreign, chill-laced panic threatening his calm. "I'll look in the outbuildings."

Demetri dismounted the bike.

"Don't let anyone else leave," Luca ordered, reaching inside his jacket for the comforting grip of his weapon. "And fucking pray we find her."

17

*"Teach not thy lip such scorn, for it was made
For kissing, lady, not for such contempt."*

— WILLIAM SHAKESPEARE, RICHARD III

Hero took the glass of red wine from Father Michael and held the bulb with both hands. She leaned her hip against the rectory's kitchen sink and stared into the glass, unable to meet his intent scrutiny. This was the last room she'd been in before John the Baptist had taken her. She'd held wine much like this. Had a similar discussion. Seemed like a lifetime ago. Like it had been some other woman standing in this kitchen, drinking this wine.

"First of all, how are *you* holding up?" Father Michael also leaned against the counter, moving close and adopting her posture. He faintly smelled of candle wax, sandalwood, and clean linen.

Hero eyed the black cassock hanging off his body and suppressed a chill. "I thought you wanted to discuss Connor." She hoped he couldn't hear the wariness seeping into her voice.

"I do," he murmured. "That doesn't mean I'm not concerned about you."

She looked up at him. His soft brown eyes, once so open and mild, now seemed to be shadowed with secrets. With shame? She sought refuge in the wine, but stopped herself before taking a drink. Could it be poisoned? Drugged? Had she made a mistake in following Father Michael here? No. *No*, she trusted him. Didn't she? She was out to prove he was the wrong suspect.

Still, she set the glass of wine on the counter. It suddenly smelled sour.

"I'm doing *great*." She emphasized the word and forced a bright smile to give it more credibility. "No need to worry about me."

"Impossible," he said kindly. "After all you've been through? Are still going through. And a new relationship on top of it all. Do you think that's wise?"

"Do you think that's any of your business?" She closed her eyes and sighed when Father Michael recoiled as though she'd slapped him. That came out wrong. God, she hated who she was turning into. If she couldn't even recognize herself, how could she recognize her killer?

"I thought... over the past few years we'd become more than priest and parishioner. I've considered us friends," he said carefully. "Forgive me if I crossed a line."

"No," Hero amended, lifting a hand to her forehead and rubbing at the pressure gathering there. "No, it's my fault, Father Michael. I feel like I've been on the defensive for so long. I'm questioning everything I've ever known. Everyone." *Even you,* she added silently.

"I ask because I care, Hero." He caught one of her hands in his, running a finger over the raised scar. His touch felt jarring, clammy, and the pressure on the damaged nerves of her hand was unpleasant. A thrill of unease burned up her arm. Was it his voice? Could the silky tones be lowered to the sing-song Latin she'd heard that night? "I care—probably more than I—"

"What the *hell* is this?"

Hero jerked her hand out of Father Michael's grip and then regretted the guilty action. But Luca's gun was out, trained on the priest and for a split second, she actually feared he might shoot.

He lowered it to the floor and flipped on the safety, but didn't holster it. Instead he swung his chilling black eyes to her throat, his left hand curling into a tight fist.

"Jesus *fucking* Christ, Hero!" he managed between gritted teeth. At Father Michael's gasp, he let out a sound of irritation. "Sorry, Father," he mumbled, not sounding sorry in the least.

"It's all right," the priest said evenly.

"You can't just disappear like that and not tell anyone where the *fuck* you are! Sorry, Father."

"Don't worry about it."

"Did you *not* hear me say to stay with your brothers? You scared the fucking shit out of everyone! Sorry Father."

"I understand."

"You're angry," Hero tried to sound soothing. "I'm—"

"You haven't *seen* me angry, goddammit!" he roared. Then he muttered again, "Sorry, Father."

"It's my fault, I'm afraid, Agent Ramirez," Father Michael offered an amused and conciliatory smile. "I invited Hero to join me here."

Luca turned his narrowed, glittering black gaze on the priest and Hero jumped in to save him from Luca's considerable wrath. "He just asked me back here to discuss some concerns over Connor for a minute. We're all so worried about him."

"Oh, and if a stranger told you he had some candy for you in his van, would you just climb on inside?" he asked testily, though he'd stopped shouting and was opening his suit jacket to holster the gun.

"I hardly think the metaphor is applicable," Father Michael sounded genuinely insulted.

Rown rounded the corner to the rectory kitchen and pulled up beside Luca, scowling at her in an almost identical way.

Did they teach a certain kind of disapproval frown at Quantico or something?

"Sorry about all this, Father Michael, but Hero's not supposed to go anywhere without us and she *knows* that." Rown was a bit out of breath, but nothing like Luca, who panted as though he'd run a marathon.

"I understand both of your concern for her welfare." Father Michael put his glass of wine down with a shaky hand. "But I assure you she's in no danger from me."

Both agents ignored him.

"I thought you saw me wave to you that I was coming over here," Hero said to her brother. "The door was open and you were in ear shot." She gestured to the door of the rectory, which opened to the bottom of the hill from the cathedral, just barely out of sight from where Rown had stood at the chapel steps.

"You should have made sure," Rown scolded.

"You should have stayed *put*," Luca spat, dark gaze bouncing from her to the priest with barely-leashed hostility.

"I'm sorry, am I a suspect here?" Father Michael

put both hands up in a gesture of surrender. "Because I'm trying to focus on what's happening with Connor, that's *it*."

Hero's gaze clashed with her brother's and she saw the worry that had drawn her here mirrored in his expression. Something had to be done about Connor. Her oldest brother was falling apart in front of them and they'd all somehow missed it, dealing with the more imminent danger of her frightening situation. The guilt nearly choked her. And when Father Michael had approached her about discussing a solution, Hero had followed him, driven by the need to focus on someone else's problems for once. To not feel so helpless and afraid. It had been a stupid decision, she knew that now.

Rown came to her rescue. "Ramirez, why don't you drive Hero to the house? Send Demetri in here and we'll stay and talk with Father Michael about Connor. Tell Mom and Pop that we'll be there in time for dinner."

Luca took a second to turn to his colleague. Hero held her breath. Even though Rown was the only other one in the family who'd inherited freckles, the defined, masculine angles of his face usually made them invisible. They stood out beneath the harsh florescent lighting of the kitchen, and Luca was staring at a particularly dark one by his mouth as though he thought it was a good place for his fist to go.

"You good, Ramirez?" Rown asked, raising his eyebrow.

"I'm good." He *so* didn't sound good.

"See you at the house?"

Luca nodded, then turned to grab Hero's elbow. She let him steer her toward the door, not daring to offer any one of a thousand objections as to how these two agents had just man-handled her.

Luca turned and pointed his finger at Father Michael, who didn't hide his involuntary flinch. "I'll be back to talk to you." *Talk* sounded like a euphemism for something infinitely more sinister.

Father Michael picked up his glass and took a fortifying drink of his wine. "I'll be here."

Hero had to give the priest credit, she thought, as they wordlessly made their way across the lawn, he was brave. But then, when you devote your life to God, maybe you're not afraid of dying.

Demetri spotted them from where he was chatting with someone in a truck, holding up the short line of cars waiting to leave the parking lot. No one honked. People in Portland were too nice for that. He patted the door twice by way of farewell and sauntered toward them with his long, easy stride. But Hero knew her brother's relaxed demeanor was deceptive. There was tension in the way he held his helmet in his left hand.

"The fuck, kid?" His dark, unhurried tone didn't match his question, but then Demetri never raised his voice. He usually didn't need to. "You scared us. Plus you made me look bad in front of your boyfriend." He tapped Luca's shoulder gently with his helmet, using his most disarming smile. "Like I need another cop up my ass."

Luca's mouth quirked a little, but he didn't loosen his death-grip on her elbow.

"We've already established I'm in the wrong here." Hero took up the role of defensive, impatient little sister. She knew this dance well, deflect and redirect. "Rown and Father Michael want to talk to you in the kitchen. It's about Connor."

"'Kay." His dark features tightened and his leather jacket creaked as he expanded his wide chest with a troubled breath. "Tell Mom and Pop we'll be a minute."

Hero nodded.

"And *don't* start eating without us," he ordered over his retreating shoulder.

Luca resumed his silent, brutal march toward the car, eating up the grass with his incredibly long legs. Hero struggled to keep pace, fearing he'd just pick her up by the arm like a recalcitrant child if she didn't keep up.

"Ya mind?" she finally said, uselessly tugging against his punishing grip.

He whirled to face her, pulling her up short and glaring down at her with the temerity of a junkyard Doberman at the end of his chain.

Hero opened her mouth, hoping to calm him down, but he moved before she could get a word in, and Luca's tongue forcing its way past her lips made talking impossible. His body slammed against hers. Or rather, slammed her against him as arms the texture of tempered steel trapped her elbows to her ribs. He snarled a warning into her mouth, his lips pressing hers against her teeth.

Hero's first instinct was to fight him. What was he, a freaking caveman? How dare he try to dominate her in this way? Her hands couldn't lift very high, trapped as her arms were, but when she pressed them to his waist, she felt the violent tremors there. In fact, his entire torso trembled, quaking with waves of vibration that seemed to start at the base of his neck and shoot down his spine. There was desperation behind the threatening sounds his throat made, and Hero suddenly understood what was happening.

She gave up all thought of fighting him then, relaxing against his hard body and softening her mouth, opening to him with a gentle sound of submission.

It was what he'd needed. His arms became cradling instead of crushing. His strong fingers kneaded her shoulders, her back, and lower, as though he had to reassure himself by filling his hands with her flesh. He tasted sweet and sharp, like expensive whiskey and costly sex. As hard as the kiss was, his lips were too full to be firm. They pillowed her mouth, infusing her with his exotic brand of passion.

Hero tried, but she couldn't stay passive in his arms for long. She strained to get closer to him, using the space his arms now afforded to reach into the heat of his jacket and feel the hard body that beckoned to her hungry fingers from beneath his thin dress shirt. She found the smooth leather of his shoulder holster and the cold steel of his gun. The wave of lust that followed her discovery nearly crippled her.

She wanted him to fuck her wearing that gun. She wanted him like *this*. On the edge of his control, wild and angry and afraid. She wanted him to pull out the erection pulsing against her stomach and slam it into her without even bothering to take his pants off. She wanted his belt to bite into her skin while she watched his wide shoulders to strain against the leather of his holster.

She wanted it right *now*.

With a ragged sound, Luca ripped his lips from hers as though fighting against a powerful adhesive. When he wasn't bending to kiss her, his chin was just above her head. He lifted his face to the sky to suck in a few breaths. Hero watched the eye-level muscles of his throat strain and his Adam's apple struggle against a few frantic gulps of air. The tremors quieted and his heartbeat seemed to be reined in like a runaway horse. He'd gathered his temper back into his glare when he bent his head to look at her again. She expected him to rip into her. To be profane and cutting. She kind of deserved it.

"You can't do that to me." The gentleness in his voice shocked then melted her. It sounded more like a plea than a command. "I'll lose my shit, Hero. Understand?"

"I'm sorry." She reached up and cupped the nape of his neck, pulling his forehead down to rest against hers. "Forgive me for being so thoughtless. You are right, you've been right all along. I need to be more careful. I'm sorry."

Luca let out another shaky breath. "If he gets to you—"

"He won't."

Strong fingers wrapped around her arms and gently but firmly set her away from him. "You're *damn* right, he won't," Luca said darkly. "Because from now on, I'm going to be on your ass like a fat kid on cake, got it?"

Hero smiled provocatively. "Promise?"

"Don't start," he warned, his hands tightening on her shoulders.

"Hey, who kissed whom? I'm getting some conflicting messages here," she teased.

His eyes snagged on her mouth again, and her chin lifted in invitation. But instead of taking her up on it, he released her and paced a few lengths away, one hand on his hip and the other running through his close-cropped hair. Once he'd reached what he deemed was a safe distance, he turned back to her. "You know that wasn't—I didn't mean to—*God*, Hero, you put me in an impossible position."

"Again, I apologize." She threw as much suggestive heat into the look she gave him. "Tell you what, anytime you want, you can return the favor, though I've never met a position I couldn't handle."

His eyes raked her body with a look so hot it should have set her boots on fire. Turning away again, he glared toward the cathedral and started passionately gesturing at the building as though it had done him an injustice. "*Dios, no me lo puedo merecer esta mierda...*"

That's it, Hero decided as she watched him curse in his rapid, guttural native language; she was going to learn Spanish as soon as possible.

"Let's go to dinner. I'm starving." Turning, she strolled past him on her way to the car, clenching her fists at her sides to keep from reaching for him.

He stopped his rant and glared at her as she moved, waiting until she passed him to follow. Hero could feel the burn of his eyes though her dress. Her legs were still a bit wobbly, blood still singing at a low hum of consistent sexual awareness. She'd thought she was in control here. That she was breaking him down until he gave her what she wanted. What they both wanted. But as she slid into the passenger seat of his car, a slight anxiety began to unfurl against the empty ache in her loins. With every other relationship—scratch that—with every other man she'd taken to her bed, *she'd* been the one in the driver's seat. She'd always decided where, when, how, and how long. Even with Alec, she'd never exactly expected or demanded fidelity and had easily moved on after his deception was discovered. The professor was the first, the only, man she'd really even allowed herself to imagine a future with. Once he'd proven himself untrustworthy, she'd been hurt, but couldn't remember shedding too many tears over it.

This *thing*, this pretention with Luca. It was different. It was in danger of becoming more real than anything else in her life had ever been.

Hero looked over at him as he maneuvered the car out of the lot, his foot a little too heavy on the gas. Men always drove too fast when they were horny. She liked him like this, on the edge of his control. It made her feel powerful and pursued all at once. The feminine thrill of being hunted like this would make their sex indescribable. She just knew it. But his kiss had done something to her. The way he'd dominated her had peeled back a thick layer of control and exposed something she didn't like to admit existed. Weakness. Submission, maybe? The danger was that for the first time in her life, she couldn't predict how this would end between them. After he was done making good on his promise to fuck her sideways, would he put on his suit coat and leave? What if it surpassed this carnal, primal chemistry between them and entered the realm of the relationship?

Her heart began to pound in her ribcage as she realized that she might not be okay with losing him. The thought of life without him seemed empty. Frightening. Luca wasn't the kind of guy that settled down. He was like her. Free. Single. Independent. She'd always been that way, but something was beginning to shift. What if this whole awful experience had changed her? What if she didn't just want him, but began *needing* him? What if he didn't need her back?

18

"It is as sure as you are Roderigo...
But I will wear my heart upon my sleeve
For daws to peck at. I am not what I am."

— WILLIAM SHAKESPEARE, OTHELLO

Portland's posh and vintage neighborhood of Laurelhurst was known for its narrow streets and large gardens. Eoghan and Izolda Katrova-Connor's home was no exception. As homage to their city, a well-kept thicket of roses lined both sides of their walk. In the December chill, they were severely pruned into neat hedges. The Victorian-era home looked much smaller from the outside than it was on the inside. It stretched deep, rather than wide, and boasted five bedrooms, a parlor, entertainment room, gigantic kitchen, and a dining room that could comfortably seat fifteen adults. Apparently, Izolda was an optimist.

Luca remembered his first visit to the home. It'd been like he'd stepped into a catalog peddling domestic bliss. Mrs. Katrova-Connor, the strikingly beautiful, golden-aged matron, had greeted him with an apron tied over a waist too small to have contained her six dynamic children. He'd stepped from a large covered porch that smelled like the heather and fuchsias spilling out of the window boxes, into a home that smelled like baked goods and happiness.

That day in October, he'd sat on their comfortable leather couch and proceeded to explain to them that their youngest child had, indeed, become the latest victim of a serial killer. Hero had still been recovering from surgery in the hospital at that point. They'd taken it like people used to such tragedy. Instead of falling to pieces, casting blame, or making accusations, they'd asked pertinent, solution-based questions. Tears had run down Eoghan's leathery cheeks, but his voice had been strong and his fury well-contained.

Luca liked and respected them instantly. And later, the genial curiosity with which Hero's father and mother accepted the idea of their relationship made this whole deception a lot easier. Though, he still had to fight a bad case of very real nerves at actually spending an evening with his pretend girlfriend's family.

Taking Vince's advice, he pasted on his best I'm-not-sleeping-with-your-daughter smile and trailed after Hero to the door. Serial killers, drug lords, and terrorists he could handle. Parents? That scared the bejezus right out of him. Maybe it was because he'd kissed her again. Goddammit. Couldn't fathers smell that kind of thing? On top of that, he'd promised to— well it was better he not think about that just now.

One. Two. Three. Four...

The heavy arched door wrenched open, but the Katrova-Connor wearing the frilly apron was the last one he'd expected.

Hero's compact body was enveloped by six foot two, two hundred five pounds of laughing Light-heavyweight. "You guys made it!"

"Knox, you remember Luca, my boyfriend." Hero gestured in Luca's direction.

He gave his only little sister a sloppy kiss on the forehead before reaching over her to offer his fist to Luca. "Of course." Knox's smile widened. "It's good to see you man, under much better circumstances."

"Likewise." Luca reached out and fist-bumped what had to be the most valuable knuckles in the country. Instead of TapOut gloves, they were encased in oven mitts decorated with grapes and wine bottles and lined with lace. They matched the apron stretched to the limit of its capabilities over the professional fighter's torso.

Lennox Goodfellow Katrova-Connor wore grey slacks and a burgundy shirt unbuttoned at the collar and rolled up past the elbows. He would have looked almost respectable if not for the alternative black tips on his copper faux hawk and the countless Celtic tattoos peeking below his shirtsleeves and above the neckline. Who could pull off neck tattoos? Cage fighters, biker gangs, and tattoo artists. That was a pretty short list.

If Luca took a picture of him in the apron get-up and the wide cheeser, he could have sold it to the paparazzi for millions. Trying not to be a bit star-struck at eating with the man whose career he'd followed for the past five years, Luca decided not to mention that he was a huge fan.

"You have to come into the kitchen, Hero," Knox insisted. "I have a surprise for you." He stepped aside and swept his mitts to usher them into the house, searching behind them for more people. "Where's Rown and Demetri?"

"They stayed behind to talk to Father Michael. They'll be a few minutes," Hero evaded.

"Sweet." He shut the door behind them, and smells both mouth-watering and savory assaulted Luca's salivary glands. The rug-lined wood floors creaked beneath their boots as they made their way past the parlor on the right. The dining room was to the left across the entry hall and attached to an enormous remodeled kitchen that could have been in a French country decorating magazine.

"I finally talked Mom into the two ovens so one of them can be convection," Knox said conspiratorially over his shoulder before they reached the kitchen door. "Tell her you like them."

"I heard that, Lennox." The sultry Russian accent was punctuated with the sharp taps of a very large knife against a cutting board.

"Really Ma?" Knox volleyed back. "Didja hear me say not to help with dinner? Because I'm pretty sure I said *that* loud enough."

Luca entered the kitchen behind Knox and Hero just in time to see Izolda slap her son's hand as he reached for the knife. "I am a dangerous woman with a blade, son," she brandished the weapon at him with a challenging smile. "Try to tell me not to cook in my own kitchen again, I dare you."

She sounded like an old-school bond villain but looked like an old-school bond girl. Her black hair, threaded with silver, was tucked into a chic, messy braid that fell down to the back of her pearl silk blouse. She'd kicked off her pumps, but still wore her pencil skirt and hose that Luca had seen at church. The woman was tall, maybe close to six feet, and towered over her husband in those shoes. Though, Eoghan hadn't seemed to notice, let alone mind.

"Agent Ramirez!" Cat-like brown eyes lit with warmth and pleasure as she noticed his presence. Still clutching the knife, she went to him and gripped his shoulders, pulling him down for two solid kisses, one on each cheek. "I call you Luca now, as you are Hero's *krasavchik*. And you call me Izolda until you are comfortable calling me Mama."

Krasavchik? Luca gulped. *Mama?* "Great. Mrs—Er —Izolda. Thanks for having me to dinner." Was he still supposed to shake hands after she'd kissed him? What was the official protocol? No one had ever seemed so glad to see him before. Like. Ever. He hadn't been kissed by anyone over fifty in as long as he could remember. God, it was suddenly way too hot in the kitchen.

"Of course, of *course* you come to dinner. Hero never brings a man home for me to feed. Is about time, this is what I think."

"What's this about a surprise for me?" Hero cut in with a little too much eagerness.

Knox hurried around the wide island in the middle of the kitchen. He pulled up to the top oven and opened it, giving it a moment for the initial wave of heat to dissipate. Reaching in, he produced a covered roasting pan and set it out on a cork trivet.

He put his mitt on the lid of the roasting pan and paused for dramatic effect, his impish brown eyes sparkling at his sister. "*Et voila.*" A puff of steam escaped the unveiling of a round, unidentifiable meat that actually smelled incredible.

"What is it?" Luca couldn't stop himself from asking, peering into the roasting pan.

"Tofurkey made from *scratch*," Knox beamed

proudly. "With a sage, mushroom, wild rice pilaf and smoked bacon stuffing."

"Awww!" Hero squealed. "Knox! I love it!"

Knox gave an exaggerated cocky nod and tapped at his cheek. Hero kissed it and then bent to stick her nose over the pot.

Luca wrinkled his brow in confusion. "I thought you were a vegetarian."

"I am." Hero closed her eyes to savor the smell. "Thus the Tofurkey."

"But there's bacon in it."

She shrugged. "Well yeah, but it's bacon."

Knox nodded his agreement.

"Bacon is meat. It comes from a pig." Luca said.

"It doesn't *count* as meat because it's bacon." She was looking at him as though *he* was the one who'd lost his mind.

"That makes no sense."

"It doesn't have to make sense, bro," Knox said sagely. "It's bacon."

Luca couldn't really disagree on any particular point, so he just nodded like he accepted infallible logic. At least breakfast between him and Hero might have a chance.

Hero's sister entered the kitchen from the hall with a cell phone tucked to her ear. "I told you the deposition was going to be on Tuesday. So you need to get that affidavit signed *tomorrow* or we're screwed." With thick-rimmed glasses and dark auburn hair held in a messy bun with a number two pencil, she looked more like a librarian than a high-powered ADA.

"Timandra, we're about to have dinner. No working! Is Sunday." Izolda scolded.

Andra ignored her mother, padded to the fridge,

took two bottled beers and opened them by slamming her hand on the tops against the counter like a champ.

Luca blinked. Color him impressed.

"I thought you government employees got the weekends *off*," Knox added. "Like my man, Luca, here."

Luca was saved from having to cover his guilty look by Andra's universal 'shut up, I'm on the phone' wave. She grabbed both bottles in one hand and magically used one of the same fingers to cover her free ear. "What? What are you talking about the formatting was wrong? I swear to God, I'm going to strangle that new paralegal with her own telephone cord. If her brain was even half as big as her tits, we'd be in business." The rest of her conversation was lost as she ducked past Luca with a mouthed 'hello' before disappearing out the opposite door of the one she'd entered. Luca assumed it led to the dining room.

The two Katrova-Connor girls were each gale forces of nature in their own, completely opposite ways. Luca met Hero's eyes across the corner of the island. She smiled at him and raised a sarcastic eyebrow that said, *Aren't you glad you came?*

His own amused smile said, *Actually... Yes.* Were they doing that couple thing where they talked with their eyes? Because that was just fucking new territory. Luca had an overwhelming urge to reach for her hand. He just—needed to touch her. The realization that he actually could in this scenario came a second too late.

Eoghan's dynamic presence entered the room a split second before he did, preceding him with a kinetic energy that may have presented on the Richter scale. "Is that you, kitten?" he sang in his Irish brogue before setting down his beer—presumably from

Andra— and planting a kiss on Hero's cheek. "Did you invite that Latin lad of yours? I just set him a place at the— oh, there he is!" The Irishman's copper beard split in a wide grin when he turned and noted Luca standing against the wall. "Welcome, son!" he boomed, grabbing Luca's palm with the mitts he called hands and pumping it in an enthusiastic hand-shake. "'Tis good to see you bringing me girl to church."

Luca's mouth went a little dry at the man's use of the word 'son.' Just how serious did the man think he and Hero were, exactly? "I'll admit she's the one who brought me, not the other way around."

The man's grin only widened. "In any case, I hope you both brought your appetites, there's enough to feed a small army here."

"Thank you, sir," Luca balefully eyed the pot full of faux meat.

"Call me Eoghan," he cuffed Luca on the shoulder and turned back to his daughter. "What took you so long to get home? Where is the rest of everyone? And what in the name of the holy infant Jesus is that?"

Luca took everyone's unruffled acceptance of Eoghan's rapid-fire questions as indication that such dialog was commonplace.

"It's tofurkey," Hero supplied.

"Smells decent, at least." Eoghan peeked into the roasting pan they now all surrounded. Luca had to ad-mit, it was the most edible looking meat substitute he'd ever come across, not that the standard was set high.

"I know what took you so long to get here." Knox nudged Hero with his elbow. "You two were making out like teenagers in the car. You were parked at the curb long enough before you came in."

Luca felt the blood drain from his face. He knew he was blanching about as white as a brown boy could go. Curbside, he'd been on the phone with Vince, going over status reports and surveillance details for tonight. But he *had* nearly devoured Hero on the cathedral lawn, in front of God and anyone else who wanted bear witness. "That wasn't what we—we weren't—I didn't—" Cue the I'm-not-sleeping-with-your-daughter-smile. Was it working? Was Izolda still holding that huge knife?

Hero's father laughed and clapped his arm again. "Don't worry yourself, son, I'm not your priest, and frankly, I don't want to know."

Luca's relieved breath delighted everyone, and laughter nearly drowned out the sound of the front door closing.

Rown strode into the kitchen looking like a Viking in a tailored suit followed by the black leather-clad Demetri. Before addressing the room, they each took a turn to bend and kiss their mother's offered cheek as though paying respect to a medieval royal.

"What did I miss?" Rown asked, giving a meaningful nod to Hero. They'd discuss Connor at a better time.

"What smells so good?" Demetri shouldered in-between Hero and Knox and scowled down into the pot. "That looks like warmed over—"

"It's *tofurkey*," Hero explained for the umpteenth time. "Knox made it for me."

"From scratch," Knox amended, picking up a wooden spoon and smacking Demetri's hand as he poked the structurally suspicious loaf of tofu. "Don't touch it! *God.* You haven't washed your hands."

"What are the rest of us going to eat?" Rown asked with a curled lip.

"A whole lotta this." Knox took his left oven mitt off, unveiling his middle finger.

"Don't be vulgar in the kitchen, Lennox," Eoghan reprimanded with a smile. "Your mother doesn't like it." He turned and slid his wide shoulders between Hero, Knox, and the ovens. To Luca's astonishment, he reached up to both of his middle sons and planted hello kisses on each of their masculine jaws. "Demetrius." (smooch). "Berowne." (smooch). "What kept you?"

Luca shifted a little uncomfortably at the very strange, *very* un-American custom of related men kissing, even if it was on the cheek. But, he supposed, if anyone wanted to question the men of the Katrova-Connor family about their masculinity, they could step *right* up. Probably would end up chewing on their own balls before they were finished, but he'd pay money to see it.

"Sorry to be late, we were talking to Father Michael," Rown said, and left it there.

"But seriously, what's for dinner?" Demetri wandered to the ovens to investigate.

"I braised *you* jack holes lamb shanks and am just finishing them in the oven. Then I made my garlic/rosemary potatoes, blanched asparagus, and homemade seven-grain bread." Knox held out his arms as though to graciously receive his accolades.

Luca's mouth watered. Who knew the most dangerous cage-fighter alive was also a master chef?

"Braised?" Rown queried.

"You sear the juices, rub them with *herbs de Provence*, and then simmer them in my secret sauce."

"Yeah, I've heard you like to smear 'em in your secret sauce," Demetri snickered.

Hero and Eoghan joined in the brothers' laughter,

so Luca felt it safe to follow suit. He liked a family who could crack dirty jokes.

"Demetrius!" Izolda said from her corner of the kitchen. A smile quivered at the corner of her mouth, though her dark eyes flashed with temper.

Luca cut off mid-laugh.

"I said *not* in the kitchen." Still chortling, Eoghan took one glance at his wife's face, sobered, and then biffed Demetri upside the back of the head.

Luca instantly stiffened, his fists clenching at his sides. The action instinctively stirred his temper and set fire to his blood. A father shouldn't humiliate his son. Shouldn't strike him. Especially on the head. Luca took a reflexive step toward Eoghan before he caught himself.

Wait. This wasn't *his* family. Wasn't his problem. Probably wasn't even a big deal.

Forcing a deep breath through his nostrils, Luca watched a still-laughing Demetri reach up and grab his dad's hand on the back swing. "Sorry, Ma," he threw over his shoulder as he sucker-smacked Eoghan's solid chest.

"You're goin' to be sorry," Eoghan vowed. "When I knock next week into you."

"It's knock you into next week, Dad," Knox corrected.

Laughter exploded around the kitchen as everyone alternately goaded and dodged the laughing, slap-boxing pair. Luca forced his shoulders to relax. It was all a joke. He slowed his breaths. They were playing.

They loved each other.

"You okay?" Hero stepped over to him, entwining her fingers through his.

Luca swallowed his heart. "Yeah." He even sounded like he meant it.

Izolda had traded her knife for Knox's wooden spoon, which she brandished like Excalibur. "Take that out of my kitchen or I'll bruise you both." Father and son turned from enemies to refugees as they ducked the flat side of the spoon and escaped into the dining room.

Eoghan popped back in to distract his wife with a kiss while he grabbed his abandoned beer, then ducked back out with a wink at Luca.

"Gets pretty chaotic around here," Hero said apologetically.

Luca was saved from having to come up with a reply by the oven timer.

Knox demonstrated his famous reflexes as he lunged for the lower oven, extracting a much larger pot. "Let's see these beauties."

A sizzle and a puff of steam preceded the most appetizing smell Luca had ever come across. "I think I'm dating the wrong sibling," he joked. "You'd be surprised at what kind of things I'd lower myself to do for that kind of food."

Knox grinned at them both. "All you have to do is keep my baby sister happy."

And alive. Luca added silently.

Izolda opened two bottles of red Zinfandel and poured them into separate decanters. "I will put these on the table and then tell Romeo is time for dinner."

"Oh, is Connor here?" Hero asked. "I didn't see him."

"He's in his bedroom," Knox said with a meaningful glance while artfully arranging the lamb on a platter and spooning the reduction from the pan over the meat.

"*His* bedroom?"

Knox nodded gravely. "Shanna left him two nights

ago. They were fighting because she didn't want him to retire, but after twenty years, I don't think he's got any more to give the military, you know? We've all seen it. He's not... the same."

"I know," Hero whispered, her chin wobbling a little. "But she just... left him?"

"She failed him," Luca said without thinking, then winced. This wasn't really his business.

Knox regarded him with approval, though. "Fucking A, she did," he agreed. "Fourteen years down the shitter, just like that. She's filed papers, the whole works, and he's acting like it's nothing. He even left her the house and moved in here until he figures shit out. Sounds like she's going after everything."

"Even his pension?" Hero asked, appalled.

Knox shrugged, but didn't look optimistic. "He won't talk about it, but you know how she is."

"I know how she waited to do this until after her little 'procedure' was paid off," Hero snarked.

"Ain't nothing little about those," Knox made a gesture as though gigantic breasts took up the length of his arm.

Luca chuckled.

"Come to think of it, that bitch *never* called me," Hero ranted. "Haven't heard from my own sister-in-law in the past two months. That two-faced cow. You know what? I'm going to—"

"Romeo! Dinner!" Izolda's call interrupted as she walked down the hallway to the back stairs that led up to the second floor bedrooms.

Knox made a *zip-it* motion with his hand across his mouth and picked up the platter of lamb.

"Romeo, Romeo! Wherefore art thou, Romeo?" Izolda called sweetly.

Silence.

The matriarch swiftly changed strategies. "Are you going to make me come up there, *mal'chik moy*? Because we both know I will."

The house held its breath for what seemed like an entire minute before a door opened and closed and a deep, muffled voice carried down to the kitchen.

"Thirty-eight years old and Connor's still afraid of Mom." Knox gestured to Luca with his head and then to the large pan on the stove. "You mind grabbing the potatoes?"

Luca nodded and reached for the pot, which was still warm, but not hot enough to need protection on his hands. "I'm a little afraid of your mom," he only half joked.

"Don't let Knox fool you," Hero laughed as she grabbed the asparagus and followed them to the dining room. "We all are. Even Pop."

"Speak for yourself." Eoghan made room for the food at the large round table and ducked out of the way. "I've learned over the years how to disarm your mother. It's not easy, but it can be fun." He gave a suggestive waggle of his ginger brows and a sinister smile.

A chorus of disgusted groans and one or two feminine 'Ewwwwwwws' erupted around the table. Eoghan ducked with a merry snicker as a linen napkin sailed toward his head.

"What's this?" Izolda asked from the entry.

Eoghan whirled around. "Nothing at all, my love." He pulled out a seat for her and she took it with a suspicious lift of an eyebrow.

"Told ya," Hero murmured.

Unburdened of his dish, Luca stood by the round table stuffed with nine chairs and wondered what to do next. He was suddenly very aware that he'd never done this before.

Family dinner.

Sure, he'd dined with people, usually at restaurants. But growing up, his family barely ate food, let alone *with* each other. He and Coach Peck usually ate in front of the TV like proper bachelors were supposed to. He'd carried the tradition into his adult life. Not that he only dined in front of the TV. He sometimes ate in the car. At his desk. At a pub for lunch with colleagues. At a nice place with friends or on a date, but by the time they got back to someone's *house* they were hungry for something else. Something that never, *ever* led to dinner with the parents. As far as he was concerned, this shit only happened in the movies. Or, like, in the fifties.

After Connor lurked in and took the empty seat to the left of his father, Luca noted a seating pattern emerge. Oldest to youngest. First Conner, then Rown, followed by Andra, Demetri, Knox, and finally Hero, who grinned and patted the seat between her and Izolda.

Hero's mother was already dishing a generous portion of potatoes onto his plate and Hero picked up the decanter and filled his glass with wine.

Luca stared at his plate as food appeared on it. The unobtrusive chandelier cast a golden glow on the table, warming the soft colors of the food along with the atmosphere and suddenly he couldn't seem to swallow. Couldn't breathe. For two months, he'd wondered to himself how Hero could have survived that awful night. Everyone said it was a miracle. That it would have taken superhuman strength of will to fight through the pain, the blood loss, the hypothermia, the surgery, and the painful recovery. Not to mention all the emotional blowback.

But she'd had to, he saw that now. She had to make

it back *here*. To this meal. To this family. Luca would have fought off the reaper single-handedly, too, if he'd had so much to live for. She had a *home*. Not just any home, one filled with laughter and chaos and pure, protective acceptance. Maybe there was a heaven, maybe there wasn't. But if someone told him that paradise was better than this, he'd slit his own throat to get there, because he just couldn't imagine it.

"Luca," Izolda's voice prodded gently.

He blinked at her, feeling like a sentimental chump.

"I do not allow jackets at my table." Her smile was penetrating and a little sad, as though she'd just been inside his thoughts.

"Oh. Yeah. Sorry." He looked down at his suit coat as though he'd never seen it before. Then undid the buttons before remembering something. "What are your rules regarding firearms?"

Her look said it all, and he stepped out to put his gun holster and jacket on a hook in the entry next to Rown's. Returning, he stepped around his own seat, pulling it under him and set his napkin on his lap.

"Let us pray." Izolda reached out and gently took his hand. Hero took the other one.

They lifted their faces, rather than bowed their heads. Luca stared at his hands, encased in the soft palms of two women, and wondered how much deeper down the rabbit hole he could get.

Eoghan prayed. "Oh Mary, conceived without sin, mother of mercy and hope, help every human being of every race and culture find and embrace peace on this, your day of feast. Amen."

Even Luca mumbled an "amen," because regardless of his lack of faith, who couldn't agree with such a request?

Izolda gave his hand a gentle squeeze before she let it go, and Luca couldn't make himself move until the lamb dish was handed to him.

"The more rare cuts are on the left," Knox said. "And the medium ones are on the right."

He dished himself a rare portion and passed the food along, then dug right in.

"So Luca, tell us about your family, do they live close by?" Eoghan asked.

Luca almost choked on the lamb melting in his mouth. Beside him, Hero stiffened. These were questions he was supposed to answer, right? Parents usually asked boyfriends this kind of stuff.

"My mother is buried in El Paso, and my father— lives in New Mexico," he supplied. They'd never need to know more than that.

"Oh, I'm very sorry." Eoghan crossed himself for the loss of his mother, and glibly moved over a sensitive topic. "What sort of work does your father do?"

Not the best place to bring up a New Mexico chain gang or drug-running for the local cartel. "He owned his own auto-body shop," Luca couldn't taste the perfectly cooked potatoes as he took his next bite.

Eoghan's face lit up. "I'm sure Hero's mentioned I own a European import machine shop myself."

"Yeah, she did. I'd like to see it some time."

Hero's father seemed pleased. "What kind of cars did your father work on?"

Stolen ones.

Luca fixed a smile on his lips, deciding to redirect the conversation. "You know what I noticed? Hero's just about the only white person I've met with a name as long as mine, do you all have middle names to go with the hyphenated last name?"

Connor groaned, earning a sharp look from his mother.

"*Romeo*'s middle name is Valentine," Izolda supplied, letting him know what she thought of her eldest son using his surname as a first name.

He'd known Connor's name was Romeo, of course. They all had files on them back at the office. But he had to get them talking about something—*anything* other than himself. Though, it took all of his considerable training to hide his amusement at Connor's somewhat ironic name.

Izolda gestured down the table. "Then, Berowne Fortinbras"

Rown sent him a look that said if Luca spread that around the office, he'd retaliate.

"Timandra Perdita."

Andra shrugged and smiled.

"Demetrius Balthazar."

Demetri seemed more interested in what was going on with his plate than conversation.

"Lennox Goodfellow."

Knox gave a grinning salute.

"And you know our Hero Viola."

Luca smiled at Hero. "Shakespeare fans, huh?"

"You could be sayin' that," Eoghan laughed.

Hero tapped her fork against her teeth, considering Luca. "Did I hear you say you had a long name? You're not just Luca Ramirez? How did I not know that?"

"Sure do." Luca wiped his mouth with his napkin.

"Well, let's have it then, son," Eoghan prodded.

"It's Luca Rodrigo Ramirez-Dimas."

Hero's parents turned to each other, their faces radiant with a secret pleasure. Izolda grinned, and Eoghan threw his hands up in a 'eureka' movement.

"Rodrigo!" they chimed in unison and kissed each other soundly.

For not the first time that evening, Luca was rendered speechless and confused.

Hero leaned in to him, her warm breath brushing against his ear. "Shakespeare," she whispered.

"Shakespeare?" Luca asked tightly.

"Rodrigo is in Othello," Izolda informed him before biting the head off an asparagus.

Luca swallowed, alternately hating and loving the way the fine lines on her still-lovely face crinkled at him. He saw expectation in that smile. She was a woman who believed in omens and in her world, his hastily given middle name was a pretty fucking big one.

"Must have missed that," he said, and took another bite of his own, chewing furiously.

Glancing to Hero on his right, he watched her cut into her tofurkey. Her eyes sparkled over at him as she chewed and Luca knew that even though this entire evening was a sham, he'd leave a little bit of his heart at this table.

Conversation drifted comfortably this way and that, driven mostly by Rown, Andra, Knox, Hero, and their parents. Luca chimed in around bites of incredible food. Topics included Knox's upcoming Pay per View bout in Canada, a million dollar Italian car Eoghan had in his shop, Hero's Friday art exhibit, and a myriad of more inconsequential topics. No one brought up the case. No one mentioned the impending divorce. All inflammatory conversations were saved for another time. Seemed like a cardinal sin to fuck with family dinner. Serial killers, trauma, and relationship failures came second to chocolate Guinness potato cake. As it should, Luca decided, helping himself to a second piece while Hero handed him a tiny steaming cup of espresso.

Deep in his trouser pocket his work cell beeped unobtrusively, but the longer vibration grated against the wood of the chair, piercing the conversation. Luca leapt on it, taking from the look on Izolda's face that technology at the table was another cardinal sin.

"Sure," Andra teased. "The new guy gets away with it."

It was Vince. "Excuse me, its work." Luca stood, ignoring Rown's intent stare. He stepped into the hallway and accepted the call.

"Getcha ass down here, we may have nabbed the motherfucker." Vince's excited proclamation was almost lost in some kind of surrounding chaos. "And he's losing his damn mind, so hurry."

Luca cringed and looked back into the dining room. There's no way they could have heard, but still. He clutched the phone tighter. "What are you saying?" he demanded.

"Are you deaf? I'm saying we may have John the *fucking* Baptist in custody!"

19

"And thus I clothe my naked villainy;
With odd old ends stol'n out of holy writ,
And seem a saint, when most I play the devil."

— WILLIAM SHAKESPEARE

Hero could have been in any cop film. A dark room. Concrete walls. Large, one-sided window set deep into the wall in front of her, and bordered in silver. Intercom and speakers to the right, two agents in suit coats on the left. She rubbed the scars along her palms, trying not to look away from the scene unfolding in the interview room.

She looked over at Rown and Vince, and bit her lip so hard she tasted blood. "What's wrong with him?"

Rown's mouth pulled into a tight line as he squinted through the window at the grimy, hollering bearded man that strained against the cuffs imprisoning his hands behind him. "What's *not* wrong with him?" He flicked a look at Vince. "Who is he?"

Vince shook his head. "He was nabbed by a surveillance team while lurking in the woods around Hero's house. He won't give his name, and it was a *bitch* getting a fingerprint from him. Once Ramirez gets a hit, he'll go in and grill him."

"Are you going to go in there too?" Hero asked Vince fretfully. She didn't like the idea of Luca in there alone with someone so obviously unhinged.

"Naw, this is what Ramirez does best. He's a mutha fucking maestro in there. It's some kind of God-given talent."

"Interviewing people?"

"Breaking people." A demonic glint sharpened the Southie's smile. "I just like to watch."

Hero stepped closer to the mirror and whispered, "I think he's already broken."

Rown put his arm around her shoulders. "Do you recognize him?"

Hero studied the man's face, barely distinguishable behind a layer of grime. His brown hair and beard hung to the middle of his chest streaked with grit and grey. As he screamed and squirmed, little strings of spittle caught in the unkempt bush. She couldn't exactly get a good idea of his size as he was sitting and layered with the requisite homeless winter uniform of sweaters and an oversized jacket. "I don't— I don't think so." She flinched as he surged powerfully against the chain, but it held fast.

"Let me out of here! I can't be in here! I have to be outside!" The chair he occupied faced a cold copper table with an identical chair on the other side, minus the restraints. He faced the door, and the window through which they watched was situated so the voyeurs would see the side profiles of both interviewer and suspect.

"What about his voice?" Rown prodded gently. "Anything?"

Hero shook her head. "John the Baptist didn't

scream that night... not once. He chanted, almost sang. He whispered." She held her hands up. It seemed that her head just wouldn't stop shaking side to side, as though rejecting the memory, the sight in front of her, the screams, and the whispers.

The man turned his face toward the window and for a moment, all Hero could see was the desperation in his ice-blue eyes. "Let me goooooooo!"

Rown stepped forward and pressed the mute button on the intercom. "You don't have to listen to that."

The interview room door opened just wide enough to admit Luca. He carried nothing but a file folder and a sinister expression that was equal parts hostile and hopeful. *Try something,* it said. *I dare you.* Even from behind the window, *she* was ready to confess. He would have broken her without saying one single word.

Hero reached past her brother and depressed the mute button again, turning the sound back on. "I want to hear this." She didn't, really. But couldn't seem to help herself.

"Get me the fuck out of here, man." The prisoner snarled and lunged for Luca, but grunted as the metal of the cuffs bit into his wrists. "I don't deserve to be here. Get me Agent Orange. Get me *out!*"

Luca looked different then he had at the house. Gone was any trace of the unsure, overwhelmed boyfriend. Or later, the relaxed and charming dimpled man who'd settled into his place at her table with amazing ease. Like he'd always been there. Like he belonged there.

This Luca was someone else entirely. Suit jacket off. Sleeves rolled up. Gun and badge nowhere to be found.

"Sergeant First Class James Mazure," Luca read softly from his file, his voice like snagged silk even through the com.

At this, the struggling Sergeant quieted, though he didn't stop straining against his restraints as far as Hero could tell.

Luca continued reading. "United States Marine, 2nd Division. Veteran of Operations Desert Storm *and* Desert Shield. Awarded the Purple Heart for injuries suffered at the battle of Khafji and again, along with the Medal of Bravery, at the Kuwait airport in nineteen-ninety-one." Luca closed the folder, slapped it down in front of Mazure and took a long moment to inspect every inch of the man's garb as though less than impressed before adding without a trace of inflection, "Your country thanks you for your service."

Beside her, Rown hissed in a breath and Hero grabbed his hand.

"Hey, *fuck* you!" Mazure snarled.

"No, fuck *you*." Luca got right into his face, which was a gutsy move, in Hero's eyes. The man had already established he wasn't too ashamed to spit. "Fuck *you*, Jimmy, for killing those girls."

"I *didn't* kill those girls!" He was yelling again, looking like he could already hear the bars slam behind him, locking him forever inside.

"Really?" Luca smiled. There was a hint of the devil in that smile. "You didn't leave a bouquet threatening one of your victims? The one who got away?"

The beard twitched a few times. Hero couldn't tell what emotion that conveyed on a face like his, but the sun-browned forehead wrinkled. "I did that. I left the flowers. But I didn't hurt no one." Though the admission made her lungs suddenly feel heavy, the trembling in the man's voice tugged at Hero's heart. It reminded her of the tremors her own terror had caused as she'd pleaded for her life. She marveled that Luca could look so cold in the face of such a lack of human dignity.

"I know you did. You left a partial print on the plastic. Sloppy work. We couldn't tell it was yours for sure until we dragged you in here and reprinted you. You've dropped off the grid." Luca leaned against the table and studied the gleam on his expensive boots with an unaffected, rather satisfied air. "I have a feeling you don't like enclosed spaces, Sergeant. You want to see the outside of this room sometime in the next forty-eight hours? Tell me something I *don't* know."

"I wasn't threatening Hero." James Mazure's voice strengthened with conviction.

Luca slammed his palm on the table with the speed of a viper, causing not just Mazure, but both agents and Hero to jump. "Don't *fucking* say her name."

Her heart kicked into overdrive. Not just because of the startle, but because of her name on the lips of a stranger. One who'd left her the beware bouquet. The one who'd nearly taken her life?

"I-I wasn't." The desperation was back in his eyes. "I was *warning* her. He's after her still. I wanted to protect her from him. Just like you, man."

"From who?"

"You know who. From *him*."

Luca leaned in again, his eyes narrowed in consideration. "You got someone else up here, Mazure?" He tapped the man on his grimy forehead. "Is that what you're saying?"

"You don't know *dick*. You insolent kid. You *civilian!*" The Sergeant's blue eyes cleared like a summer sky for a moment, revealing a stunning amount of intelligence.

"I know you're too young to have fought in Vietnam." Luca smirked as the other man resumed his squirming. "So who's Agent Orange? Is he the one telling you to kill these girls?"

"No! *No*, I never killed a woman. Would *never* hurt one!"

Luca's black eyes glittered, like they tended to do right before he was going to do something dangerous. "*Never*?" he repeated with that silky softness. "You've never caused the death of a woman? Not even over there?"

Mazure's head lolled back on his shoulders. Then he used his legs to surge up once more, lunging for Luca who sat just out of reach. His speech dissolved into maniacal screams again.

Rown shook his head beside her. "I heard Ramirez was brutal but... damn."

"Just wait until he *really* gets started," Vince piped in. "Oh shit!"

Mazure had thrashed about so much that he tipped the chair that was supposedly bolted to the ground and rolled out of it, shooting for the mirror. Hero jumped back as he slammed his body into it. The cuffs still held his hands behind him. "Tell them it wasn't me!" His wild eyes searched the mirror blindly, frantically. "I pulled you *out* of the river. I couldn't leave you in there to die. Tell them to let me go!"

Luca recovered from his surprise quickly and had Mazure bent over the table with his face ground into the cold surface and his arm wrenched at an awful angle in one graceful move.

Hero's eyes widened as the prisoner said a few

choice things about Luca's ethnic heritage that would have put that racist anchor from Fox News to shame.

Luca's dimples appeared, though a smile didn't exactly materialize.

The man writhed beneath his strong grip, though he had to be in considerable pain. "Let me go! Tell them to let me go! I can't be in here. The walls. The walls will burn! I need to get out!"

"It's not him," Hero whispered.

Rown took her elbow. "Come on. Let's go get a cup of coffee. You don't have to see any more of this."

"It's not him!" she gasped. Wrenching her arm away from her brother, she lunged for the intercom and punched the speak button. "Let him go, Luca. He didn't do it. It isn't him."

"Get her out of that goddamn room Di Petro," Luca ordered through gritted teeth over the screaming man in his vice grip and Hero's impassioned voice echoing back at her through a delay in the com.

"He can't be in there any longer!" she insisted. "He's afraid. Oh, God. He's *just* afraid."

Vince exploded into the interview room, righted the chair and helped his partner wrestle the squirming man back into it. Hero hadn't even heard him leave the observation room or gather the other agents armed with tasers and more scary-looking restraints.

Rown grabbed her hand away from the intercom. "You can't *do* that shit, Hero, not here."

Director Trojanowski wrenched the door open. "What the hell was that?" Hero surmised he must have been watching the whole thing from one of the many cameras stationed in the corner ceilings of the interview room.

"It wasn't him. I'm certain of it. Don't let them lock him up. He's not John the Baptist."

Trojanowski visibly wrestled with his temper at her antics, obviously better at it than Luca. He was the kind of man that turned colors like red and purple when he was angry. "How do you know?" he demanded.

"He's too tall. I couldn't tell until he stood up, but his legs are way too long. Please get him out of there, he's so scared!" Hero cried.

"Hero, he'll be fine." Rown stood behind her, blocking her view of the chaos in the interview room.

"He was still caught trespassing on your property," Trojanowski pointed out. "And we can't be sure he wasn't involved, somehow." He looked like a man with the answers to all his problems turning to silt and slipping through his fingers.

"I don't *want* to press charges." Hero begged, "Please let him go. Can't you see he's traumatized?"

Trojanowski's balding pate shone with sweat even in the dim light of the observation room. "Are you one *hundred* percent certain it's not him."

Hero nodded. "He's at least a *foot* too tall. He's almost as tall as Luca—er—Agent Ramirez. John the Baptist was *not*. If I know anything, I know that. It sounds like he was the one who pulled me *out* of the river, doesn't it? That he's just been watching me?"

"Take her somewhere to relax," The director ordered Rown, still staring at her as though she'd taken away his birthday. "I'll take care of this."

"Yes, sir." Rown took up her elbow again. "Come on, Hero."

"What are they going to do to him?" she asked as she allowed her brother to drag her away. She tried to peek over his wide shoulders back into the interrogation room.

"They're not going to hurt him, Hero. They'll do their best to keep him from hurting himself."

The observation room dumped them into a hallway with a glass wall. The wide, open room on the other side of the glass took up one entire floor of the Federal Building. Outside walls were lined with offices, supply closets, record rooms, and one very large conference room which offered a view of the airport. Herman Miller cubicles bisected the rest of the open floor with shoulder-level grey walls the texture of the fuzzy side of a Velcro strap. Some people tried to brighten and personalize their allotted spaces with family pictures, inspirational calendars, and comic strips hung by push-pins. As Hero allowed herself to be steered past them toward the conference room, she stifled a feeling inside not unlike the ones Sgt. Mazure had demonstrated in the interview room. If she had to spend eight-plus hours of her life in one of those grey boxes every day, she'd be as loony as he was before long.

"What happens now, Rown?" She looked up at her brother and he shook his head at her, flicking a glance at the handful of agents milling around the doorway to the interview room. They all watched her, some with mild interest, and others with frank and intense curiosity. Hero supposed that for a homicide unit, she was somewhat of an anomaly. A survivor. A victim that remained among the living. Someone who carried the wounds of death on warm and vibrant flesh, and the memories of a serial killer locked inside her head.

She took Rown's unspoken hint to stay silent and studied him for a minute. He belonged to this place.

To the grey fuzzy walls and uniformed suits. He was so structured. Out of everyone in her family, he was what people would call the most *normal*. Not exotically handsome like Luca, but large and angular with an almost barbaric masculinity that contrasted with his savvy ways and clinical acumen. This was his world in a way that it would never be Luca's. Luca attacked every case as though his own redemption depended on it. He took down each criminal as though they'd done him a personal slight. He looked evil in the face and saw himself.

Rown enjoyed the puzzles, the mysteries, and knowing things that were stamped *Confidential*. She bet he even liked the politics and the mind games. The travel and the overtime. The hours of dedicated monotony punctuated by moments of adrenaline-fueled danger.

"I bet you're good at your job," she told him as he settled her into a grey swivel chair by the door. He took the one across the corner from her at the head of the table, looking like he belonged there.

His grim mouth turned up at the corners. "What makes you say that?"

"Those men out there, they respect you. I can tell. And you're obviously terrified of your wild, hippie little sister doing anything to embarrass you at work."

That dragged a laugh from him. "It's not like that, Hero. This isn't my case. Hell, this isn't my floor. I have to maintain a certain level of professionalism if they're going to allow me to be here with you."

The yells and screams of the restrained man still filtered down the hall, along with the commands and cajoling of the agents. Rown stood to shut the door before sitting to face her again.

"I guess everyone has to be a little different here at

work. Not quite themselves." She murmured, peering out the glass wall at the sea of dark and empty cubicles. Talk about Federal transparency. The place was a ghost town on a Sunday. The only people here were called in for the special circumstance and likely lingered to log overtime hours and be present just in case the suspect turned out to be the killer.

"You mean Ramirez?" Rown correctly assessed.

Hero exercised her Fifth Amendment rights.

Rown considered her for a moment, his fingers templed in front of him. "What you just saw *is* Ramirez, Hero. That's who he's always been. The man who sat at our table tonight was just an agent doing his job, and I'll admit, he's damn good at it."

"What are you saying?"

"I'm saying he's been at *many* tables. He's dined with Mexican drug cartels, got drunk with the Highway 101 rapist to get a confession, and most recently partied with a bunch of South Asian sex traffickers. Our parent's table isn't any different in his mind. It's the job, Hero, nothing more."

"You don't know that," Hero whispered.

Rown made an exasperated sound. "What scares me is that *you* don't know that." He leaned forward and took her hand, green eyes glimmering with deep emotion. Her father's eyes. Her own eyes. "You've been through hell, are still facing fear and danger and a lot of uncertainty about the future. You've got to be emotionally vulnerable right now."

"Do *not* patronize me, Berowne," Hero warned, pulling her hand away.

"Do *not* fall for this guy, Hero," he warned back.

"What makes you think I am?"

"Well, you didn't deny it, for one," he said pointedly. "And I watched you grow up. I know how you are." Rown grabbed her hand again, gripped it this time with the strength of his emotion. "Remember when you were eight and got bit on the hand by that Pitt Bull you were trying to pet?"

Hero nodded, looking down at the hand held within Rown's. A larger, deeper scar covered the old bite wound now.

"You sat next to that dog's cage at the shelter while they put him down. I remember Mom and Pop trying to drag you away, but you were having none of it. You cried and cried while he snarled and snapped at you from the metal cage, and you didn't move away from him until the drugs kicked in and he was gone. You were apologizing to him the entire time."

Tears pricked Hero's eyes at the memory. She'd felt so guilty, because *she'd* reached through the chain link fence. The dog had been so obviously mal-treated and neglected, she'd only wanted to offer it friendship. The owners hadn't even shown up or fought for the dog when animal control had taken it away. In the end, she'd understood why she'd been bitten, and couldn't live with the idea of the animal dying alone.

"Agent Ramirez *is* that Pitt Bull. If his leash ever snaps, he's going to hurt someone. And I'll be damned if that someone is going to be you."

Hero nodded. She usually didn't like when her family got high-handed with her. She hated being treated like the baby sister. Well, most of the time. But the love in Rown's words was demonstrated honestly and carefully. He usually wasn't the most demonstra-tive of the bunch.

Her brother leaned back in his chair with a tired smile. "On the other side of that coin, Pitt Bulls make the best guard dogs. There's no one else I'd rather have working this case, or watching your back. So long as he keeps his eyes where they belong."

Hero gave her brother a chastised look. Luca had tried to behave himself, and she'd been acting like a shameless flirt. Going so far as to blatantly invite him to have sex. More than once. Was this the adult version of sticking her hand through the chain-link fence? In the past, she'd been able to open her bedroom door, but keep her heart closed. This time, she'd done things differently, through no fault of her own. In the space of a few weeks, Luca had punched a hole through quite a few firsts that had been denied almost any other man. He'd slept at her house more than a few times. He'd gone to church with her. Had dinner at her parent's house. All without having sex with her, or even a date. Had she put more emotional importance on that then she should have? She *knew* it was his job. But did she assume that it had been more than that to him?

She thought of the possessive, desperate kiss they'd shared only hours ago. The heat and the tension swirling between them like a separate, tangible entity. Something dark and wild and very forbidden.

I'm not your boyfriend, Hero.

I know.

Do you?

Did she?

"I don't think you make it easy on the guy," Rown said perceptively. "Not dressing like that."

She looked down at her mini dress. "I've always dressed like this."

He released her hands, adopting a very put upon frown. "Don't I know it? You've kept four older brothers very busy over the years."

Hero tossed her head unrepentantly, but rose with

Rown to give him a warm hug. "I know, and I love you for it."

"I love you, too." He held her close for a minute. "I don't know what we all would have done if we'd lost you."

"Don't even think about that." She swallowed some more emotion and stepped away from him. The screams had stopped, but it seemed that Sgt. Mazure's claustrophobia was somehow contagious and Hero wanted to be anywhere else but this cold, grey office building. "Can you get me out of here?"

Rown nodded. "Yeah, let me, ah, get an update on what's going down." He left her to confer with Trojanowski and a few others for a moment. The director and his men cast disappointed, almost antagonistic looks at her.

She kind of understood how they felt. This could have been it for them. They could have called press conferences, added this serial killer to their statistics, patted themselves on the back for a job-well-done, and moved on.

Not now. The hunt was still on, and she was still in danger. Though, it wasn't *her* fault they had the wrong guy.

Rown returned. "Let's go. We can wait for Ramirez in the parking lot. Shouldn't be too much longer." He showed her to a non-descript back door that led to a rear staircase. Just to change up the color scheme, the stairs were beige instead of grey, interrupted by dark wood doors with badge scanners on each floor. The entire building was dark but for auxiliary lighting and Hero found herself glad Rown had his gun with him. She followed him down three flights of stairs, through two separate doors where he had to swipe his government ID badge to get out of the building.

They broke out into the night through very heavy glass doors, and Hero was instantly grateful she'd brought her heavy jacket instead of her sweater. As they made their way to the parking lot, she felt the tension in her brother's stride. His awareness of their surroundings. It made her feel safe.

"What happens to Mazure now?" she asked him.

"They'll finish fingerprinting him, just to make sure he's in the system. They'll check his name against all the national and international databases, and probably talk to someone in the Marine Corps just to make sure no one wants him for anything."

"Then?"

"Then, since you're not pressing trespassing charges, they'll have to release him. Though they'll probably be watching him closely until all this is over."

They stopped by Luca's black Charger and Hero leaned on it, suddenly exhausted. "Luca was so... mean."

"Don't be too hard on him for that," Rown said hesitantly. "Ramirez *did* think the man was a serial killer at the time."

"I know." Hero sank deeper into her coat, her eyes and shoulders incredibly heavy. "Watching that man fall apart, all I could do was wonder if that's where Connor is headed."

Rown let out a deep breath as they both watched an airplane take off and circle to the south. The flashing lights eventually became another one of the many mobile beacons in the night sky. His shoulders drooped as though they contained the same weight she'd only just been contemplating.

"I read the file on Mazure. In the last battle Ramirez mentioned, he was trapped inside a tank that had been set on fire. It would have felt like he was being cooked to death."

Hero gasped.

"He got out, obviously, but he had serious burns over the lower half of his body and was medically discharged from the military after that. I guess that's why he can't be inside. He's not only afraid of small spaces, but of buildings catching fire. Connor's trauma, however severe, was nothing like that."

"What did Father Michael say?" Hero felt an almost desperate need to be focusing on anything, *anyone's* problems but her own right now.

Rown hesitated. "Not much, honestly. He said he couldn't break a confession confidence."

"That's it?" That was less than nothing. Maybe Father Michael *had* been lying about the whole Connor thing to get her alone. Maybe it was good that Luca had barged in when he did.

"Well, basically he said that Connor had confessed something that worried him, but he stressed that he can't mention the details unless Connor was going to be a danger to himself or others."

"And he didn't say either way?"

"Not in so many words."

"Good thing he wasn't being vague," Hero muttered sarcastically.

Rown's sarcastic noise was an explosion of breath and irritation. "None of us know what to do. Not Mom and Dad. Not even me."

"He won't talk to you?"

"I tried, but..." Rown stared into the darkness for a long time.

Rown had followed Connor into the Army right out of high school. While Connor had made a career out of it by swiftly snatching up an opportunity to become a Ranger, Rown had put in nearly a decade as a sniper while finishing his graduate degree and then he'd opted out to pursue his own career with the FBI. They had both been deployed to the Middle East, Africa, and places they weren't allowed to mention. Being the two oldest boys, their deep bond as brothers had only increased as soldiers. Rown had been Connor's best man at his wedding. They'd attended their Army buddy's funerals together, even if it meant flying across the country. Everyone in the Katrova-Connor family was glad they had each other, because no matter how well-meaning and loving the rest of them were, they could never truly empathize or understand what the soldiers went through.

Hero leaned forward and put her forehead against Rown's lapels. "Do you know what I've realized I hate more than anything in the world?"

"What's that?"

"Feeling helpless. It's got to be the worst kind of torture. Helpless to stop someone else's hatred. Helpless to stop someone else's pain. Or crawl away from your own. It blows."

Rown squeezed her shoulders. "Get used to it, baby sister. In my experience, you spend most of life pretty damn helpless on both accounts."

She smacked him in the ribs, mostly because they were accessible, and pulled away from him. "Good thing you never opted to become a therapist. You would have sucked at it."

He laughed, but the smile didn't permeate the sadness in his eyes.

"Also, I'm not your baby sister. I'm twenty-six."

"You're twenty-five."

"I'm going to be twenty-six in, like, three months."

"I think you'll stop being my *baby* sister when

you're old enough to not to round up a year anymore."
Rown winked. "Then you'll just be my little sister."

The crunch of the door handle drew Hero's attention to the front of the building. Her heart clenched as
Luca and Vince emerged from the building on either
side of Sgt. Mazure, whose hands remained locked behind his back. Luca was saying something to the man,
giving some kind of orders in his serious, don't-fuck-
with-me voice.

Mazure stumbled into the open air and took in
great gulps of breath, as though the oxygen inside had
been contaminated somehow.

Hero was vaguely aware of Rown grabbing for her
as her feet carried her across the black top. The
golden lights of the parking lamps blurred as moisture
burned in her eyes. She blinked it away, picking up
speed as she jogged over to the front of the building.
Mazure's own lurching steps toward her were shuffling and uncertain, as though his boots were suddenly lined with concrete.

"Stay back, Hero." She didn't have to look at Luca
to know exactly which scowl of disapproval he directed at her.

Her feet didn't stop until she stood directly in front
of Sgt. James Mazure's chin, looking up into his craggy,
bearded face. The red rims of his eyes made the
piercing blue that much more stunning. The whites
had gone pink from tears, and the puffy bags beneath
deepened the wrinkles born of age and exhaustion.
Under the grime and the sun damage, he was pale, as
though he'd just seen a ghost. In fact, he stared down
at her with the expression of a cynic witnessing a
miracle.

They stood for an eternal moment just like that,
the parking lot and its inhabitants disappearing in the

wake of the rare and intense connection that existed between them. Savior and victim. If not for his horrific experience and the resulting emotional disturbance, she wouldn't have survived.

His face crumpled and fresh tears began to run into his beard.

Hero threw her arms around him and supported his weight as he buried his bushy face in her neck and sobbed. He trembled in her grip, his grief interrupted by body-wracking gasps and hiccups. Hero held onto him as though he would drop if she let go, filling her palms with huge handfuls of his oversized jacket. Soft, unbidden noises of comfort escaped her throat now swollen with emotion. They were the sounds someone offered to a screaming baby in the middle of the night, or an overwrought child after a traumatic fall.

She refused to look at anyone, to see the censure on their faces. This man was, in a word, a hero.

"Thank you," she whispered. "Thank you." Her eyes kept blurring with tears, and she let them fall onto the canvas-like material beneath her cheek.

A few repeating metallic clicks sounded, and she blinked Luca's face into view. He didn't look happy, but he gently removed the cuffs from Mazure's wrists. That done, he kept his eyes averted as he stepped back to stand with Di Petro, who gave a suspicious sniff.

The man literally crying on her shoulder made no move to hold her, he just stood passively, trying to contain himself.

"I'm sorry," he finally whispered against her hair. "I'm sorry about that night."

"What could you possibly have to be sorry for?" Hero pulled back, taking his cheeks between her hands. "You saved my life."

"I *left* you there." His voice was raw, the words

having to find their way through the thickness of his mustache. "I tried to stick around, but they—they threw me in that police car and I—I panicked." His shoulders tightened on another hiccup and a noisy sniff. "Then I scared you—with the flowers." He stood straight and looked down at his big, scarred hands like a chastised boy. "I usually head to California for the winter. But knowing that bastard was still after you, I couldn't leave. I wanted you to know that I was still around. I didn't think what it would look like."

"Why didn't you just approach me?" she asked softly. "I've wanted to thank you ever since that night."

A gusty sigh disrupted his whiskers. "The news kind of made it sound like I coulda done it. And I didn't know if they were after me for breaking the police car's window to get away. Plus, I'm... well I just don't approach ladies. You know?"

Hero tossed a questioning look at Luca and Vince.

"There may or may not be an attempt to locate on a suspect for destruction of police property and evasion of arrest that night," Luca muttered.

"Your name's not attached to it, because no one knew it before now," Vince said to Mazure as he flicked a careful glance at Rown. "We sort of didn't bring it up to Trojanowski on purpose."

"Not my department." Rown nodded.

Mazure gave a jerky nod, but didn't turn away from Hero. His stance was uncertain, his eyes full of shadows and tears. "I was gonna just leave you alone," he said wobbly. "But I kept seeing you in that little bundle, bleeding and pale and so tiny... I didn't want you to go through that again."

The bouquet *had* frightened her. It had also confused the details of the case, causing the investigators to wonder if there had been someone working with

John the Baptist. But Hero couldn't bring herself to blame the man in front of her for the trouble he'd un-wittingly caused.

"They told me that I can't watch out for you any-more." He threw a surreptitious head tilt toward the agents behind him.

Hero smiled. "It's a free country."

That drew a smile from Mazure's eyes. Again, she couldn't be sure what his mouth was doing.

"Can we drop you somewhere? Can you go in a car if we keep the windows down?"

Swiping his jacket across his face did little but smear the tear tracks in his weathered cheeks. "Maybe back by the river behind your place. I left Agent Or-ange there."

Ignoring Luca's death glare, Hero asked gently, "What's Agent Orange?"

Mazure's eyes softened and he sniffed again. "He's my cat."

Luca said something foul beneath his breath.

"Of *course* we'll take you to him." Hero took a turn of her own glaring down the three agents in her vicin-ity, heedless that other federal personnel began to file out of the building, tossing them goodbyes and cu-rious glances. If Luca refused, she'd get her car and drive the man her *damn* self. It was the least she could do seeing as he saved her life and all.

Mazure's beard twitched and his eyes crinkled a smile at her again. "Do something else for me kid?"

"What's that?"

"Stay close to that agent man of yours." He leaned in, but didn't really bother to lower his voice. "He's a military-grade asshole, but he's a dangerous man hell-bent on keeping you alive."

That produced a choked laugh from Vince.

Hero gave a little two-finger salute. "Yes, sir."

Any trace of a smile disappeared. The solemn clarity that turned those blue eyes to ice must have served him very well in the military all those years ago. "I mean it, Hero. He's the only chance you got against the evil that's after you."

20

"Tis best to weigh the enemy more mighty than he seems."

— WILLIAM SHAKESPEARE, HENRY V

Hero could barely hear Luca muttering to himself as he drew his gun and put her key in her deadbolt. "Agent Orange. His *damn* cat. Frickin' ridiculous." They were the first words Luca had spoken since they'd left FBI headquarters. Needless to say, the drive home had been quiet and uncomfortable. Which made sense, she supposed. They all had a lot of thinking to do. After they'd retrieved the cat, Hero had sent Mazure to St. Andrew's with a note to Father Michael. They had outbuildings and garages that might work as a temporary but open shelter, and Mazure seemed more than grateful for a respite from the winter chill.

"I don't know, I thought the name was clever." Vince said from behind her. He'd followed them home in his Camero, as Luca's Charger wasn't an official transport vehicle with the safety cage, and no one liked the idea of the unstable Sgt. Mazure sitting behind them while they were at the wheel. "Little orange bastard was kinda cute."

"He tried to bite you." Luca said mirthlessly.

"Yeah, but all the kitties do that," Vince replied with a wicked grin.

Hero turned to Vince with a laugh. "My father would call you a scallywag."

Vince gave her his most winning smile. "Your father would call me a lot worse than that before I was through with ya."

"Consider me warned."

Luca pulled the slide to his weapon back and let it chamber a round with a little more force and noise than was strictly necessary. "Let's just clear the house so I can get some sleep," he said testily as he opened the door and went straight to the alarm pad to enter the code. "It's been a long day."

Hero stepped aside so Vince could follow him into her loft. He gave Hero a conspiratorial wink as he slid past her. They'd pushed Luca far enough for now. She wandered in after them while they did their thing. Her apartment looked plenty normal. Warm, inviting, eclectic and familiar. Hero's eyes went to the fridge and she froze in place until Luca opened it and checked inside.

He paused and made a sound of disgust.

"What?" A familiar surge of anxiety drained the blood from her extremities. "What is it?"

"Just trying to figure out how a fridge can be so full of *nothing* edible," he bitched.

Hero let out a breath on a laugh that was too high-pitched to be identifiable as her own. No dead animals in her fridge, not from a butcher, a deli, *or* a serial killer. Whew.

Letting out a beleaguered sigh, Luca disappeared into her pottery studio.

Di Petro's voice carried from her bedroom. "Batshit psycho *sonofabitch*!"

Luca leapt out of her studio. "Don't move," he ordered as he followed his gun into her room.

Hero swallowed. It wasn't that she obeyed him directly; she just couldn't move on feet that she couldn't feel anymore. A strange permeating numbness radiated from somewhere in her middle and froze her into place. John the Baptist had been in her bedroom. She was certain of it. The voices from inside sounded like they were very far away, or maybe underwater.

"I don't even know what code to call in," Vince said, disgusted. "That's a metric fuck ton of blood."

"I don't think there's a code in the book for this," Luca sounded closer now. More grim than angry, but if Hero knew anything about Special Agent Luca Ramirez, the anger wasn't far in coming.

"God," Vince exclaimed. "This John the Baptist has some balls the size of—"

"What I want to know is where the hell the surveillance team is. Weren't they supposed to be sitting on the house?" Luca clipped, his voice getting equal amounts louder and deeper.

"Probably they followed Mazure and everyone to Headquarters after that all went down."

An expectant silence followed. Some shuffling feet. Vince let another sound of disgust.

"Where the hell are you?" Luca demanded. Another protracted silence told Hero that he was on the phone. "I ordered you to sit on the residence." More silence, shorter this time. "Who approved you to leave after the take down?" Pause. "You *analyzed* the situation? Well, tell you what, get forensics together and get down here so they can help you *analyze* your gigantic fuck up!"

There it is, Hero thought with an amused sort of detachment. Anger. Right on time. Hero lurched toward her door, still numb, but glad the paralysis had been temporary. She watched rather than felt her hand reach for her doorknob, which was sort of unnecessary as the door was already about two-inches ajar. She could have just pushed it open. But still, her hand needed to wrap around something solid and cold and metal to anchor her back into her body.

"Did I fucking stutter?" From the projection of his voice, Luca stood right on the other side of the door. Hero was pretty sure if she opened it, it would run into him. "Yeah? I haven't *begun* to show you a hostile work environment, dickwad. And while you file that personnel complaint make sure to mention your gross incompetence, your insubordination to the agent in charge, and your idiot *analysis* that resulted in a felony incident on a high-profile case. Now quit wasting my *fucking* time and get to work."

"What a mess," Vince muttered. Hero couldn't tell if he referred to whatever horror awaited her in her room, or Luca's conversation. Her hand tightened on the curve of the door knob. She took a few deep breaths.

"I've got to tell Hero." Luca sounded as though he'd rather face the firing squad.

That was her cue. She opened the door until it jammed, probably against Luca's expensive boot, which didn't give her much time. She plunged through the space just big enough for her body and was inundated by the color red before Luca blocked the view with his big frame.

Blood. Buckets and buckets of blood.

"Hero, no. I told you not to move."

"I'm not one of your agents," she quipped, though she sounded more breathless than she'd meant to. She hadn't been aware how difficult breathing had become until she needed enough oxygen to speak. "Let me see." She pushed against him. Compared to her bloodless, trembling hands, the skin beneath his shirt was hot and solid.

His nostrils flared, eyes crackling with an onyx storm. His fists curled at his sides as though considering the option of picking her up by the shoulders and bodily carrying her back into the other room.

For some reason, that strengthened her resolve. "I *need* to see. It was meant for *me*."

He stood for a second longer, then cursed. "Don't touch *anything*," he ordered, and wrenched open the door, palming his phone as he strode from the room, leaving her with the horrific tableau that her bedroom had become.

Hero barely registered Vince's presence until he stood next to her in his favorite loose-limbed posture. "Any idea what it means?" he asked softly.

Hero could only shake her head as she stared, unblinking—unbreathing. She'd known there would be blood. They'd said *blood*, hadn't they? And she'd expected— well honestly, she couldn't really say *what* she'd expected. A dead body, maybe? Another crucified prostitute? Tonight was the Feast of the Immaculate Conception, they'd expected him to kill again, and it looked like he had.

But who? There was no body. It looked like Jackson Pollock broke into her bedroom and used blood as the pigment for his next piece. The metallic tang hung in the air, not as thick as paint or pervasive as death, but light and almost sickly-sweet. The macabre artist had to have stood where they did now, because the wall at their backs was the only one unscathed.

No, that wasn't true. The white space right above her bed had been spared the indiscriminate carnage. It was there the artist had *really* done his work. A monochromatic masterpiece. And they studied it as though it hung in a gallery, inviting their interpretation. *What could the artist have possibly been trying to convey*? They would ask, rubbing their chins and offering obsequious and self-important answers.

Two circles, painted in thick, bloody lines lay one inside the other. Their symmetry was stunningly perfect. Between their outlines, spaced as meticulously as the numbers on a clock, seven block letters mocked them. Vince grabbed her elbow and held her back, pointing at the thin, drying splatters of blood at the foot of her bed. But as soon as she was settled back by his side, he also squinted up at the wall. "YASMODA?" he experimented, but didn't sound convinced. "Maybe it's an acronym for something, or could be an abbreviation. Is it at all familiar to you?"

Hero was pretty certain she shook her head in the negative. At least, he didn't repeat the question. She couldn't seem to tear her eyes from the intricate, confusing design within the inner circle. A vertical line bisected the circle in half, and the left side of the line was conspicuously empty but for what was obviously the forked tail of a devil. The right side of the line however, contained a number of confusing swirls with no particular rhyme or reason.

It occurred to Hero to be alarmed with how numb and cold she felt. It was as though she'd cycled past acceptance, anxiety, horror and hysteria back to a calm sort of analytic remoteness.

This had been John the Baptist. It *felt* like him, and regardless of what Luca thought about feelings and energy, Hero was as certain of it as if his signature graced in the lower right hand corner of the strange depiction. Which, of course, it didn't.

Hero realized she'd given John the Baptist a perfect canvas. Though she generally dressed and decorated in vibrant colors, her bedroom had been the opposite of all that. She'd done it in different shades of white and off white. Up until this very moment, she'd fancied that when she woke up to her simple, white room every morning, it reminded her that her day resembled the clean tableau. It was a blank canvas for her to paint in whatever shade of life she chose. It had been a break from the constant clutter and chaos of the world outside. Clutter and chaos she invited and accepted into her life, but not her bedroom. When she'd fall asleep at night, she would sometimes imagine she slept in a cloud. The visualization would help her separate her consciousness from the world, and she'd drift off with no problems.

Now, her fluffy eggshell comforter had depressed into a bowl for an obscene amount of blood that was currently congealing into a soupy mixture of liquid and—other. Before today, Hero hadn't really known that blood still tried to clot, even separated from its host. She swallowed a few times to keep from contaminating the scene with a reappearance of Knox's Tofurkey.

She suddenly became very aware of her body's reaction to what she was seeing, though her mind still seemed strangely detached from it. Cold seeped through her bones, but her skin felt as though it had caught fire. A deep, trembling vibrated through her, but the hand she held in front of her was absolutely steady. Her mouth was dry and her palms were wet. Her breathing was rapid and her heart pounded everywhere but in her chest. Sound didn't seem to process correctly, and come to think of it, she couldn't trust her vision, either.

Luca returned from the other room. "Trojanowski is rounding up the CSU so they can start their investigation on whatever the fuck that is." He pointed to the macabre sigil on the wall.

"What is he trying to tell me?" Hero wondered out loud. Her voice didn't sound like her own, but like it belonged to someone much younger, someone standing in another room, perhaps. "If he wanted to threaten me, he's certainly pulled that off but... what does that—that *thing* mean?"

Luca reached for her. "Let's go sit down," he said gently. "You really shouldn't be in here."

Hero brushed him off. "I'm serious! Couldn't he have just scrawled some sinister 'I'm going to get you' message like any other self-respecting serial killer? I mean *come on*."

Vince cleared his throat uncomfortably. "Most serial killers don't really..."

Luca shot him a look, and he shut his mouth.

"Does he plan on desecrating every room in my house? Whose blood is that? And how the hell does he keep getting in here? The alarm was on." The hysteria caught up to her. She visibly shook now, chasing the skitters of nervous chill bumps down her arms with her hands. Her skin crawled. The air smelled and tasted like pennies and dirt. Her mouth was full of it, and she couldn't take in a breath through the rot and the stench that seemed to be growing stronger with every second. Shadows crept into her periphery, but they were crimson instead of black.

"Hero." Luca sounded concerned and far away. "Hero, breathe." Strong hands caught her ribcage and jerked her upright before she even realized she'd buckled. Beneath his grip, her ribs struggled to expand with breath, but her body wouldn't seem to cooperate. Panic flared. She was suffocating again, drowning in a puddle of blood and muck, taunted by a ridiculous talisman on her wall that didn't mean shit to her.

The feeling of being lifted off legs that didn't exist anymore tilted her world sideways. The surreal and insistent pressure of his grip against her ribs and beneath her knees grounded her back into some sense of reality.

She still trembled and nausea roiled around in her belly, but had since stopped clawing its way up her throat. She gripped him, leaning her head against his shoulders and inhaling his salty scent and subtle cologne. He was warm—always so warm against her —and strong. He ate up the length of the loft in a few strides and deposited her on the couch much too soon. Hero didn't want to be without him, and to her pleased surprise, he didn't leave her to go back in the bedroom, but sat next to her and settled one of her throw blankets around her shoulders.

"This is our fault," he muttered, rubbing big hands up and down her arms as though her trembling was a result of the cold. Oddly enough, it helped. "The surveillance team should have stayed at the house until the suspect was confirmed. Heads will roll for this."

"Don't be angry at them." Hero leaned her head against his chest, part of her cheek pressing into his leather holster. His gun was tucked into the other side. "They thought this was over, we all did, for just a second there."

Luca's arm went around her, pulling her in close. She could hear the pounding of his own heart against his ribs. He was taking deep breaths, short in, long out. Familiar with the concept, Hero synchronized her breaths with his and instantly felt a little stronger.

Vince came out of her bedroom. He paused when he saw how they were sitting, but if he disapproved, it didn't show on his face. "After pictures are taken of the room and we're cleared to check it out, we'll see if any windows are left open and then we'll narrow down a point of entry and exit."

Hero stiffened. "Do you think he has a key?"

"It's unlikely, but not impossible." Luca stated. His voice sounded deep, resonant, and a little bit muffled as she listened to it through his chest. "Your landlord swears up and down that she's never given anyone but her lawyer and maid a spare key to her house or your apartment. She showed me the papers that said she had the locks changed after every tenant, just in case."

Hero sat up straight, her heart rate spiking once again. "Angora!" she gasped. "Has anyone checked on her?" What if that was her blood? Oh God, what if she'd caused the death of her sweet friend?

Vince was all over it. "She was present and accounted for when they took down Mazure," he said as he headed for the door. "I'm going to go check the big house. Backup should be here any minute."

"I'm coming with you." Hero rose, but was assaulted by a wave of dizziness, and it didn't take much pulling on the part of Luca to get her to sit down, again.

"Like hell you are. You're staying right here. Vince is waiting for backup before barging into the house." He eyed his partner.

"But what if he has Angora? What if he's in there

with her?" Hero felt the hysteria bubble again. "What if we're too late!"

Luca took out his cell phone again and made a call.

It only rang once.

"I answer at this time of night only for tall, dark, and dangerous," Angora purred by way of greeting.

Hero sagged with relief.

"Mrs. Steinman, where are you right now?" Luca asked.

"Angora," the lady insisted. "And I'm where Hero ought to be, beneath you in the bedroom." She laughed at her own naughty joke.

Luca nodded, obviously fighting a smile as he asked. "Is anyone with you? Or has anyone bothered you before or after that incident earlier tonight?"

"I invited Josiah Winthrop over at about eight thirty to keep me company and calm my nerves with a little... *tête-à-tête*, and he left around midnight."

Hero smiled in spite of herself. Angora was such a lively woman. She hoped to have half her spark at that age. That was, if she made it to that age... If she made it to her next birthday.

"Should I be worried, Agent Ramirez?" Angora sounded a little less than concerned. "Was it the killer you caught in my back yard earlier?"

"I'm afraid not." Luca ran a hand over his face and sighed. "Mrs. Steinman—"

"Angora," she said more sharply. "I really must insist."

"Angora." Hero could tell Luca was trying very hard not to sound impatient. She silently applauded him. "Did you disarm the security system when Mr. Winthrop was over?"

Angora took a moment. "Only long enough to let

him in. It rearms itself automatically. But I double checked tonight."

"How long do you think that was?"

"It takes thirty seconds."

"Long enough for someone to break in here," Vince observed.

Sirens wailed in the distance and Vince made a gesture that he was going to go check the main house.

Luca nodded. "We're sending Di Petro down to check and make sure your house is safe, can you meet him at the front door?"

"Why? They already cleared my house hours ago."

Luca took a deep breath, but Angora beat him to it.

"Did something else happen? Is Hero all right?"

"I'm right here, Angora," Hero chimed in. "But... he came into my room and left me a—a message there while I was gone."

"How is that possible?" Angora whispered.

"You're absolutely certain that no one else has the disarm code?" Luca pressed.

"No. It was changed when Hero got home from Mexico and the only person I've told the code to, besides Hero, is you and Agent Di Petro."

Luca frowned, and Hero wanted more than anything to know what he was thinking. It couldn't have been Di Petro, the house was cleared after they arrested Mazure by multiple agents, and then Vince had been with them all night at FBI headquarters.

"No one has an extra key?" Luca asked. "Not Mr. Winthrop? Do either of you keep one under a mat or in your car?"

Hero shook her head. "I used to keep one in a glass planter, but you made me stop that after the incident with the goat head in my fridge. I told you I gave it to my parents in case of emergency."

Luca made an affirmative noise.

"I even took my key back from the maid service after all this business began," Angora said. Rustling on the other end sounded like she was walking in her high-heeled slippers. "I think that's Agent Di Petro at the door."

Vince's unmistakable accent filtered through the phone, though his words were muffled.

Hero blew out a breath of relief. At least her friend and landlady was safe.

"Angora," she said, effectively cutting off the woman's flirty greeting.

"Yes, darling?"

"I should—probably move out. I feel like it's not safe anymore and it's all because of me. This is becoming... There's just so much..." Blood. Danger. Death.

"You hush. I won't hear of it. I adore you, and I honestly haven't been a part of something so salacious since the Cold War and the communist scare in Holly-wood. You worry about yourself, dear, I'll be all right." She paused. "But maybe—I'll stay with Josiah a little while. Until it's safer. He's been trying to talk me into spending the holidays with him, and perhaps I'll re-lent. Just this once."

"Might be a good idea," Luca agreed. "Make sure to stay close to Agent Di Petro until they clear your house. Di Petro will stay with you while you pack and drive you to Mr. Winthrop's if you need."

"That will be *perfect*," Angora sighed. "It is always good for the man you're with to see you driven about town by someone younger with a sportier car."

Luca chuckled as they hung up, but then he sobered as he turned to Hero and saw the look on her face. The sirens grew louder, some of them already on the property and they shared a moment of extreme exhaustion just sitting on that couch and clutching each other's hands. Hero knew what came next. Knew it would take hours. They would strip her bedroom of everything and take it into their lab. She felt violated. They would paw through her things with their powdered latex gloves. Leave the impossible residue of fingerprint dust. Ask her a million gentle, yet probing questions. She began to finger the scars on her free hand.

"He just made his fatal mistake, Hero." Luca's voice interrupted her thoughts and she focused on his swarthy, brutal features. "He thinks he left us a threat, but he left us a clue, and a pretty damned precise one. I'm going to find out just what the hell that is, and once I do, I'll nail whoever put it there."

21

"O' What may man within him hide,
though angel on the outward side!"

— WILLIAM SHAKESPEARE, MEASURE FOR
MEASURE

"Mind telling me what this is?" Luca slapped the folder down on the desk in front of Father Michael and propped himself against the corner, purposely invading his space. The young priest almost jumped out of his Ikea chair, but to his credit, he regained his composure quickly.

Vince leaned against the open door to Father Michael's minimalist office, loudly chewing his gum. Luca had asked him to leave Hero with Rown to conduct these interviews. He had a feeling he'd need a witness.

"When you told me you wanted to see me for an interview, I wasn't expecting blood." Father Michael's thin lips whitened around the edges.

Yeah well, neither was Hero last night, but if *she* had to face it, then so could the men who'd just leapt to the top of his suspect list.

"Tell me what it means," Luca repeated. He knew what the symbol stood for of course. An internet image search and a few other documents had made the research relatively easy, but he wanted to hear it straight from the mouth of God, so to speak.

Father Michael picked up the picture of the symbol painted on the wall above Hero's bed, looking at it as though a monster might leap right off the page. "Where did you see this?"

"Is it familiar to you?"

"Yes. It's—I mean it's not exactly *familiar*. I would call it more recognizable—is that real blood? There's so much." His hands began to shake. "Is Hero okay?"

Luca leaned forward, keeping his arms crossed over his chest and his register at an acceptable decibel. "I don't know if you comprehend how interviews work, but the general idea is *I* ask the fucking questions, and *you* answer them."

He had to give the priest props, the man met his eyes with the steady, unwavering stare of an innocent man.

Or a sociopath.

"Are you allowed, as a government agent, to always use such foul and abusive language while interviewing witnesses?"

Luca smirked. "No, but I'll tell you right now, I'm not looking at a witness. I'm looking at a suspect in a serial murder case. Though I'm technically supposed to inform you that if you want to lodge a complaint with my superiors, feel free." He leaned in even closer. "They'll add it to the pile."

Father Michael cast a quiet plea for help to Vince, who have him a helpless shrug. "He always gets to be the 'bad cop,' I'm too handsome."

The priest returned to staring at the picture in front of him, his shoulder flexing against the fabric of his black cassock. Luca noted that, though the garment was loose and slimming, he filled out the robes better than in the previous months. Father Michael had been working out. Building his strength?

"I can't shake the feeling, Agent Ramirez, that this treatment is personal as well as professional. Have I done something to offend you?"

Luca narrowed his eyes. "Personally? I think you're worse than a wolf in sheep's clothing. I think you're a snake."

Father Michael rolled back from his desk, putting some distance between him and where Luca stood. Luca followed him inch for inch.

"I'd like you to—to stand farther off." Father Michael gestured over to where Vince remained unmoving, unaffected.

"Why, Father? I'm not going to hurt you. The door's open. There's a witness."

The words weren't meant as a consolation, and Luca's soul flared in a dark triumph at the fear in the other man's eyes as he used his feet to roll himself to the far edge of the modern, black lacquered desk. Maybe he should dial it back, he was enjoying this a bit too much, but Father Michael was the type of man who needed to be cornered before the truth came out.

"You want to know what offends me?" Luca took another step forward. "The way you look at Hero."

"I don't—I don't know what you mean." He'd backed into the plastic fichus tree in the corner of his small office, upsetting the dust on the leaves. They exploded into the shafts of light from the small window like little flurries of the priest's racing thoughts.

"Bullshit," Luca pressed. "You don't think I watch you look at her? I saw the way you held her hand in the kitchen. The way your eyes find her in a crowded room."

"No! I don't—"

"You're supposed to be a man of God, but you're a fraud, aren't you? Do you have a thing for redheads Father Michael? Does guilt drive you to ritualistically kill the ones you pay to fu—"

"Stop! *Please*! Don't say it." Father Michael held up his hands as though to ward off a physical blow. "Yes, I *look* at Hero. I may be a man of God, but I'm still a *man*. That woman would tempt a Saint. I'm just a priest! But I have never in the past, and have no intention to indulge my temptation. I'm a stronger man than that."

Just how strong was he? Strong enough to lift a cross with a woman tied to it? Luca straightened, then leaned back against the desk again.

Father Michael calmed a bit when Luca backed off, his eyes were earnest and pleading as he lowered his hands. "I've committed my own share of sins, Agent Ramirez, but I would *never* hurt those women. I understand that symbol may cast suspicion on those closely connected with the Catholic faith, but why are you targeting me, specifically?"

"We know all about your sins, Michael Sullivan," Vince said softly.

The man froze, the whites of his eyes visible now.

"They started out small, didn't they?" Vince walked closer, still deceptively relaxed. "Prep school parties, pills, some coke, a few DUI arrests, one too many charges on Daddy's credit cards to bail you out. You were rich, the original preppie playboy, untouchable by us 'government agents.'"

Luca picked up the ball. "These women aren't the first prostitutes connected to you to die of drowning."

Father Michael slowly leaned against the back of his chair, reminding Luca of a tire losing its air. His defined chin crinkled as he visibly fought a surge of powerful emotion. "That was... more than a decade ago. I was... a kid... a juvenile. I thought those records were sealed."

"We can't bring them up in court, but that doesn't stop us from using information about your past in our investigation." Luca pushed himself away from the desk with enough force to rattle the paperclip tray. "Besides, there was enough press about it in The Hamptons to make the juvenile records obsolete. Their versions are always more interesting than the official reports."

Father Michael wordlessly rolled his chair back beneath his desk and stared at the bloody symbol with unblinking eyes. "That incident was so different than this. There was no blood. No religion. No... intent. Just a few guys taking my dad's yacht for a midnight joyride in the bay with booze, drugs—hired women—and no thought for consequences." His voice was bleak and toneless. He didn't look up from the gruesome picture in front of him. "No one pushed those two women over the side. They were drinking and dancing. Then they were running. Then they were...gone. It wasn't murder, it was an *accident*. A horrible, stupid, God-forsaken accident, and I took—take —absolute culpability for it." Father Michael's tear-filled eyes found Luca's. "It's why I went into the church. I'm devoting my life to redemption, to penance."

Luca studied Father Michael for a silent beat. What would Father McMurtry call the apparitions of sorrow, pain, loss, and guilt visibly aging the young and vibrant man in front of him?

Demons. Like the one symbolized in blood on Hero's wall.

"Tell me about the symbol, Father Michael," Luca murmured. "Tell me what it means to you."

Father McMurtry's graveled voice threaded through the tension. "Is all this really necessary?"

Luca looked over his shoulder as the old man entered the room. Dressed in an identical cassock and leaning heavily on his cane, Father McMurtry stood in the doorway next to Vince. A tremor in the hand clutching his cane was the only indication of emotion the elder priest exhibited. Luca wasn't singling Father Michael out. He was there for the both of them.

"I was coming to talk to you next." Luca indicated the chair across from Father Michael's desk. "Maybe you can answer a few questions since you're here."

Vince lifted an eyebrow. The plan was to talk to them each separately, to compare their stories and their take on the symbol.

Luca shrugged. He had a feeling that McMurtry's appearance wasn't an accident. He wanted to see where this took them.

McMurtry eyed the chair with equal parts suspicion and distaste. Father Michael's office was, unsurprisingly, a direct contrast to his older counterpart's. Instead of warm-toned wood and heavy ancient furniture, it was sparsely furnished with file drawers, a cheap laminate desk, and mesh swivel chairs.

"What's that you have there?" McMurtry pointed to the open file in front of Father Michael.

"Asmodeus," Father Michael murmured, almost imperceptibly.

"Come again?" The old man limped around the

desk, shuffling past Luca with a paternal pat on the shoulder, and stared down at the picture, seemingly unfazed by the blood. "Oh, *him*. A sly devil, that one, but I don't see why he has much of anything to do with the past. Father Michael has atoned for that night in the eyes of Heaven." He gave Luca a meaningful look. "*And* the eyes of the law."

"The past repeats itself, *Padre*," Luca pointed out. "We'd be foolish to dismiss it."

Father McMurty rested both hands on his cane and seemed to consider that before he nodded. "I can't argue with that, Agent Ramirez, but I'm convinced Father Michael is incapable of being this so-called John the Baptist." He made a face and reached for the photo. "But he, *he* could be the affliction, the reason for the entire tragic affair."

"What did you call him?" Vince chimed in. "Asmodeus?"

"What do you know about him, *Padre*?" Luca asked.

It was Father Michael who answered, his gaze still glued to his desk. "We learned about Asmodeus in seminary," he said quietly. "He's one of the seven princes of hell under Lucifer, the Emperor. He has seventy-two legions of demons under his command and is responsible for all the gambling houses in the underworld."

Vince snorted. "Hero have a gambling problem we don't know about?"

"Nope," Luca denied. They had all her financial records. She was a bit of a spend thrift, but never showed any tendencies to gamble.

"Then why would this guy's freaky symbol be painted in blood on her wall?"

"I can't think of a single reason," Father Michael put a dejected forehead in his hands.

"Is that so, Father Michael?" McMurtry put a hand on his shoulder. "You can't think of a *single* reason?"

Father Michael looked over his shoulder at his superior in confusion.

Luca held his breath. Now they were getting somewhere. Asmodeus wasn't just a prince of hell. He was one of seven. And, according to his research, each prince of hell corresponded with a cardinal sin. *This* was what he'd wanted to hear from the priests.

"Lust," Father Michael whispered the word as though it was a prayer. "Asmodeus is a demon of lust."

McMurtry nodded. "Yes, there, I think, will be the answer the agents are looking for."

Father Michael seemed to have an idea. "Do you know what the *Malleus Maleficarum* is?"

Luca searched his memory. "It's a book on the practice of persecution of witches back in the day."

"The fifteenth century, actually. Asmodeus, or Asmoday as he is known to some and depicted here in this symbol, is written in the *Malleus Maleficarum* as the demon of lust. He specifically is an enemy to St. John."

"John the Baptist?"

Father Michael shook his head. "No. John the Apostle, the younger brother of James."

Luca considered this. The names were too close to be a coincidence.

"He's also mentioned in the teachings of Solomon, and, according to Pope Gregory the First, Asmodeus was once a seraphim before his fall from grace."

"Those teachings are rather apocryphal, Father Michael, and not necessarily the canonized traditions of the church." Father McMurtry held out his hand. "I have some other reference material on these demons if you'd like to follow me into my office."

Luca looked at Vince who nodded.

"Come with us, Father Michael." McMurtry limped toward the door. "You may learn something new."

22

"The lunatic, the lover and the poet are of
     imagination all compact:
One sees more devils than vast hell can hold."

— WILLIAM SHAKESPEARE, A MIDSUMMER
                        NIGHT'S DREAM

"You sure you're up for talking to Professor I-used-
to-bone-your-girlfriend after all of that?" Vince
asked.

Luca's hand tightened on the steering wheel as he
merged on to the I-5 toward the University of Portland.
"Hero's *not* my girlfriend." Was he the only one who
seemed to remember that?

"Oh yeah?" Vince made a rude noise.

"You got something to say to me?"

"Yeah, actually. Why the hell not?" His partner
seemed to come to a decision. "You two are kinda perfect for each other."

Luca glanced over at him. "Have you lost your
damn mind?"

"Hear me out. Just because it doesn't look good on
paper doesn't mean it's not the right thing. I mean, say

you two wait for this case to be over to avoid career consequences. How could that be wrong?"

"Let me count the ways."

"You could at least, I don't know, get her to work your bone a few times, she obviously wants it, and then you'd be a hell of a lot easier to live with."

"No I wouldn't, trust me." Luca fixed his eyes straight ahead for a few silent miles. That was the plan, wasn't it? After the danger passed, they would rip each other's clothes off and fuck the tension out of each other.

Then what?

As cavalier as both he and Hero were about relationships, whatever brewed between them was different, and they both knew it. If he took her to bed, he might not leave the next morning. He'd spend a weekend. She'd make him coffee. He'd go to work. They'd make plans to do it again. Suddenly he'd have a drawer, then room in the closet. A toothbrush. They'd start to mingle their groups of friends. That thought made him smirk, but the smile quickly vanished as the more long-term vision stretched out before him, as congested and dangerous to navigate as the freeway.

There were no rose bush hedges and double ovens in their future. No picket fences or joint bank accounts. She'd push him for something he couldn't give her. He'd try to dominate and control her. She'd withdraw, or worse, be dishonest. He'd lose his temper and do something he'd regret for the rest of his days. It was a cycle he'd seen time and time again, and not just in his own life. He just—couldn't let that happen. Not to her. Not to them.

"Can I have a pass at her, then?" Vince asked glibly. "I'm pretty sure I got the wrong assignment, here."

"Try it, and I'll rip your guts out your ass and use them as a jump rope."

Vince just laughed. "That's what I thought." He unzipped the leather binder on his lap and picked the memory chip from the pocket recorder and paper-clipped it to the priests of St. Andrew's files before selecting a different one for their upcoming meeting with Professor Graham. "Priests, man." He moved on to safer territory. "Is it just me, or do they always seem guilty because of all the times they play the creepy bad guy in the movies?"

Luca welcomed the change of subject. "I don't know what to think. They certainly had a lot of religious information about the demon symbol. None of it particularly helpful or relevant, but I don't know a lot of religious professionals so well-versed in all that historical minutiae. Seems like shady bullshit to me." They'd spent the better part of an hour reading canonized texts on the very creative historic details of the Catholic Church regarding their take on the denizen of Hell. They learned of lesser demons in the Legions of Asmodeus, famous reported possessions and exorcisms of his throughout the ages—both male and female—and numerous anecdotal narratives of confrontations with him, all with little to no supporting evidence. Luca didn't feel any closer to understanding just why this demon was linked with Hero, specifically. Was it because she inspired lust? Was that the connection with the prostitutes? Seemed like kind of a weak link, but worth exploring further.

Vince shrugged. "I don't know a lot of religious professionals, period. But pretty much everything they did seemed suspect to me. Anyone willing to take a vow of celibacy just freaks me the fuck out. That shit is unnatural." He shuddered as though someone just walked over his grave. "You get those medical records on Father McMurtry back from Ireland?"

Luca shook his head. "Could take weeks, it's been so long since he lived there, and he hasn't really visited any one here in the states for complications related to his hip."

"Well, there's definitely tension between those two. I don't know if Father Michael is covering for the old man, or McMurtry is threatened by someone younger and more hip in his territory, but there's something going on there." Vince's shrewd assessment paralleled Luca's own thoughts, precisely.

"If you think about it, Father McMurtry would have to have faked that limp for thirty years in order to have pulled this off. I mean, that's just... fucking excessive. Also, why wait until now to commit these murders? Why not do it when he's younger and more capable? I mean he's got to be in his sixties."

"You trying to talk yourself out of suspecting him, Ramirez? You got a soft spot for the *padre*?"

Luca thought of the conversation he'd shared with the old man in his office.

There are many ways to exorcize a demon, Agent Ramirez.

Had he been trying to tell him something? Was it a confession? Had he been pointing the finger at himself? At Father Michael? Or had he just been doing his job, offering spiritual counseling to someone who'd come looking for answers?

"The only person I have a soft spot for is your mom." Luca joked as he took the exit onto Lombard Street and turned toward the university. "She treated me so good last night."

"Yeah, she said something about your spot being

soft." His partner made a lewd gesture and chuckled, then began to fiddle with the recorder.

Luca smiled, too distracted to think of a comeback. He found himself thinking about how he'd been on this very drive the night Hero had been fished out of the river. He had to admit, it was much more comfortable to consider a perverted asshole like Professor Alec as the perpetrator of these crimes. He had all the traits. Narcissism, predatory behavior, a practiced and grandiose charm, and the pathological ability to lie without remorse.

Had Professor Alec taken refuge at the college that night after dumping Hero in the river? Had Luca been driving past John the Baptist on his way home from work every night for the past year?

The thought caused tendrils of ice to lick at his extremities. The Burlington Bridge crossed the Willamette exactly halfway in between the University of Portland and Cathedral Park. It would have been the easiest thing in the world to release a dying Hero into the river and hide out at the college.

Vince's initial question had been appropriate. Was he up for talking to the professor? On Luca's list, the guy rated somewhere between fuckwad and shit-stain, and that was just his personality. Toss in the fact that he'd slept with, and subsequently cheated on, Hero, and Luca had to force himself not to instantly dick-punch the guy on sight. An image of Hero wrapped in those bloody vestments reared in his mind's eye, and he barely escaped running a red light. Sometimes in quiet moments, he saw her reach out for him with those holes in her hands. Pictured her bruised and swollen face as she fought for her life in the hospital, and a little bit more of his humanity chipped away and disappeared.

If Professor Alec was responsible for that night—well—Luca's sixth kill might not be so righteous, legal, or particularly quick. Hell, he might just be forced to brush up on his Old Testament and nail the professor's ass to the wall. Or a railroad tie. Whatever was handy, really. A dark satisfaction surged through him. Eye for an eye, motherfucker.

"Don't get that look," Vince warned. "I know that look. It's the I'm-going-to-do-something-that-will-cause-my-partner-paperwork look. You just lock that shit down, Ramirez, I swear to God."

"If I do what I'm thinking about doing, there won't *be* any paperwork," Luca promised. "They'll never find the body."

"Yeah well, make sure they don't," Vince said in that voice that made Luca wonder if the guy was really just kidding. "I don't want to break in a new partner, and I *especially* don't want to be lead on this case. No thanks. I'll take the next serial killer. Maybe I'll get lucky and it'll be your average, run of the mill, the voices-in-my-head-told-me-to-do-it kind of thing. None of this demons, and priests, and prostitutes, and professors. It's all a little too *Da Vinci Code* for me, not to mention the alliteration."

"Tell me about it," Luca muttered as he pulled onto Willamette Blvd. The river came into view sporadically in between dense greenery and the occasional nineteen forty's neighborhood. A large portion of the older homes were sub-divided into rentals, like Luca's, providing housing for the transient nature of a student's lifestyle. He resided a little north and west of the college in a nicer neighborhood that mainly catered to students with families and even a few adjunct professors.

Luca turned into one of the many lots and parked,

then waited for Vince to get the malfunctioning digital voice recorder sorted before they stepped out of the car.

The University of Portland's layout was much like any other college campus established more than a hundred years ago, complete with the requisite stately brick buildings, towered bell clock which chimed the hour, and landscaped academic quad in the center crisscrossed by sidewalks full of students. The further you traveled from the center, the more modern and less elegant the buildings became. Luca had always been disappointed by this. When he'd attended college, he'd appreciated the ponderous monuments to academia built by the founders. They'd established a sense of place, an affinity for education and knowledge. Outer buildings usually felt like some architect with a boner for the unfortunate fifties threw together the building equivalent of a fold-it-yourself cardboard box complete with florescent lighting, confusing hallways, and stupid student renderings of "art" that no one particularly liked or understood. Being a Catholic institution, The University of Portland fared better in that respect than some state colleges, but barely.

Luca and Vince were a bit conspicuous during their short walk to the Buckley Center. Their suits and ties stood out amongst the sparse but assorted co-eds splattered among the campus.

Vince's eyes followed one particular blonde into a building across the way and he bit into his knuckles. "*God,* I miss college."

Luca opened the door to the Buckley building and consulting the helpful map tacked to a corkboard, which was rapidly disappearing beneath advertisements for roommates, bands, and one very concerning amateur acupuncturist. Finding the correct room number for Professor Graham, they navigated the nearly empty hallway in silence.

Some of the more tenured faculty members wore what seemed to be the accepted professorial uniform of wrinkled slacks and light-colored blazers, some equipped with elbow patches, or dull roped sweaters. Apparently, intellectualism was mutually exclusive to hairbrushes and shaving regularly.

Luca reached up and ran a hand across his black hair, cut short enough to the scalp to hide its tendency to curl, and peered over at Vince, whose light brown hair was clean cut and disciplined with a comb and some gel.

Christ. Conspicuous didn't begin to cover it. They stood out like Mormon missionaries at a swinger's bar.

Wide gazes followed them the entire way. Some feminine eyes banked with naked interest, the male ones with curiosity or, in some cases, suspicion.

They turned the corner to the hallway where they would find Professor Graham's office clustered among those of his colleagues in the History Department. His next hour was set aside for office appointments for his theology grad students to discuss their final grades.

They'd just have to reschedule.

A receptionist, who could have stunt-doubled for Bea Arthur looked up from her desk where she sat and polished bifocals hanging from a chain around her neck. "Can I help you?"

Vince drew his badge from his suit-coat pocket and threw some extra wattage into his smile. "We're here to see Professor Alexander Graham."

"You're not students," she informed them.

"No, ma'am," Luca said. "We're with the Federal Bureau of—"

"I can read your identification, sir," she interrupted, glaring up a Luca with a look that told him she'd already made up her mind not to like him. "Do you have an appointment?"

"We don't," he confessed.

"Then, do you have a warrant?"

Luca flinched. She'd just said the word that made every law enforcement officer across the nation cringe. Getting a warrant just to talk to someone meant you didn't have enough evidence to arrest, interrogate, or search, and the suspect didn't have to talk to you or allow you into their home or place of business. Which was true in this case, and also a huge pain in the ass.

Luca could almost see Vince pull up his big-boy pants and accept the challenge posed by the battle axe in front of him. Vince never met a woman he couldn't charm. His partner checked her nameplate and his smiled turned from friendly to fiendish.

"Mary-Louise St. Clair. Is that Mrs. or Miss St. Clair?"

"It's *Ms*," she said sourly.

"Fair enough. We're working on a very important case, and we're hoping that Professor Graham can use his expertise to help us identify some iconography. I've heard this department was the best in the state."

The woman's pinched features relaxed a little, interest flaring in her gaze, whether for Vince or the case, Luca couldn't be sure. "We do have a sterling reputation. Is this iconography religious in nature?"

"I can't discuss the details of a case, Ms. St. Clair. I have to keep my secrets," Vince chided with a devilish grin. "But, I'll tell you what, clear the professor's schedule for the next half hour and you can grill him about what we discussed. I'll bet you can be *very* persuasive."

She preened beneath his attention and Luca rolled

his eyes. It was like the Southie had some kind of voodoo mind-control powers.

"Come on, Mary-Louise, we all know who runs this office. You can make anything happen."

She returned to cleaning her glasses, obviously discomfited. "And what is the... the nature of the case? Is it very terrible?"

Vince leaned on her desk. "The worst you can imagine," he said conspiratorially. "The details would shock and appall you."

Returning her glasses to the bridge of her hawkish nose, she considered Vince for a moment. "I can give you fifteen minutes."

"I'd consider it a personal favor." Vince threw a victorious smile over his shoulder, and Luca just shook his head in amazement.

"You'll find Professor Graham down the short hallway, second to the last door on your left." She pointed past a cluster of front offices behind her desk and down a hall haphazardly lined with file cabinets that often overlapped tall wooden doors.

"You're a gem, Mary-Louise." Vince strolled past her desk, rapping his knuckles on it.

Luca nodded at her, but by the time she inclined her head at him, all the warmth had left her eyes. Figured.

Professor Graham's office door stood slightly ajar as though he expected visitors. Luca enjoyed a stab of perverse pleasure at the man's reaction to his presence in the doorway. He smothered the initial shock and displeasure with a chillier expression. He shot for polite condescension, but the arrow landed closer to agitated impatience.

"Agent Ramirez." He clicked a few things on his laptop and snapped the lid closed before he stood and offered his hand over the desk. "What brings you here?"

Luca shook hands briefly as he could get away with, noting that the professor surreptitiously wiped his palm on his tan slacks when they were through.

Feeling's mutual, douche bag. "This is my partner, Agent Di Petro."

"Professor." Vince's handshake was a bit friendlier.

"Call me, Alec, please." He casually piled a few papers and files on top of his closed laptop. "I'll admit I'm quite surprised to see you here. Is something amiss?"

Luca and Vince exchanged a look. Amiss? Seriously?

"We're here in a professional capacity, actually." He reached his hand out to Vince, who gave him the folder with the macabre photo. "We needed help deciphering a symbol."

Alec regarded the closed folder with unrestrained skepticism. "Don't you have people who can do that? I imagine the FBI has quite an intelligence department." He motioned to the organized chaos that constituted his desk. "As you can see, I'm very busy. I'm in a rush to finalize grades before the holiday and I have scheduled meetings with students today."

Luca was this close to grabbing the pretentious dipshit by his toolbag sweater and grinding his face into his own desk. He took a deep breath in through his nose, released it while counting and summoned a smile.

Professor Alec blanched.

Must not have been the right kind of smile.

Flipping open the file folder, Luca held the picture suspended over the cluttered desk. "We've exhausted our resources." He peppered his lie with some truth.

"Even went so far as to consult with Catholic clergy, but it was decided we needed a more *expert* opinion. As you happen to be the only iconography expert I'm acquainted with, I thought I'd give you a stab at it. But if you're not able, I'll just—"

"That's Hero's bedroom." Alec snatched the photo out of Luca's hand in a quick and desperate move, bringing it closer to his face. "Jesus, is she okay?"

The reminder that the professor was acquainted with Hero's bedroom almost had Luca leaping across the desk. "She's safe," he forced out through tight lips. *Safer than you are right now, asshole.*

"This was *him*, wasn't it? John the Baptist?" Alec's eyes touched every detail of the page, whether scanning or savoring, it was hard to tell.

"That's the theory," Luca confirmed, watching the man's face very closely. "It's the symbol of Asmodeus, a demon—"

"Lust." Alec's gaze flicked to Luca, both meaningful and secretive. "Apropos, wouldn't you say?"

Luca's nostrils flared as he had a fantasy of setting Professor Alec's scholar-meets ken-doll face on fire and then putting it out.

With a hammer.

Vince saved the professor's life by reminding Luca there was a witness. "So we know the demon's name. We know he's supposedly one of the seven Princes of Hell whose patron sin is lust. The Catholic priests told us as much. They weren't so clear about the origin of the symbol though, nor did they have much of an idea why it would end up on a victim's wall."

"That's because they only had the education of a Catholic perspective." Alec stepped from behind his desk, gave Luca a wider berth than needed, and ran his fingers over a series of old leather-bound resource books on the floor to ceiling shelves that lined the far wall. Probably, he had the resource material available in digital format, but Professor Alec was the kind of guy that liked to pose with an old book in his hands.

"Asmodeus or Asmoday as the symbol indicates in the picture has origins much older than the Catholic church. Older than Christ, if my memory serves." Selecting a book, he opted to reclaim his place behind the desk, which amused Luca to no end. Was he trying to establish authority as the one behind the desk? Or did he just need a barrier between them? Either way, it was a good strategic move.

Luca noted the soft, effeminate fingers as they flew through pages and his lip curled in disgust. Those hands had touched Hero. Probably everywhere. Had they pleasured her? Had they been worthy of the epic morning after coffee?

He swallowed a sudden onslaught of nausea. Jealousy had never been a problem of his. Scratch that— He'd always been smart and careful enough to understand the chemical equation of his territorial tendencies combined with any feelings of possession and fear of losing something he cared about was a volatile concoction. He avoided it like the red button on a missile launcher. Tie that together with his short fuse and the fact that he was perpetually armed, and the situation became downright explosive.

As he stood in the quiet, sun-lit office of a man who'd once been Hero's lover, feeling his blood begin to catch fire, Luca forced himself to focus on the one thing that could bring him back from the brink. The cipher in blood.

Professor Alec's movements were frenetic and excited as he searched through the reference book. He seemed less perturbed by the blood than by the symbol, itself. Could that be because he'd put it there? "Here we are!" He smoothed out a page with an almost exact replica of the symbol in front of him, this one stamped on the acid free paper and the size of a small thumbnail in thick, dark ink.

"Before Asmodeus became a Catholic demon, he was Asmoday. According to the Apocryphal and Gnostic Gospels, he was a fallen arc-angel who followed Satan during the Great War in heaven. Before that, he was a Talmudic Judaic demon by the name of 'Ashmedai' who was the result of an adulterous affair between the Devil and Lilith, Adam's first wife before Eve. But in every incarnation, his main reason for existing was promoting the excess of lust and all the foreboding variables thereof."

"Such as?" Vince prompted.

Alec didn't look up from the page as he shrugged. "Oh, the usual stuff, perversion, rape, incest, homosexuality, adultery."

"Prostitution?" Luca supplied.

"Of course." Alec's finger skimmed the page as though caressing a lover, causing Luca to shudder in revulsion once more.

"It says here his genesis was Persian, the name derived from the words *ashma daeva* literally meaning 'raging fiend.' So there are also violent connotations connected with his origins." His eyes again found Luca and he recited his next words, not glancing down at the book once. "According to ancient Persian texts, those afflicted with an *ashma daeva* are forever cursed to be a prisoner to their lusts, and not necessarily those of a sexual nature but, more specifically, their lust for vengeance and blood. Those possessed by this particular demon tend to raid and conquer, to pillage and steal things that were not theirs to begin with."

Luca's vision narrowed into a tunnel, focused entirely on the unspoken suggestion in Professor Alec's sardonic expression. Was lust a component of this case? Absolutely. Prostitutes were the economically available fulfillment of sexual desire. His own lust for Hero may or may not be taken into consideration by the killer. Her actions to incite lust remained in this unequivocal grey area. But here was an unexplored aspect that had completely escaped them all until this very moment. What if the message *wasn't* intended for Hero?

"May I see that?" Luca's voice sounded decidedly less threatening as he reached for the book splayed on the desk.

"Of course." Alec picked up the book and handed it to him. "Be careful not to break the spine."

Luca clenched his teeth, but nodded, feeling like he'd just been handed someone's newborn. His heart wasn't just pounding, it threw itself against his sternum as though trying to beat its way out of a cage. The words blurred a bit as he scanned them. Apparently, there was no recourse available if afflicted with the *ashma daeva.* It was some karmic blight of birth. The victim, or deserving villain depending on your perspective, was damned to spend his life fighting non-stop lust for power, vengeance, and death until their deeds stained their soul beyond any hope for redemption. In this life or the next.

Vince, who'd been reading over his shoulder, made a thoughtful sound. "Respect to those ancients. They were hardcore."

"Yes," Alec agreed. "With a perspective like that, it's little wonder the more accepting and forgiving traditions of Christianity, Islam, Judaism and Buddhism took root with the masses."

"I think there are several million corpses who would argue the idea that neither Christianity, Judaism, nor Islam offers much in the way of forgiveness or acceptance." Vince's eternal cynicism dripped from his voice like acid.

"Perhaps not for the mortal body," the professor conceded. "Yet outlined within all Abrahamic scripture, be it the Bible, Apocryphal texts, the Torah or the Quran, are rather precise, specific, and often interchangeable commandments for procuring the safety and redemption of one's eternal soul."

Alec turned to address Luca, once again, "You see, our Id might be worried about the survival of our physical forms, but our Ego and Super-Ego can't process the idea of our consciousness ceasing to exist after death. As such, we endlessly search for ways to impress a Universal Creator so He may allow us to continue on as we are or furthermore, to cosmically advance somehow. Because of our predatory natures, this tends to turn into climbing to the top of a mountain of martyrs to reach out to God. The Super-Ego convinces the Ego that each kill is righteous. That each soul, though a creation of your God, or theirs, continues on as will yours. And thus, instead of robbing someone of their life, you've only facilitated the inevitable soul's meeting of the Divine, be that what it may.

"It's truly an ingenious way to explain away our more... barbaric tendencies, wouldn't you say? When sanctified by God; hate crimes, sectarianism, torture, murder, even genocide all become..." Alec spread his fingers as though to encompass all those things. "Acceptable."

Luca wrinkled his forehead. "Yes, but society as a

whole has decided that all of those things are *not* acceptable."

"Only *very* recently," Alec argued. "Who's to say? Are these tendencies evil? Or merely animal? Humans are arguably the only sentient creatures who feel true empathy. We don't cull the herd, as it were, or abandon our weak." His thin features curled into a wry form of amusement. "At least, civilized society likes to think so. We're the only ones on the planet who have the tendency to feel remorse for ending another's life. Doesn't it logically follow, then, that we'd scramble to smother that remorse with excuses for our unavoidable inhumanity toward each other? Why take responsibility for your own selfish brutal behavior toward your fellow men when you can blame it on the influence of a devil? Better yet, why allow your soul suffer the eternal consequences when a demigod will do it for you?"

"You mean Christ?"

"Christ, yes, and the myriad of other allegorical virgin-born, half-human/half-God, bringers of light, enlightenment and saviors of humanity—many whom were resurrected from the dead, by the way—including Krishna, Horus, Apollo, Mithras, Baal, Osiris, Adonis—"

"We get it." Vince held up a hand. "What are you saying, all this has to do with John the Baptist?"

The professor's lips pulled away from his teeth in a victorious smile of relish he likely never showed to his students.

Luca decided to steal his thunder, just because he was sick of hearing the guy enjoy the sound of his own voice. "Serial killers are regarded as a particular kind of evil within our society because they tend to kill without remorse." He speared the professor with a meaningful look of his own.

"Precisely my point, Agent Ramirez."

Luca nodded. The FBI labeled serial killers as psychopaths or sociopaths because of the driving force behind their kills or because of the horror of the crimes, themselves. But from the beginning of this ordeal, it was evident that John the Baptist was a different breed of killer. Hero had described the drops of his tears on her skin. The uncontained signs of remorse for his actions. That had been a game changer. And the symbol in front of him was yet another.

Vince's eyes bounced between them. "Am I the only one *not* getting the point? Use smaller words."

"The point is, Agent Di Petro, whoever painted this symbol of a demon on Hero's wall had a powerful message to convey. Perhaps the priests are right, and it is directly tied to Asmodeus's connotations of lust and Hell and hedonism." Alec picked up the photo and scrutinized it again with a mysterious half-smile. "Or maybe, this has nothing to do with sex, but instead the killer is merely fulfilling a bloodlust for other stimulating physical releases such as violence and vengeance and possession." He placed the bloody symbol on top of the open pages of the book, right beneath Luca's nose. "Or he's trying to communicate with someone attached to the case who personifies those aspects of the *ashma daeva*. Let me ask you this, Agent Ramirez, what is a politically correct word for vengeance, revenge, or retribution? How can a man commit socially sanctioned violence without fear of the same?"

Their eyes met and held. A breathless moment came and went, rife with all kinds of inconceivable impulses. Violence, vengeance, and possession. All those things leapt through the currents of air between them and only the twitch of a muscle would have manifested them in the most primal way. Evil or animal? Luca felt the pull of both sides of his nature. The animal would squelch a threat, take down his prey, and establish dominance for the sake of survival and propagation. The evil would gloat over the victory and enjoy the kill.

A cold smile stretched Luca's lips as he saw his own knowledge reflected in the way the shorter man's eyes flicked away from his. Either way, Luca would have won any contest between them. They both knew it.

"Lemme see that." Vince broke the moment by grabbing the book and discarding the photo to the desk as he scanned the page and then turned it to the next one. He had a talent for scanning a document and picking out the important things.

"Yes well," Professor Alec busily shuffled papers, the universal symbol of dismissal. "I hope I was able to shed some illumination on the case."

"Ramirez, take a look at this." Vince turned the book to face him, pointing to yet another image on a subsequent page. "It's a picture of our demon."

Luca leaned in and then gaped. Asmodeus was illustrated as possessing three heads, the middle one that of a man, the left one a goat or ram, and the third an angry-looking bull.

Holy shit, another piece of the puzzle snuggly clicked into place.

"May I ask who else was murdered?" Professor Alec asked quietly from where he'd reclaimed his seat.

"What?" Luca turned to face him once again, reaching for the photo and returning it to its folder.

"All that blood, to whom did it belong, if not

Hero?" Alec's eyes followed the picture back into the jacket, morbid curiosity shone in his symmetrical face and Luca narrowed his eyes at his apparent lack of concern, convinced now, more than ever, that the guy was just this side of a full blown psychotic. "Or have you been able to ascertain that?" There was the condescension again.

Prick.

"I'm not allowed to disclose that to the public." Luca enjoyed lumping the pompous blowhard in with the general populace. "Thanks again for your time."

"I don't imagine that will be the last blood spilt before this is all over."

Luca paused at the door. Was that a threat or an observation? Or both?

"Give Hero my regards, would you?"

Fat fucking chance, psycho. "Sure thing."

Vince tapped on the receptionist's desk as they departed. "See you around, Mary-Louise. You're a peach."

She visibly fought to maintain her frown. "I thought I was a gem."

"That too."

Luca barely heard as he blindly took the corridor, his mind spinning like the tires on his car, laying some rubber on the inside of his skull. Probably he was going in the right direction.

"Soooooo...that guy's a knob," Vince said, catching up with him.

"That's not the only four-letter word that applies."

"The bull's blood makes a lot more sense now. I mean, I was glad when it wasn't human blood all over the bedroom, but the whole animal thing has had me more than a little confounded."

Luca nodded. What they'd kept from Professor

Alec was that the buckets of blood in Hero's room had been identified as pure bovine. Not a single trace of human DNA in the entire mess.

Bulls had a somewhat fringe connotation in regards to western religion, but it had cast one more shadow on an already maddeningly cluttered case. Now a new, infinitely frightening possibility swam to the forefront of Luca's churning thoughts. A goat's head. Bull's blood. All they were missing was the body of a man. So far, the only victims they knew of were female. The consideration whispering through his thoughts was somewhat of a long shot, but the dread gathering in his gut told him it was too much to ignore. What if the symbol in the bulls' blood had nothing to do with Hero? Or at least, not directly. What if the demon symbol was meant as a warning for *him*? Professor Alec had been more than helpful. If he was their perpetrator, was he counting on this visit so he could finally point the investigation in the right direction? Was he that desperate for the real message to be heard?

The professor's chilling questions echoed through the near-empty halls of the college. *What is a politically correct word for vengeance, revenge, or retribution?*

The answer was *justice.* Luca was certain of it.

How can a man commit socially sanctioned violence, even kill, without fear of same?

That was easy. He could become a soldier...

Or a Cop.

23

"I see that the fashion wears out more apparel than the man."

— WILLIAM SHAKESPEARE, MUCH ADO ABOUT
NOTHING

"I can't wear this! What was I thinking? *Who* let me decide that buying this was a good idea?" Hero's voice reached from her bedroom to where Vince and Luca sprawled uncomfortably on her couch. Right after leaving for a long weekend with Josiah Winthrop, Angora had paid for a professional bio-cleaning service to take care of Hero's bedroom as an early Christmas present. Included in the offer was a brand new bed, which was now buried under Hero's entire wardrobe as she discarded candidates for tonight's Art Gallery exhibit.

"You look nice," Stef decided. "Very—uh—professional. Successful."

Luca squirmed. Hero's friend should stay away from words with so many S's in them. Also, despite the man's sexual proclivities, Luca didn't know how he felt

about another dude in the room while Hero dressed...
and undressed.

"I look like Hillary *freaking* Clinton!"

"No, you do *not*!" Stef insisted. "That bitch looks
powerful. Also, she puts mad amounts of highlights in
her hair."

"What, are you saying I look helpless?"

"*No*. No no no." Stef backpedaled. "I'm saying she's
all, 'fuck with me and I'll make your family disappear,'
you know, all Whitewatergate style. And *you* look really... nice."

A tick of silence went by. Then, "Get me out of this
without messing up my hair."

"Yes, ma'am. Luckily, we bought five different
looks. One of them will work."

Luca checked his watch. If they left this very moment, he'd only have to break a few speed laws to get
downtown on time. Any later, and he'd have to resort
to lights and sirens to make it to her art exhibit. He
shifted to alleviate the pressure mounting in his back.
Fucking couch.

Friday night snuck up on him faster than he'd expected. Office hours had been busy and torturous in
the aftermath of the Sgt. Mazure debacle. He'd been
wading through reports, paperwork, and inquiries
with a machete. He'd coordinated an agent for Hero's
Yoga class replacement tonight, on the off chance that
Reese "Two Rivers" Donovan showed up. Organized
and approved press releases, and checked in with the
Irish Embassy about those slow-moving medical
records. When he appeared for his evening shifts with
Hero, she was polite, but distracted, spending most of
her time in the studio with the door shut and the
music loud.

Luca hated to admit it, but he missed her. She

hadn't invited him to have sex with her once in almost a whole week. Not since Sunday. It felt like she was starting to dismiss him and, though Luca knew it was for the best, he despised the distance. Secretly, he was glad they were going into public because they would be playing the role of a couple again. He would get to touch her. She'd be forced to look into his eyes, an action she'd been avoiding for days.

"She's been sleeping on the couch, you know," Vince murmured quietly as not to be overheard in the other room. He sat to his left dressed much like Luca in loose-fitting designer jeans and a tight t-shirt/jacket combo. "After you leave in the morning, she just collapses into it and sleeps until noon."

Luca was glad to hear she was at least sleeping a little. "It's still not enough."

"Yeah..." Vince motioned to the row of new gallon-sized cylindrical cans perched patiently against the wall. "She says she can't sleep in her room until she paints it. She can't look at the white."

"At least she's talking to *one* of us," Luca muttered.

Vince cast him a speculative look. "What happened between the two of you Sunday night? Something's changed. Did you—say something to her?"

"I didn't say anything." Luca searched his memory. "I don't know what's going on." It frustrated the hell out of him, and the last thing he wanted to do was talk about it right before they spent an entire night out together. He checked his watch again. "What's taking her so long? We're going to be late."

Vince waved his hand toward the door absently. "She's a chick. They always take forever to get ready."

"She's generally pretty low maintenance when it comes to this kind of thing," Luca said.

"Hmm," Vince considered. "Let me see something.

Hey, Hero," he called loud enough to be heard in the next room. "You have any competition you're expecting tonight?"

"Talia Malone," Hero called back. "She works in bronze, and she *hates* me. That bitch ripped off one of my ideas and sold it for five thousand dollars. So I got her sculptures banned from the gallery."

"Ouch," Vince laughed.

"I know." Hero sounded disappointed. "That's bad for my karma, but it felt really good at the time."

Turning back to Luca with a knowing smile, Vince said, "See, my man? Rule *numero uno* of female modern warfare: Thou shalt lookest finer and more bootylicious than thine opponent."

"No one says *bootylicious* anymore."

Vince shrugged. "Just sayin'."

"That rule makes no sense and yet... explains so much. How do you know all this stuff?"

"You forget I've been married like, two-and-a-half times."

Hero appeared in the bedroom door. "What do you think?" she asked breathlessly as she held her arms out and rotated for a full three sixty view.

Luca became abruptly glad he was sitting down. He couldn't have formed a response if he'd tried. She wore a soft skirt in butter yellow that flared from the hips and ended above her knees paired with a silky cream tank draped in gold beads. Her hair was pulled back and twisted on top of her head in some kind of braid thingy Luca guessed was held in place by gel, pins and probably magic.

She was a lemon-drop wet dream and all Luca wanted to do was puddle the silky fabric on the floor and lick her from head to toe. In a word, she looked delicious.

"Meh." Vince made a skeptical sound. "That green dress you brought home the other day made your ass look better, plus it's probably more appropriate for an almost-Christmas show. Not that this one doesn't look great, but it makes me think summer, you know?"

"I told you so!" Stef sang from the bedroom.

Hero looked thoughtful, and then smiled. "Got it, the green one. Thanks!" She tossed Luca a look of disapproval and disappeared back into the bedroom.

Luca shook his head as the spell broke. He instantly turned on Vince. "What the fuck, man? She looked incredible. Not to mention it's time to *go*."

"I know, but if you always just tell a woman she looks good in whatever, she'll think you don't really pay attention," Vince said sagely.

Luca made a sound of extreme irritation. "How did you manage to get divorced, anyway? You seem to be an expert in all the feminine rules."

"Depending on whom you ask, I'm sexually selfish, I don't make enough money, and I work too much." Vince ticked the reasons on his fingers. "Oh, and I'm an asshole, that one comes up a lot."

"You *are* kind of an asshole."

"That's the only one I agreed with." His partner threw him a rueful smile. "I work over time to make more-than-decent money and I'm a genius in the sack. A mother fucking revelation. At least, that's what they're screaming until they get angry with me."

"I'll take your word for it," Luca smirked, shaking his head. "Oh, and Vince?"

"Yeah?"

"Comment on Hero's ass again—"

Vince cut him off with a deep laugh. "I know, I know, you'll knock me so hard I'll be shitting my own teeth for a week. Roger that."

"Roger what?" Hero asked.

"Oh, nothing. I'm an asshole. Let's get out of here." Vince heaved himself out of the couch and strode toward the door.

Luca stayed rooted right where he was, his eyes glued to Hero.

The green dress sheathed Hero's lithe body like a caress. It was the kind of dress that either enhanced a flawless form or exposed every lump and imperfection. Made of a shimmery material that begged to be touched, it grazed her pale thighs in a way that mocked and summoned at the same time.

"What do you think?" A little knowing smile shined on her glossy lips.

Luca's hands curled at his sides. *Well. Shit.* He was fucked up one side and down the other. What did he think? He thought she was asking for trouble in that dress. The kind of trouble he ached to give her. The kind of trouble that had you walking funny the next day.

"I think you look too good to leave the house," he aimed for casual, and other than a hoarse thread in his voice, he was pretty sure he hit his mark.

Stef bopped around Hero posing in his studded and carefully ripped skinny jeans and a baby-doll tank, complete with heart-shaped sunglasses he wore over the now bright, cherry red tips of his hair. "Thank you!" he sang. "But ain't nobody going to keep this queen from gracing her subjects tonight." He did his signature head toss and sashayed to the door. "Also, shotgun."

Vince opened the door for him and grinned. "Okay, but I'm driving."

"Works for me." Stef checked him out from head

to toe. "You look like a man who knows how to handle a stick."

Vince's smile stalled and Stef giggled, flicking polished fingers at him. "I'm just teasing you, sugar; don't get your knickers in a knot. I can tell you're strictly for innies, not outies and I'm too busy to change your mind. Now, let's get this drag show on the *road*!"

Luca stood, making a surreptitious adjustment of his jeans, then he held his hand out to Hero. Just for the sake of Stef. Didn't matter that the guy was halfway to the car by now. "You ready?"

Hero's smile dimmed as she put a small sparkly bag with a gold chain over her bare shoulder. She regarded his hand as though trying to figure out what to do with it. "Just let me get my coat," she murmured, turning back into her room.

Luca considered her bedroom door with a dark frown. Hero was still avoiding physical contact with him. He should be grateful. He should be promoting this behavior. He should appreciate the ease the distance created and use the extra bandwidth to focus on the case. But as he stood there feeling like his favorite toy had been taken away from him, he decided that was just one too many *shoulds*.

What was she trying to pull? Did his constant refusals finally sink in? Was this her playing *hard to get*? Pulling some kind of reverse psychology on him? Maybe she thought if she didn't seem interested anymore it would bring him to heel. Problem was it was fucking *working*.

HERO'S favorite part about these gallery shows was the

after parties. What she needed was a damn drink. Preferably something sweet, tropical, and expensive with enough top shelf alcohol to pass as an elephant tranquilizer. She could afford it. She'd cleaned *up* tonight.

The *Terpsichore Gallerie D'Art* was smack dab in the middle of Portland's Alberta Arts district, a posh area just northeast of downtown. Situated in a converted brick building that may have been a mechanic shop in the neighborhood's more blue collar days, the outside of the gallery was as dazzling as the inside covered in ever-changing free-handed street murals. Since Hero's pieces were all sculpture and pottery, the gallery had combined her show with a local land and seascape artist named Chloe Whysper, though Hero doubted that was her real name. But, who knew? When it came to strange names, she was in no position to point fingers.

Chloe was in her mid-thirties, but dressed like she was still twenty-one. Tonight she wore a long mesh tunic with black leggings. In deference to propriety, bright red pasties covered her nipples beneath the mesh. She bounced up to where Hero stood against the far gallery wall, taking momentary refuge from the dimming crowd. "Club Françoise is having a Mardi Gras practice weekend." Chloe tossed her black, red and platinum streaked hair over her shoulder. It made her look like a comic book character, but in a good way. "I wanted to see if you were interested before I posed it to everyone else, seeing as it's your big night and all."

That explained the pasties. Chloe would get Mardi Gras beads just for showing up. Hero plastered on a smile for her and did her best to project warmth into it. "It's *our* big night. And I'm down for whatever everyone decides." Everyone being Stef, their mutual friend, Summer Dawn, who owned a gluten-free bakery in Laurelhurst, and a few other artist acquaintances of both Hero's and Chloe's. One of whom was, unfortunately, Talia Malone.

"That's just great!" Chloe gushed. "Well, this night calls for a celebration. I haven't made this much money since the recession hit." She winked and bounced away, drifting into the crowd to spread the word about their late-night plans. What she hadn't mentioned was that Hero's recent ordeal had created a certain celebrity around her work. More than a few prospective buyers and members of the press had shown to take a gander at the surviving John the Baptist victim. People who shook her hands lingered over the scars, some going so far as to ask about them. Hero had thought it wouldn't trouble her. But the idea that her art would sell because she'd been a victim rather than on its own merit bothered her more than she had expected it to. She did her best to shrug it off. A sale was a sale, and this night would keep her until the summer festival circuit and then some. How many artists could say they made a living doing what they loved? She didn't want the universe to think she was ungrateful.

Hero went back to scanning the crowd. As per usual, her gaze jumped to the most powerful, salient presence in the entire place.

Luca.

Hero had already said goodbye to her family, who'd all come to show their support. Her mother and father had left only moments ago, and Luca now stood by the door in a crowd of her brothers, Andra and Vince, exclaiming over some fight reconstruction video on Knox's tablet. As Luca and the Katrova-Connor men stood head—if not shoulders—above the rest of the crowd, they drew as much attention as any of the art on display, mostly from the female contingent. Hero had to admit, though she was related to most of them, it was hard to find that much handsome muscle packed into such a small space.

She noticed Luca positioned himself in the circle to face her, and as though he could feel her regard, he looked up from the tablet and speared her with his solemn gaze. He hadn't taken those observant eyes off of her once the entire night. In fact, he'd barely taken his *hands* off her, which had been both titillating and troubling. He'd been her constant shadow as she mingled with friends, strangers, and customers, his big warm fingers possessively resting on her lower back, on her elbow, or dancing where only a lover's might. He'd been all smiles and dimples and *pleasure-to-meet-you*s, though his black eyes remained restless, constantly searching the crowd for a threat.

Hero offered him a tentative smile. He jerked his chin at her in acknowledgement, then glanced back down at whatever the guys and Andra found so amusing. Something had shimmered across his features before he'd hid it from her. On a less masculine face, she would have called it hurt. But that couldn't be right, could it? What could she possibly have done to hurt his feelings? This entire week, she'd been behaving herself. Working and allowing him the space to work. She'd been doing her level best not to dick-tease, touch him when she ought not too, or otherwise toss out invitations that might land him in trouble. Wasn't that what he'd wanted? Was he still mad at her for talking to Father Michael on Sunday? Was he upset about their kiss? About Mazure? Dammit, what did he want from her?

She blew her breath out in a frustrated puff. She

certainly knew what he *didn't* want from her, at least not enough to go for it. And considering her conversation with Rown, perhaps that was for the best. Hero tried for the millionth time to really self-examine her feelings for him. Could her brother have been right? Was she just misdirecting vulnerable emotions onto him because he made her feel so safe? If she continued to pursue this, would Luca end up breaking her heart, or worse? She'd never really been afraid of that happening before, but then, a few uncommon terrors dogged her steps nowadays. Now she had to be afraid of everything. It helped keep her alive.

Feeling suddenly very heavy and emotionally exhausted, her eyes moved on, studying the rest of the crowd. She picked up the other two agents attending the exhibit. They appeared to be gallery-hired security guards, and people seemed to accept that they were loss-prevention or whatever.

No one realized they were on the lookout for a serial killer to jump out of the shadows and nab her at any moment. Hero put one arm around her middle, her fingers brushing over the healed spear wound on her side, and told herself she was being melodramatic. However, anxious questions swirled around her head reminding her of the stars or birds after a cartoon head wound. Had John the Baptist come tonight? Had she shaken his hand or offered him a smile? Had he bought one of her pieces?

Was he watching her right now?

"You look like you could use this." A wine glass appeared in her hand at the same time a thrill of unease raised chill bumps over her skin.

"Alec." She dropped her hand from her side and turned around to face him. "What are you doing here?"

His wounded expression was much more practiced than Luca's and smacked of insincerity. "I came to support a dear friend. I wanted to see the lovely pieces that came out of my kiln find good homes. Was I mistaken in thinking I'd be welcome tonight?"

Hero shook her head. "No, no, I invited you." That had been before John the Baptist, Luca, and the demon symbol, but still. "You just startled me, is all."

"It looks like you've done well tonight." He motioned with his own wine glass at the many empty columns and daises that had once displayed her pieces.

She nodded, wishing she could feel the pride and pleasure she ought to be feeling, but it just wasn't there. It seemed her eternal well of sunny thoughts and optimism suddenly dried up and she mourned that fact more than anything. "It's been a—lucrative night."

Alec raised his glass for a toast and she obliged, but merely stared into the wide glass bulb at the thick red liquid inside. How come everything reminded her of blood?

"It's bad luck not to drink after a toast," Alec prompted.

She blinked up at him. Well, she'd take her chances with the bad luck.

An expression both thoughtful and dissatisfied crossed his handsome features, and Hero noted how his cream sweater brought out the gold highlights in his hair. He'd been so fascinating to her once. Older and mysterious and a little forbidden. Was this some kind of emerging trend she should be worried about?

She found Luca with a quick and nervous glance over her shoulder. He'd just noticed them, and a dark frown clouded his already swarthy features. He said something to Rown and Demetri that was probably excusing himself, and he detached from the circle.

"Are you hungry?" Alec motioned to one of the waist-coated waiters wandering with *hors d'oeuvres* trays. "They have these delightful goat cheese brochettes that I think you would appreciate."

Hero narrowed her eyes. Had he just emphasized the word *goat*?

"No, thank you." The thought of eating goat *anything* made her nauseated.

"I'll take one, if you please." Father McMurtry intersected the waiter and helped himself before turning to Hero as he took a bite.

Where had he come from? She hadn't even seen him come in. Hero summoned a warm smile for him, as well, feeling like she may be running out of those before the night was over. "Father, how kind of you to come!" She opted not to offer him a hug as he was busy with chewing and brushing crumbs from his cassock. "Did you bring Father Michael with you?"

Father McMurtry's blue eyes smiled at her, and he gestured over to the curator's table by the door with the second half of his goat cheese *hors d'oeuvre*. "He's paying for our purchase, dear. Congratulations on the success of the exhibit."

As long as she didn't look at the black cassock, her heart maintained its usual rhythm. Mostly. "Thank you! But really you were under no obligation to buy anything."

"Aye, well, he was taken with that rather... creative piece you did of the virgin Mary."

Hero's eyes widened. If he was talking about the piece she thought he referred to, then he was going home with a mash-up of the more traditional renderings of the blessed virgin and an ancient Irish figure called the *Sheela na gig*. Basically, it was the Mother of God with her legs splayed while she held open her exposed labia for inspection.

She'd meant it to be somewhat ironic, excusing the piece because many old churches in Ireland had a depiction of the very same over their doors and carved into their walls. But still, staring straight into the eyes of the man who'd christened her as a baby, she couldn't suppress a blush.

"Oh... well...um..."

"Luca, my boy, it's good to see you again!" Father McMurtry shoved the rest of the treat in his mouth, wiped his fingers on his napkin, and eagerly shook Luca's hand.

Hero tilted her head at them in confusion. *My boy?* She'd heard all about their interviews before and after the symbol had been left on her wall and from what she understood, Father McMurtry was still very much a person of interest. Yet Luca's smile seemed genuine as he shook the Priest's hand.

"*Padre.*"

A little shiver of pleasure made its unbidden way through her bones. Though Luca didn't usually have an accent to speak of, whenever he said a Spanish word, his tongue rolled deliciously over the more vibrant consonants of his native language. It never failed to make her entire body come alive and take notice.

"Any luck finding out who was responsible for that unfortunate symbol, Hero, my dear?" Father McMurty asked sympathetically.

Hero looked to Luca to answer, unsure of what she was supposed to say.

"Yes," Alec chimed in. "It's been on my mind all week, Agent Ramirez, since you consulted me about it."

Father McMurtry's head owlishly swiveled on his neck toward the professor. "And who are you that he would consult you about such a thing?"

The condescension in his voice surprised Hero. Father McMurtry was usually a kindly, easy-going man. "Father McMurtry, this is Professor Alec Graham. He's an expert in the field of history, theology, and iconography."

"You must be the religious expert Luca mentioned." Alec held out his hand.

Father McMurtry took it, but his shake was brief and much less friendly than the one he'd given Luca. "Hmmm," he said aside to Hero. "Has the look of an atheist about him."

Alec nodded and shrugged at the same time.

Puzzled by the complex undertones she read in this strange interaction, Hero was relieved to see Father Michael hurry up to their little group in brisk, excited strides.

Luca tensed beside her, and his hand slid to the small of her back.

"Hero, look what I just bought." He reached into the gallery's designer bag and pulled out the Virgin Mary/*Sheela na gig*. The veiled head of the sculpture looked pious and thoughtful, her downcast lashes a suggestion of contemplative prayer, though her spread thighs and the position of her hands suggested something else, entirely. "That'll get some attention at church, wouldn't you say?" He wagged his light eyebrows at her, though his smile dimmed when his eyes flicked to Luca.

"Undoubtedly." Hero's own smile felt tight and uncomfortable at the realization that she was currently surrounded by Luca's top three candidates for John the Baptist. Her smile beamed from one man to the next, wondering all the while if one of them wanted her dead.

God, this was horrible.

It was Chloe who became her unlikely savior. "All right, girl. Game on! Club Françoise it is, after tonight I'm ready to get my grind *on*." She bumped Hero's hip with hers before noticing the particulars of the crowd. Her chocolate eyes widened at the priests, especially as Father Michael stood frozen with the somewhat vulgar statue in his hand. "*Nofuckinway*, you bought *that*?"

Father Michael inspected it with a nonchalant shrug. "Why not? These symbols are both synonymous with the Irish Catholic church. I think it demonstrates as sense of... diversity and history, don't you?"

Chloe's eyes darkened at Father Michael with unconcealed feminine interest, and Father McMurtry's lip curled with disgust as he took in the woman's choice of wardrobe.

Father Michael seemed not to notice as, even though he'd been addressing Chloe, he hadn't glanced away from Hero. The earnest admiration in his soft eyes now made her uncomfortable, as did the slight tremor in his hand as he tucked the statue away in its plush protective bag. Damn, she never used to notice that kind of thing before.

Oblivious to all of this, Chloe turned to face her and Luca after a flirtatious "hello" and a wink up at Alec. "You bringing this sexy new man of yours?" she asked brashly, sweeping Luca from head to toe. "He looks like he could wreak some destruction on a dance floor."

Hero giggled in spite of herself, and glanced up at Luca who looked half-pained and half-flattered.

"I don't know about destruction." His dimple appeared. "But I've been known to do a *little* damage."

"Well, you kids enjoy yourselves tonight." Father McMurtry kissed Hero on the cheek, his lips and skin dry and clean against her skin.

Hero breathed in his familiar scent and truly smiled at him for the first time that night. He fondly patted Luca on the back as he cleared a pathway through them all with his cane. "Don't do anything I wouldn't do."

They all stalled and blinked at him awkwardly, unsure of what to say.

Father McMurtry's silver hair glinted in the flattering overhead light as he turned back to them with a bit o' mischief sparkling in his eyes. He chuckled as though vastly amused with himself. "Little priest humor there."

Hero let out a breath and then joined their relieved laughter.

Father Michael pressed her arm gently. His hands felt cold and clammy against her over-warm skin and goosebumps erupted once more. "Congratulations again," he murmured.

She nodded a thank you and watched them leave with a troubled frown.

Luca leaned down from behind her, his warm breath tickling her neck. "Don't think about it," he whispered. "I'm here. You're safe. Enjoy your night."

His words released the constant ball of anxiety that had taken residence in her stomach and she sighed a bit and allowed herself to lean against him. Problem was, she could feel the tension corded in his own muscles. Could see the wariness every time she looked into his eyes. The knot tightened once more as she saw the expression on Alec's face. He wasn't looking at her, but over her shoulder. If she had to hazard a guess, it was Luca's own eyes he stared at so intently. He didn't move. He didn't speak. Just stood there for a few seconds with a completely fathomless look in his eyes.

Hero was afraid for the wine glass he held in a death-grip as she felt Luca's lips brush the nape of her neck. "You ready to get out of here?" He threw some extra silk into his voice.

"I know *I'm* ready," Chloe said.

Stef wrapped Chloe in a hug and they hung on each other for a moment of glee now that the night was mostly over. "Let's do this," he goaded. "These high-heels will only last so many hours."

"See you around, Professor," Luca said casually.

Alec seemed to be pulled out of his trance, and he nodded at Luca.

"Later." Hero waved.

As she allowed Luca to lead her away, she thought she heard Alec's low voice.

"Goodbye, Hero."

"When you do dance, I wish you a wave o' the sea, that you might ever do nothing but that."

— WILLIAM SHAKESPEARE, THE WINTER'S
TALE

And she'd been afraid she wouldn't have fun. Two hours and three Irish Car Bombs later, Hero was swimming in a happy haze of her father's people's finest contribution to the human race. Guinness, Irish cream, and Irish whiskey.

"Have you ever noticed that the more I drink, the straighter I get?" Stef slurred into her ear as he handed her a drink. "See that *gorgeous* woman over there in the lime-green leggings? I'm taking her home... I'm going to lose my *girlginity* to her. To both of them, because right now there are two." He held up *three* fingers, counting his thumb.

Hero searched the bodies lit by strobes, color, and writhing to a mash of music she and her friends had just dubbed "electro-techno-gangsta-voodoo-blues." She found Stef's conquest with almost no trouble. "I —don't think that's a woman."

"Really?" Stef swiveled around on unsteady legs to squint closer. "What makes you say that?"

Hero laughed. "Well, for one 'she' has two lumps that a woman should not, and one of them is an Adam's apple."

Stef collapsed against her. "Oh, thank God. I'm too old to be sexually confused again. I barely survived the first time. How come I didn't notice that?"

Shrugging, Hero looked down into the caramel-colored liquid shot in her hand. "What's this?"

"Bourbon," Stef clicked his glass to hers. "This is fake Mardi Gras, girl, you've been drinking like its St. *Practice* day."

Hero tossed the sweet drink back and enjoyed the burn. She didn't usually drink whiskey made on this side of the Atlantic, but *when in Rome*, and all that happy horseshit.

Stef grabbed her hand. "We've all been standing around talking too much, let's go shake something *loose*."

Hero turned to Vince who was chatting up Chloe. The woman seemed ready to make him her stripper pole in one more drink. "I'm going to dance with Stef," she yelled over the music. Most of their group had already hit the dance floor, except— "Where did Luca go?"

Vince motioned toward the bar with a meaningful wink. "He went to get Chloe and me another drink."

Hero was smiling when she rolled her eyes. Luca was nothing if not a consummate wingman. "Thoughtful," she teased, scanning the bar.

She saw Talia Malone's fake blonde highlights first, and knew the tall, broad shadow she was using the crush of the crowd as an excuse to press her tits against was Luca.

"Uh oh," Vince winced.

"I could pop her implants with my plastic olive pick," Stef offered.

Hero put on a very wide, fake smile, mostly for Chloe's sake.

I'm not your boyfriend, Hero.

She took Stef's bourbon from his hands and finished it in one swallow. "Let's go dance," she rasped.

"I don't have to tell you to stay on the edge of the crowd where we can see you and you can see us." A thread of steel laced with Vince's casual tone.

"Roger that!" she waved.

They wound their way to the glittering particle board floor surrounded with pillars and picked a spot halfway between the tables and the speakers. She usually liked to get lost in the crowd. She loved the crush of bodies, the anonymous movements, passing from one dance partner to the next in a wicked parody of something she'd never dare do. The edge was fine, though. Lil' someone-or-other was telling her to 'get low' and she was more than happy to oblige.

Hero was born with almost no performance talent. She couldn't act to save her life, she couldn't carry a tune in a bucket, but if she could do anything, it was *dance*. She let the thrum of the beat overtake the fibers of her muscles and her movements were barely her own. They belonged to the rhythm. She refused to look at the bar, back to the table, or anywhere but the DJ booth where an intricate lightshow synchronized with the music to create some very cool ambiance. The music seamlessly transitioned from remixed R&B to something that sounded more like The Bayou-meets-the-Latin-Quarter.

Stef smacked her ass before wandering toward his lime-legged 'lady.' Hero didn't mind, she was in full

Mardi Gras mode now, a part of the writhing, grinding, sweaty mass of bodies performing the 'vertical expression of a horizontal desire.'

She lost count of how many bodies brushed against hers, how many hands found her skin, or how the hot spread of her increasing buzz numbed her ability to truly feel any of it.

Until a warm body connected with hers from behind.

Instantly her soul came alive. The funk she'd drifted through the past couple of days didn't just lift, it was singed away by the arc of pure, electric energy sparking between them. Hero's lips parted and her eyes closed as the scent enveloping her told her exactly whose strong hands fitted her ass snuggly against him.

"Teaches me to take my eyes off you, even for a second," Luca purred in her ear. "You shouldn't be out here alone."

"I wasn't sure you could keep up," she challenged breathlessly.

His purr turned into a growl as his big hand flattened against her belly, pulling her harder against him as his body undulated into a sexy hip swivel that took her on a sensual ride through the music.

"*Never* worry about that, *me encanta*." His body drove her movements. His knees nudged her thighs to bend, his hips moved against hers in an alternating slow and fast rhythm that made her head spin. His hands were everywhere as she caught his vibe and their bodies moved as though they were already joined.

Eat your heart out, Talia Malone.

Luca had been modest when he'd said he could do

some damage on the dance floor. He didn't wreak any destruction either. No, neither of those words applied.

He dominated it.

More appropriately, he dominated *her*. Pushing her away from him, he caught her arm and pulled her around to face him in a move that made her feel like a freaking pro. His eyes were two impossibly dark flames as his thigh wedged its way between her legs.

Hero all but rode his leg as the crowd swallowed them. They weren't the only ones in this very same pose on the dance floor, but Hero was pretty sure she was the only one this close to orgasm. Every word they'd been avoiding slid between their interwoven gazes and his grip became bruising on her hips, pulling her higher so he could grind something *else* against her. Something just as hard and plenty thick.

Their sex would be just like this, she thought. Luca would drive. He would dominate. He would ride her hard until she was so crazy out of her mind with lust she'd do anything, anywhere just for a taste of the pleasure he could give her. Pleasure that powerful was almost like a punishment. What if he gave it to her, then took it away?

Fuck that, her Irish blood whispered to her. She wouldn't be the only one begging on her knees before they were through with each other. Maybe it was the alcohol, maybe it was the fact that she could die tomorrow, or that one dance with Luca was probably better than any sex she'd had in her entire life.

Surging impossibly closer, Hero drove her lips against his. As she'd expected, she didn't have control of the kiss for very long. He thrust his tongue right into her mouth, simulating the rhythm of his gyrating hips. It was hot and wet and all she could think of was how she wanted any willing part of his body inside her, his fingers, his tongue, his cock.

Right now.

"Take me somewhere," she demanded against his mouth.

He pulled back to look at her and his dimples appeared. "I didn't drive us here, remember?" The matching breathlessness in his voice comforted her.

She scowled at him then bit his lip, reveling in his sharp intake of breath and the insistent thrust of the ridge of his desire against her. "Think of something," she challenged.

He buried his face in her neck and let out a laugh mixed with desperation and aggravation. Hero smiled victoriously, knowing he was hers for the taking. She twined her fingers through the short hairs at the nape of his neck. "I need..."

He thrust his thigh higher against her, grinding against the place where she throbbed for release. "You need what?"

Well, shit. He'd taken back the control, hadn't he? He knew damn well what she needed. He was going to make her say it?

"You," she gasped.

"Not good enough."

She hated him. No, she loved him. *No*, she *wanted* him. Needed him to—

"Make me come," she said, then nibbled on his ear, just because he deserved it.

Luca's head snapped back and the look he gave her damn near scorched her panties off. His eyes flicked to their surroundings. The crowd on the dark floor crushed ever closer as more late-night revelers flocked to the club. The dancing all around them had become hedonistic. Vince, Chloe and Stef were God-knew-where. No one was paying them any mind. Or everyone was. In either case, Hero didn't care. She was nothing but a flaming ball of wet need and reckless desire.

Luca's took her mouth with his. His hands were suddenly everywhere. Her shoulders, her ribcage, her waist, her ass.

Then he did the unthinkable. The impossible. Something Hero had never before imagined herself doing. He braced her hips with one strong arm against his thigh and angled it right where she throbbed for him. He whispered something in Spanish against her ear. She didn't catch the words over the music, just a rush of rolled *R*s and lavish sounds. They drove her higher as movements intensified.

Luca was so skilled, so perfectly discreet. He didn't pull up her dress. He barely even touched her. Just rolled his sinewy leg against her again and again, taking her dress and panties with it, and pressed it against her clit.

It only took two more rolling motions of their connected bodies to break her, she was already that far gone. Hero twined her arms around his neck and held on as the orgasm rocked her. Her thigh muscles clenched and trembled, spasms of aching pleasure slowly rode her major muscle groups before singing along her connective tissues. The pulses of ecstasy melded with the thrum of the music until Hero felt as though she would continue to climax through the vibrations of the floor.

Just as she became afraid her body would collapse, he pulled back and made sure her dress was straight before wrapping his arm around her back and pulling her close in a more tender position.

"Fuck," he breathed.

"Yeah," she agreed.

His erection twitched and pressed against her, pulsing insistently against the zipper of his jeans. "You're going to kill me," he groaned.

Hero thought that the orgasm would release the pent up tension and desire driving her damn-near crazy, but it didn't. It made everything worse, if possible. Now she was incredibly slick and ready to take that hot length throbbing between them inside her body.

"Let's get out of here," she said into his ear, speaking loud enough to be heard over the music. "We can take a cab."

"Hero." Luca groaned her name like a damned man begging at the pearly gates. "I *can't*. Not when you're drunk. It's not right."

"Fuck what's right." She scored his back with her nails. "I'm not too drunk to consent to this. Hell, I'll sign something."

He hissed a breath out through clenched teeth and ten seconds ticked by. "Ask me tomorrow, when you can stand without stumbling," he said tightly. "I don't want you to hate me after."

It became increasingly apparent that the two double shots of bourbon she'd downed before dancing just started to compete with all the Irish alcohol she'd had before. Standing on her own did seem like a dangerous undertaking at the moment.

"But I *won't* ask you tomorrow," she said plaintively. She was enough out of her right mind to know what it would do once it returned.

"Why not?" he demanded.

"Because you're a Pitt Bull."

"What?"

"You're going to bite me. Rown thinks so, too." Her

head began swimming in earnest, the lights suddenly becoming overwhelming to her senses. "I can't let you do that, Luca. I can't... Not now that I feel all this—"

"Hero, you're not making any sense. I can barely hear you."

"I know." She held a hand against her temples, wishing the moment hadn't turned this fast. "Nothing makes sense anymore, does it?"

The music faded and the DJ, a fast-talking, handsome Polynesian asked everyone to make some noise.

The crowd erupted in ecstatic cheers.

"This is a very special night for someone!" the DJ continued. "I don't usually do this, but this next song is tight."

Dancers went wild again, even though no one could have any idea what *this* referred to.

"I'm throwing on the band *Broken Social Scene*. This goes out to a Hero, from your boy J to the B."

"Luca!" Hero clutched his hand, all pleasure, emotion, and blood draining from her and replaced with pure adrenaline. "He's *here*."

The dancing started again as the pulsing beat of a remix reached the floor.

Then the lyrics began.

Thought you were the sweetest kill... Did you even know?

"*Puta Madre!*" Luca barked, his eyes bouncing from the DJ box to the entrances, and frantically scanning the blissed-out faces of the crowd. "Follow me," he ordered, but then tucked her into the safety of his body.

People melted before Luca as his wide shoulders pushed through the press of partiers, towing her in his wake. He made it through in miraculous time and Vince was already at the edge of the crowd waiting to meet him, his eyes anxious and a red cocktail glass in a latex-gloved hand.

"This came to the table the moment the song started," Vince informed them.

Hero stared at the brightly mixed drink uncomprehendingly as Luca's arm rested around her shoulders and pulled her in to the protective arc of his body just as the second verse began.

Clenching her hands together, she hid the deep marks on her hands. "What is it?" she asked in a trembling voice.

Vince looked uncomfortable.

"The drink, what's it called?"

"I asked the waiter..." He paused as they were joined by Stef, Chloe, and a few others who closed around Hero in a protective circle. "It's like a Bloody Mary but with beef bullion."

"What. *Is*. It?"

Vince let out a breath. "It's called a *Bloody Bull.*"

"*Christ.*" Luca grit out, then pulled out his phone. "Get a team down here, Di Petro," he ordered. "We need to sweep this place, subpoena the security cameras, and question everyone." He turned on Hero. "I'm getting you out of here," he snarled. "Even better, I'm locking you the fuck away until this bastard is caught!"

"I called a team the moment this song started," Vince said.

Hero shook her head, her stare stuck on the thick red liquid in the skinny, tidy cocktail glass.

Thought you were the sweetest kill...

"No," she murmured, her voice whisked away by the music.

"The hell you say?"

"This is what we wanted, isn't it?" She found her voice, lent nerve by a probably still climbing blood-alcohol level. "We wanted to draw him out. I agreed to be the bait. This is *supposed* to be happening." She didn't mean it like that. None of this was *supposed* to be happening, but as long as she was the focus of this nutcase, no one else had died. That fact helped her sleep at night. If you didn't count the goat and the bull... may they rest in peace.

Vince put a hand on Luca's shoulders. "She's got a point, man. He's getting more reckless. He's closing in on her."

Luca said some things that even made Stef's eyes bulge out of his head. Then he went to work.

"Get security to cover the exits. No one leaves until I say. Shut off that *fucking* music and put the DJ in a room by himself. Also, isolate the club manager and the bartenders."

Hero looked up at Vince, who didn't seem to like where this was going. "Chances of him still being here are wicked slim, Ramirez."

"Do I look like I care?"

Though he addressed Vince, the entire group shook their heads in the negative.

"I'm saying we should wait for the team to show," Vince argued. "We can't shut a place this size down by ourselves."

Hero flinched away from the murder gleaming in Luca's eyes.

"Watch me."

25

"And oft, my jealousy shapes faults that are not."

— WILLIAM SHAKESPEARE, OTHELLO

L uca grabbed his duffel from the trunk and trudged up the walk to Hero's house on the brink of collapse. He'd left the club with only enough time to eat, shower, change, and show for his evening shift.

In the last fifteen hours, with the help of the local PD, they'd collected two hundred statements from club goers, bouncers, bartenders, and one very irate night manager. The lab processed the note on an emergency priority bases, and Luca finished the day with fruitless scans of shoddy club security footage that covered three out of four possible entrances to the building because *Who needed to watch the kitchen dock?* The manager wanted to know.

Dumb ass.

All this was done with half an erection and a full-on bad attitude.

Vince had stayed through the interview with the DJ, and then was instructed to take Hero home. According to Mr. "Slamsquach," a note with the song request had been handed to him by a "red-haired skank" along with a hundred dollar bill. Interestingly enough, the waiter who'd delivered the Bloody Bull gave a matching story.

Luca did his best to get pictures taken of club goers before they left, but after so long, it was impossible to hold a group that large for questioning. In the end, the only patrons they could keep around were the ones who agreed to stay, and those people ended up more voyeurs to the case than witnesses to anything helpful.

The waiter, the DJ, and the security staff were shown what pictures they could get of the club goers, but no one recognized anybody from the photos as the mysterious red-haired woman.

Trojanowski told Luca to go home hours ago, but he refused to comply until every spare inch of the club had been searched, every last person interviewed, and every other direction considered.

Frustrated, exhausted, and sick to death of dead ends, Luca felt like he could sleep anywhere right about now. Even Hero's couch.

Unlocking the door, he stepped in and punched the security code. The sounds of Hero's laughter and the beat of provocative music drifted from her bedroom. Vince's low words were lost between the walls separating them, but Hero's delight could be heard loud and clear.

Bedsprings. *That* sound was un-*fucking*-mistakable. Luca froze. His heart became a battering ram against its chamber. His hand actually went to his chest as though to contain it.

Not Vince. Not his *partner*.

Can I have a pass at her then?

The words toyed with his sanity. Luca braced himself with one hand against the wall separating the entry from the room. Could this be the reason for Hero's distance that week? Had something bloomed between her and Vince during their long days together? Had she finally tired of Luca's scruples and decided to move on to an easier conquest?

His goddamned *partner*.

His hands shook as a familiar patina of red laced through his vision. As the rage spilled over him and settled somewhere low in his gut, Luca knew no amount of counting would fix this. There wasn't a visualization he could muster that wouldn't involve his partner jack-hammering the women he— Luca reached for the door. He should leave. *Now*. He should turn around and get in his car and drive as far away from the house as possible until he calmed the fuck down. He should take off his shoulder-holster and leave his weapon.

"Yes! *Yes*." Vince's breathless, straining voice burned like lava in his ears. "Angle to the left...Yes... That's good... *Fucking* hell."

"Like this?" Hero's throaty response was equally as breathless.

"Just like that. Brace your hands there and I'll do all the work."

Time slowed, and a peculiar yet welcome rushing sound pulsed into Luca's ears, blocking out their voices. His skin was hot, but his veins flowed with ice. He couldn't say how he got from the entry across the loft to her bedroom, but when he wrenched the door open, the handle almost came off in his hand.

Vince stumbled backward a bit, as he'd been bracing himself against the closed door. To Luca's surprise, he was not only completely clothed but smeared with paint.

"Thank God you're here!" Vince smacked his shoulder. "Warm up, man. This thing weighs as much as your mom."

Wordlessly, Luca turned his head to see Hero's brand-new gigantic wooden bed frame blocking the bedroom door.

"I know what you're thinking. You're thinking, 'But Hero just had this delivered the day before yesterday.' And you'd be right, my man." Good-natured sarcasm dripped from Vince's voice.

"When you're done with your bitch circle, I'm ready to move this bad Oscar," Hero's muffled, teasing voice came from the blocked entrance to her room.

"I'll go around and push, you get it from this side." Vince paused, his expression turning to puzzlement as he noted Luca's face. "You okay?"

Luca stared at him uncomprehendingly for what felt like a full minute and waited for the red to wash from his vision. It didn't, even though he registered the situation. Violence still vibrated through him with each palpitation of his pounding heart.

"Something happen?"

"I—" Luca blinked at the bed frame again, turned on its side to fit through the door. "I didn't smell paint."

"It's non-toxic," Hero said proudly. "I bought the kind with zero volatile organic compounds."

Of *course* she did.

"We just moved the bed frame into the middle of the room while we painted the walls," Vince informed him, still unaware of how close he'd come to a beating. "But now *someone* wants to do the ceiling, so we have to shove this son of a bitch out here."

"It doesn't match," Hero insisted.

"So she keeps saying." Vince rolled his eyes conspiratorially and then headed for the bathroom and its connecting door to Hero's bedroom. "Careful," he called. "The mattress is leaning against the linen closet wall here in the bathroom."

Luca still hadn't processed what was happening. He felt like he'd just stepped into one dream and then been dropped down the rabbit hole into another. He couldn't wrap his mind around it, nor could he quiet the thunder rolling through him.

"You ready?" Vince asked from the other side.

Shaking his still-pounding head, Luca grabbed his side of the bed frame, figuring some heavy lifting would help.

"One, two, *three*."

He lifted and pulled while Vince pushed, and the bed frame shot through the door. It was a heavy bastard, but Luca felt like he could lift cars and shit with all the various masculine chemicals swimming through his veins.

Vince's cell beeped and they abandoned the bed frame next to the dining room table.

Hero appeared in the bedroom doorway, and Luca didn't even hear Vince's brief conversation. His heart kicked up again. Tiny grey sweats cut off into shorts and a tank bared her pale, toned limbs. Her hair was clipped into a messy pile on top of her head. Cream paint smudged random swaths of her skin interrupted by a few smears of teal. She had on no makeup, but her color was high from exertion.

She was the most goddamned beautiful woman Luca had *ever* seen.

As she noticed him, Hero's smile faded and the teasing in her eyes was replaced with distance that bordered on wariness.

"Well kids, I've got plans, so I wish you luck on the

ceiling." Vince was already by the door. "Catch you tomorrow, *suckers*."

Luca said nothing as the front door closed. He just stared at her, hoping his eyes didn't give away everything going on inside him.

"Hi," Hero murmured quietly before turning and disappearing back into her room.

Hi? What the fuck did she mean, *Hi*? Luca marched to the front door and threw the deadbolts, then stormed back into her room.

Hero stood facing away from him toward the wall her bed used to rest against. The wall where a demon symbol had been painted in blood. Now a deep teal marked it an accent wall where the others were a lavish cream. Luca paused in the middle of the room. His fingers curled at his sides to keep from reaching out to her.

He could tell by the way her spine stiffened that she knew right where he was.

"I'm thinking about doing a peacock mural here," she said in a voice made too bright by sheer force. "Maybe one that fans out from the headboard. I could get some beaded wall lamps to match and—"

"Hero."

She flinched and turned around, her eyes doing a quick sweep of his appearance. When she reached his face, her eyes widened, something flaring in their depths. Fear? Excitement? Both? "You look—tired," she said softly. "Did you work all night?"

Luca gave a sharp nod. He looked like shit warmed over. He felt even worse. But that wasn't what caused her to blink so rapidly and look uneasy. She could see the darkness that had been awakened in the entry. She was perceptive enough to sense the intensity of his current emotions. Maybe she could read the fact that his entire body vibrated with the need to claim her.

"Maybe you should get some sleep. I'll get the mattress and put it in the living room..."

If she hadn't backed up a step, she might have had a chance. But it was that one small movement of retreat that sent him leaping after her like a hungry predator.

The rage and adrenaline that hadn't yet drained from him quickly transformed into something equally as powerful and ultimately more dangerous.

Violent need.

"Luca, wait," she whispered as he snatched her from where she stood. But the hands she lifted to ward against him were weak as he claimed her mouth.

HERO TREMBLED as his arms locked her against his hungry lips and angry body, one hand behind her head, the other filled with the curve of her ass. His kiss wasn't a question or a punishment, not this time. It was a declaration.

This was happening. No more words. No more waiting. No more promises. Their explosive desire had just tipped the scales and overcome all other emotions. Patience. Fear. Hell, *common sense* had no room between their melded bodies now. Just carnal, primal, *animal* need.

She couldn't remember why she'd been putting the distance between them. None of it seemed to matter now that he'd given in. When she'd seen him in her living room she'd known something had changed. Had wondered what happened to unleash the dark violence in his eyes. But now he kissed the questions out of her, and Hero was helpless to do anything but let him meld her pliant body into his with demanding hands.

His tongue made wet, delicious promises against hers. His heart pounded in his chest like a jackhammer beneath her hand. His skin was hot and hard underneath his shirt. And speaking of hard, his long, impossibly thick erection strained against his zipper, digging it into the tender flesh of her belly.

The reckless arousal from the night before slammed into her once again, this time unenhanced or unimpeded by drink. Unable to move any of her limbs, she melted into him, submitting to his dominance. Her knees weakened, but her mouth felt strong next to his as she returned the kiss with equal force.

Damn, those lips were made for sex.

Hero's surrender had the opposite effect than she'd expected. Instead of softening, Luca growled deep in his throat and curled the hand in her hair, pulling her head back and imprisoning it there, exposing her neck. His eyes were demon black and triumphant as he ran his full mouth down her jaw, spreading hot kisses on her neck, using his teeth in little bursts that made her gasp for air.

They had a lot to say to each other, but none of it seemed to matter as she drowned in a pool of her own longing rivaled only by the man-turned-beast imprisoning her against him. Maybe she *was* possessed by a demon of lust. Maybe *Luca* was that demon and at the moment she'd gladly lose her soul for the hard fuck he was about to give her.

A pleading sound escaped her chest and that seemed to snap his last thin reserve of self-control. With a few foreign curses, he let go of her hair.

Her shorts disappeared.

Her panties disintegrated in his hands.

Then he was palming her ass with both hands while fusing their mouths, and lifting her against him as he staggered forward a few paces and shoved her up against the freshly painted wall. It was wet and sticky against her shoulders and ass, which she found erotic as hell. She latched on to him with her arms, launching an assault on his lips that made him snarl a warning against her teeth.

His body ground against her, helping one arm hold her in place as his other hand reached in between them to wrench his zipper down. His knuckle brushed against her spread sex with the movement, and as her hands gripped his wide, straining shoulders, the leather of his gun holster bit into her palms. This was exactly what she'd wanted, to watch his long, predatory muscles strain against that holster as he came inside of her.

His hand came away wet and was instantly replaced by the hot, blunt head of his cock. She arched helplessly, still unable to move much but feeling the need to facilitate his possession. He drove into her with such force her body resisted a little, creating an incredible friction for them both.

A low, desperate noise vibrated between them, but Hero couldn't tell who'd made it.

He didn't give her the time she needed to adjust to someone his size, but before he began drilling her into the wall, his hand reached up and cupped the back of her head, protecting it from injury and paint.

His strokes were long and brutal. His teeth bared and startlingly white against his dusky skin. His eyes black holes of mindless need. Buried beneath all that was something that surprised Hero yet again. A reverent disbelief. A tender awe that reminded her of someone lost in a fantastical dream and seized with the terror that it could end at any moment.

That wasn't going to happen. Hero cinched her ankles together around his waist. She was never letting go of him, and he'd just have to deal with it.

He groaned and hiked her higher on the wall, repositioning his thick shaft to saw in and out of her in such a way that her breaths became pants of exquisite torture, then moaning, demanding explosions of vulgarity, culminating in strong, high cries of incomprehensible pleasure as her body clenched around his in the most vicious, unrelenting climax of her life.

Hero could have climbed the wall to escape it as the sensation of being fucked with a lightning rod suffused her nerves with raw, electric pleasure so intense, it bordered on pain. As she squirmed, Luca's grip tightened and he continued to plunge into her with awe-inspiring power and efficient grace.

She sagged against him when the storm passed, her limbs trembling and limp.

Luca grunted and drove her higher and harder, his strength and stamina astonishing and impressing her at the same time. He seemed intent on a single-minded focus, and for just a moment, Hero wondered if he was struggling to find his own release.

Now that she sagged forward against him, the hand behind her head plunged between their bodies, his thrusts becoming faster and shallower as his thumb found her clit and made small, insistent circles around the tight, smooth bud.

Suffused with this new sensation, Hero made a shocked sound as she convulsed around him again, feeling his cock grow impossibly harder inside of her as a second throbbing orgasm rushed into her core.

Luca dropped his head into her neck, his hand

pulling from between them and bracing against the wall. As he thrust deep once again, his body rubbed against her sensitized clit. His movements became violent jerks and then shuddering tremors. He bit her shoulder gently, and then harder, drawing her orgasm from her sex into a full body experience. Pulsing inside her, he tried to say her name, but could never quite manage it as his whole body locked up with pleasure for several intense, beautiful moments.

The aftermath was quiet but for their labored breathing and the pulsing sounds of the music from the other room. The wall was cool and slippery behind her. Luca was still hot and slippery inside her. Hero closed her eyes, a sense of calm and rightness settling over her as she held him close. She ran her nails through the softer hairs at the nape of his neck and turned her head to kiss his scratchy jaw.

Her name finally sighed past his lips and a deep sense of contentment and connection flowed between their joined bodies.

Until. "Fuck," he cursed, his muscles stiffening as he withdrew from her and lowered her to the plastic covering her floor.

She missed him instantly, but gave him space to pull himself together and zip up. Still naked from the waist down and mostly covered with paint, she frowned at him. "What?"

"Hero, we didn't—*I* didn't use anything. Are you on the pill?" The fear in his voice made her smile a bit.

"I wouldn't touch the stuff," she said. "But I'm due to start my period any day, so I'm not ovulating."

He shook his head and blinked a lot. "That doesn't necessarily mean—"

Hero stepped forward, tracing the line of his gun holster. "Don't worry about it, I have some condoms in the bathroom, but first I need to shower." She gave him the most suggestive look she could muster, hoping to distract him and knowing she succeeded. "I'm very dirty, and I'll need help washing my back." Turning around, she wriggled her ass at him, now mostly smeared with teal paint.

He swallowed and she peeled her soiled tank off, the only clothing she had remaining. "Think you're up to it?"

Luca's dimples appeared, the fear draining from his face. "It may kill me," he admitted. "But at least I'll die smiling."

He shrugged off his holster and carried it with him into the bathroom.

26

> *"Give sorrow words.*
> *The grief that does not speak whispers the o'er-*
> *fraught heart, and bids it break."*

> — WILLIAM SHAKESPEARE, MACBETH

L uca almost fell off the couch as his arm flailed out to slap at his vibrating phone and push the button to shut it up. From where she sprawled on top of him, Hero made a sleepy noise and snuggled closer beneath his chin. His body ached from passing out on the too-small couch with one leg braced on the floor to support both of their bodies and sleeping for God-knew-how-long in the same cramped position. He checked the window, still disoriented from so much sex and so little sleep. It was still dark outside, but he couldn't tell if the feeble glow through the slats in the blinds came from the neighbors' lights or the beginning of dawn.

Who cared?

Luca squinted at the screen. A little indicator told him he had a text message. Neither Vince nor his boss ever communicated through text, especially about a case. The lab and everyone else could wait until after he'd had his morning after coffee.

Letting his phone drop to the rug, he adjusted his hips against hers, stretching his waking erection against her silk wrapper as he gathered her closer. God, she smelled good. *Felt* good. Felt... right. The clean musk of her shampoo reminded him of the long, hot shower they'd taken. Luca had helped Hero scrub until her pale skin grew pink and most of the paint was gone. He'd washed her intimately, worried that he'd bruised her delicate flesh with his brutal behavior.

With a mischievous smile, Hero had informed him that she'd enjoyed his loss of control, and went on to show him with her hands, and talented mouth, just how much. By the time the water turned cold, he had her pinned against the smooth shower wall as he pumped into her from behind, bringing them both to a shuddering climax.

Exhausted beyond words, they'd enjoyed takeout in relative silence, smiling like idiots at each other across the table, their meal interrupted by a casual caress or secret smile.

They'd crossed some invisible threshold last night and a momentary peace, a sense of true release, settled into the air between them. Perhaps that was why they'd said very little. There was still so much *to* say, and maybe the words would remind them of all the pitfalls they faced with or without each other.

No matter how Luca looked at this, a part of him knew this might be the biggest mistake he'd ever made. As grateful as he was for yesterday's catalyst to their mind-blowing sex, he had to examine the reasons he'd lost control. What if he had found Hero and his partner in bed together? What would have happened?

Squeezing her closer, Luca fought over a difficult swallow. He knew exactly what would have happened.

It had happened before.

A familiar guilty disgust twisted in his gut.

"What?" Hero asked, pushing herself up on his chest to gaze down at him with those soft green eyes. "What is it?"

Luca tucked a wild piece of auburn hair behind her ear, crinkled from sleeping on it while still damp. His heart clenched painfully at everything he saw shining on her face.

Sleepy satisfaction—*damn right*—hope, tenderness, affection, and something that surprised him, because he usually considered it a masculine trait.

Possession.

That look on any other woman's face would have sent him running in the other direction like his ass was on fire. He probably still should. Simply because it was the last thing he wanted to do. Because he couldn't bear to see the day where the trust shining in her eyes was extinguished by disillusionment and fear. It would kill him.

"Stop thinking so loud," she whispered, feathering her fingers over his lips before leaning down to kiss them softly. "You should be too satisfied to look so troubled."

"I was wondering why you weren't making me morning after coffee." Luca covered his mounting disquiet with a teasing smile. "I think I've earned it."

With a sound of outrage, she reared up and tweaked his nipple. "After what I did for you on my knees in the shower, I think *you* should be making *me* some damn coffee."

Heat flared at the mention of it and he pressed his hips upward again, settling his hardness in the hollow of her thighs separated only by his boxers and her silk robe. "I could just return the favor," he offered, his tongue snaking out to lick at her lower lip before catching it with his teeth and slowly drawing it out.

Hero's breath hitched on a sigh, but interest and rejection warred in her gaze. "Wait until I recover feeling down there," she smiled. "Or at least until I stop walking funny."

His smug smile drove her off of him, and Luca enjoyed watching the way her silk robe billowed as she padded to the kitchen. Yeah, she was going to make some coffee. He was such a lucky bastard.

A chill in the air shuddered through him now that the heat of her body was gone, and Luca scrubbed his face with his hands, reached for his gun, and went for his duffel bag in search of clean clothes. His slacks and shirt from the night before hadn't survived the ordeal unscathed by paint, and he couldn't contain what was no doubt a dopey smile as he dressed. He'd thought that when it came to sex, he didn't have any 'firsts' left. Sometimes being wrong wasn't so bad.

He had to filch his belt off of yesterday's slacks, but it looked no worse for wear. Tucking in his shirt, he zipped up, checked his gun, donned his holster, grabbed his phone from the rug, and wandered to the half-wall to check on coffee progress.

His timing was perfect. Hero set a cup with sugar on the ledge for him with an impressive yawn before grabbing hers with both hands and curling her upper body around it like an addict would his next score.

Luca's phone vibrated deep in his pocket, reminding him he had an ignored text. It was only five a.m., which was about the time Luca usually woke, but was still incredibly early for Hero. Their sleep patterns the past week had both been so fucked-up and they'd passed out early on the couch.

Taking a tentative sip, he hissed cooling air in over the tongue-burning ambrosia as he fished out his phone and rubbed his thumb over the screen to un-lock it.

"My parent's invited us to dinner on Christmas Eve and also to Midnight Mass," she said through a lazy yawn. "It's kind of tradition. They put your name in for the gift exchange and Mom said you pulled Pop, and Andra pulled your name. We're not supposed to spend more than..."

Her words drifted into the background as the coffee turned to ash in his mouth. Luca read the words on his screen again and again, wishing desperately that they didn't mean what he knew they meant. *Son of a bitch.* He needed to act. Now. But it was already too late. He knew he'd have to kill the light in Hero's eyes at some point. He just hadn't known that moment would come so soon.

Hero's words died and her eyes became huge. She'd seen the look on his face. The one that told her someone was dead.

"WHO?" She sounded like a deranged owl, but couldn't help herself. Hero's mug grew heavy and began to shake, so she set it down on the counter hard enough to slosh the liquid over the side. Dread stormed through her stomach, pitching its contents and squeezing a band around the center of her chest. "Tell me," she demanded hoarsely.

The creases of his fingers had gone white where he clenched his phone. "Hero... Maybe you should sit down."

"Who *else* has he murdered?" Hero could hear her voice raise a full octave as she raced out of the kitchen and around the half wall. "Someone I know. I can see it in your face!"

Luca looked down, came to a decision, and extended his phone to her.

She has been freed from sin.

A simple, single line turned her heart to ice. The note left with the goat head in her freezer only weeks ago had scripture with a line similar to that one. *He that is dead is freed from sin,* it had said.

A sharp sob escaped Hero as she read the name of the text's sender. There was only one bubble, as no text had ever been passed to Luca previously, though the screen indicated they'd talked on the phone recently.

"Angora?" Her face crumpled, and the phone slipped through her fingers. Bewildered, hurting, and utterly shocked, she looked up at Luca, whose jaw worked bitterly and a vein at his neck jumped and pounded against his mocha skin. "*No,*" she gasped. "Why? Why her? *Why?*"

The question kept ripping from her in gasping sobs. Luca's arms pulled her in and braced her weight as her knees gave.

"I have to call this in, Hero," Luca mumbled softly against her hair. "I have to get a team over there."

Hero stiffened as a horrible thought dawned on her. "Mr. Winthrop! Josiah! Do you think he's all right?"

The look on Luca's face told her he doubted it as he bent to retrieve his phone before pulling her against him with one arm while punching the screen with his finger.

"John the Baptist doesn't kill men," Hero found herself insisting desperately. "Maybe he left him alive. Maybe he's hurt."

Luca didn't answer as he held the phone to his ear. He rocked her softly for a minute as she sobbed out equal amounts of pain and guilt, feeling as though the warring emotions would rip her apart. She knew he didn't say anything because he couldn't get her hopes up.

He called an ambulance, a CSU team, and local PD to Josiah Winthrop's house, Hero cried even harder as he told them to expect a dead body. Luca then called Trojanowski, and they spoke about triangulating the whereabouts of Angora's cell phone. His next call was Vince, and all the while he supported her weight with his body and rubbed his free hand up and down her spine.

Because of the timing, Vince had been dressed, ready, and drinking his own coffee before heading to her house. He and Luca made somber plans to meet at Winthrop's residence ASAP.

Hero tried not to think of how her friend might have suffered. How the same fear and pain could have been inflicted on the frail but vibrant older woman.

"I'm coming with you," she insisted.

"I can't take you on scene," Luca said grimly. "And I can't leave you here alone. I'll need to drop you at headquarters with Rown."

"Take me," she begged. "Angora was like family to me. She doesn't have anyone else."

"I can't, Hero." Luca held her face tenderly and

wiped a tear from her eye. "Let's get you dressed. I have to go."

Hero had every intention of dressing quickly, but she took one moment longer than she should to cling to Luca, to his strength, his solid, masculine, wonderful-smelling body that pleasured, shielded, and protected her so well.

"I'm sorry." His hands moved to either side of her head, and he gripped her gently as he pressed a soft kiss to her lips. "I'm *so* sorry about your friend."

Hero nodded, though the hot tears streaming down her face and the swelling lump in her throat kept her from responding.

Luca supported her while she staggered into her bedroom. She started going through her closet, not really making out any of the clothing through her tears.

The sound of her phone vibrating on the bathroom counter distracted her. She'd left it there while painting because it seemed like a safe place. It was one short vibrate, not a long succession of them.

Which meant she had a text waiting.

Her eyes collided with Luca's before she raced into her bathroom and snatched it up. Her toes gripped the shaggy lime-green bath matt and her hands shook so badly she almost couldn't navigate the screen to recover the message.

Letting the counter hold her weight, she handed the phone to Luca, who'd been at her heels the entire time. "It's nothing we don't already know," she said, sounding as hollow as she felt.

Luca's *modus operandi* was equally as predictable at this point. He slammed his hand against the wall and said things that would cause a sailor, a truck driver, and even a soldier to blush.

Hero took her phone back, fearing for its safety in his hands and stared down at the words still illuminated on her screen, sent the same minute the text had gone to Luca's phone.

Tell Agent Ramirez he can't stop me from setting you free.

27

"It will have blood, they say;
blood will have blood."

— WILLIAM SHAKESPEARE, MACBETH

"We found the cell phone." Trojanowski's weary voice sounded tinny on the line as Luca sped toward Josiah Winthrop's house after dropping Hero with Rown at FBI Headquarters.

"Was it with the body?"

"No. It was tossed in a dumpster downtown." Trojanowski sighed. "Mrs. Steinman washed up on a Hayden Island sandbar. I'm at the scene. The Medical Examiner just got here, and he said she's likely been deceased for a couple of hours, though we can't tell how long she's been in the river yet."

Shit. That meant she was dumped in the middle of the night. "Same M.O.?"

"Mostly. Hands, spear, everything. Though, the wounds look like they're *post mortem*, thank God. She put up a hell of a fight."

"Mostly?" Luca queried.

"Well, it looks like the bullet from a .38 was what did her in. Di Petro said they haven't found a gun at the scene yet, but Mr. Winthrop was also shot in the chest."

Luca wondered how much of this information he could protect Hero from. "As far as I knew, Mrs. Steinman wasn't a redhead," he remembered.

Trojanowski was silent for a moment. "He put a wig on her."

Luca reigned in his mounting rage in front of his boss, but barely. *Damn.* He'd liked Angora. She was— had been— a vibrant, funny, generous old broad who, under all that makeup and melodrama, was one of the most genuine people Luca had ever met.

"She had something wrapped around her wrist," Trojanowski informed him. "I think it lends credence to your Irish Saint theory."

What they needed now was more than a theory, they needed some fucking evidence. "What is it?"

"The medal of some saint or other. I'll snap a picture and send it to you."

"I'm on my way."

"No, you head to the hospital."

Luca's heart sputtered. "The hospital?"

"Winthrop's in critical condition, but he survived. Di Petro is already there, but I want you both to talk to him when he comes to."

"Yes, sir." Luca's chest filled with a reckless kind of hope. Another survivor.

Another witness.

It took him less than fifteen minutes to make the twenty minute drive to the Legacy Emmanuel Medical Center. The distinct smells of blood, sterilizer, and misery assaulted Luca as he hurried through the halls, and he tried not to remember that the last time he'd been in this ICU, Hero had been fighting for her life.

Vince met him in front of Josiah Winthrop's room, but neither of them was allowed in until he was more stable.

"It was ugly," Vince said soberly. "A lot of blood, no surprise there, but JTB, he... did things."

"Like what?"

"Like this." Vince sent him a file from his phone. The file was entitled: *Winthrop Crime Scene Photos*. Even Luca winced as he flipped through the gruesome pictures, not the least of which was the now familiar symbol of Asmodeus carved into the wrinkled, aged skin of Josiah Winthrop's chest.

"Poor bastard," Luca muttered.

"How's Hero holding up?" Vince asked.

Luca shook his head, unable to meet Vince in the eyes. Guilt was like a burr in his shoe, pricking at his more tender skin, a constant reminder of what he and Hero had spent the night doing while sweet Angora Steinman and Old Man Winthrop were going through hell.

An email from Trojanowski was highlighted as new in his inbox, and Luca opened the attachment. The photo of a saint medal on a silver chain pulled up. The medal looked like real silver, if a bit tarnished. Luca had to ignore its placement, and how it draped across the wounded and mangled hands of someone he'd known and liked.

"What's that?" Vince asked.

"It was found on Angora's body." Luca told him, reaching into his briefcase for his tablet.

"Another saint?"

"Looks like." Luca downloaded the image onto his

tablet and did an image search on the internet browser. He didn't find a hit right away and had to scroll through some very weird Gaelic pictures and advertisements before he hit pay dirt.

"There." He clicked on the picture.

"St. Kentigerna," Vince read aloud. "Am I saying that right?"

"Who knows?" Luca shrugged. He clicked on the website and began to read her story. "Says here she's Scottish, not Irish." Choking on his mounting frustration, Luca scanned the long Catholic text, searching for anything that might be of some help. Vince had started to fidget in his shoes and check his watch before he found it.

Luca shoved the tablet at his partner. "According to this, she was married to the supposed grandson of King Arthur. She bore him sons, who were also sainted, some of them in Ireland. She was known for being a good and faithful wife, even if her husband wasn't, and when she was widowed, she devoted her life to converting the pagan people of the Highlands to Catholicism."

Vince narrowed his eyes and pursed his lips. "Draw the parallel for me here, because I think it's a stretch."

"It may be," Luca agreed. "I think this is more of an explanation to us of *why* Angora was killed, aside from being Hero's friend. Angora was a showgirl before she married and divorced about five different times to amass her fortune. Out of all those marriages, she never had any kids."

Vince started nodding, but said, "I don't think I like where this is going."

Luca agreed, feeling uncomfortable even as he

spoke the words. "In the eyes of a zealot like JTB, I don't think Mrs. Steinman was much above a well-paid prostitute who sold not just her body, but her name for a rich husband's money. Also, birth control is kind of a hot bed sin right now in the Catholic Church."

Sighing, Vince reached for his tablet and scanned the article. "I was right. It's a stretch, but a plausible one."

A pretty, young blonde dressed in pink scrubs walked up to them holding a clipboard. "Excuse me, but we don't have a next of kin for Mr. Winthrop. Do either of you know if he has family who should be notified?" She flashed him a white smile that said she was open to conversation and possibly more.

Luca pulled up the case files, knowing that Josiah Winthrop had been enough in Hero's orbit to merit a folder. "He has a daughter who's stationed with her husband near Atlanta." He gave the nurse the daughter's contact information without even looking at her nametag, and then dismissed her.

It took three extra hours for them to be cleared to see Mr. Winthrop. Aside from the gunshot and the gruesome carving in his skin, the seventy-three-year-old man suffered a head wound from being knocked unconscious, and also ligature marks on his wrists and ankles.

The dimmed lights in Josiah Winthrop's room caused the monitor screens around him to emit a florescent glow all around his tall, willowy form. Cords and wires disappeared beneath the white blankets attached to every damn thing. His mottled, leathery hands twitched beneath the oxygen sensor on his fingers, and Luca noted the very angry bruises around

Mr. Winthrop's wrists. Older people bruised ugly, and this guy was no exception.

Doctor Karakis stood on the far side of the bed, insisting on monitoring the patient while he spoke. Luca exchanged nods with the Mediterranean doctor, remembering he'd done right by Hero.

"Let's stick to what's important," Karakis said quietly. "I don't want him straining anything, not with his concussion."

Luca nodded his understanding, and then met Mr. Winthrop's cloudy, gun-metal grey eyes. The old man licked his dry lips with a drier tongue and spoke. "You find her—body?" He croaked. "She was—already *gone* when he—when he took her." A tear slipped out of the corner of his eye, but his stare never wavered.

"We found her, Mr. Winthrop... We're incredibly sorry for your ordeal. And for your loss." It felt lame even as Luca said it, but an acknowledgement needed to be made.

A shoulder that looked like it had been wide and strong twenty years ago twitched in the weak semblance of a shrug, or maybe a grimace. "I went through worse as a POW in Korea. It'll just take me longer to heal this time, I think. But this... this makes me glad I'm an old man, because I'll hear Angora's screams every night for the rest of the time I have left." He speared Luca with those intense grey eyes. "Hope you never have to listen to the dying screams of the woman you love."

A raw, desperate chill speared through Luca and settled as roiling nausea in his gut. He had to clear his throat before he could speak. "Mr. Winthrop, as you know, we're with the Federal Bureau of Investigation. My name is Agent Luca Ramirez and this is my partner, Agent Vincent Di Petro." They flashed him their badges, taking comfort retreating into their duties. "I hate to ask you to relive your attack, but if you can remember anything, it might be helpful in catching the man who killed Angora Steinman."

Winthrop lifted a shaking hand to hover above the white bandages wrapped about his chest peeking above the hospital blanket. "I'm pretty sure he's after *you*, Agent Ramirez."

Vince made a tight noise.

"Excuse me?" Luca asked.

"He said—for the ritual to be complete—that a man who has been infected by the taint of the demon must be bled." More tears shimmered in the dim light, threatening to follow the grooves carved by age and sadness through the old man's face. "He said it was either me—or *you*."

Luca ignored the shocked stare of the doctor and Vince's sharp intake of breath. He compartmentalized that information for later. Winthrop was fading and they didn't have much time. "Sir, can you give me a description of the man who attacked you? Anything you remember will be of help. Age. Size. Identifying characteristics. An accent, maybe?"

Winthrop's hand continued to hover, his bruised wrists standing out in stark blacks and purples. "I couldn't say as to the accent, he spoke mostly Latin in a deep, chanting voice."

"You said he spoke to you. You understand Latin?"

Winthrop shook his head, and winced.

"Please remain still, Mr. Winthrop." Dr Karakis shot Luca a warning look.

"Italian, French, and Spanish," the old man said. "I grew up an army brat in Europe. I tried to communicate with him...to plead—" Tears spilled freely into Mr. Winthrop's silver hair and his breathing sped. "We spoke briefly in Italian. He seemed pleased I could speak it. He said it's one of the languages of God."

"Did you get a look at his face?" Luca prompted, worried over the increasing slur in the old man's speech. *Come on, old man, give me something I can use.*

Winthrop was careful not to shake his head this time. "No, when I arrived home, I immediately heard Angora's screams. They were coming from the bedroom. There was a man's voice. I thought maybe he was—that she was being sexually assaulted. I didn't think. I just grabbed my pistol from my study and charged in there."

His hand lowered back to his sides where he fisted it in the bed sheets. "I should have called the authorities. I should have taken a moment to be smarter. To *think.* But my blood was filled with her screams." His voice broke, and he took a moment to contain himself. "The sound of her pain. It drove me out of my right mind. I don't know if you understand my position, Agent Ramirez, but—" He trailed off, lost in a nightmare forever branded in his memory.

"I believe I do, sir," he admitted.

Josiah Winthrop had burst into that room ready to die for the woman he loved, and Luca could see the regret that he hadn't done so glimmering in the tears streaming down his temples.

Luca felt so compelled to check on Hero, his hand twitched.

"He was waiting for me." Mr. Winthrop's voice began to shake. "She was already tied to the bed with her arms spread, screaming like a banshee. They tell me I was hit in the back of the head. I remember the gun going off in my hand... When I came to, *I* was tied to the bed and blindfolded, as well. Angora was quiet, and somehow... I knew... she was..." He broke down, no longer able to speak through the force of his grief.

Luca regarded the man with sympathy. Winthrop may have tragically been the one to end Angora's life when his gun had gone off. Luca hoped the man *never* found that out. By his way of thinking, her quick death had been a blessing, under the circumstances. She hadn't had to live long enough to experience a painful crucifixion, stabbing, and drowning.

"He started carving on me," Winthrop said woodenly. "Chanting in Latin. Praying, I think. That's when we talked. I'm ashamed to say I screamed. I begged. Something I *never* let the Koreans make me do... He said he was saving us... from each other. From *him*."

"From himself?" Vince asked.

"No," the old man's voice faded to a whisper. "From the demon. Then he—he shot me—shot me with my own gun."

Doctor Karakis injected something into his IV then touched Mr. Winthrop's good shoulder "I think that's enough for now." He directed this at Luca, who nodded his assent.

"Thank you, Mr.—" Winthrop was already knocked out, so Luca followed Vince and the doctor into the hallway.

"The bullet missed his heart by inches. Millimeters even," Karakis gravely informed them. "It's my professional opinion that it was meant to be a kill shot."

Luca agreed. "Thank you, Doctor."

"The press is gathering," Vince said ominously.

Luca let out a weary breath. "Better here than the river. The hospital staff will keep them away from Winthrop."

"Where to? I'll check to see if Angora's body has

been taken to the ME's office, or should we check in on Hero?"

Luca straightened his jacket and adjusted his case, considering the gathering bodies swathed in tailored suits and holding microphones or cameras. "I say we send this motherfucker a message of our own."

28

"Wherever sorrow is, relief would be:
If you do sorrow at my grief in love,
By giving love, your sorrow and my grief were
    both extermin'd."

— WILLIAM SHAKESPEARE, AS YOU LIKE IT

Hero tried to blink open swollen eyes. Her nose felt numb, and her face puffy, so she just buried it deeper into the pillow, still damp from the storm of her grief.

Rown had helped her situate her bed in the middle of the loft for the time being, and put her mattress on it. She hadn't let him in her bedroom, as the dried paint on the teal wall still told a pornographic story. She'd have to redo that wall. Or maybe she'd leave it as a delicious reminder of Luca's reckless passion.

Curled on her side with her pillows and a throw, Hero stared at her brother as he sprawled on her couch, watching the news on his tablet. "Ramirez is in *so* much trouble," he muttered, his hard mouth drawn into a thin line. "This press conference was *not* cleared with the Bureau."

Hero barely heard him. She'd honed in on the unmistakable sound of Luca's voice on the news, silk with an undercurrent of hard steel, heated by determined rage. She knew he stood in front of the hospital where poor Josiah Winthrop fought for his life. "My message to the killer who calls himself John the Baptist is this: Your latest two victims are dead and we're closing in. While you wait for justice, let me direct you to Deuteronomy 32:35. '*To me belongeth vengeance and recompense; their foot shall slide in due time: for the day of calamity is at hand.*'"

Hero had to admit; hearing Luca quote the bible was odd. But, she supposed, he was trying to speak to JTB in a language he understood.

Luca's next words speared her with equal parts fear and pride. "There will *be* no repentance for you. In the bible, the Lord claims both vengeance and mercy for himself, but before you meet your God, vengeance will first be claimed by me, the innocent victims whose lives you destroyed, and by the people of Portland. And I assure you, I will show *no* mercy."

Hero heard applause, and the gathered reporters began to vie for statements and answers to questions, to which he gave neither. Eventually, the female newscaster's voice took over, her voice a few husky octaves lower than before. That brought a tremulous smile to Hero's lips. Luca could have that effect on any woman.

"Oh man, he just fucked himself," her brother groaned.

"Sounds like he's beyond caring." She could relate. It was time this madness ended before anyone else was hurt. Before more dead bodies were fished out of the river. One way or another, they needed to finish this.

"Yeah, but you just don't make promises like that in public. Not if you aren't damn sure you can keep them." Rown frowned at her. "Why do you think he would lie to the press and tell them that Josiah Winthrop is dead? We know that's not true."

Hero was certain that Luca had every intention of keeping those promises. As to lying about Josiah Winthrop's death? She didn't have a clue why he would do that, but he probably had a plan.

Twenty minutes later, a key slid into the door and Rown stood, instinctively palming the butt of his weapon.

Hero found it amazing that she knew Luca by the sound of his distinctive, predatory walk in those costly shoes. The security system beeped as it was reset and then all was quiet.

Hero didn't have the strength to move, so she lay where she was curled facing Rown but away from Luca.

"That was ballsy, Ramirez, I'll give you that." Rown gathered his things, hanging his suit coat over his forearm. "But I don't want to be you when Trojanowski gets wind of it."

"Vince is meeting him at the ME's office," Luca said quietly. "He'll run damage control."

"Let's hope he's as good as his reputation," Rown's wary smile didn't reach his eyes. "You think it'll work, calling him out like that?"

"I hope so. I feel like I've been trying to have a fist fight with a shadow."

Her brother reached down to squeeze her shoulder before stepping around the bed and out of sight. "I hope you know what you're doing. Not just for your sake."

"I'm ending this."

Hero didn't turn to see whatever silent communication happened between them before Rown left, and she didn't really want to. Once the door closed and she was alone with Luca, the tears started flowing again as she listened to him come closer.

"Did you see her body?" she asked, trying to keep the tears from her voice. She could feel him looming on the other side of the mattress, silent, dark, and angry.

"No. Vince is attending the autopsy."

Hero pushed up onto her elbow so she could look over her shoulder at him. "Why didn't you go with him?"

He looked haggard, stark, and dangerous, looming above her bed. "After talking to Winthrop I needed—" His jaw flexed a few times as he tracked the trail of a tear down the curve of her jaw. "I needed to check on you."

Touched, Hero rolled over and rose to her knees, bringing them face to face. She wiped at her wet cheeks with shaking hands, but it seemed the dam had finally broken, and fresh ones rolled into the space.

His dark eyes softened as he reached up and took both of her hands into his. He didn't offer any worthless platitudes. He didn't tell her not to cry or that everything would be all right. He just turned her hands until they were both palm up in his larger ones. Her skin looked very pale, almost translucent next to his. The fine blue veins in her wrists pulsed softly beneath his grip. A shudder of sensation rippled up her arm as he softly caressed the skin next to her puncture scars, as though he understood that touching them was unpleasant.

She'd been so hesitant to let anyone else inspect her healed wounds. To touch them. It was too personal. Too intimate. But she sat passively as Luca lifted her left palm, then her right, and pressed his warm lips to the raised skin in a reverent kiss. It felt like a ritual. Like worship. And Hero's tears flowed for a completely different reason by the time he lifted his head.

"She died before any of this happened," he murmured. "She didn't suffer this pain."

She searched his eyes for an eternity, probing for a gentle lie. His gaze was steady, unblinking. A ragged sob ripped from somewhere so deep, Hero hadn't realized that place existed. It was a fear born of memory. A helpless dread that a loved one had been tortured and terrorized in the same way she had.

"Thank God," she gasped, crumpling into his arms as little explosions of gratitude and anguish burst from her soul. A cyclone of loss and anger and grief tried to rip her away from herself, and it seemed the only things holding her together were Luca's solid arms. His chin rested on her head as he let her cry out her misery. Her pain. Her confusion and fear and all the other emotions she hadn't allowed herself to examine during the past few months. She'd tried so hard to not let this horrific experience change her, or make her bright world darker. But with each day that passed she could feel a little bit more of the constant threat turning her hopes in to fear. Her faith into doubt. And her open heart into something broken and unrecognizable.

After a long time, the storm mellowed to a light, sniffling trickle. "What if he wins?" Hero whispered against his chest. "What if he breaks me?"

Luca's finger reached beneath her chin and lifted her face away from his soggy shirt. His black eyes were uncharacteristically tender as he leaned down and brushed his lips against her wet cheeks, her eye-lids, her forehead, and chin.

"I won't let him." His vow was no less powerful for its lack of volume, and Hero instantly felt the constant flow of now-familiar electricity crackle through innumerable atoms vibrating out of control in the air between them.

His muscles hardened against her body, and he paused for a desperate moment, his lips hovering above hers in silent question.

Hero closed the gap. He tasted of her salty tears and cautious desire. They'd never kissed like this, not once. Instead of frantic, unspent passion, and wet, penetrating thrusts, the kiss was full of comfort and tender regard.

Luca moaned and cupped her face in his hands, his thumbs brushing her tears away with heart-melting care. His full lips swept against hers like the caresses of butterfly wings, lighting the nerves of her mouth on fire with a gentle drag and release.

Their passion was a whisper where before it had been a roar. It snaked through the room as tangible and indefinable as the wind, blowing away errant pangs of hurt and sorrow until they were suffused with warmth and ardor.

Hero's body released a wet rush of desire in answer to the hard length he pressed against her hip. As Luca fused their mouths together, she reached for his jacket and pushed it from his shoulders. He worked at his holster and simultaneously stepped out of his shoes as she undid his shirt buttons.

Their breaths came faster now, feeding the flame

between them, giving each other sustenance as neither of them was willing to separate for long enough to breath. Her shirt was a stretchy halter-top that Luca pushed down instead of up, taking her leggings and thong along with it. His tongue swept into her mouth with a hot caress as he undid his belt and slacks, letting them fall off his lean hips and puddle at his feet.

He laid her down, his arms cradling her as he followed, settling in-between her legs. The inferno built between them as their bare skin contacted and then merged, fitting together now as though they belonged. As though they'd been doing this for lifetimes upon lifetimes.

Hero sighed in relief as he filled her sense of loss and emptiness with hot flesh and pleasure. His tongue and hands continued to stroke and caress her as he rocked his hips against her, entering her body and retreating with long, slow, exquisite strokes. Their mouths swallowed each other's moans, taking them just as deep. The friction of their warm skin sparked and crackled until Hero was certain she could feel the essence of him inside every part of her, from where they joined, to the tips of the finest hair follicle.

For a man so constantly on the edge, he exercised unnatural control and precision in bed. Once he found what made her gasp, he never altered, just pressed his hot sex against her sensitized inner flesh until she jerked and dug her heels into the mattress, her nerves pulsing with an aching, relentless climax.

To her surprise, Luca pulled out of her, bending his knees and trailing his mouth from her lips to her chin, and down the vulnerable skin of her throat to her breasts. He paused there, licking and tugging the small pink nipples into jutting peaks, moaning at her soft sighs of pleasure before moving on.

Hero bent her neck to watch him drift lazily down the flat plane of her stomach, the pale skin unmarred but for the healed jagged gash in her side. Luca didn't ignore it, and the muscles in her stomach quivered as his raw growl rolled over her.

He didn't speak, and neither did she. Somehow it seemed that words would cheapen the moment, would profane the sensations and emotions flowing between them that language was not meant to contain. That Shakespeare, himself, could not properly describe.

Black lashes drifting over his sharp ochre cheekbones, Luca hid his expression from her as he pressed kisses to each of her hips, nudging her pale thighs wide enough to accommodate the broad expanse of his shoulders.

The air felt chilly against her warm, wet sex as she exposed it to his hungry gaze. He lost no time, his head dropping, his pink tongue reaching out from behind those wicked lips to split her with a long, sinuous lick.

She moaned so loudly it echoed back at her from the walls of her spacious loft.

As with his kisses, the feel of his mouth against her core was intensified because he barely touched her. He hovered above her clit, his hot breath creating both sensation and aggravation. For just a moment, his eyes speared her over the expanse of her trembling body, a brilliance of emotion shining from the darkness she always saw there.

She mouthed his name, her tight throat unable to produce a sound, even a desperate one.

His arms plunged beneath her thighs and locked them open, one hand spreading across her torso, the other settling on her mound as he parted her and opened his lips over her sex, pulling her flesh gently into his mouth.

Hero's entire body clenched and strained at the incredible sensation. His hands held her lower body prisoner as he rolled the flat of his masterful tongue over her, sucking on her with subdued strength.

She couldn't breathe, and then she was screaming his name as fireworks went off behind her eyelids. She was aware of the bunch of his biceps against her as he battled with her straining, trembling thighs as wave after wave of crippling pleasure called for her to curl into herself before it killed her. He didn't allow it. He stuck with her until the pulses became painful and over-stimulating, pulling away at just the right moment.

Hero panted and shook, but he still wasn't finished. Releasing one of her thighs, he traced his middle finger down the slit of her body, found the entrance where she wept both desire and release and invaded with a twisting thrust.

Hero enjoyed this with the lazy, disconnected amusement one felt after two mind-blowing orgasms. She liked the contrast of his thick, masculine arm made darker and more exotic by the paleness of her stomach and inner thighs. Biting his full lip, glossy from her pleasure, he joined his middle finger with another, and then another, stretching her replete muscles as his tongue snaked out to softly tease at the engorged nub of her clit.

She came again. Hard, unexpectedly fast, drenching his hand and riding his fingers to a burning conclusion. He turned his head and nipped at sensitive flesh of her inner thigh, leaving a slick path there.

Luca crawled up her body, a new rigid intensity

vibrating through his big frame. He'd given. And now he was about to take.

He found the opening to her body without a hitch and lingering pulses of her orgasm pulled him deep inside. His gentle eyes had hardened. All thoughts of comfort and languor evaporated as he looped his arm beneath her bent knee and stretched her high and wide, enough to press their hipbones together.

He cursed. She arched. And then they were pounding against each other, the connection going deeper than their thrusting flesh, deeper than their grinding bones, speeding through the very fibers of their DNA, their smallest molecules, until it reached that part of their being that everyone knew was there, but no one agreed on exactly what to call it. Their spirits. Their souls. The part of the construct that is built and unraveled by forces unseen. As he drove her to a peak she'd never thought possible, Hero lost track of how many times she said "yes." Only that she chanted it like a prayer, hoping he heard it as the answer to any question he'd ever dare ask her.

He followed her to that place, his bliss seeming to last for an eternity as he clutched her to his straining body, and grit his teeth as though afraid he'd say something he couldn't take back.

———

HERO DOZED in the comfort and warmth of Luca's arms, her mind working too much to let her drift off into sleep. Guilt and loss didn't belong in the aftermath of their lovemaking. There would be a time and place for grief, but not here. Instead of dwelling on Angora's death, she did her best to think about other things. Upcoming holidays instead of funerals. The safety of her family instead of the cruelty of the world. Falling in love with Luca instead of the hatred of a madman.

Luca's fingers lazily drifted from her elbow to her shoulder and back again in a soft caress. A lover's caress. Hero's own hand explored the enticing ripples of his strong abs, finding places that made him purr and others that were sensitive and caused his skin to twitch.

His jaw cracked on a yawn and he pulled her in closer. As she listened to the breath fill and cycle through his lungs, she rejoiced in what they'd found in each other. He'd pleasured her beyond comprehension. Expressed his feelings with his mouth in ways that words would never begin to touch. It would likely always be that way between them. Luca wouldn't bare his soul or expose his needs and feelings to her with words. He was too proud for that. Too damaged, maybe. But he was a master at expressing these things with his body. His care showed in the way he protected her. The way he controlled his strength when handling her. Putting her needs, her safety, her comfort, and her pleasure before his own.

In the past, Hero always thought she'd wanted someone like her father. Steady but pliant to the whims of the woman he adored. Quick to smile and slow to anger. Doting and long-suffering and level-headed. Well, for an Irishman.

Who would have guessed she would end up with a feisty, exciting, passionate Latino with an anger management problem? Hero smiled to herself. If anyone could handle Luca Ramirez, it *would* be her. If anyone could offer him the love, patience, support, and sense of family he'd never known, she would do it gladly. She could spend the rest of her life trying to make up for his past. They could heal each other, building a co-coon of strength around their love constructed of trust and shared experiences, and years of every type of passion they could devise.

She was all in. Both feet. Luca Rodrigo Ramirez-Dimas was *her* man. And she was his woman, patriar-chal societal constructs be damned. Hell, she'd prob-ably even marry him.

"We'll have to figure out last names," she realized aloud.

"Hmm?" he asked drowsily.

She kissed his ribs. "Well, we can't hyphenate, right? I mean, Katrova-Connor-Ramirez-Dimas? *I* wouldn't mind, but that's just mean to the kids. What about when *they* get married? Where would the mad-ness end?"

His relaxed muscles instantly went rigid, nearly bouncing her off of his chest. "*Kids*?" he echoed in-credulously. "Hero, what are you talking about?"

Of course Luca would be afraid of their future. Afraid of the depths of their rare and intense connec-tion. He'd need a little time to get used to the idea. She sat up, expecting to find an expression of abject terror on his face. She wasn't disappointed.

She decided to back up a few steps. "I'm falling in love with you," she said in a low voice.

He jerked up, as well, pulling the blanket over his lap while flashing the whites of his eyes. "Wha— just —cut it out."

She gave him a patronizing smile. "I can't. In fact, I'm already done falling. I'm in deep. I love you."

His scowl darkened. "Well—*stop it*."

Hero wanted to laugh, but knew now was not the time. "You can't tell me not to love you. I'm not asking for you to say it back to me, I'm just letting you know how I feel. If it takes you longer to identify your emotions for me, I acknowledge and understand that." She felt so enlightened. Emotionally aware and together for the first time in months.

His eyes went from wide panic to a narrow glower. "Why the *hell* would you go and do that, Hero?"

"I can't help it," she shrugged. "It's kind of your fault."

He cringed away from her like she held a tarantula in his face. "Is this because I just had sex with you?"

"You just made love to me," she corrected.

Luca jammed the palms of his hands into his eye sockets and then scrubbed them across his face. "That wasn't—I mean—your friend just died and I—wanted to comfort you."

"I know that's part of it. But you can't tell me you didn't feel what just happened between us." Hero crossed her arms over her breasts, calling him on his emotional limitations. "Don't go pretending that was all pity sex because examining your emotions makes you uncomfortable. I thought you were more evolved than that."

He blinked at her, a familiar storm of fury gathering across his handsome features. "Don't put words in my mouth, Hero, that's not what I—"

"If you want to comfort someone, you give them a hug, not more orgasms than can fit on one hand." Hero interrupted, winding up for a much-needed tongue lashing. "Don't cheapen what happened by acting like you were doing me a favor." She grabbed his hand in both of hers and pressed it to her heart. "Look, I'm not trying to pressure you into anything right now. I'm just telling you that *this*, between us, is something rare and incredible. It's not pretend anymore. This is *real*. Instead of fighting it because it scares you, why not, for once, take a chance on something that matters?"

Luca stared at the hand she cradled in both of hers like it betrayed him. His jaw worked as though he chewed on a particularly gristly problem and he wasn't sure if he was going to swallow it or spit it out.

Coming to a decision, he rolled away from her and stood, reaching for his briefs and pants and jerking them over his hips. "I'm going to say this once," his voice was low, his teeth clenched. "I don't do relationships, and I sure as hell don't do love. After this is over, I'm walking away from you, Hero. I *have* to."

Hurt speared through Hero's chest. "That would be the biggest mistake you ever made, and we both know it."

"What do you know about the mistakes I've made?" Luca boomed. "Listen to yourself! You don't even know what the fuck you're talking about!" He zipped up and bent to grab his shirt, grappling with it in his temper. "Look," he said, controlling his volume. "Don't go mistaking gratitude for love. *That's* the problem here. You're young and traumatized and more than a little distraught right now—"

"Why do men insist on treating me like I can't know my own self because I've been a victim? I *love* you, Luca Ramirez. I know I do."

"Stop. Saying. *That!*"

"No! It's the truth," she insisted.

Luca's lip curled with a calculated cruelty she'd never before seen on his face. "Grow the fuck up!" he bit out at her. "You've spent your entire life bossing around your older brothers and charming your way into getting what you want, but you can't pull that shit with me." He threw his arms wide. "*Yes!* I fucked you. That doesn't mean you get to start naming our kids, and it doesn't make me a dick for not wanting them. I only did it because I thought you were the kind of woman who got what this was."

Hero stood, needing to feel solid ground beneath her, and wrapped the blanket around her naked body. "Yeah, well, John the Baptist made assumptions about what kind of woman I was, too."

"Don't do that." He tucked his shirt into his pants, more like shoved it in short, furious motions. "Don't bring *him* into this. This is between you and me."

"Regardless of how much they scare you, I know you have feelings for me."

"You want to know what happened to the last woman I loved?" He growled, pacing away from her.

"Yes."

"She filed assault charges and a restraining order."

Stunned, Hero just blinked at him a few times. Feeling like he'd doused her with freezing water. "Wait. What?" She hadn't thought it was possible to look angry and ashamed at the same time, but he did.

"In college. I came home from studying one night and found her fucking a third-string Quarterback on *our* bed. I put him in the hospital, Hero. I broke his bones with my bare hands. Ended his football career, and I got kicked off the team. The *only* thing that kept me from jail was that he admitted to reaching for me first. But I did something worse that night. I pushed my girlfriend down when she tried to get in between us. I put my hands on her, Hero, on the woman I thought I loved."

She tried to keep the utter shock off of her face, but judging by the look of grim victory spreading across his features, Hero could tell she'd failed.

"You know what they say," he continued, knowing he'd succeeded in shutting her up. "Once a man—

does something like that— he's liable to do it again. That kind of behavior escalates."

Hero's mind raced. She knew the statistics, knew this was a major red flag, but a part of her was unwilling to accept defeat. "But you can choose not to. People can change." She wished her voice sounded stronger. That her argument wasn't so weak.

He made a raw sound of derision and shrugged on his holster. "Not in my experience. Look, by some fucking miracle of paperwork, I was accepted into Quantico, and this is what I've chosen to do with my life. Put my past aside, my job is not conducive to a wife and kids, and I'm not willing to give it up."

Hero snorted. "That's such a pussy thing to say."

"Excuse me?"

"Plenty of FBI agents have *strong* marriages." She held up her hands to stave off his interruption. "Yes, I'm aware of the divorce rate, but things would be different for us. You keep weird hours? Great! So do I. If you want it bad enough, you make it work."

Luca shook his head, suddenly looking more exhausted than angry. "I *don't* want it."

Hero stared at him quietly for an eternal moment. "You think you're being noble, Luca, but you know what you are?"

"Enlighten me." His voice was so dry and rough, she could have lit a match against it.

"You're a coward." Hero let the blanket fall, turned, and walked stark naked into her bedroom. A part of her wished he would come after her. That he would come to his senses and realize the truth. That he would understand what it was she offered him.

He didn't.

29

"I do desire we may be better strangers."

— WILLIAM SHAKESPEARE, AS YOU LIKE IT

Luca's simmer was about to boil over as he scowled at the various projections and whiteboards smeared with *his* work by the fuck-sticks they sent from DC to take over his case.

Agent Corelli and Agent Reinhardt were about as different from Luca and Vince as they could possibly get. Dressed in identical black suits, sporting identical haircuts, and lean, yet unimpressive builds, they gave off a very "Men in Black" vibe. All they needed were the matching shades. Reinhardt was the lighter copy of Corelli, as though printed out when the toner cartridge needed to be changed. Corelli had dark brown hair, Reinhardt had light brown hair. Corelli had dark brown eyes. Reinhardt had light brown eyes. Corelli was the senior agent with a very large nose that kept him from being handsome, and Reinhardt sported only one eyebrow. Not like a unibrow, but like one was missing. Under different circumstances, Luca would have wanted to hear that story. Their biggest differences, though, were that Corelli was an ass jockey whereas Reinhardt was just an ass hat.

"We boring you, Ramirez?" Corelli leaned on the conference room table. His East Coast accent wasn't endearing like Vince's, but irritating in a way that made him sound like he belonged to a canceled episode of Jersey Shore.

"I'm just taking notes on *my* case." Luca offered him a disingenuous smile from where he leaned back in his conference room chair jammed between a still-furious Trojanowski and Agent Donahue, his colleague with the longest elbows in the history of the world. *Jesus.*

Vince was at Hero's doing the day shift protective detail thing. Luca couldn't decide which place he least wanted to be. Here getting his ass handed to him by a fuck-stick, or there getting his ass handed to him by Hero.

This was less painful. But barely.

Corelli eyed his yellow legal pad, and then cast a pointed look at everyone else's laptops and tablets. "Maybe you should have taken notes on Agency Policy and Procedure, Ramirez."

Luca's teeth ground together. Corelli was, of course, referring to the impromptu press conference, the final straw in Trojanowski's decision to bring in the big boys from the DC office.

Maybe you *should eat shit and die,* Luca thought, but kept it to himself. What do you know? Personal growth.

Corelli's eyes gleamed victorious as he turned to the whiteboard. "Due to some poor decision making on your part, we believe our unsub is about to do something desperate and dangerous, possibly harming a large number of people."

He used the appropriate term *unsub*, short for unknown subject, refusing to call the killer by his media-given name. Agent Corelli was by-the-book.

"How do you figure?" Luca asked. "That's not even remotely close to his M.O."

"He strayed from his M.O. the moment he attacked Ms. Connor," Reinhardt said, cocking his non-eyebrow. "And his erratic behavior has only escalated since then. Historically, the next step has been something akin to mass-shootings, murder-suicides, or terrorist activity."

Luca contained an epic eye-roll, waiting for the new guys to tell him something he didn't know. "Look, he was thrown off his game because Ms. *Katrova*-Connor is still alive, despite his best attempts to get at her. *That's* why he changed strategies, not because of something I or the Bureau did or didn't do."

"Sounds like he's not the only one becoming desperate." Corelli smirked.

"We should *all* be desperate to stop him from reaching his goal," Luca insisted. "I've been following this asshole for a year. I know him as much or better than anyone. He's intelligent, fanatical, and utterly focused on *one* thing. Killing Hero." He pointed to the photo of the Asmodeus symbol on one of the corkboards. "He's just waiting for the appropriate time to strike."

"I hear you, Ramirez," Agent Reinhardt said in a placating voice. "And we'd agree if not for the most recent incidents with Mrs. Steinman and Mr. Winthrop. A firearm was used, a man was tortured, and the woman ritualistically disfigured *post mortem*. It's sloppy, it's desperate, and the use of a gun has every one of the profilers convinced that John the Baptist is going to break with his predicated actions."

"Well, the profilers are *wrong*." Luca slammed his notepad on the conference room table. "You have the texts he sent. You have the interview of Josiah Winthrop stating that *he* was the one who likely shot Angora Steinman. I believe the gun was used because it was readily available at the scene. It doesn't have anything to do with escalating behavior. John the Baptist thinks that Mr. Winthrop and I have been somehow tainted by this demon he's after. We're both supposedly *involved* with his victims. In my opinion, his actions aren't out of the realm of his scope, but another part of the puzzle. If we—"

"Your opinion is noted, Agent Ramirez," Corelli cut him off. "But we can't rely on Mr. Winthrop's drugged testimony as fact. He said the gun went off. We can't be certain he was the one to shoot Ms. Steinman when he was attacked. We can't verify that the .38 involved belonged to him, as he has no registered firearm under his name. We can't wake him long enough to *properly* question him. Hell, we can't even be sure he's not involved with the killer."

"Don't be an idiot." A burst of temper drove Luca to his feet. "He's not even on the suspect list!"

"Maybe that's because the suspect list is narrow and weak!" Corelli shot back.

Reinhardt put a hand on his partner's shoulder, drawing him back from where he and Luca bent so far over the table, they were almost nose to nose. Maybe their relationship was more like his and Vince's than Luca had originally thought.

"You've done some exemplary detective work, Agent Ramirez," Reinhardt said, trying to toss buckets of water on a fire already out of control. "But in light of all the circumstances, we feel it will serve this case better to step back and cast a wider net."

"Fuck the circumstances!" Luca growled.

"Sit down, Ramirez," Trojanowski ordered.

Luca ignored him, staring Corelli down. "John the Baptist is one of those people on my list. It's the priests or the professor. *Maybe* Reese Donovan. Cast the net wider and you'll only end up with more dead bodies, *starting* with Hero!"

Trojanowski also stood, his heightened color beginning to telegraph his own temper. "Ramirez! My office. *Now!*" He turned on his heel and stalked out of the glass door propped open to circulate air. The other few agents at the table sat absolutely still, watching the drama unfold before them, unwilling to take sides or make waves. All motion and sound pollution had ceased on the entire floor, as well, heads popping over their cubicles to see what Luca would do.

Luca held Corelli's glare for a moment longer, valiantly battling the urge to haul off and pop the guy in the gigantic schnoz with a career-ending but ultimately satisfying fist to the face. Instead, he shoved off the table with both hands and stalked toward Trojanowski's office.

"How the hell could you do this to me?" Luca went directly on the offensive once the door was slammed behind him. "How could you call in those DC douche monkeys to take over *my* case? We were closing in, Hank. Mark my words; they're going to royally fuck it up." He slapped the metal door frame in frustration. "Dammit, I was *this close!*"

"You were too close," Trojanowski said softly from behind his desk. "You *are* too close."

Luca stalled, his heart lurching as he pinned Trojanowski with a scrutinizing stare. What did he know? Had he found out about what happened between him and Hero?

Trojanowski let out a long sigh as he wiped his forehead and then leaned to prop his weight on the desk with one hand. "I don't know if it's become too personal between you and John the Baptist, the fact that he may be targeting you, or something to do with Ms. Connor, but you've let this case get to you."

Luca stood silently for a moment, struggling to get himself under control. "It didn't affect how well I did my job." He kept his voice low and chose his words carefully.

"That's debatable." Trojanowski considered him a moment, his eyes softening. "I didn't get to where I am without knowing and facing the many dangers of this profession. You're a good agent, Luca. One of my best. I chose to see your fire and your ability to take risks as a strength I could use, rather than a weakness, and I've been right nine times out of ten. But Dammit, your *head* isn't in the game anymore because your heart is."

Luca dropped into the chair in front of his boss's desk mostly because he couldn't think of what else to do.

"I don't want you to let this fuck with your head too much, Ramirez. It happens to every agent at one point or another in his career. We all have that one case that defeats us a little. I had to do something be-fore it puts you down, entirely."

Luca huffed, but couldn't bring himself to deny anything.

"Is it the woman?" Trojanowski asked. "Hero?"

Luca's head snapped up and his boss chuckled.

"Yeah." He wiped his hand across his balding pallet again and heaved another sigh. "It's usually the woman."

Luca blinked at him, stunned. "Sir?"

"What? You think you're the first type-A, gun-toting, danger-loving, alpha dog to fall ass-over-end in love with the damsel in distress?" Trojanowski actually laughed out loud. "Don't flatter yourself."

Luca's shoulders pulled back and stiffened as though an electric rod was just shoved through his spinal column. "I'm not ass-over-*anything*," he insisted. "Especially love."

"Bull shit."

Luca's palms began to sweat. "It's not like that, Hank. The acting just became intense, somehow— it was too..."

"Real?" Trojanowski supplied.

"*No*," Luca said quickly, shaking his head, unwilling to share with the man who could crush his career, but ultimately wanting to talk to *someone* about it. In the few days since Hero told him she loved him— and he'd rejected her—a pit of biblical proportions opened right where his heart should be and threatened to pull him inside out. The cavernous silence went beyond awkward to straight up excruciating. Twenty times a night he talked himself into going to her room and taking it all back, just so he could get back in her arms—*pants*. He meant pants. Because that's all this was between them, at least on his part. An intense, rare kind of epic physical chemistry that would likely remain unmatched for the rest of his god-forsaken life. For her part, it was maybe a serious case of transference. But both of those things would eventually die, given the opportunity, and what would they be left with? A ridiculously incompatible pair of miserable people with the power to mutilate the shit out of each other's souls.

Also, probably one unemployed FBI Agent.

Luca still couldn't believe she'd offered him her heart. *I don't want it,* he'd said.

He was such a fucking liar.

Luca's eyes flicked to Trojanowski, still shocked as all hell that he wasn't flipping out over this.

"Can't say falling in love wasn't something I considered, though I wrongly guessed it would be Vince. That girl's one powerful piece of temptation. She's sweet, brave, bendy, and has an ass you could bounce a quarter—"

"Jesus Christ, Hank." Luca squeezed the bridge of his nose with his fingers, a headache pricking behind his eyes. "Look, I'll admit that, toward the end there, this case became more about keeping her alive than actually catching the killer. But, I'm going to say this one last *goddamned* time. I'm *not* in love with Hero."

Trojanowski wore an expression of disbelief tinged with laughter. "I believe Shakespeare had an appropriate saying for moments like this. 'The lady doth protest too much, methinks.' Or the agent, in this case." He chuckled, obviously finding himself very witty.

Luca surged to his feet, saying some very choice words in Spanish that only fueled Trojanowski's amusement.

"It's Christmas Eve and no one wants to be working," his boss said, pulling at his suit coat in a fashion that declared he was getting back to business. "But Corelli and Reinhardt think that JTB is going to maybe strike during Midnight Mass at St. Andrew's. They want to station several agents there and set a trap for him. Ms. Katrova-Connor has already been briefed and has agreed."

The fact that he'd been left out of the briefing by the DC agents lit Luca's blood on fire. "They're willing to risk the safety of the entire congregation?"

Trojanowski shook his head. "With a target on her

back, Hero makes every Kmart, McDonald's and Star-
bucks that she visits a possible crime scene. In this
case, we'll be ready."

Luca decided not to point out to his boss that he
just named three places Hero wouldn't be caught
dead. Er—fuck—bad analogy.

"The place will be swept for explosives beforehand
and FBI Agents will be strategically located."

Luca cursed. "You can't sweep for explosives. You'll
tip off the priests. If it's one of them, then he'll know
the plan."

Trojanowski also stood, looking uncomfortable for
the first time. "Corelli and Reinhardt think..."

"I doubt that," Luca grumbled.

"They've all but dismissed the priests of St. Andrew's as suspects."

"They *what*?"

Trojanowski shrugged. "There's no van on the
premises or such vehicle registered in either name.
The night the bull's blood was left in Hero's room, surveillance teams were sitting on both of them. According to them, no one left St. Andrew's that night."

Luca knew all of this. "Yeah, well, we both know
what a cluster fuck the surveillance team caused. That
still doesn't mean—"

"Luca." Trojanowski's voice sharpened, all trace of
friendly confidant disappearing. "Go get some sleep,
something to eat, work out, whatever the hell it is you
have to do to get your head in the right place, then report to the Katrova-Connor residence. As I understand, you and Di Petro are invited to a Holiday
supper. Keeping in mind that you're not only charged
with keeping Hero safe, but the rest of her family, as
well. Then you can thank the Almighty that you still

have a job when you accompany them to St. Andrew's for Midnight Mass."

"Where tweedle-dumb and tweedle-shit-stick are in charge?" Luca snarled.

"Precisely." Trojanowski strolled to his door and opened it. "Are we clear?"

Luca stared at his boss for a full ten seconds, then turned on his heel and stalked toward the elevator.

30

"In time we hate that which we often fear."

— WILLIAM SHAKESPEARE, JULIUS CAESAR

By the time Christmas Eve dinner was over, Hero felt as brittle as paper mâché. Luckily for both her and Luca, Vince had somewhat stolen the show, charming her parents and siblings with his usual easy-going aplomb. Luca had rallied admirably, as well, summoning his dimples and smiles at the appropriate moments. He'd bought her dad a year subscription to his favorite car magazine and tickets to the Portland International Auto Show in February. Hero tried not to be bitter that Luca didn't bat an eye when her *father* demanded they set a date for the wedding. Luca had thought her pop was kidding. She knew better.

Her family already loved him.

They loved a lie. And the shitty thing was, so did she. Even still.

Her favorite Shakespeare quote played through her head as she watched Luca cautiously open her present to him. *"Reason and love keep little company together nowadays."*

He'd avoided touching her all night, but when he unwrapped the large, heavy box she'd hauled in for him, his hands seemed less coordinated than usual. She hadn't pulled his name, but couples traded gifts in Hero's family, too, and she'd bought him a life-time supply of yellow legal pads. He'd stared at them, rubbing his hands across their smooth newness with an unreadable expression.

Remembering himself, Luca had kissed her, but only on the cheek, which her family found amusing and her brothers thought was appropriate and respectful. His reaction to Andra's gift had been much more passionate, but that was because she'd scored him an exclusive invitation to an early private sale and showing of the Salvatore Ferragamo spring shoe line at Saks Fifth Avenue.

As he hugged her sister in a way that set her family into peals of hilarity, Hero saw the reason the soft feelings of love and understanding still overrode the antipathy and wretched disappointment he evoked within her. He seemed lost and amazed. Like Christmas presents and laughter were strangers to him. Behind the soul of the lonely and dangerous man that he'd now completely locked away from her, she could picture the tough, mistreated street-kid with a yearning for home. She wondered which one she'd fallen in love with first.

It was eleven-thirty, and everyone filed from the entryway out to their cars to head to St. Andrew's except Connor, who pleaded a migraine and stayed behind.

As the quick taps of Hero's heels on the brick walk echoed her racing heart, Knox slid his arm around her shoulders and squeezed her in close.

"You okay?" he murmured, flicking a worried

glance toward Luca who was behind them, talking to their father about—what else? — classic cars. Hero heard her pop invite Luca to attend the car show with him, and she had to blink away tears. Luca gave him an affirmative-sounding non-committal answer and she realized at that moment just how good he was at playing this game. Rown had warned her, hadn't he? Why hadn't she listened? Why did she always have to learn everything the hard way?

"I'm good," she lied to Knox. "Just... overwhelmed." She hoped he bought it. Knox had a way of being eerily perceptive, which came in handy in the ring.

He kissed her temple with a loud, cheerful smack. "Don't think about the heavy stuff. It's Christmas!"

Hero leaned on him, grateful for his sunny disposition, letting it lift her as it always had. "What are you doing tomorrow morning?" she asked him.

Knox grinned as wide as the Grinch, making his once-too-many broken nose look equal parts treacherous and endearing. "I just bought myself a mansion for Christmas. Want to come over and see the kitchen?"

Hero gasped. "You bought a *mansion*?"

He shrugged as if to say that it was no big thing. "Well, this last title fight earned me a seventh figure and... I got that cereal box promo gig check coming in so, you know, seemed like the thing to do." He popped a toothpick between his teeth and chewed on it a little, causing his muscular jaw to flex and doing interesting things to the Celtic knot tattoo crawling up his neck. "Plus, it has a built in stone fire oven. I can make homemade pizza." His eyes lit up like he'd just had a good idea. "I can make *real* naan! How do you feel about Indian Food for Christmas?"

"What does a brother have to do to get invited?" Vince asked shamelessly.

"Just bring your appetite." Knox elbowed him. "And just try not to kiss the cook,"

"No promises," Vince joked, opening the door to Luca's Charger for Hero. "We'll see you guys over at the church."

Hero climbed in the passenger side and Vince got in the back. Luca finished his conversation with her pop and slid into the driver's seat. The ride was tense and full of expectant silence. The nightscape flashed by in a colorful string of Holiday lights and sparkling frost, the artistic atmosphere of the city accentuated in its decorations denoting every possible winter holiday for anyone willing to celebrate one. Hero tried to feel some peace and joy and love for her fellow man, but instead all she could focus on was the sword hanging over her head. Not telling her family about the night's plans had been torturous, but even Rown said it was for the best.

"Do you think this will happen the way they say it will? That he'll try something dangerous tonight?" She turned to Luca, who kept both hands on the wheel and both eyes on the road.

"I think this idea is a fucking waste of time and re-sources," he snapped.

Hero nodded. He hadn't really answered her ques-tion, but he didn't seem inclined to at the moment.

"I still can't believe Trojanowski pulled your case," Vince piped in from the back seat. "That was a dick move, bro."

"Might have been the right one," Hero thought she heard him mutter as the familiar spires of St. Andrew's came into view. The church glowed against the night sky with lights strung on the bare trees, candles in every window, and warmth spilling from the open doors. Their parking spots had been saved close to the doors and Luca pulled up next to the black SUV that held Corelli and Reinhardt.

Luca and Vince used the darkness of the car lot to spot-check their firearms.

"What if—" Hero flinched as magazines were checked and driven home, sights tested, and then guns returned to various holsters. "What if *nothing* happens tonight? What if he doesn't show?"

"Then we go back to the drawing board," Vince sighed. "The only point I agree with DC on is that he's going to make his move soon, though it probably wasn't going to be tonight."

Luca remained silent, keeping his opinions to himself.

Corelli stepped out of the driver's seat and opened Hero's door for her before Luca had a chance to come around.

"You look beautiful," he complimented her. His eyes alight with masculine interest. Hero thanked him. She'd opted for a long, form-fitting burgundy velvet skirt with a billowy gold blouse that let all the cold air through it. She shivered in her coat, ready to go inside.

Vince was out of the car and the malicious glint in Corelli's stare told her that the dark, silent presence behind her was Luca.

"How are your nerves, Ms. Connor?" Corelli asked, shaking her hand with both of his. He had the audacity to feel for her scar through her mittens, and Hero jerked her hand out of his grasp.

"It's Katrova-Connor," she corrected. "But you can call me Hero." She gave him a disingenuous smile. No use pissing off the people charged with keeping you alive.

Corelli fake-smiled right back at her, annoyance dampening the admiration in his deep-set brown eyes. They weren't a dangerous black, like Luca's, but the color of mud, bland and uninteresting. He obviously didn't like being corrected, especially in front of people.

Reinhardt had come around the SUV, his doe-eyes and young face tagged him the more companionable of the two. "Just a quick brief before we go inside. We have an agent stationed on the corner of both the front pews and Corelli and I will be covering the rear of the church. You'll be sitting in-between Ramirez and Di Petro, and your brother is also on duty tonight, though his main concern is the safety of your family."

Corelli motioned to a dark van hunkered like a prowler beneath a large tree next to the church. "Surveillance and operations is in there, along with backup."

Hero nodded, suddenly unsure. "Do you think anyone is going to get hurt?" she asked, fretful for her family, for the people inside.

"Not if we can help it."

Hero didn't appreciate Corelli's shrug, or his attitude, so she turned away from him and slipped her arm into Luca's. "I'm ready."

Luca tensed where she'd gripped his arm and a pang of hurt preceded a longer stab of irritation. "Oh, relax," she hissed. "This is just for show, remember?"

He stood frozen for a beat, then began walking across the crunchy grass to the sidewalk. Vince followed them, and the other two agents hung back in the shadows, probably to enter more inconspicuously.

"Hero—" Luca began hesitantly.

"Save it," she cut him off. "Just... hold me up. I have to get through tonight."

Luca let out a long breath through his nose, the frost reminding her of a dragon, before he reached over and put his other hand over hers. "No matter what happens, I've got you," he rumbled.

Hero looked up at him and knew, in that moment, that he spoke the absolute truth. A little of the dread coiling through her released, and she clung to his arm, leaning on his strength as they walked up the stairs to the cathedral doors.

A large, powerfully-built, grizzled man with slicked-back hair and an ill-fitting suit stood at the entry and handed out programs. He looked more like a bouncer than a parishioner, but Hero absently thanked him as she took a flimsy red program.

"Psst, Hero," he muttered out of the side of his mouth. "I need to ask you a favor."

She froze and Luca's arm flexed beneath her fingertips, but as she stared up into familiar ice-blue eyes, she felt her mouth break into a wide, genuine smile. "Jimmy Mazure! Don't *you* look sharp?"

The skin beneath his newly-trimmed beard colored and he stared at the programs in his hands.

Hero reached for him, and squeezed his shoulders. Luca made a negative sound and Mazure replied with a disgusted face. Still no love lost between these two.

"Where's Agent Orange?" she asked, looking around for his cat.

Mazure's grey beard revealed a fond smile this time. "He likes to sleep in the nursery around back where it's warm and he can dig in the soil."

"That's wonderful, Jimmy, I'm so glad to see you here. What favor did you need from me?"

Luca made another rude noise, and Hero elbowed him.

Mazure's expression turned sour as he stared at

Luca and his hands trembled a little, but his features were soft by the time he swung his gaze back to her. "I wanted to take communion tonight," he announced.

Hero's grip tightened on him. "But that would mean going inside," she said gently.

His shaking intensified, but he swallowed and nodded. "I think I can do it. It's just a trip up the wide isle and back out again." He motioned to her family taking their customary seats in the middle pew. Three empty spots were left at the edge for her, Luca, and Vince. "If I get to you, do you think you can... go with me?"

"Oh, Jimmy." Moved by his request, she tried not to let her chin wobble. "I'd be *honored* to. I'll wait for you."

"You'll have to go up with *us*," Luca motioned to himself and Vince, who looked like he suddenly realized communion would be part of the deal.

"Am I going to get hit by lightning if I take the sacrament?" Vince asked.

They all ignored him.

"I figured *you* would be close by," Mazure said to Luca, sounding as though he disapproved. This puzzled Hero as he was so adamant that they should do just that when last they spoke. He was probably still sore about his treatment in the interview room.

"You look well, Jimmy." She gave him a final squeeze and then released him. "I'll see you inside?" He nodded, looking alternately relieved and troubled.

Poor man, Hero thought as she made her way up the isle to her family's unofficial pew. He must be terrified of what he was about to do, but it was a big step and Hero felt grateful to be a part of it. Flowing with a little more of the Christmas spirit, she stepped back to let Vince slide in next to Rown, then she sat, and Luca took the edge.

She spotted the other agents right away from the way they tracked her progress into the church. One was a short but stocky blonde man who'd been at her art show, and the other a woman she'd never seen before but looked like she threw on a skirt beneath a work blazer that didn't exactly match. They took seats in the alternate front corners of the congregation on either side of the dais where Father Michael, dressed in a black cassock with a white robe, was giving a pep talk to the choir. Father McMurtry impatiently pushed at the step to the podium with his cane, positioning it at just the right spot before he limped over to ask the organist for help straightening the red sash over his resplendent golden robes.

A pre-teen with a tight ponytail strangled *O Holy Night* on the harp and Hero found herself thinking the girl's parents were cruel to let her do that in public. To the girl *and* the congregation. Feeling guilty for the ungracious thought, she cast a surreptitious glance over her shoulder to Mazure, through the people filing inside to take their seats. She saw him hand programs to Corelli and Reinhardt. He seemed to be studying the seams of their suit coats and hips, as though he could see through their clothing to the weapons beneath. Jimmy *was* ex-military. He probably knew exactly how to spot those kinds of things. His head snapped toward her with an incredulous look, and Hero gave him an encouraging smile and a little wave.

"Did he seem off to you?" Luca murmured into her ear. His hot breath conjured a sneaky memory of him biting that earlobe in her shower and the repercussions branded all the way down to her panties. "I mean, more than usual."

She would only have to turn her face a tiny bit to bring their mouths flush, and she fought every cell in her body that screamed at her to do so. "Don't. Start," she said, whipping around to face forward. Great. Now she was aroused *and* irritated. If she didn't love Luca so much, she'd really hate him.

Maybe that was his plan.

Frowning, Hero caught Father Michael's gaze from the dais as he helped Father McMurtry to step up on the podium. Instead of smiling at her with sparkling eyes, as he was wont to do, he guiltily snapped his gaze away from her. Her frown deepened to a scowl, which felt foreign and uncomfortable on her face. Like it didn't belong there. Because, well, it didn't. Sagging in her seat with a frustrated sigh, Hero focused on Father McMurtry's familiar and comforting voice.

"Thank you, Jenny Bower, for that lovely prelude music," Father McMurtry started before leading into his flowery Christmas welcome message.

"Wow. He said that with a straight face," she marveled to herself, and next to her Luca covered a snort of laughter with a quiet cough.

Hero felt a flare of victory at cracking his 'stony face,' as she'd come to call it. She spent the first half-hour of the service alternately scanning the crowd for someone with obvious serial-killer eyes, and trying not to notice the cut of Luca's muscular thighs beneath his slacks.

Man, she was weak. Maybe there was something to this whole being possessed by a lust-demon thing. She looked over at Vince, also a hot male and a whole lot better in the disposition department.

Nothing. Well, looked like it was just that pesky being in love thing.

Dammit.

The organ started playing after the call to communion, and Hero stood with her family, but waited out of the way for Mazure. She did her best to encourage him with her eyes as he dragged his feet down the wide, but crowded aisle. She was certain he'd have preferred it to be clear so he'd have nothing to impede his exit, but the crowd was polite and as long as he kept eye contact with Hero, his resolution didn't waiver.

Once he reached her, she held out her hand to him and he took it, much to Luca's obvious displeasure. But Hero detected no impropriety in the older man's shaking, sweaty grip as they made their slow progression toward Father McMurtry.

Luca walked in front and Vince behind as they trundled up through the line to partake of the Eucharist. As had become her habit, Hero wondered if JTB was here. If he was watching her right now, wishing her violence and death.

Hero bent her head toward Mazure, trying to distract herself. "You're doing great," she whispered. "Almost there."

His head jerked in one nod while he seemed to search out all exits with wild eyes, but he squeezed her hand even tighter. They reached Father Michael first, who administered the wafers. Hero tried to send him an encouraging smile, as well, just because he looked like he needed it.

"B-body of Christ."

"Amen," she answered.

His hand seemed unsteady as she opened her mouth and presented her tongue. He dropped a wafer on the carpet, which happened from time to time, but it seemed to take a long moment for him to recover the next one and actually place it on her tongue. Hero waited for Mazure to finish receiving his wafer before moving on to Father McMurtry, who watched Luca intently as he drank the wine.

McMurtry cast her a fond expression as she stepped to him next and bowed her head. "Blood of Christ." He administered the wine and then gestured with his head to Mazure. "Thank you," he mouthed, winking before she moved on.

Hero beamed as Mazure seamlessly partook of the wine, a companionable look passing between him and Father McMurtry before he shuffled down off the dais.

"There." She groped for his arm and gave it a little squeeze. "It's nearly over." To her distress, he felt even more stiff and unsteady than before, and she worried that his courage was wearing down. Following Luca down the right side of the aisle, past the parishioners awaiting communion filing up the right, she tried to gauge the distance to the door.

Halfway, Luca excused them between the lines and cleared a path to her family's pew. Hero made to follow him, but Mazure's elbow dug into her back and desperately urged her forward. "Keep going," he stage-whispered to her as the gap in the line-closed ranks.

She searched for a way to explain her situation. It wasn't like she could leave the agents, but if she kept walking to the door, Luca would notice and follow them both. She didn't want to abandon Jimmy Mazure now. Besides, Corelli and Reinhardt were at the back of the church, watching for her. She couldn't see them—should have worn heels—but she'd watched them come in.

"I mean it, Hero. Just *keep* walking." He nudged at

her back, harder this time, and Hero realized with a dawning horror that the hard jab against her spine wasn't his elbow.

It was cold through her thin blouse. Hard and unmistakable.

A gun.

The faces of people she'd known for a lifetime blurred into each other as Hero's mind surged from utter panicked emptiness to teeming with scenarios, all of them ending with someone innocent getting hurt. Because of her. Because they'd tried to do this *here*. *Why* had she ever agreed to this?

"I'm getting you away from *him*," Mazure explained as Hero took a few halting steps forward, her mind suddenly blank from shock and fear. "I'm *saving* you, just a few more steps and we'll be free."

Suffused with a singular terror at the word *free*, Hero couldn't think of anything better to do than to keep walking. If she got Mazure away from the crowd, then they, at least, would be safe.

Was Vince still behind them? *He* obviously couldn't see the gun. Where were the other agents?

"Hero?" Luca's voice lifted above organ music and the shuffling of the crowd, drawing the attention of the entire quiet congregation.

She glanced back to see Luca maybe only two or three paces away from her, pushing his way back out of the pew toward her with a surly frown on his face. Vince had been detained somehow up at the dais, and was now behind Rown, who played shepherd to the rest of her family.

"Luca," she gasped. Knowing he probably couldn't hear her, but hoping he would read the panic in her face.

He did, but not before old Mrs. Werner in the aisle next to her shouted, "Gun! He has a gun!"

The three seconds it took for Luca to get to them felt like thirty. Someone pushed the pause button on time, freezing everyone to their spot.

Hero kept walking through the pathway of people who ducked out of their way, prodded forward by the steel pressing into her back.

"Don't look back at him," Mazure snarled, though his eyes still held that wild, frightened animal look. "We're almost free," he said again.

"Don't do this, Jimmy," Hero begged. "There are children here."

"Hero!" She thought she heard her pop's voice, and tears sprang to her eyes as she prayed he didn't try anything stupid.

"*Freeze,*" Luca commanded, and Hero looked back again to see Luca's gun pressed up against Mazure's temple from behind. She didn't know if she should be relieved or even more terrified.

Her body picked terror, and began to shake and she needed to pee emergently.

"Put. The gun. Down." Luca's voice was hard and cold.

"I'd rather shoot her then hand her back to you!" Mazure yelled, his eyes growing wilder, latching on the doorway rather than Hero.

"I'm giving you three seconds." Luca's eyes were black holes, boring into Mazure as savagely as his bullet would.

A few desperate souls from the back of the church lunged for the door.

Hero turned forward to see Corelli and Reinhardt moving against those that fled, but doing their best to get as many people out while still trying to reach her.

Maybe she should make a play for Mazure's gun while he wasn't watching her. Glancing back and down over her shoulder, Hero realized what Mazure meant to do, and that Luca couldn't see because of his position behind the big man.

"Luca! He's—"

It almost seemed like Luca was blown backward before the explosion of the gunshot ricocheted off the stone walls in a repeating succession. Hero screamed and lurched toward Luca as he fell, clutching his ribs, but Mazure grabbed her around the waist and started to drag her out of the church.

Pandemonium erupted like Hero had seen in the movies. People ran in every direction. Some toward the front exit off to the left of the dais, others toward the large doors of the cathedral, putting themselves in Mazure's way. They shoved and trampled long-time friends and neighbors to reach the possible safety and cover of the darkness outside.

Hero could feel herself being jostled and bumped in the madness, but all she could bring herself to do was chant Luca's name, searching for his body between the legs of what had become a mob.

She couldn't see him. Oh God! Was he dead?

The other agents. Where were they? Could they get to him? She searched the isle in front of her, and saw that Corelli and Reinhardt had their guns out and were shouting commands at Mazure, but Hero understood right away why they didn't take action.

They couldn't shoot into the crowd.

Mazure was shouting back at them, pointing the gun at one agent, then the other. "Let me out! I need to get outside!"

Hero knew for a fact that if he got her outside, it would mean the end for her. Remembering something

Knox had taught her long ago, she let her body go completely limp, sliding from Mazure's erratic grasp like a heavy bag of wheat.

To her shock, he didn't fight her much. The moment he was relieved of her weight, he lunged toward the door, clearing a path the only way he could see how.

Thunder erupted inside the stone cathedral. Mazure's shot at Corelli landed right in the center of his chest. He got his next shot off at Reinhardt before the first agent staggered and hit the floor, swallowed by the crush of screaming bodies pressing toward the exit. Blood spattered from Reinhardt's shoulder, as he spun from the impact and slipped beneath the sea of people.

It sounded like a flurry of gunshots rather than two as the noise bounced in between the terrified screams of the congregation. "I'm sorry," Mazure yelled at her over the commotion. "I tried to save you —I'm sorry." He joined the dash toward the arched doors with jerky, panicked motions.

Somebody stomped on Hero's hand while another body stumbled and kicked her in the ribs. She cried out before strong hands hooked beneath her armpits and dragged her above the stampede and against a cold, square chest.

Dark hands roughly skimmed every inch of her torso, and she looked up into Luca's harsh, black eyes just in time for him to shove her back into the aisle.

"You're alive!" she croaked as another pair of arms scooped her into a similar cold, unyielding chest.

The hell?

"I've got her. Go, go, *go!*" Rown had her tucked into his side and her mother into another. From behind them, her father's voice ordered Andra to stay down and Hero had *no* idea where Demetri and Knox were.

She looked back to where Luca had plucked her out of the crowd, but he'd vanished. She clung to Rown for a moment as he swept them into the center of a pew, searching for Luca's dark head above the crush of the crowd.

"We're safer here, now that the shooter is outside," Rown yelled, gathering her family into the same row and letting the panicking herd of people filter slowly by. "Stay together and stay *down*."

The female agent from the front of the room ran by with her gun drawn, the husky blonde man right behind her. They expertly elbowed through the crowd and out the door in pursuit of Mazure, announcing their presence as FBI. She couldn't see Luca *or* Mazure and Hero tried not to drown in a sudden despairing anxiety. Luca *had* been shot. She'd watched him get shot.

After a second, the unnatural rigidity of Rown's torso began to make sense. He wore a Kevlar vest. Which meant Luca did, as well. She'd have known that if she'd touched him at all that night.

"Thank God," she breathed. Maybe the other two agents she'd watched Mazure shoot down had survived, as well. She sent a silent prayer on their behalf. How could this be? How could Mazure have been John the Baptist all along? He'd been so damaged, so lost. He'd been in custody when—

"Rown!" Demetri's deep voice lifted over the din of screams, and they turned to where he and Knox's hands waved above the crowd back toward the dais several rows ahead of them. "Officer down! It's Vince!"

"Vince!" Hero cried. "Is he alive?"

"There's a lot of blood!" Knox answered.

"*Shit!*" Rown swore, frantic indecision flashing in his emerald eyes as they bounced from Hero to his downed colleague and back to his family.

"Go," Hero shoved him toward the isle. "Help him!"

"I'm not leaving you unguarded!" Rown insisted.

"I've got them, son. Like you said, John the Baptist is outside." Her father squeezed Rown's shoulder. "Help Vincent."

The cathedral was finally beginning to empty, and Rown deftly leapt over several benches before braving the center aisle.

Her father turned to her mother and gently inspected a growing lump on her cheek where it looked like she'd been elbowed or punched. Blood ran from her lip.

"Mama, are you all right?" Hero called.

"I'm fine," Izolda uselessly slapped at her husband's hands. "I've survived worse."

She had?

"Let me see that right now, Izolda, or I swear on this the day of the Lord's birth, I'll bend you over my knee," her father ordered.

Andra already had her phone out and was yelling into it with a finger over her ear.

Hero heard her name called in low, desperate tones, and she wrenched around to see where it came from. No one left in the cathedral seemed to pay her any mind. The sea of people was thinning out, but she still couldn't tell where the plea had come from. Then she looked down, and noticed a trembling hand reaching up at her from across the aisle, attached to a blood-soaked sleeve. "Help me, Hero."

"Oh God!" she cried, and ducked away from her family to assist. How many people had been shot?

How had any bullets reached all the way back to Vince? She couldn't remember anyone shooting back that far, but gunfire had seemed to echo loudly from every direction once the shooting started. Plus she'd fallen on the ground. Had Mazure shot into the crowd after that?

Hero knelt down and clutched the hand reaching up to her, hoping to create enough space around the prone body so they could stand. "Oh, my *God*, are you all right?" The hand, steady now, grabbed her back with surprising strength, and by the time she saw the gun, it was too late.

31

"Some rise by sin, and some by virtue fall."

— WILLIAM SHAKESPEARE, MEASURE FOR
MEASURE

L uca sprinted into the night, his breath coming in short, painful gasps. He was pretty sure the bullet had cracked a rib or two at point blank range, but breathing or not, he was going to run this mother-fucker into the ground.

Adrenaline had dumped into his veins the moment he'd seen the panic on Hero's face. Rage had strengthened the initial surge until Luca felt like he could run down a pack of stampeding wildebeests. He raced after Mazure down the cathedral hill, training his gun on the man's fleeing back, but unable to get a clear shot.

Mazure was tall and fast, but running after and pile-driving someone into the ground was something Luca had done since high-school. He lifted his gun as soon as he broke past the last terrified parishioner. His long legs ate up the slippery grass, and when they hit concrete to chase Mazure across a paved square and toward the church garden, he began to close the gap between them.

"Stop," he wheezed the command. "I'll shoot." Fucking vest was becoming too tight.

A manufactured outbuilding loomed ahead, and the plastic sheeting of the Parish nursery covered half of a garden, now bare and glistening in neat, frosty rows. On the other side of a slatted fence, a neighborhood of upscale townhouses backed up to the church property. Luca didn't want to chance a shot going wild into a window, but also didn't want to stop and take aim, possibly losing his gain on the gunman.

Who was he kidding? He didn't want to *shoot* Jimmy Mazure.

He wanted to tear the man apart with his bare hands.

He was maybe five yards away and closing in. Luca holstered his gun and summoned a burst of speed fueled by murderous wrath. Three yards. Two. They were back on the grass now. He needed to pounce before Mazure reached the fence. If he did, Luca's vest and other hidden gear, along with the fact he'd just been fucking shot, would give Mazure the advantage when it came to climbing, and tight neighborhoods were easy to disappear into. If Luca lost him now, Mazure would be a ghost.

Calculating the distance, Luca dove, caught the kind of air that would send a football stadium roaring to their feet, and crashed his heavy shoulder into Mazure's kidney, tackling him to the ground and driving his face into the grass.

The nine-millimeter in Mazure's hand went flying, but the man recovered surprisingly fast, and caught Luca in the jaw with his elbow.

Luca's peripheral vision dimmed and stars exploded in the night sky as Mazure twisted his body from beneath him and began to scramble away. Fighting an enveloping darkness born of not-enough-oxygen and a soundly rung bell, Luca surged to his feet, grabbed Mazure by his fleeing shoulder with enough force to swing his big body around.

Luca saw the haymaker aimed for his temple just in time to block it, simultaneously landing a quick jab to the throat. Taking advantage of Mazure's stunned gasps for air, he boot-stomped Mazure's knee out from under him. The crazy bastard screamed and crumpled, giving Luca one more chance to connect with a hay-maker of his own. The crunch of Mazure's nose beneath his fist was better than any Christmas present Luca could have imagined. He stood over Mazure's writhing body. Reaching for the cuffs strapped to the back of his belt, he paused halfway back by the butt of his weapon.

"Get up, you son of a bitch," Luca's voice came stronger now, victory returning some of his breath. "Give me an excuse to *end* you."

Mazure groaned and spat blood onto the ground, but stayed down. "I don't care what you do to me," he said from behind the hand that caught the blood pouring from his nose. "I know Hero's safe, and by now, she knows all about who you are."

Pinning Mazure to the ground on his stomach, Luca slapped his cuffs on one wrist and quickly reached for the other hand, now slick with blood from cradling his nose. "I told you not to say her name," he said against the psycho's ear.

"You won't get to her now, John the Baptist!" Mazure screamed. "He'll tell her who you are!"

Luca froze for a shocked breath. "*What* did you

say?" he demanded, jerking Mazure onto his back to face him.

The madman smiled, revealing blood from his nose and mouth etched into the gaps of his teeth. "I know *all* about you," Mazure rasped, his chest heaving from exertion and pain. "It's been you all along killing those girls. Who would suspect the agent working the case?"

A nauseous dread spread through Luca's gut, turning his extremities cold. "*Who?*" He shook the front of Mazure's blood-spattered shirt. "Who said that?"

"How could you do it, you sick fuck?" Mazure's eyes looked as ill as Luca felt. "Pretend to protect her while terrorizing her? When did you plan to kill her, tonight?"

Luca couldn't believe what he was hearing. Mazure had been duped, and only one of two people could have been pulling his strings all this time. In a fit of desperation, Luca drew his gun and shoved it against Mazure's forehead. "Which one of the priests told you that?"

"Just kill me," Mazure hissed. "I'll be one more stain on your black soul."

"I just might," Luca's finger tightened on the trigger. "But not before you say his name."

Mazure's face was a mask of hatred and blood, illuminated by the light pollution from the festive city. "He told me that it's not your fault," he spat. "That you're plagued with demons, but I don't believe him. I think you *are* a demon and you're going to burn."

Fuck.

Luca frantically searched the night for backup. The church still glowed like a beacon on a hill, shadows milling about, shouts echoing through the darkness, the wail of sirens piercing the distance, but no one was running to his aid yet. He and Vince had forgone the telling signs of an ear-bud, so all communication with his team was effectively cut off.

Luca did the only thing he could think of. He pistol-whipped Mazure on the side of the head, effectively knocking him out, then leapt off his limp, handcuffed body. A tight pain in his ribs set his head to spinning, but he let as much breath out of his chest as he could and regained his balance.

He had to get to Hero. She was still in danger, and now he knew who wanted her dead.

Heart pounding, he raced back up the hill toward the cathedral. Taking out his phone, he pushed the button that would wirelessly connect him to the other's ear pieces. "Gunman secured by the gardens!" he yelled into the receiver, which was mostly true. "Someone get their hands on the priests and cuff them!" He didn't hear the reply as he leapt up the church steps two and three at a time. Most of the people had scattered or were gathered in the parking lot, wrangled there by the FBI and Portland Police arriving on scene. An ambulance pulled up as he tore into the cathedral and took in the shocking scene in front of him.

Andra was still on the phone, barking at what sounded like a 911 dispatcher. Reinhardt was being checked by Trojanowski, but seemed mostly okay. The blond agent, Drexler, was kneeling by Corelli, working on undoing his battered vest. Rown and the rest of Hero's family huddled around a prone form in the middle of the aisle.

"*No*," Luca gasped as the band around his chest tightened. Was he too late? Racing across the plush carpet, he wedged his way in-between Demetri and the female Agent, Brighton, too petrified to care about what happened to whoever got in his way.

Brighton had a finger to her ear piece and she lowered it before informing the gathering that the ambulance had arrived.

Luca pulled up short to see Knox putting pressure on a bleeding wound in Vince's thigh. "Jesus Christ!" he swore, unable to believe his partner had been shot.

Hero's father crossed himself, turning his curse into a prayer.

Dropping to his knees, Luca inspected his closest friend for other wounds. "How did he get you?" Vince had been *behind* them, hadn't he? He lay too far up the aisle to have been shot. This made no sense.

Skin waxy and he sweating profusely, Vince was in obvious pain, but he was still conscious. "It—wasn't Mazure," he gasped through pale, pinched lips. "I was shot from behind." From the looks of it, the bullet had gone clean through the meat of his leg, but missed the artery.

"Where are the priests?" Luca snarled, turning to Agent Brighton. "Where's Hero?"

Vince's face went impossibly whiter. "She's not with you?"

"I left her with Pop," Rown said.

Brighton seemed more defensive than worried as she explained. "Drexler and I followed you outside, but you'd disappeared by the time we pushed through the crowd. When we returned, Hero was missing and Di Petro, Corelli, and Reinhardt were down—"

"She should be fine," Andra said, leading the paramedics up the aisle. "We saw her helping Father Mc-Murtry outside toward ambulances. Some idiot kicked his cane out from under him and he was almost trampled." She shook her head, disgusted as the para-medics went to work.

Luca stood and said a few things that God would never forgive him for. A white-hot terror the likes of which he'd never known sliced through him.

"What's the matter?" Rown asked. He wouldn't know. He hadn't had an ear bud, either.

"He's got her," Luca's hoarse words stunned the family. For the second time that night, Luca found it impossible to breathe as he drew his gun. "McMurtry is John the Baptist!"

Leaving them with the fallout of that nuclear in-formation, Luca raced for the door. He searched every wide-eyed face in the darkness for Hero. Her shim-mering gold shirt should have reflected the bright lights. He saw police-issue flashlight beams from the direction of where he'd left Mazure, but no sign of Hero or McMurtry. He felt like a volcano about to blow its top. "Fuck, fuck, *fuck*!"

"Agent Ramirez?" A shaky male voice called out to him from the shadows of the street-side steps.

Luca whirled to see a pale Father Michael laid out on a stretcher, his white robes soaked with blood at the stomach.

"I knew that was you," the priest said. "I—I think he took her—he shot me—I can't believe..." He trailed off.

Luca advanced on him. "I swear to Christ if you had something to do with this, I'll—"

"Sir, please!" A large African-American paramedic stood with her hand up, as though that would stop him.

"I didn't!" Father Michael held out a hand to Luca and struggled to sit up, but the paramedics wouldn't allow it. "There's—a van. We borrow it from the Hebrew Senior Center sometimes." He winced and gasped in a few pained breaths.

"Where?" Luca demanded.

Father Michael shook his head and lifted his hand as though to point. "It was parked—across the street today—didn't think about it ..."

Luca looked to where the wounded man gestured. An empty spot big enough for a van interrupted the line of cars parked along the road.

"Did you see him leave? Where did he take her?"

Father Michael just shook his head, his eyes closing.

"We've got to move him," the paramedic said. "*Now*."

Luca pushed past her and shook Father Michael by the shoulder. "Where did he take her?" he yelled as the priest's eyes popped open and he looked around as though muddled.

"I didn't know..." A tear streaked down his cheek and he kept shaking his head like he couldn't believe what was happening. "I didn't—see," his speech was beginning to slur.

Luca bit out some more obscenities as he left the priest and ran down the hill toward his car. He had a hunch about where Father McMurtry had taken Hero.

To the place this all started.

As he yanked his door open, Luca grabbed his phone and pressed the button to his boss's cell. "Come on, come on, come on," he chanted.

"Where the fuck are you, Ramirez?" Trojanowski screamed in his ear. "You just left the gunman on the ground beat all to shit and trussed like a Christmas turkey. I have three agents and a priest down, and what's this I'm hearing about the crippled father taking Hero? Tell me what the hell is going on!"

Luca was blocked by the front end of some officer's shitty Crown Vic, and he did the guy a favor by backing into it and pushing the car out of the way. Both entrances to the parking lot were likewise blocked, so Luca flipped on his lights and sirens and jammed his foot to the floor, clearing the sidewalk, grass, and curb with some air to spare.

"He took Hero in a van belonging to the Hebrew Senior Center." Luca ignored all his boss's questions. "I want the information on that vehicle given to all units in this fucking city."

"Ramirez, don't do anything stupid," Trojanowski sounded panicked and Luca could hear the squeal of his own tires burning the road through his phone as Trojanowski raced outside in time to see him leave. "Where the hell do you think you're going?" he demanded.

"I think he's going to try to kill her at Cathedral Park," Luca said, then threw his phone to the seat beside him and focused on driving.

Street lines and traffic lights blurred in front of his tunnel vision. He navigated through the sparse late-night traffic like a getaway driver and for the first time in his life, he *prayed*. He prayed like a dying man that he was right about where to find her. That he would get to Hero before it was too late. Because God, the devil, the holy fucking Roman Empire couldn't protect *anyone* from what he would do if something happened to her.

32

"When sorrows come,
they come not single spies,
but in battalions."

— WILLIAM SHAKESPEARE, HAMLET

F or the second time in her life, Hero regained consciousness tied up in the back of a windowless van. Grey-lined upholstery abraded her cheek, and she knew, without a doubt, she'd been here before.

This time, her hands were secured behind her, rather than to a cross, and her ankles were free. She did her best to breathe through the initial wave of panic pounding through her body exacerbating the throbbing in her head. She needed to gain her bearings.

They were moving. Very fast, as far as she could tell, and making a few jerky, frenzied turns, so they were not on the freeway. She couldn't hear any sirens behind them. Which meant no cops.

Balls.

Terror seized her muscles, though she tried to re-

main absolutely motionless so Father McMurtry
would think she was still out cold.

A cowardly part of her wished she were still unconscious. As much as she wanted to live. To fight. She
knew what was coming next. Spikes and hammers and
spears. Torn flesh. Drowning.

Father McMurtry would make certain she didn't
survive this time. Maybe he'd even shoot her first.

She valiantly held on to a sob by gritting her teeth
so hard her jaw ached. How could it have been Father
McMurtry all along? She'd known him her *entire* life.
She'd been so very fond of his sweet, sparkling eyes
and his dashing, wrinkly smile. He was so kind and
gentle and pious. A shocked part of her was still
swamped by disbelief.

He'd shoved a gun in her face and told her to walk
out with him. When she'd refused, he'd pointed the
gun at the back of her mother's head. He'd told her he
could kill most of her family as they gathered around
Vince before Rown had a moment to react. His voice
told her he would regret the deaths, but his eyes told
her he would relish them.

How could she not have followed him out of the
church? She'd *gladly* give her life for any one of her
family.

No one had paid them the least bit of mind as
they'd limped down the Steeple Hill and across the
street milling with panicked victims. Hero had desperately hoped someone would catch her eye. That she
could telegraph her need for help. That Luca would
leap from the shadows and rescue her.

She'd seen a ridiculous amount of the people who
were supposed to protect her gunned down already,
and the rest were desperately trying to deal with the
ensuing chaos. Luca, no doubt, went after Mazure,

and God only knew where they both were. Or if he was all right.

The last thing she remembered before McMurtry knocked her out was his limp disappearing as he rushed them to the awaiting van.

Her heart squeezed in her chest as she thought of Luca and also Vince. What if both of them were dead? God, that would be... unthinkable. Compounded with the tragedy of the loss, her family wouldn't know to suspect McMurtry until it was too late.

A dark hopelessness bloomed and threatened to take control, but Hero fought to contain it. Even though she wasn't exactly religious, if her parent's faith had taught her anything, it was to cling to hope. On the other hand, their pragmatism had taught her to remain calm and consider your options in a desperate situation.

It didn't get more desperate than this.

She needed to see more of her surroundings. She was curled on her left side with her feet facing the double-doors and her head toward the driver. Chancing that McMurtry couldn't see her on the floor, she tilted her head back. A black metal cage, like the one found in a police vehicle, protected the driver. It ended halfway down and was bolted to a metal paneling that made up the rest of the van's interior.

Well shit. There was no bum-rushing the bad guy while he was driving. Which, now that she thought about it, happened a lot in movies but was probably a bad idea. She'd be tossed like laundry in the dryer if the van ended up rolling.

The rest of the interior seemed pretty standard and infuriatingly clean. Hooks where seats could be installed or removed spaced evenly for up to three rows. The carpeted floor had been recently vacuumed.

Hero scowled, her gaze beginning to bounce around the inside as she fought to maintain her composure.

Then she saw it. A hook in the carpeting in the corner right by her head. If having a mechanic as a father wasn't handy enough, having him lecture about checking in any trunk for tools and tire changing implements may have just given her a chance.

She'd have to roll over and shimmy her body to the corner so her hands could lift the carpet. If she stayed low behind the panel, she should be able to pull it off. Holding her breath, Hero waited until the next erratic turn to roll her body, hoping her captor thought she'd shifted with the movement of the van. She froze after that, listening for any signs she'd drawn his attention, then cautiously, she began to use her feet and body to push her hands toward the driver's side corner.

"Are you awake, Hero, my dear?"

She froze again and squeezed her eyes shut. What had once been a lilting and lyrical accent now sounded creepy and sing-song in a way she'd never heard before. *Unhinged* was the word that came to mind.

"Of course you're awake. I can hear you moving back there."

She needed some noise to cover her sounds. What better than her voice?

"Why are you doing this?" she asked loudly, not having to reach too deep to throw some confusion and fear into her voice. "I thought—I thought we were friends. That you cared— about me." The strain in her voice came from her bending her body in half to fit in the corner while reaching for the loop with her fingertips from behind. Hero hoped he heard it as the tension of panic and tears.

"I care for you *very* much, sweet girl. Consider yourself lucky, that you'll meet your Heavenly Father with your soul cleansed of all demons. Pure and unsullied. Where the dark lord will have no claim to you."

The dark lord? What was this, Harry Potter? Hero stifled a hysterical giggle that had her doubting her own sanity as she groped behind her and found the loop in the flooring.

The carpet came up, but not without a slight ripping sound as it rubbed against the panel. "I don't understand! I don't *have* a demon, Father," she said quickly. "I'm not a prostitute like the others. I'm Hero, you've known me my *whole life*." A little trepidation speared her when it came to blindly groping in the space beneath the carpet. What if there were spiders down there? Or dead body parts?

She needed to get a hold of herself. What if there were *weapons* down there? Weapons that would save her life? What was a spider bite compared to a hole through the hand? Suppressing a shudder, she secured the folded carpet with her elbow and leaned back to grope behind her with her bound hands, connecting with something hard and metal.

"Come now, girl," McMurtry said gently, his voice filtering through the cage. "You may be strong enough not to submit to the demon's will and sell your body, but I've seen the face of Asmodeus on you time and time again, reflected in your actions and the actions of those around you."

A gasp of real outrage escaped her. She'd seen a picture of the demon on the internet, and Hero found herself affronted on a level she'd never thought would enter the equation here.

Vanity.

Asmodeus was an ugly three-headed cretin. "Thanks a lot," she muttered, remembering she had a job to do. "When did you see his face?" she asked louder this time. "What did I do to deserve this?" Some real, intense emotion escaped on this question, as it had dogged her since the night of her attack. "I volunteer at the church. I know I don't attend as much as you like, but that's hardly a reason to—"

Her groping fingers identified the cold metal rod of a tire iron, and she forgot what she was saying. At first she was excited, but then realized her issue. *Damn.* The implement was too big to conceal and no sharp edges to work on what felt like leather straps cutting into her wrists.

She redoubled her efforts and kept looking.

"Of course you've been a good girl!" McMurtry's graveled exclamation sounded like a parent trying to encourage a child, which was creepy as hell. "But, my child, once a demon attaches itself to your soul, you're nearly powerless to stop him. That's why I have to save you. It's your actions that let him in, yes, but they're not above redemption."

"What actions?" she asked.

"You prey on the weaknesses of men's flesh." McMurtry's voice turned stern, disapproving. "You deliberately arouse their carnal thoughts and encourage them to sin."

Hero cringed. Yeah. She kind of did that. Like a lot. But she didn't believe as he did. She didn't see sensuality, sex, pleasure, and love as a sin. Though she wasn't about to make the argument.

Her fingers groped beneath the tire iron, but couldn't seem to move it without making noise, so she worked on peeling the carpet back further.

Father McMurtry continued, which a relief

because she'd run out of things to say. "I thought Asmodeus was contained to fallen women, to prostitutes, until I saw you that night in the kitchen with poor Father Michael."

"What?" Hero searched her memory of that night, while desperately trying to pull a crowbar that was stuck down deep. She couldn't use it as a weapon yet, but if she could get the sharp sides to wear through her bonds, she'd be in business. "There was *never* anything between Father Michael and me," she insisted, breathless from the strain. "I would never!"

"I *saw* the demon in your smile that night. Realized you had the red hair of his priestesses," McMurtry said sharply. "You can't have missed the lust in Father Michael's eyes as he shared the wine with you."

"I—" Hero couldn't bring herself to deny it. She'd enjoyed the appreciation of Father Michael back then. It had seemed harmless at the time.

"I knew Asmodeus had done the unthinkable." McMurtry growled. "He'd infected my congregation. He'd taken one of the souls I'd found most dear."

"What if you're wrong?" Hero asked, attempting a different angle. "I survived the crucifixion and the stabbing. What if that was God's will? What if he wants me to live because I'm not really possessed?" She was beginning to sound too desperate. A sheen of sweat broke out above her upper lip.

"This isn't your fault, alone." A weighty remorse filtered through the cage on his words, ignoring her logic. "Asmodeus has plagued me all the days of my life. I think he's always known I was the one God chose to defeat him. I thought I *had* back in Ireland, as my mother was the first woman I was forced to save there. The others that followed her were tallied among the casualties of the Troubles."

Hero gasped. He'd killed his own *mother*?

She'd had heard *all* about 'the Troubles,' the Irish name for the centuries-old war between the Catholics and the Protestants, from her father. In the past fifty years, a lot of people had died violently. It would have been easy to prey upon the women walking the streets of Belfast.

"The demon traced my steps here, though," McMurtry continued wearily. "And I'm both proud and sorry that it is incumbent upon *me* to send him back to hell. Though, I hadn't intended it to be tonight. Those new FBI agents forced my hand and I had to ask poor James Mazure to be a soldier of Christ."

Hero was going to be sick. Poor Jimmy. He really had thought he'd been saving her.

After one final turn, McMurty brought the van to a stop and Hero *really* began to panic. She'd found nothing useful in the floor of the van, and now her time was running out.

"Wait!" she called as McMurtry opened the door and climbed out.

His walk was steady and sure on the ground as he came for her.

Hero's fingers brushed something and hope rose in her chest, then died before it truly could clear the ground. It was little more than a metal tire pressure gauge. Mostly harmless.

As she heard him slide the key into the back door, she swiped it anyway and slid it beneath the leather thongs binding her hands. The carpet burned her legs as she wriggled her body back down toward the door and poised to make one last desperate move.

The moment the gun appeared in his hand, Hero kicked out at it with all the impressive power of her legs.

McMurtry yelled in surprise as the gun went flying. Hero kicked at him again, this time catching him in the chest.

He staggered backward, fighting for purchase in his flowing robes, and Hero plunged into the freezing night, running for her life.

It would never have occurred to her how important her arms were for balance. How strange it would feel to not have your hands to protect your face from the hard ground if you should fall. Cursing her heavy velvet skirt, she flew through the night, her eyes tearing from the wind and the cold enough to block out the terrain. Hero had no idea where she was, but ran toward lights instead of darkness, hoping to find a miracle.

A part of her had been certain McMurtry would recover his gun and shoot her in the back as she fled, but *anything* was better than another crucifixion. So when his heavy body tackled her to the ground, she lay stunned for a breathless moment of utter shock. Recovering quickly, she flailed and screamed and fought him like a wildcat.

"Yes," he hissed in her ear, pressing his heavy body against her legs to subdue them. "Your demon begins to show himself." He was so brutally strong. So solid against her. How had he hid that behind those flowing cassocks and false limp for so many years?

A press of his hips against the curve of her squirming behind brought a fresh terror slicing through her as the revolting realization that he was aroused caused her to gag.

"Even now, at the moment of his reckoning, Asmodeus tempts me to commit a sin of the flesh." McMurtry sounded as disgusted as she felt.

"Please." She hated herself for begging. "Don't!"

He jerked her up by her hair and pressed the gun to her neck, drawing a ragged sob as she scrambled to stand. "I would never so demean myself as to touch the likes of you." All traces of the sorrowful savior were gone, replaced by a spitting, angry megalomaniac. Hero was too relieved to be hurt by his words.

Blinking, she recognized the park in which they stood, the stone bridge illuminated by Parisian light posts. The Willamette River meandered by in its slow winter crawl to the ocean.

Cathedral Park.

Hero finally began to feel the hope leach out of her, replaced by a trembling, sick apprehension and a resolute preparation for the worst.

"D-do you have to pierce my hands again?" she whimpered.

"No." he sounded equally relieved. "That part of the ritual is already done. All of the required rituals are complete. You are the only remaining thread, and upon your return to our Lord, Asmodeus should be forever banished from this world."

"Upon my murder, you mean."

"Call it what you will." McMurtry pushed her ahead of him by the merciless grip in her hair, forcing her to stumble toward the river. East of the bridge, a long pier connected to a floating dock empty of any boats. He steered her in that direction and Hero knew the water would be deep.

She didn't *want* to cry. Didn't want to be weak at this, the hour of her death. But her head throbbed painfully. Everything hurt from where his heavy body had driven her into the frozen ground. Her heart clenched for the guilt her family would feel over her death. For the casualties of the day, and the pain of not knowing who'd lived or died. For the friends and strangers John the Baptist had already taken.

For the man she loved who would never have the chance to love her back.

"I—Is Luca dead?" she whispered through her tears.

"Mazure may have killed him, but likely not. There was no need for him to die. Not anymore."

His answer puzzled her. "Anymore?"

"I completed the final ritual without him, which *you* forced me to do in parts." His voice was almost back to conversational now, as he pushed her onto the pier. "God always calls for a sacrifice, in a case as serious as Asmodeus, he called for *three*. A goat. A bull—"

"And a *man*," Hero whispered, horrified. The heel of her shoe caught on a wooden plank and she stumbled, crying out as McMurtry's tight grip on her hair was the only thing that kept her from falling. The resulting jerk wrenched her neck.

"Not just *any* man," he continued, as though nothing had happened. "But one who was tempted and partook of the flesh of the demon."

Hero's eyes closed as a fresh wave of guilt and pain washed over her. The tears felt hot against her cold cheeks, but quickly turned freezing as they dropped from her chin to her chest. "You didn't have to kill Angora."

"I didn't plan to, but God showed me that she had to die." The pride in his voice angered her almost beyond bearing. He thought he talked to God, that his hatred and murder was sanctioned by heaven, and that was the worst kind of evil.

"The Lord helped me sneak away from the FBI that night," he bragged. "I drove *right* past them.

When I arrived at your house, your wanton of a land-lady was inviting Mr. Winthrop inside to fornicate with him. I was able to slip inside as she disabled the alarm and complete the ritual. You see? God prepares a way for his servants."

"God had *nothing* to do with this," Hero spat, fury and disgust overtaking her fear and pain.

"You'll see it differently when you're standing be-fore Him."

"You didn't kill Josiah Winthrop," she informed him smugly, hoping that put some freaking Vaseline in his cornflakes.

"Don't lie to me, demon!" he wrenched her hair again. "There's no way he survived what I did to him."

They reached the end of the pier and the black water lapped at the dock. He shoved her onto it and held her off kilter, dangling over the water to where she had to use the toes of her shoes for purchase.

The lights of St. John's Bridge made the water seem darker and their depths more yawning. Hero knew how cold it would be. Sometimes at night she would still feel the barbed chill as it engulfed her, and would wake up gasping for air. A last-ditch survival instinct kicked in and she struggled against the hand in her hair. But her knees were weak with fear and cold and exhaustion. The pain in her head caused the tears to flow harder and frightened sobs to break the barrier of her raw throat.

McMurtry began to sing in Latin in that terrible voice she'd never heard from him in her entire quarter century of listening to him sing prayers in church.

Except for *once*, the last time he'd tried to end her life.

As he started in on the prayer for last rights, she truly began to despair. She wanted to kick out at him, but he held her so far over the water, and if he let go of her hair, she would fall in and that would be the end of it. She'd never been a strong swimmer, and even if she *could* break the surface, with her hands tied behind her, she would eventually drown. Working the tire gauge out from behind the leather thongs she desperately wished it was something—*anything*—else. Something sharp and deadly.

The approaching roar of an engine broke through the night and Hero almost screamed out her triumph, but feared the priest would drop her right away. She couldn't turn her head toward the road to check, but she knew the sound of that engine. The distinctive roar of a patented Hemi rumbled inside the sleek black Dodge Charger.

"Luca!" she screamed, more thrilled he was alive than afraid of her own death.

Father McMurtry actually uttered a blasphemy, but his grip on her hair strengthened as he sped the resuscitation of her last rights.

He was nothing if not fanatical.

Luca yelled her name, and nothing in the world had ever sounded so sweet. The dock began to bob in the water as his heavy boots pounded up the length of the long pier.

McMurtry suddenly whirled around, bringing her with him as a shield for his body. Her cry of pain stopped Luca in his tracks.

Or maybe it was the gun the priest held to her head.

33

*[I will] translate thy life into death, thy liberty into
 bondage...
I will kill thee a hundred and fifty ways. Therefore
 tremble...*

— WILLIAM SHAKESPEARE, AS YOU LIKE IT

Luca fought to maintain a steady aim of his
weapon, but because of the darkness, the
shaking of his hands, and shifting of the dock, he
couldn't get a precise kill shot without putting Hero in
danger. Usually he was steady as a rock, but a strange
weakness in his arms caused a strange and unsettling
tremor. What the fuck was the matter with him?

Hero's cry of pain wrenched at his insides and
smothered the relief at finding her alive with a familiar rage.

McMurtry was going to die. *Tonight.* Slowly, if Luca
had his way.

"I'm doing you a favor, Agent Ramirez," McMurtry
called from the dock. "I'm releasing you from this Succubus. You'll no longer battle the pull of her
temptation."

"Put the gun down," Luca ordered, taking a threat-ening step forward.

"One more step and she dies now!" McMurtry jammed the gun hard against her temple.

Luca could hear Hero's whimper amplified by the acoustics of the stone bridge and the water. He drank in the sight of her. Helpless because she was so close. *Alive*, and yet out of his reach. The front of the golden blouse that had made his mouth go dry earlier that night was now soiled with dirt, and wet as though she'd sprawled front-first into the grass.

Had McMurtry hurt her? He couldn't see any blood, but what if he'd been tempted to—

Luca's temper was usually hot like a roiling fire in the center of his chest. Tonight, the fury felt different. Cold. Dark. Half fire, half ice, pulled from the deepest recesses of hell.

"No matter what happens tonight, I'm going to kill you," Luca told him.

"You think that matters to me?" McMurtry looked taller now that he wasn't stooped over. His shoulders were wide for not being hunched with age and pain. His body stocky and well-built. "I will go to the Lord as his servant. His warrior on this earth. You'd be doing me a favor."

"No, I wouldn't," he said coldly, using the informa-tion from the frantic phone call he'd made on the reckless drive here. He never thought he'd be so happy to hear Professor Alec's voice. Never thought he'd be so thankful to receive information from the man. "Your ritual isn't complete."

"What do you know of it?" McMurtry snapped.

"You need to sacrifice a man, one fornicating with your demon."

A peaceful smile appeared on McMurtry's face

that affected Luca worse than all the horrors he'd ever witnessed. Combined.

"Already done. The Lord tells me he accepts Mr. Winthrop as a sacrifice."

"Mr. Winthrop isn't dead," Luca said. "I lied on the news to draw you out of hiding."

Come on, let her go, he thought. *Come after me.*

"Lies!" McMurtry screamed, causing Hero to jump and gasp.

"He's in room fourteen-oh-three, eating pudding and enjoying a visit from his daughter."

McMurtry seemed to consider this, the gun easing a little away from Hero's temple.

That's right. Point it over here.

At the worst possible moment, the familiar sounds of sirens and tires merged onto the park, strengthening the priest's resolve.

The cold affected Luca's vision, and he had to blink several times. The pier felt like it swayed wildly beneath him, but that had to be wrong. Only the dock rested on the water. He shook his head to clear it and felt an overwhelming pressure against his lungs. Fear had never affected him quite like this before. He felt different now, though. Hero was his world and he might be forced to watch as he lost everything.

"It's true," Hero said, her eyes wide and terrified, glancing behind him to the approaching army of police, FBI, and medics.

"Shut up, demon!"

Car doors slammed. Voices yelled in the distance.

"Stay back!" Luca ordered over his shoulder, but no one seemed to listen.

He swung his eyes back to see McMurtry's finger twitch on the trigger, and Luca lurched forward before he could stop himself, putting out his other hand.

"Don't!" His command came out sounding more like a plea. "Can't you see she's not a demon? She's an *angel*. Let her go and you can have me. I'll complete your ritual."

"*No!*" Hero gasped.

McMurtry's hand went from her hair to around her throat, squeezing her protests silent and cutting off her precious breath.

"I love her!" Luca yelled, stunning more than just the three of them. "God help me. I love her. Don't —*you won't* take her from me." He repositioned his gun, his cloudy vision clearing by the force of his sheer will.

McMurtry's lips moved in the semblance of a prayer, and Hero's eyes widened impossibly further as she fought for air and registered his words. They locked with Luca's, full of love and hope and a message he couldn't identify.

McMurtry's gun swung toward Luca in the same moment a flash of metal caught the light as Hero's shoulders jerked back. Did she have a knife?

A bark of pain escaped the priest's lips. His gun went off, but the shot swung wild.

Hero dropped down, giving Luca all the room he needed for a kill shot.

By the time the sound echoed off the stone and steel of St. John's Bridge, McMurtry was in a freefall off the side of the dock. At the last moment, he grabbed for Hero, pulling her into the water with him.

Ignoring the shouts of his colleagues, Luca barreled down the bridge and dove into the river, following the sheen of Hero's gold blouse. The weight of his vest and gear made it easy to reach deep enough for her. She stopped struggling once he caught her around the waist, but his equipment fought him on the way up. His limbs felt unusually heavy, but he locked her tightly in his grip and kicked as hard as he could, doing his best to ignore his screaming lungs and the soul-stinging cold of the water.

Something was wrong with him. A creeping blackness blocked his vision of the surface. The pervasive pressure against his lungs grew strangely painful. He let out his breath in a flurry of bubbles, but it didn't help. Hero was kicking her legs, too, but they didn't seem to be ascending fast enough.

Luca fought the darkness. Maybe it was his punishment. Maybe it was his demons weighing them both down as he'd feared all along. But before they claimed him, he would give Hero her life.

Digging deep, past the pain and the fear, and the strange, oppressive confusion of his thoughts, he gave one last powerful kick, both of them breaking the surface with a screaming gulp for air.

Except his breath refused to go very deep. It wouldn't get past that pressure in his chest.

Didn't matter. Hands grabbed for Hero, and he pushed her toward them. Watching her body being lifted from the water was the sweetest relief. He didn't even feel the cold any more. Didn't even really worry about not breathing. Hero was okay. The pressure still grew against his lungs, but it was tempered with the knowledge that the woman he *loved*—the one who'd somehow taken possession of his black heart—was finally safe.

The mad man who'd threatened and terrorized her floated face down right next to Luca, the river water diluting his blood.

See you in hell, Luca thought victoriously, as the black depths finally claimed him.

34

"Doubt thou the stars are fire.
Doubt that the sun doth move.
Doubt truth to be a liar.
But never doubt my love."

— WILLIAM SHAKESPEARE, HAMLET

Heaven was everything he'd thought it would be, Luca thought. Bright white lights, a chorus of angels, and Hero smiling down at him from above.

"What are you doing here?" Luca asked, wondering why he couldn't hear all the consonants that went in that question.

Hero blinked, sadness dimming her smile until it disappeared.

The sight made Luca feel weirdly frantic. "I saved you," he told her through a burning throat. "Go back. You're still alive."

The smile returned, and her soft voice reached into his heart, releasing some of the anxiety. He didn't register her words, not at first, but he latched on to the perfect vision of her face, convinced she was an angel.

Except...

She looked like she'd been through hell.

The corner of her bottom lip was swollen and her blood-shot eyes puffy. An angry bruise at her temple melted into her wet hair. She wore a shapeless white gown and smelled like anti-bacterial soap.

She was the most radiant, gorgeous, welcome sight Luca could ever hope for.

He tried to reach for her, and pain exploded somewhere beneath his chest cavity granting his vision a harsh clarity and returning his other senses to him with a brutal, jarring crash.

Strong but gentle hands restrained him, and he was told by a stern male voice not to move. Luca wasn't in the business of following orders, but in this case, he'd relent. He felt hot and dry and not unlike a rotisserie kebab.

He needed water.

He remembered feeling so much pressure inside he feared he would explode. That was gone, but now he felt like the victim in one of the *Alien* movies, with his middle ripped out.

"Here," Hero crooned. His eyes fluttered closed and he relaxed, the restraining hands left him and the glorious sensation of an ice chip was pressed between his lips, then another and another until he shook his head.

She really *was* an angel.

"Agent Ramirez, do you know where you are?" a male voice asked.

He lifted his lids, but only enough to squint. The bright white lights were corporate-issue florescent bulbs. The choir of angels happened to be Christmas music piping in from the hallway. "I'm in hell," he groaned.

"Close enough." Dr. Karakis made a note on his

clipboard and patted Hero on the shoulder. "I think he's going to be fine."

Did this guy just live at the hospital, or what? Luca looked down across the expanse of his chest, but bandages and a blanket restricted his view.

"What the f—"

"I'd say you're this year's Christmas miracle." Doctor Karakis smiled in that easy way of his. "Getting shot at point blank range is mighty dangerous, even with a vest on. It broke a few ribs and subsequently caused some pretty severe internal bleeding. You almost didn't make it." He shook his curly dark head like he couldn't believe it.

Luca's eyes flew wide. "Vince! Is he—"

Hero shushed him, running a cool hand over his forehead. "He's fine. Bullet went clean through, and he'll have a bit of healing to do."

Luca relaxed.

"The other agent's injuries were minor, and Father Michael is recovering close by," she informed him.

All of those gunshots and no casualties. *That* was the fucking miracle.

Karakis cleared his throat. "Well, I'm going to put in an order and grab a painkiller for your IV, then I'll be back to check on you." He quietly left them alone.

Luca drank in the sight of Hero, catching every nuance of her apprehensive expression. If anyone was a miracle, it was her, and he needed to make sure she knew it.

"I meant it," he said.

"Oh, thank God." Big silent tears slipped down her cheeks, and she released his hand to dash them away.

She knew what he was saying, but he felt driven by the need to give her the words. They scared the shit out of him, but he could no longer stand to play the coward in her eyes. "You were right. I love you. And I was afraid of it."

The tenderness in Hero's smile nearly undid him. "It's okay to be afraid. I've scared away braver men than you."

He didn't doubt it. "It wasn't you." Luca needed her to know that. "It was me. I haven't known you two months, and you made me want things I never even allowed myself to think about."

"What things?" she whispered.

The part of his brain that was ruled by self-preservation screamed at him to shut up, but the power of his emotion—probably helped by strong medications —overrode his fear. "A future, love, a mortgage, a yard, commitment, stability—"

"Let's not get carried away here," she laughed nervously. "This is *me* we're talking about."

"Babies," he murmured.

Her eyes went round, and her smile died as she began to cry in earnest.

"When you offered me everything I wanted. Everything I didn't want *to* want. I freaked out. I needed you to be as scared as I was."

"I was scared when you said it at the river," she admitted. "I thought maybe... because I had a gun to my head..." She trailed off and shrugged, her lashes sweeping down.

"It's harder to have something taken from you than it is to give it away," he conceded. "But I realized, life without you was much more frightening than any danger I've faced."

She leaned forward and pressed as soft kiss to his mouth. "Say it again," she whispered.

"I love you."

"No, the part about me being right."

That brought a laugh, which sent a sharp pain through his entire torso, stealing his breath. Doctor Karakis showed up with the blessed syringe and pumped it into his IV.

His muscles relaxed and limbs became heavy but in the most wonderful way possible. Talk about a Christmas miracle.

"Before you check out, your family wants to see you," Karakis said, gesturing to the door.

Puzzled, Luca shook his head. "I don't have a family."

"Thanks a lot, asshole," Vince said from his wheel-chair as Rown pushed him into the room making way for Hero's parents, Andra, Knox, Demetri, and even Connor. "You're already on my shit list because you'll have a longer vacation and get the better drugs."

"Is this allowed?" Hero asked.

"Not really, but it's Christmas." Karakis's whole lab coat rippled with his shrug. "Also, I'm kind of afraid of your mom."

"Join the club," Vince snarked.

Luca tried to speak, but his tongue felt heavy and his throat tightened. He blamed the drugs. Yeah. It was the drugs. Probably the sheen of moisture over-clouding his vision was the same thing.

Luca felt the darkness threaten him again, pulling him under with a soupy allure. Offering him a refuge from the swell of gratitude and hope.

"I heard what you did," Karakis said. "Chased down that gunman, stopped John the Baptist, and then fished this lady out of the river before she drowned all with internal injuries. You're a hero, Agent Ramirez." The doctor's eyes flicked toward the lady-in-question, and he chuckled as though he'd made a joke.

"My hero," she sighed dramatically and clutched his hand in both of hers, lifting it to her lips.

My Hero, Luca thought, refusing to release his grip on her hand even when a gentle sleep claimed him. They'd be there when he woke up, ready to start the rest of his life.

He couldn't wait.

35

EPILOGUE: (A SNEAK PEAK AT THE NEXT SHAKESPEAREAN SUSPENSE)

SEVERAL MONTHS LATER

"Next time you move, I'm going to be sick that day," Vince huffed as he dumped the last box marked *bedroom* on the floor. "I'm starting to think this isn't worth pizza and beer."

Luca allowed himself a secret smile as he thought about how pissed his partner would be when he saw what kind of pizza Hero ordered. Though he was pretty sure her brothers ordered something with double meat behind her back. A guy could only have so many green things on his pizza before he had to give up his man card.

The kaleidoscopic chaos that was the floor of Hero's closet stopped him dead for a long minute. "Houston, we have a problem," he muttered.

"What the hell is in these boxes anyway?" Vince continued bitching. "They're all lumpy and lopsided."

"Look if you want," Luca muttered. He ignored the sound of a box being ripped open as he tried to figure a closet strategy. How does one *take* room away from a woman in her own closet? Was that even possible? If he figured this out, he'd be right up there with the great problem solvers of humanity. Newton. Fleming. Einstein... *Ramirez*.

He liked the sound of that.

"Jesus, Ramirez, are all these yours?" Vince's question dripped with disbelief.

"That and three more boxes."

"Okay." Vince stomped over to him. "Hand it over."

"Hand what over?" Luca asked, still contemplating the closet.

"Your man card. No one man should own that many shoes. You know, unless he's Stef."

"I heard that!" Stef called from the other room.

Luca laughed. "Funny you say that," he began. "I was just thinking about my man card."

"You mean the one you don't have any more?"

A commotion of male exclamations distracted them both, and they wandered toward the living room to investigate.

Knox and Rown gingerly set his new flat screen on the entertainment stand, and stood back to admire it along with Connor, Demetri, Stef, and Vince.

"She's so beautiful," Demetri said reverently.

"Sixty inches of pure sexy," Knox agreed.

"You can have your man card back," Vince murmured as he wandered toward it like a moth to a flame.

"LCD? LED? Plasma?" Connor asked.

"Lasers," Luca bragged. "This model's the latest and greatest in badass entertainment technology."

"Lasers," they all agreed.

"Welp, fight night is at your house from now on," Demetri informed him.

"Think again," Hero said from the doorway, setting down a lamp. "I have way too many breakable objects in this house to let all you guys in here on fight night." She smiled and warmth rippled beneath Luca's skin.

"But... you were willed a *mansion*," Demetri argued. "I think that comes with obligatory hosting clauses. Also—lasers." He pointed at the television.

"Most of Angora's house is going to be converted into an academy of art, pottery, and sculpture," she reminded them as she slid into Luca's arms with a soft kiss that curled his toes.

Luca's lips lifted in a smile while still pressed against hers. They spontaneously did that sometimes, just on their own. Guess that's what happiness did to a guy. Badly-timed smiles. He just couldn't turn them off.

"I have a mansion," Knox offered, having yet to tear his longing gaze away from the television. "And you can bet every one of your asses I'm getting me one of these."

"Problem solved." Hero pulled back, but didn't leave the circle of Luca's arms. "I can't wait to officially make my bed *our* bed," she whispered to him so her brothers couldn't overhear.

Luca couldn't wait either. The bed. The kitchen table. The bar. The desk. The carpet. Hell, even the couch. Not that they hadn't had sex on all those places. But it wasn't official sex, which was like a whole new reason to do it again. And again.

Okay. Time for Hero's brothers to leave.

"Like we're going to have fight night on Slayer Street." Stef interrupted Luca's train of thought. He fluffed his artfully arranged blue frosted tips with manicured nails before noticing everyone was looking at him as though he'd produced a girlfriend. "What? I lost my adult channel subscription a few months ago and stumbled onto Ultimate Fighting. Dominant, muscled guys in shorty-shorts straining, sweating, and wrestling each other for three rounds... What's not to love?" He leveled Knox an appreciative look.

"Repeat the thing about *Slayer Street*," Connor ordered, his severe eyes narrowing at Stef.

"It's nothing, guys, forget it." Knox turned from the television and wiped his hands on his ripped and dusty jeans. "Who ordered the pizza?"

"I did," Hero chirped.

"Who ordered the pizza we're actually going to eat?" He tried again.

"Spill it, Lennox." Luca had to give Connor props. He was the only man any of the Katrova-Connor brothers actually listened to. Not just because he was older and authoritative, but he was bigger, meaner, and could probably kill them all with his pinky finger and a teacup. Also, he grew up loving and protecting them, and that meant something to them all.

Knox ran his own hand over his faux-hawk and looked supremely uncomfortable. "So... there have been a couple random deaths in my neighborhood."

"Three," Steff corrected smugly. "Some lady they interviewed on the news said that she felt like she was living on Slayer Street and the name is really catchy."

"Yeah, but only one of the deaths is for sure a murder," Knox waved it off. "It kind of happened this morning." They'd been moving Luca into Hero's loft all morning, but Stef hadn't showed up until two hours ago, so he'd had time to catch the news.

"Knox!" Hero protested. "Why didn't you say something?"

Everyone cringed, and Luca pulled Hero closer.

"Because I didn't want to worry anyone," Knox lifted his heavy shoulder to prove his ambivalence. "I'm sure it's just some *Real Housewives* meets *Law and Order* kind of thing. Besides, it's probably a coincidence. I live by rich old people, too. They die all the time, right?"

Luca's eyes narrowed at Knox. There was something he wasn't saying, but he didn't want to further upset Hero. Not when things were just getting back to normal at home and at work. "Where is that pizza?" he piped in, hiding a meaningful look to the surrounding men from Hero.

"We'll talk about this later," Connor promised softly.

"There's nothing to talk about," Knox insisted. "It's not like *I'm* in any danger."

ALSO BY KERRIGAN BYRNE

The Highwayman

The Hunter

The Highlander

The Duke

The Scot Beds His Wife

The Duke With the Dragon Tattoo

A Dark and Stormy Knight

ALSO BY KERRIGAN

The Highwayman

The Hunter

The Highlander

The Duke

The Scot Beds His Wife

The Duke With the Dragon Tattoo

How to Love a Duke in Ten Days

All Scot And Bothered (Coming in March of 2020)

ABOUT THE AUTHOR

Kerrigan Byrne is the USA Today Bestselling and award winning author of THE DUKE WITH THE DRAGON TATTOO. She has authored a dozen novels in both the romance and mystery genre. Her newest mystery release THE BUSINESS OF BLOOD is available October 24th, 2019

She lives on the Olympic Peninsula in Washington with her dream boat husband. When she's not writing and researching, you'll find her on the water sailing and kayaking, or on land eating, drinking, shopping, and taking the dogs to play on the beach.

Kerrigan loves to hear from her readers! To contact her or learn more about her books, please visit her site: www.kerriganbyrne.com